I0544663

Missionary to the Oddballs

©2020 Penny N. Haavig

Edited by Silver Lining Literary Services
106 Offutt Rd.
Clinton, TN 37716
www.saralfoust.com

Printed in the United States of America

All rights reserved. No part of this publication may be reproduced, stored in a retrieval system, posted on any website, or transmitted in any form or any means—digital, electronic, photocopy, recording, or otherwise—without the prior written permission of the publisher. The only exception is brief quotation in printed reviews.

The persons and events portrayed are fictional and not true-This is based on a true story and most characters are actual.

ISBN: 978-0-578-75345-4

Scripture quoted is from the King James Version of the Bible, which is in public domain.

©2020 Cover Design by Hannah Linder
https://hannahlinderdesigns.com/

*I will hide beneath the shadow of your wings, until the
storm has passed.*

Psalm 57:1

Missionary to the Oddballs

Based on a True Story

A Novel

Penny N. Haavig

Part One

Chapter One

1954
Miller Place, New York

It took twenty shock treatments to bring me back to reality. The hurricane winds are howling profusely as the wood shutters bang against the windows. I squint my eyes to adjust to the darkness and manage to find my way to the kitchen. I feel my way to the cabinet that might have an oil lamp. *Ah, ha! Here you are, oil lamp of my dreams. Good, the box of matches is right here. I won't allow any storm to bring me down.*

Peter's hunkering down at his friend, Vinnie's. Henry warned me by telephone earlier that he may be forced to stay in Manhattan if public transportation shuts down.

As I strike the match, I wonder if my eight-year-old daughter is hiding under her covers scared out of her noodle. "Jane. Jane. Can you hear me?"

The sound of loud footsteps pounds their existence on the linoleum flooring which connects each room in this small house. *Must be the wind.* I leave the lamp on the counter and proceed down the hall. Many a place has caught on fire because of these hazardous lamps.

"I'm coming, Jane. Don't worry, hug your pillow tight." Fear encompasses my body as I breathe in a smell of whiskey, and heavy breathing right behind me. *My imagination running wild again.* I leap to the bedroom that

I share with my daughter, open the door as she runs into my arms. She's wet with perspiration as I stroke her curly hair. "Mommy has you now, little one. Come on, let's go and sit by the fireplace."

Suddenly, strong hands are pressing down on my shoulders, and the grotesque smell of alcohol fills the small room. *Lord God, please help me right now to be strong for my Jane.*

His body is close to my back, but I manage to get my daughter and me out the door.

"H-h-h-heeeeey! Where d'ya think you are going, Violet. Can't we have a little fun while the hubby's away?" the slurred, annoying voice shouts.

Now, in the dimly lit living space area, I can see who the perpetrator is. "Mr. Léger? How did you get in here?"

He wobbles on his feet a few steps from us. "Now, now. I won't hurt you or your little girl. All I want is some companionship." Hiccup. "Shouldn't leave your door unlocked."

I back up with Jane wrapped in my arms. "Listen, Mr. Léger, your wife will be scared to death with this storm whirling around us. You better leave."

He steps closer with a sway and knocks my good lamp crashing to the floor. "Don't worry about her. She was out like a light when I left. It's time you call me Freddy, Violet. Co-o-me here and give me a big k-i-ss."

"Mommy, where's Daddy? I want my Daddy," cries Jane.

I position myself near the fireplace, so I can reach the wrought iron poker with a free hand. "Don't you take another step; do you hear me?"

Burping loudly, "So the little woman doesn't want to play, huh?"

"You need to leave this instant, Mr. Léger."

With eyes half open, unshaved face, and staggering body, "In a few minutes, okay?"

Pushing Jane behind me with a motion to sit on the hearth, I step forward with the poker. "Do you see the tip of this, sir? It could bore a nice big gouge right in that belly of yours."

The torrents of rain pound against the siding of the house as the wind whistles down the chimney. I can hear the crackle of the fire behind me.

He takes a step forward, loses his balance, and falls flat on the floor.

Jane jumps up, hides behind me, and screams at the top of her lungs. "Is he dead?"

I bring her to my side and whisper, "Stay right here, but I don't think so." I tiptoe over and poke him lightly.

"Mr. Leger. Freddy?" His face is turned away from me. I skirt around him with an eye on my daughter. There's no blood. He appears to be out cold, but he sure reeks of booze. *I don't think this man is ever sober.*

As I lean a bit closer, I can hear muffled snoring sounds.

"If God brings me to it, He'll bring me through it," I say quietly.

"Mommy, are you going to call the police?" Jane whispers with wrinkled brow.

I take her by the hands and lift her trembling body in my arms as we plop on the couch.

"No. Mr. Leger will be sleeping for a long time."

We stare at our uninvited guest as his snoring gets louder and louder.

"I'm hungry," she utters.

"How about a peanut butter and jelly sandwich? I wish I knew where your father put that flashlight though. I could hunt down some candles with it."

"I know where it is, Mommy." She slides off my lap, peers into the log holder, and pulls out a silver flashlight.

"Let's go get those sandwiches." I tap Mr. Leger's foot on purpose, but he remains out, like all the lights in the house.

Our lives were in danger for a few moments, but I know God was watching over us during the whole ordeal.

The winds continue to roar throughout the night, but Freddy Leger sleeps like a rock through it all. Not even a budge, only a loud rhythmic snore. He's a big man so impossible to move by myself. I take off his shoes, hide them and barricade him in place with logs, anchoring down the blanket around him. Any movement would get my attention for sure. Jane and I curl up on the couch with pillows and blankets. She drifts off to sleep as I stroke her soft curls. My watch reads three am.

∽⦿℘∾

"Mother, wake up. Please, wake up." Peter's voice seems so far away

"Mr. Leger's moving, Peter." Jane whispers.

My eyes pop open in confusion when I see my freckled face son standing in front of me.

"Peter. How did you get here? What about the storm?"

"Vinnie's mother drove me home a few minutes ago. The winds have died down quite a bit. I was worried about you two. What's our neighbor doing on the floor anyway?"

I throw off the blankets and leap to my feet. "Hang on to this poker, Son."

"Oh, uh, oh," grunts the bedraggled neighbor as he thrashes about.

Peter glares at his prey getting ready to stab him at the first chance. I pick up the receiver on the phone. No dial tones. Still dead.

Frightened Jane is perched on the couch with her legs folded up to her chest, rocking vigorously.

Our visitor moves back and forth enough to flip on his back. "Where am I?"

"Don't move, Mister, or else." Peter waves the poker in front of the middle-aged man's face.

I push the tool my son's holding away from the predator's face. "Mr. Leger. It's time to go home," I order.

Trying to get up, "Violet?" He looks around. "How did I get in your house?"

"Help me, Peter. Put these logs away so our neighbor can get out of here," I mutter.

"Whew. You sure do reek, fella," Peter shouts in his face.

After I remove the blankets from him. "Here are your shoes and a pamphlet I would like you to read."

Freddy holds the tract in his hands, studies it, and looks up at me. "Jesus loves me? You are kidding, right?"

Smiling with uncertainty, "Yes, He does. If you confess your sins, He's faithful, and will forgive you of the wrongs you've done."

Slipping on one shoe at a time and tying them, "That's a laugh. What sins do I have in my life anyway? A few drinks here and there don't make me a bad man."

"Get out of here, Mr. Leger. My father will deal with you when he gets home tonight," Peter yells.

I'm amazed at how mature this boy is for twelve years old.

"Okay. Okay. I hear you, boy."

We follow him to the front door and all but push him down the stairs. He turns around, rips the tract up in little pieces, and tosses them in the air. "I'll be seeing you,

Violet." He jumps over the fence that divides our property from his.

One would never know he was stoned drunk hours ago. I'm sure Henry will press charges tomorrow. Thank God, he didn't hurt us.

As I look out across the lawn and down the road, I see branches everywhere and a few power lines down on the ground. Our driveway's flooded over with water and, unfortunately, most of our car is too.

"Come on, kids, let's go and find some breakfast. I have some Sterno cans that I can light up. At least, I can boil some coffee for myself."

"I'm going to check the doors are locked," Peter shouts as he sets out on a mission.

I reach into the refrigerator, grab the milk, a box of Wheaties, three bowls, and set everything on the picnic table in the small dining area. Luckily, there a few ripe bananas too.

"Time to eat," I exclaim.

"Can we play Parcheesi after breakfast?" Jane asks.

I smile as I gaze out at the tall waves of the Long Island sound. "Sure, we can, but after one game, it will be clean up time."

Henry will be so disappointed when he sees that the two young trees he planted in the spring are no longer there. Part of the screen is ripped too. I wonder what the damage is like in Port Jefferson and if my little gift shop is still standing.

"Isn't that Mr. Leger standing on the edge of the cliff?" Peter asks.

I squint my eyes and look. "Yes. That's him alright. If he stays on his property and leaves us alone. I'm alright with that."

"Do you think Daddy will be home tonight, Mom?"

"I'm sure he'll need to hitch a ride home with a buddy. It will take a couple of days for the water to recede from the driveway."

I stand up quickly when I spot the bothersome neighbor walk along the fence line and stop a few feet from us. The children do not see him because their backs are to him.

He winks.

Goosebumps creep up my arms, and I begin to get sick to my stomach. I don't know how I'll be able to go down to work in the cellar knowing this numbskull could jump over the fence at any given time. I wish we had an inside staircase.

I turn my attention to the kids and make a move with my game piece. As the clouds try to roll away, some light manages to peek through. I don't have to look to see if Leger is still there, because I feel his eyes boring through me.

"Peter, watch your sister for a minute. I want to see if the telephone's working yet."

"Okay. Your move, Sis."

I check the lock on the back door first and then take flight to the kitchen. As I pick up the phone to listen for a dial tone, I glance out the window to the fence line. The one who invaded our privacy is gone, but where is he? Still no phone service. I race to the porch and parade around inside scanning all vantage points. I unlock the screen door and venture outside to access the damage in the back yard. The big oak tree in the other neighbor's yard snapped, leaving half of it on our lawn. I bend down to pick up scattered chaise lounge cushions, and as I come up, I catch the back of Freddy Leger going into his house.

Chapter Two

Later that afternoon, "Hey, Mom. Look what I found in my room?" Peter says.

I look in his hands. "Batteries for the transistor radio. Wonderful."

Excited at his find, "Where is that thing anyway?"

"Right over there next to the hurricane lamp."

Piercing sounds of static and mumbled voices fill the house as he tries his hardest to find a news report.

Peter loves to take things apart and put them back together again. He's so tall and very thin in stature. He's almost taller than me.

"Most of Long Island is under a flood watch, especially the towns on the South Shore. Hurricane Carol blew across the sixty-mile span with winds from 90 to 120 mile per hour. The damage is excessive as crews span out to assess the damage. Reports are coming in from the Long Island Lighting Company there are over 275,000 homes without power currently. Governor Dewey asks all residents to remain in their homes until power has been restored," states the news reporter.

Fortunately, I filled several pails and a few jugs of water before the power went off. That way, the toilet could be flushed, and dishes washed.

Sitting on the couch with a Look magazine. "Grandpa and Daisy are supposed to drive out from Brooklyn for the day next week. I sure hope everything is back to normal by then."

Jane giggles and plays with her Ginny doll. "Grandpa's so funny, I hope he brings his puppet."

"He's a little odd if you ask me," chimes in Peter as he tinkers with a model airplane.

"Now, Peter. He's an entertainer. They're a bit different due to their creative spirit.

"Daisy loves the beach and diving off the rock too. Did you tell her to bring her bathing suit?"

"Yes. I did. Speaking of the beach, I'm going to check out the condition of the cliff and the shoreline. I'll be back in a jiffy." As I stand on the edge of the cliff at the end of our back yard, I look down at the waves roaring over the entire beach. The white caps on the dark, angry waves create havoc for any kind of boat. I scan off to my left at the steps going down to the beach that Henry and several men from the community worked on last week. They estimate 150 steps and one landing to completion next year. *I can't believe they're still there. The waves are eating the cliff away. The kids do love to run up and down to go to the beach. Otherwise, walk down the road to Gully Landing.*

"Those waves look ugly, don't they, Violet?" shouts a familiar voice.

I turn to my left and scowl at Mr. Leger. "Yes, they do."

"You sure are pretty, even when you don't smile."

"Keep your distance that's all I have to say." I flee to the safety of my house. I lock the screen door of the porch and do the same with the inner storm door. I breathe a sigh of relief.

"What does it look like out there, Vi?"

I spin on my heels and fly into my husband's arms. "I'm so glad you're finally home safe."

With a hug around the neck and a few kisses, "Peter claims you had an unwanted guest last night?"

"Yes. Freddy Leger was under the influence again. Luckily, he passed out on the floor before any real harm was done."

"I think I better go to the police and file charges tomorrow."

"Try to reason with him first?"

"Be reasonable, Violet. He could have hurt you or Jane."

"God loves him as a person."

"Religion can't help someone like that fella."

Peter weaves between us. "Dad, the radio said some of the power has been restored in Nassau County. Do you think ours will be back on soon?"

"I would think so but, in the meantime, let's go and collect some of those smaller branches for kindling. We must keep the fire burning through the night. In lieu of what happened here last night, I suggest we all camp out right here tonight."

I scrounge around in the refrigerator, "Let's roast frankfurters over the fire for supper. I was able to pick tomatoes and cucumbers from the garden before the storm hit and, look, a can of baked beans to top it off."

Henry shakes his head. "The thing about the neighbor still bothers me. I'll try to sleep on it and wait until morning to do something about it. Come on, Son, let's gather some wood."

The morning sunrise beats down on my face as I try desperately to hide from it. I peek at my watch with amazement when I discover it's 7:30 a.m. Everyone's sound asleep on their makeshift beds. Jane's on the other end of the couch, and I don't want to take a chance of waking her.

I sure would love a cup of coffee but no electricity. Where there's a will, there's a way.

I slither to the floor and creep into the kitchen. Boiling water in a pan over the Sterno and instant coffee will work.

I have what I need now. I'll wait until everyone gets up and has breakfast before I check out the cellar. It would be so nice if we could build an addition with a master bedroom, bath, a bigger living room and art studio. If the tile business continues to be prosperous, it might come to fruition. The tile conventions I have been attending have opened the doors to big orders from major contractors

It's Labor Day weekend, and everything's pretty much back to normal. Henry had a visit with the Leger's when Freddy was sober. There haven't been any recurring problems since the hurricane. Jane and I are at the Violetile's gift shop in Port Jefferson since the boys are fishing. No interior damages from the storm, but a few shingles are missing. Luckily, the flood waters kept rolling down the hill into the lower areas of town.

"Mommy, I'm hungry. Can we eat lunch at the Schooner? It's fun there because it was a real sailboat."

Chuckling as I wipe off her chocolate milk face, "We can do that. Let's check out all the yachts and sailboats at the mariner too. If we're lucky, we should see the ferry too. I have to price the last of the gifts in this box before we go."

The cool, salt air's blowing through our hair as we walk along the docks jutting into the Port Jefferson harbor. A few people are picking up the debris on their vessels.

"Aren't these boats huge, Jane?"

"Yeah, they are. Do people sleep on them?'

"They sure do. Sometimes for weeks at a time, except during storms such as Hurricane Carol. Let's sit right here and soak in the sun before we head back to the shop. Your mother wants to sketch some of these beautiful boats."

So, this is how the rich and famous live? I love sailboats, and this well-appointed one is a perfect specimen. Why does that handsome man keep staring at me? I wish he would stop. Oh no. Here he comes.

He hands me a business card as he shakes my hand. "Hi. My name is Louis Dormand. I'm a freelance photographer, and I would love to have you pose for me."

I want to grab my daughter and run, because for some reason I don't think this man is for real. Instead, I slowly pack up my pastels, pencils, and sketch pad.

"Miss, you're exactly what I've been searching for. The model I select will be on thousands of postcards to be distributed on the island as souvenirs. Ask around and you will find out I'm on the up and up."

Out of respect and curiosity, I shake his hand. "My name's Violet Pearl Funk. Give me a few days to get back to you. Come on, Jane. It's time to go."

As we walk away, I can feel his eyes roaming all over the back of my body.

"Who was that man, Mommy?" my little one asks as we head back to the shop.

"Oh, a gentleman interested in the tiles. Don't worry about it, alright?"

"Can we go to the library on our way home today?"

Looking at the little clock on the wall, "I guess we can. You'll have time to pick out a couple of books. In the meantime, play with your dolls while I catch up on my work." I smile as I watch her scurry to the play area I set up. *I wish her left eye would straighten out though.*

I pick up the business card handed to me moments ago. Louis Dormand. Hmm. A photographer from

Manhattan. This business could blossom overnight if this fella is legit. Henry knows so many influential people in Metropolitan Life. He'll check this Mr. Dormand out. I could be the newest celebrity in Suffolk County. Come on, Violet, stay away from becoming famous. Focus on the Lord, not the things of this world. I can't believe I found these candies. Coward's violet mints. A unique flavor experience of a floral and fragrance blended. Now, I have an area designated for violets. These lavender folded hankies are beautiful, and two hand-painted china sugar and creamer sets top off the display.

Stepping back to admire my new exhibit, I catch myself in the full-length mirror.

Louis Dormand is right. I would make a perfect model.

Chapter Three

We're having a perfect September on the North Shore. The children are back in school, and I don't have to drive them. Peter gets frustrated with his sister because she's always dilly-dallying along the trek of close to a mile. I made the mistake of teaching her about fairies and gnomes hiding in the forest. She is convinced they're flying amongst the ferns and moss-laden logs along the route, so stopping periodically goes with the territory.

I wish we didn't always have to drive an old, used-ten-times-over jalopy. This 1949 station wagon is a gem, all right. Ripped seats with stuffing coming through several enormous holes, and the passenger door is tied shut with a rope, so the only way in or out is the driver's side. Henry won't ever buy a new car again. Says it is a waste of money. Last week, he found dough to buy a new table saw though.

"Violet, I have the contract papers for you to sign," comments Mr. Dormand, entering the shop.

"I'm glad that my husband checked around about you, Mr. Dormond. I feel better now."

"Please call me Louis since we'll be spending a lot of time together over the next couple of weeks."

This is the third time I have been near this man, and each time he makes my heart race, and my face blushes with delight. His sense of fashion is up-to-date and the perfect fit every time. The corduroy, burgundy sport coat with an open-collar, white oxford shirt and dark brown tweed trousers sure suit him well.

14

Leaning over the counter with a wink, he says, "Violet, can you take the time to look these over?"

His deep brown eyes send me into a trance within seconds. "How perfectly rude of me. Come here and sit down while I get you a cup of tea. It's time for a break anyway. I read fast."

"You look ravishing today in that white gauze peasant blouse."

We are locked in each other's gaze for a moment.

"Thank you. They'll print 5,000 postcards with my picture?" *I'm shocked that my stipend will be ten thousand dollars.* "I'm excited about this project, Mr. Dormand."

He touches my hand and sends goosebumps to the top of my head. "Please call me Louis."

I sign my name and date the document. "There you go, Louis, we have a deal."

"I need your measurements, so we can get the perfect swimsuit for you. My assistant in the city is waiting for a phone call so she can shop. The photo shoot will be a week from today at the marina. I have an agreement with the captain of the largest clipper in the harbor for the sole purpose of taking your picture. You'll be able to change into a swimsuit in the bathroom on board."

Jotting down my measurements, I hesitate. "Here you go. Do you need anything else?"

He raises his eyebrows as he reads the numbers in front of him. "Just what I thought. A perfect figure."

"It's time to close, Louis. I have to pick my husband up at the train station in twenty minutes."

I grab my shawl and pocketbook and head to the door. I feel him at my heels, breathing down my neck.

He opens the door. ""You smell lovely, and you have a gorgeous head of hair too. What's that fragrance? Gardenia?"

I slip past him into the cool early night. "Good night. I'll see you next week."

He reaches out and strokes my hair. "I'm looking forward to it."

He disappears into the parking lot across the street as I lock the door.

"Are you sure the children are all right by themselves, Honey?" asks Henry on the way home.

"I called once, and Peter called me once. The doors are locked, and they're watching *Annie Oakley*. It's all right, honestly."

"Did you hear from Mr. Dormand?"

"Yes, as a matter of fact, he was at the shop today with the contract. The photo shoot is next week."

"Do you remember when we first met, and I said you would make a great model?"

I chuckle and give him a love punch on the arm. "How can I forget all of those pictures you took of me in so many crazy poses?"

"You still have what it takes, my beautiful lady."

"Did you know I will get ten thousand dollars for this job?"

"Really? That's a lot more than what he told me."

"You mean, Louis actually told you what I would get paid?"

"Louis? Aren't we getting a bit too personal?"

Henry and I have so little time to talk during the week. He catches the train at Port Jeff Station every day at six in the morning. By the time it stops at every town through two counties, the poor man doesn't get to his

16

destination until 9:00. He leaves the Met at 5:00 and arrives back home at 7:00. Supper in front of the television quickly follows this routine. All of us have learned that no one says a word when Daddy is watching the evening news. His bedtime is the same as the children. Nine o'clock.

"Daddy, can I have a doggie?" Jane screeches as we walk in the door.

He lifts her into his arms. "A dog? Are you going to take care of it?"

Peter stands beside his dad. "The Delaneys are giving away some puppies."

"Who are these people, and where do they live?"

"Lulu and Gladys are my dark skin friends from school. They live near Paulette."

He looks at me with a wink. "If it's all right with your mother, then it's fine with me. I hope it's a hound because they make good watch dogs."

I smile as I bring my daughter to me. "As long as you kids take care of it."

We enjoy TV dinners as we each sit at individual tray tables, but I'm preoccupied with the events of the day and the man whose name is Louis Dormand.

Chapter Four

Business at the shop is booming with last minute shoppers trying to find a perfect gift for Christmas. The Louis Dormand photo shoot went well. He tried hard to get me alone, so he could flirt more effectively.

On the last day of the three-day shoot, he asked, "How about dinner tonight, Violet? Tomorrow afternoon I head back to the city for the winter months, but the postcards will be ready for distribution in March. The publisher will be calling you about how many you would like for your shop."

I stay behind the counter in the shop. "I have to go to prayer meeting at church tonight, Louis. Sorry about that. I sell a lot of postcards during the summer months, so it will be nice to get something new."

Looking back at the customer by the door and leaning closer to me, he whispers, "We could've had a great time together, my dear. You're attracted to me. Face it."

I call his bluff. "Do you know how much God loves you, Louis?"

"Okay. Okay. That's enough of that. I'll be here tomorrow morning with your check."

With a nod and a wink, he walks out the door.

After spending time in prayer about this Casanova, I came across an article in a Christian magazine. I cut it out, made it into a thank you card, and gave it to him.

"Positive Thought"

If God had a refrigerator, your picture would be on it. If He had a wallet, your photo would be in it. He sends you flowers every spring and a sunrise every morning. Whenever you want to talk, He'll listen. He could live anywhere in the universe; He chose your heart. What about the Christmas gift He sent you in Bethlehem; not to mention that Friday at Calvary!

Face it, He's crazy about you!

I never saw Louis Dormand again.

ᶜᵉᵃᵍᵒ

I pull into the parking lot at the school one snowy morning after dropping Henry off at the train.

"When will we get our Christmas tree, Mom?" Peter asks.

"Oh, you know how your father likes to traipse through the woods until he finds what he thinks is the perfect tree."

"It's always dark when he comes home though. The boy scouts are selling them at the post office for a couple of weeks. They're really nice."

"When does the Montgomery Ward's Christmas catalogue come, Mommy?" shrieks Jane.

Laughing as I get out of the car, "Come on you two or you'll be late for school. There's the bell. You better run."

I'm reminded of the tile orders that must be filled by next week and the almost empty rack at the shop. Henry and Peter shoveled the walkway to the driveway and to the entrance to the cellar too.

I better let the dog out first.

"Come on, Lucky. You go out while I go too."

It's wonderful having a dog with me during the day especially. Lucky's a great watch dog, and I'm thrilled to have a telephone in the basement now. Last month, Henry called the telephone company to install another phone jack downstairs.

Now, I feel so secure when I'm by myself. Deuteronomy 31:8 says, "It is the Lord who goes before you; He will not fail you or let you go."

I love Jesus because He first loved me. The evil spirit that controlled my life just a few years ago is gone forever. The Holy Spirit lives within me since Jesus came into my heart.

"Come on, boy. Let's get some work done." I check out Leger's house before heading down the cement stairs. Thank God, he stays to himself these days.

I flick the lights on, lock the door, and turn up the thermostat. I really have everything I need down here except a bathroom, but I do have that old commode. Today's agenda is to paint two dozen tiles. *Good food requires a loving hand and one dozen nautical. I must at least create the beginning of one new design.*

I breathe in a sigh of relief as I gaze around the cement block walls, the ceiling with exposed insulation, and shelves of plain tiles. The ugly spirit of the demonic world certainly had a grip on me. *Because God lives, I can face tomorrow. "You believe that God is one; you will do well. Even the demons believe and shudder." James 2:19.*

"Thank You, Lord, for dying on the cross for me and all of my sins. My Redeemer lives." *Now, instead of demons around me, there are angels everywhere.*

Astrid Olson, my artist neighbor two blocks over, will be here at 2:00 to paint in some colors. She just went through an ugly divorce, but I wait for an opportunity to tell her about God.

The new record player has two speakers attached, so music infiltrates the room.

Nineteen-fifties Gospel Classics is one of my favorite records. "Give me that old time religion" makes

20

me want to dance. I can envision the angels doing the jitterbug.

"Get to work, Violet," I mumble. I pour some fresh turpentine in the cup, uncover the ceramic paints, and arrange my brushes with the utmost organization. I glance over at Astrid's work area. "She's always so organized."

"It's getting chilly out there, but it's nice and warm in here," Astrid comments a half hour later.

My attractive blonde friend has lost weight over the last few weeks.

I turn the record player off. "Do you think we'll have a white Christmas?"

"I don't want to think about that. Too depressing for me to talk about."

"Your son will be with you, I hope."

"We don't talk about the holidays at all. His job at the United Nations keeps him in Manhattan most of the time. His girlfriend lives in the Bronx, so he spends weekends with her."

"Can I pray about this with you right now?"

"I don't mean to be rude, Violet, but I just can't grasp a hold of this God of yours. I have no problem if you want to pray for me when I am not around."

Closing my eyes, I mumble a quick prayer. "I understand, Astrid. Okay, please fill in the green on the tiles."

Later that day while waiting for Henry's train to pull into the station, I grab a *Newsday* from the newsstand.

It's hard to read under the dim lights inside the ticket office, but an article catches my eye.

Gertrude Crawford, a forty-nine-year-old widow from Queens opens a 24-room hotel for displaced homeless veterans. Thorn-Mel Hall is in Mount Sanai on the North Shore of Long Island.

The estranged men came from Northport Veteran's Administration Hospital. One man described his new home as a Swiss chalet without the mountains. "I'm ashamed of my neighbors because they're rude and inconsiderate of these warm-hearted human beings," noted Mrs. Crawford.

As the train pulls into the station, I smile at this act of kindness one woman is taking to help folks in need. *Maybe, God can use me too.*

My husband meets me on the platform. "Hello there, beautiful."

We exchange hugs. "I got you the newspaper. There is an interesting article about a new home for homeless men in Mount Sanai."

We pass right by it on our way home. Although it's dark and impossible to see any buildings from the road, Thorn Mel Hall's small sign is illuminated by our car's headlights.

"Now, you must be very careful when you drive around here by yourself, Violet. No telling what these guys will do."

"Henry, they're probably harmless. It's a wonderful thing for a woman to do. She wouldn't do it if her life was in danger.

On Saturday after the first snowfall, we pull on our boots, warm winter coats, hats, and mittens to venture out to hunt down a Christmas tree. We pile into the station wagon, drive it to the end of Sea Cliff Avenue, and hike uphill through the snow.

"Daddy, this is so far. I can't walk anymore," whines Jane.

Peter points and runs ahead. "Look over there. Pine trees."

The smell of the green needles fills the air. The trees look too big for the small living space in our house.

Henry looks at one lonely tree from top to bottom. "If I saw the trunk right here, then it should fit perfectly."

"It's too big, Henry," I shout.

He pats his head. "What do you think, Peter?"

Peter wrinkles his brow and points off in the distance "That tree over there is a lot smaller."

Two hours later, after some hot cocoa and chocolate chip cookies, Henry and Peter drag the tree into the house. Too bad there isn't a hole in the roof because then it would be the right size for sure.

I try to contain myself from a hysterical laughing outburst.

We go through this process every year. Poor dear. He won't break down and buy a precut tree.

"Peter, help me unwind the lights so we can get these on tonight," orders Henry.

"Do I have to? Can't we do this tomorrow? It's Sunday and we have all day."

I'm feeling frustrated with the whole situation. "I was hoping we could go to church in the morning."

Henry yawns. "No church for me. I like to relax on Sunday morning with the newspaper. I'll take the kids to get hard rolls and cold cuts for lunch. You can go to church, Violet."

Jane rushes to my side. "I want to go to church with you, Mommy."

Weekends come and go so fast. The Monday routine seems to always be the same, until today.

As I pass Thorn Mel Hall, I see two shabbily dressed men walking along the side of the road. I slow down and stop the car on the side. I watch them proceed without gloves, hats, or boots.

These poor men must be freezing. Should I give them a ride?

"God, show me Your will here. Henry fixed the door on the passenger side, and there's room in the back too. Should I offer them a ride? Amen."

The wind picks up. I pull alongside them, roll down the window, and smile. "Can I give you a lift someplace?"

Looking at me in astonishment, the taller of the two says, "Uh, yes, Ma'am. That would be nice."

"Where are you going?"

"To the Miller Place Library."

"Hop in. It's on my way home."

Chapter Five

Most folks are deathly afraid of my new-found friends because they smell rather odd and their clothes are ragged or plain worn out. God has virtually healed me of the psychological problems that plagued my life until recently. Maybe, that's why I'm not afraid to be around them. They fought in the war for the great United States of America, and that alone makes me completely indebted to them.

"What's your name, Miss?" asks the older of the two.

"Violet. What's yours?"

"Well, Violet, my name is William, but my friends call me Captain Bill, and this here is Sammy. He doesn't say much."

We're almost to the library. "Do you boys live at Thorn Mel Hall by any chance?"

"Ah, yep. We do. Now, you're sorry you picked us up, right?"

I slow to a stop. "It was nice meeting you both. Do you have a ride back?"

Captain Bill reaches his hand out to mine. "Yes, we do. Thanks for the lift. You're a mighty kind lady."

Christmas is over, but the children are still on vacation. The pond across the street from the school is a perfect place to ice skate. It's the gathering place for all the children in the neighborhood. Jane's tickled pink with her brand-new white figure skates. Although a bit wobbly at first, she's becoming quite the skater. Today, we're skating as a family, which is a very rare occurrence. The pond is a part of Randall Farms. Someone always builds a nice bonfire with logs, so we have someplace to keep warm.

Jane wobbles over to me, and I grab her hand for support. "Mommy, who are those strange men over there? They keep staring at us."

I wave to the men. "Captain Bill, Sammy, come here."

Jane hides behind me and latches on to my jacket. "No. No. They scare me."

"Hi, fellas. Come sit here by the fire and warm up."

A few boys leap to their feet. "Let's get out of here. These men are crazy. No telling what they'll do."

"This ain't a very good idea, Miss Violet. We don't mean anyone no harm," stammers Captain Bill.

My daughter flees from the scene, yelling, "Daddy, Daddy."

In an instant, Henry is by my side, and I can feel the hostility rise within him. "It's time to go home, Violet."

I take a deep breath. "Henry, these are my new friends from Thorn Mel Hall. You know, the hotel for veterans of war right down the road."

"Your friends? What are you talking about?"

Peter and a few of his friends are standing nearby with mock hockey sticks ready to strike at a moment's notice.

Captain Bill pulls Sammy to his feet. "We'll be seeing you, Violet."

I grab Captain Bill's arm and glare at my husband. "Wait a cotton-picking minute."

"Get out of here, you dirty old men," Peter Paten, a heavy-set teen, shouts out.

26

I place myself in front of my guests. "The Bible says don't judge lest you be judged. You don't know anything about these two. They're the nicest people I have met, and all they want is to be accepted."

Mr. Salovey, our next-door neighbor, roars a bellowing laugh. "So, you're a religious fanatic now, huh?"

"Kids, get your skates off now. We'll be leaving this instant. Violet, get in the car," Henry shouts.

I face Captain Bill and Sammy. "Do you have a ride home?"

With sadness in his eyes, Captain Bill mutters, "Mom Crawford is picking us up after she does the grocery shopping and gets the mail. Goodbye, Miss Violet."

The tears roll down my cheeks as I watch them walk away toward the far side of the pond.

"Bon voyage, jerks," yells Peter Paten. I turn on my heels, then I pull up all the energy within me and push that big brute of a kid flat on his back.

My son, with skates slung over his shoulder, grabs my arm. "Mom, we must go now. This kid's father is the school principal."

Shocked at what I just heard; I still manage to kick the kid in the leg before he gets up.

"Ouch. You better run Peter with the freckles, because you'll be a-hurting when I get on my feet. Mrs. Funk, you're in big trouble with my father."

That night, after the children are in bed, we change into our pajamas and robes. Henry stokes the fire, pours two glasses of red wine, and covers us with the afghan his mother gave us.

"Listen, my dear Violet, the friends you are making are a bad influence on our children. Poor Jane's frightened out of her wits. She told me that you have driven those two men several places with her in the car. That's dangerous for both of you."

"I can help them. They trust me. I want them to know Jesus like I do. I desire the same for you, Henry."

"Now, you are talking like a quack. I hate to say it."

"You were with me when a nervous breakdown nearly broke me for good. My heart was shattered, and the demonic world was out to get me. If I didn't turn my heart to the living God, where would I be?"

"I'm grateful for the change in you, sweetheart, but this religion thing is yours and yours alone. I'm simply not buying it. That's it. End of discussion."

I lean my head on his shoulder. "Okay, but you can't stop me from praying for you and the kids."

He strokes my hair. "That's fine. Now, let's enjoy the beautiful fire and each other's company before turning in for the night."

"Jane does love going to Sunday school."

He sighs. "That's because you're the teacher."

After several minutes of silence, I speak. "Henry, I want you to know one thing."

"What's that?"

"Prayer does change things."

For some reason, the winters on the island are not hard to endure. Maybe the salt air has something to do with it. There always seems to be enough snow to go sleigh riding and some great hills for the kids to do it. Now that Peter is going to be a teenager in a couple of days, he doesn't want his little sister tagging behind him everywhere he goes.

I don't know why, but my daughter is always so sad. She rarely smiles, and if I didn't reach out to the few little girls in the neighborhood, she wouldn't have any friends. Lucky is the best thing she has going right now. Lord, I pray that she will never succumb to a nervous breakdown the way my dear mother or I did. Please protect my daughter from self-destruction. I love her so much, Father.

"What's for supper, Mother?" asks Peter as he sniffs like a dog around the kitchen.

"Your favorite. Pot roast."

"Yum. Aunt Flossie said in her letter to me that she's coming for my birthday and staying over one night?"

I flip the meat over in the pot to brown. "I'm so glad she'll stay over. She likes to drive rather than take the train."

"Mom, where is she going to sleep? There are four beds and four people already."

I chuckle and wrap my arms around him. "Son, I will sleep on the couch. Auntie can bunk with your sister."

He shakes his head. "Does she know that?"

I look around the room for Jane. "No, but she'll be fine with it. So, don't worry."

Peter seeks out his erector set to complete an invention. "Where's the dog anyway? He's not outside."

"He's probably in your sister's room on the bed." I venture down the short hall and open the door.

In a serious coloring mode, she scowls at me. "Can I have a snack?"

I look on the bed and floor of the small room. "How about an orange? Have you seen Lucky?"

She jumps from her chair. "He was on the front steps when we came home from school."

Within seconds, we sling the front door open. "Lucky. Here boy," we call out.

"Lucky! Lucky!" Jane squeals and bolts out the door, down the steps without a coat or hat.

"Peter. Come quick. Get your sister back in the house before she catches a cold. Jane, get back in this house immediately. Your brother will find the dog."

She freezes in place with her arms folded. "Where's my doggy?"

Dressed in his winter garb, Peter coaxes his sister. "Sis, come in the house where it's warm. I'll find him, okay? Can't be too far."

c౭౨ౚ

It's getting dark, and Peter has been gone an hour already. The dog never goes any farther than the Showalter's house a half-mile down the road. Lucky loves to play with their beagle when it's outside.

I'm so glad that Henry took the car and left it at the station today. He should be on his way home and will pick Peter up on his way. I have tried to avert Jane's attention by coloring with her, but she keeps on crying anyway.

I lift her in my lap and rock her. "Shush. Shush, sweetie. Your doggy is probably playing in the snow with a new friend somewhere."

She drifts off to sleep in my arms, and I start getting drowsy myself. Everything is silent except for the drip, drip, drip of the kitchen faucet.

Peter and Henry burst through the front door and startle both of us. Jane rubs her eyes, grabs her teddy, and flies down the hall. "Daddy, did you see Lucky?"

Peter rushes to my side. "I found Lucky dead on the side of the road," he whispers.

Henry drops his briefcase on the floor and picks his daughter up. "Come, Tot. Let's have some supper. Your father is famished."

"Where is he though?" She sniffs.

Peter grabs her tiny hand. "The neighbors are keeping an eye out for him, Sis."

Somehow, she accepts the fact that the dog is lost and falls asleep for the night. Peter's a strong boy and seldom shows his emotions, but we knew finding Lucky dead on the side of the road was tough. "I'll be in my room if you need me," he calls out as he leaves the room.

Cuddling together on the couch, Henry softly speaks, "Whoever hit the dog, moved him to the side of the road. Lucky was still warm, so must have happened recently."

A few tears roll down my cheek. "Where's the dog now?"

"We got a box from the cellar and put him in that. I'll bury him in the morning. The ground is soft under the snow, which is good."

"Who did this, Henry? Our little girl is going to be heartbroken."

"I know, honey, but her love of all animals will be the comfort she needs. She's been asking me when she can have her first riding lesson. Spring is coming, so I can make that happen."

⚮

Today is Peter's thirteenth birthday and winter vacation from school. The warm snap practically melted all the snow. A light dusting remains, which means children get mighty bored with little to do outside. The Monopoly game fills the small table, Ginny's dolls and clothes are strewn everywhere, and pillows and blankets fill the floor for mock sleeping bags. My aunt will be here soon. Henry met her in Queens, and they will drive home together.

"Come on, kids, pick up this mess. Your father and Aunt Flossie will be here any minute."

"But she loves to play Monopoly, Mom." Peter scowls.

"Peter, I have to set the table for supper. You can always take it out after cake and ice cream."

"I thought Auntie Flossie liked Chinese checkers better," screams Jane as she continues playing.

"Put those dolls away right now."

She tunes me out, as usual.

Her brother puts the game on the shelf and proceeds to grab the dolls out of his sister's hands.

With crocodile tears rolling down her face, she sits on all her doll clothes. "Leave my friends alone."

I check the roast chicken in the oven and the potatoes boiling on the stove before I tend to the brewing ordeal waiting to explode. Anger starts to have its way with me.

Picking up the dolls and the girl playing with them, I yell as loud as my voice will go, "Go to your rooms, now."

The siblings scramble to their rooms as the front door opens.

Confusion flickers across my aunt's face but words cannot find a way out of her lips.

With a pile of pillows, blankets, and other things in my arms, I hug her as best I can. "Auntie. Oh, Auntie. It's so nice to have you here for a visit finally."

Dressed in a black seal coat with a fur collar, donning a matching hat, and carrying a beautifully wrapped package, she moves into the living room.

"Let me take your coat, please?" offers Henry after putting down her suitcase.

She sweeps her gaze over the whole family living area. "Where are the children? It appears that I might have come at a bad time."

"Peter, Jane. Come here please and greet your auntie."

Sheepishly, they slink out of their rooms.

"Aunt Flossie, I'm glad you're here for my birthday," Peter says as he hugs her.

Flossie smiles as she removes her hat and coat. "I wouldn't miss it for the world."

Peter's absolutely thrilled with the wood burning kit his great aunt gave him. After a chicken dinner with all the fixings and a couple of rounds of Chinese checkers, the children go to bed. "I so wish we could afford to build an addition to this house. It's so small, Auntie. There's no place for a guest to have privacy."

Henry grunts and groans from his big chair. "An addition, huh? Do you know how much that would cost?"

I drain the sink and wipe the counters. "Thank you, Auntie. Go relax in front of the fire for a while. I'll join you in a few minutes."

"I'm eager to hear about this idea, Violet. Loans are easy to come by these days, so it could be a reality soon for both of you."

If my aunt likes the idea of an addition, I'd better jump at the chance to show her my drawings. My hear jumps for joy.

Pulling out my sketch pad, I flip the pages to a drawing of the potential wing. "Here, look at this."

Now, Henry's wide awake with curiosity as he joins us at the table. "Looks like you have been thinking about this for a long time."

"The tile business is flourishing, and I could use an art studio with substantial office space included, among other things."

Auntie smiles as she examines the layout before her. "So, this wall would come down, and a new living room would be here, a hallway, a nice, big master bedroom, walk-in closet, large bathroom."

"Can I take a gander?" Henry asks with enthusiasm.

He looks it all over with a fine-tooth comb then winks at Auntie. "I see you even added steps to the cellar and, of course, a studio of your dreams."

"This is so professional, Violet Pearl. I'm very proud of how talented you are." Auntie smiles.

Henry removes himself from the table to stoke the fire. "I don't mean to burst your bubble, but I don't think we can afford this, honey. Not at this time anyway."

"Henry, this place is way too small for the four of you, and my niece needs a bigger place to work out of," suggests Auntie.

He shakes his head. "I suppose you gave it to an architect for an estimate already, Vi."

"I've been praying about this for some time now."

"Tsk. Tsk. My dear niece, money's what you need, not prayer."

I hug Henry from behind. "Actually, there's a young architect that just moved in down the road."

Chapter Six

Spring, 1955

I'm learning not to be anxious about anything but instead go to God in prayer about what ails me. I prayed unceasingly for a new wing on our little house, and I know God interceded and led me to a Christian architect. Since the ceramic tile business is doing phenomenally well, I was able to apply for a loan. Auntie graciously paid the architect. Henry grumbled for a few days, but now that the constructions almost completed, he's enjoying the progress. God is good.

"I'm so excited, Henry. The contractor says that we should be ready to paint in less than two weeks. Don't you have some time off soon?"

"I do. I bet you want to save a little money and do the painting ourselves. I like the idea, but the studio has such high ceilings and will be difficult to paint between the beams."

"Sam Clark from Port Jeff does paint on the weekends. Perhaps he can do one room for us. You're almost done with the tile floors in the bathrooms, aren't you?"

"The master bath is finished, but the guest bath needs two feet of tile yet. Tough on the knees. Last night, I was working on that thing until midnight."

I lay my head on his shoulder as we watch the fire burn out. "Just think, in a matter of weeks, we will be able to sleep in the same bed every night and the kids will have their privacy too."

◦⦿ℛ◉◦

It's hard to find time to spend with the children these days. I'm either up to all hours of the night, painting and firing tiles, working at the shop, or delivering orders all over the island. Mrs. Crawford from Thorn Mel asked me to drive two of the men to the Port Jefferson Library every Tuesday since it's so close to the shop.

"Thank you, Miss Violet," Walter utters, getting out of the car.

"Ah, yep. Tanks, Miss. Much obliged," shouts Sammy.

"I'll be at the shop, if you need anything, okay? Otherwise, I'll see you boys next week."

There's a lot of summer merchandise to order, but it's fun sprucing up the store with lots of artificial violets. All Christmas stock is 50-75% off, which leaves a few bare shelves in the small nook upstairs.

Ding a ling, the door chimes as it opens.

Hearing the sound, I prevail down the creaky stairs. "Good afternoon, may I help you?"

The attractive woman has long, jet-black hair with a perfectly made up face. The bright red wool velour swagger coat matches a straight skirt of the same color. Her accessories of black patent leather pumps, handbag, and gloves offset the ensemble.

She reaches her hand out to mine. "Are you Violet?"

"Yes. What can I do for you? Miss?"

"How rude of me. My name is Jean Tish from Ridge."

"Not too far from where I live in Miller Place."

She smiles at me. "Of course. I drive through there on occasion because it's so quaint."

"I just marked down the remainder of my winter merchandise and, as you can see, spring is busting out all over."

She chuckles. "I would like to hire you to paint tiles for my new swimming pool."

"I would love to do that. Please sit down, Jean. May I get you a cup of tea?"

"No thank you." She pulls out a simple sketch of three different fish.

I glance over the artwork before me. "Interesting design. Would I have to copy this precisely?"

"This is just a rough idea. You'll have time to draw a sample for me if you choose to do the work."

I hand her a business card. "I'll put together designs based on this artwork. Call me in two days to set up a time to meet."

"I'll do that. We'll meet at my house so you can see the pool and measure."

cseлgo

The days are getting longer, grass is greener, and the tulips I planted are in full bloom. Henry has plowed space for a little vegetable garden to the right of the driveway. Look at that house now, Violet Pearl. I wave to Jane. She's waving at me through the picture window in the new living room. I grab the groceries from the back seat of the old station wagon and slam the doors shut with my buttocks.

Jane rushes to my side. "What's for supper, Mommy? I'm hungry."

I hand her a small bag to carry as we go inside. "Where's your brother?"

"In his room, of course."

"Peter? Are you doing your homework?" I yell.

He shouts back through closed door, "Yep. Be out in a few minutes."

I chop up three tomatoes, open two cans of tomato sauce and one can of paste, and mix it all in a large Revere Ware stock pot. Jane sits on a stool at the new Formica counter; so she sees everything I'm doing. I chop an onion, garlic, and green pepper. "How was school today? Do you have homework?"

"Charlene's having a birthday party, and I wasn't invited."

"That's not nice of her, is it? Any homework?"

"Arithmetic."

"Your daddy will help you with that after supper. In the meantime, I think *Fury* is on television right now."

She nearly falls off the stool. "My favorite. I love that horse."

It's amazing that she got over Lucky so quickly, but horses have taken over her whole life, it seems. There. The sauce is simmering, the water's ready to boil, and the garlic bread will go in the oven when Henry comes home. The used 1950 Nash Rambler he bought last week is a Godsend.

"I'm home. What smells so good?" Henry asks as he hugs me.

"Spaghetti and garlic bread. Come on, kids. Turn off the television. Supper time."

I've added a line of unique stationary with designs of mostly violets at the shop. Since we have a lot of tourists that come through over the course of the summer, postcards are the most reasonable souvenir.

What a beautiful day out there, I muse as I pull the revolving rack out of the box. *Good. Right by the door.*

Five for twenty-five cents. I'm so glad that I arrived an hour earlier today, because this box of cards will take a while to categorize. The magnificent ferry, the harbor, Schooner restaurant, the historic Dunford's hotel and, oh my goodness. It's me. Stacks of postcards of me. My legs look so white.

The ring of the telephone brings me back to reality. "Hello, Violetile's Shop."

"Violet, this is Jean. Jean Tish."

"Hi, Jean. How are you today?"

"Can you break away for lunch at my place today? I want you to meet the mason."

The red wood, ultra- modern structure has three tiers, and to the naked eye, proves to be an unusual sight. Beautiful landscaping of various shrubbery embraces the color of the wood. The house sits by itself on five acres with pine trees on either side of the long driveway.

With a box of tile samples in my arm, I ring the doorbell.

"Violet, please come in," offers Jean.

"This is a lovely house, Jean. So artistic in design."

Walking up six steps to the main floor, I'm amazed at the view of the backyard. "That's going to be a good-size pool."

She laughs. "Do you swim?"

"Yes. I love to."

"Well, you'll be my first guest to swim with me. How does that sound? I hope you like oyster stew."

"How did you know it's my favorite seafood meal?"

She points to a well-appointed, set table. "Please sit here while I dish up the stew, and enjoy the Waldorf salad and warm croissants in the meantime."

After we share the duties of clearing the table, "Come to my office while we wait for Billy Weston, the mason, to arrive. He'll be here shortly."

"Can I do the dishes for you?"

"Thank you, Violet, but the maid will tend to it."

No wonder this place is spic and span. No dust bunnies in sight anywhere. That's why she has perfect nails, hair, and makeup too.

"Jean, I brought these samples for you to look at. You can choose six- or four-and-a-quarter-inch tiles for the border around the pool. Either way, I'll have to make up a silk screen for the designs you choose."

She looks them over with a smile. "I love all three of them. The colors are brilliant. Maybe you can design every fourth tile with coral or sea grass?"

"I could certainly do that once we see how many tiles the mason will need."

A gong-like doorbell brings me to my feet.

"That's probably him now." She scurries out the door.

Billy is short but very muscular. His grey hair is long and straggly but pulled back behind the ears. Donning a black leather jacket over a plain white tee shirt and jeans indicates a possible rebellious spirit.

"Violet, this is Billy Weston. You'll be working with him from now on."

He winks at me, which sends my heart into a fast, pulsating beat.

I reach out my hand to his. "Nice to meet you, Mr. Weston."

He chomps on his gum. "Are these the tiles you were talking about, Jean?"

"Yes. Violet is a well-acclaimed artist on Long Island."

"The pool business is booming these days, and I have customers that would pay good money for hand-painted tiles like these. Have you ever done something like this before?"

"No, but I've done murals for fireplace facings and backdrops for kitchens too."

"The pool will have to be measured to determine how many tiles needed. I have another appointment this afternoon, but maybe we can measure tomorrow."

Looking at her watch, Jean stands up. "Come tomorrow afternoon around 2:00. I should be here, but if not, please go around to the pool and do what you can. My daughter has a soccer match at the high school, and I promised I would watch. I'll catch up with you two. Tootles."

Billy grabs my hand, but I pull away. "Let's go now. That's if you are up to it, pretty Violet."

This fella makes me feel very uncomfortable and being alone with him is not something I wish to do. I can hear the clanging of dishes in the kitchen so that tells me the maid is still in the house. I get up, grab my pocketbook and the sample box, and head to the door. A warm tap on my bottom makes me leap forward.

I turn on my heels and glare at him. "Don't ever do that again."

He lets out a loud laugh and another wink. "Well, excuse me, Miss Prude."

I keep my distance as we head out the back door to a massive deck and down two flights of stairs. The waterless, oval-shaped pool has a three-foot walkway around the entire opening. Cement steps lead down. Landscapers are busy planting shrubbery gardens in each corner as we stand in the middle of the empty space.

"It will be beneficial to use six-inch tiles rather than the smaller one," Billy suggests.

"I agree. I'm sure you're very good in calculating how many we'll need after the measurements are taken tomorrow."

41

He ascends the steps. "Meet me here at 2:00, Violet. I have an industrial tape that measures up to 100 feet. We can get this thing measured in no time."

Billy's leaning against his van staring at my car when I drive away a short time later. *I really don't want to be alone with that character. He gives me the creeps. Good thing Jean will be here tomorrow.*

∾⊙≈⊚∽

"I tell you, Henry, the mason is very strange, but Jean is so educated and from a very wealthy family. She wouldn't hire anyone that came with baggage of any kind. His work is known all over the island."

"So, he made a pass at you. You are very attractive, you know."

"His eyes. They are shifty and untrusting. He made me feel very uncomfortable."

He wraps me in the safety of his arms. "Honey, this order is the biggest one for the year. You'll be able to pay off the loan in no time if you keep getting business like this."

"I'm glad tomorrow's Saturday, so you'll be home if I should need you. Are you taking the kids for their first riding lesson?"

Silence fills the dark bedroom.

"Henry?"

Faint, rhythmic snoring tells me it's time to call it a night.

Lord God, grant me peace about Billy Weston. He needs a Savior. He needs you. I tend to judge people for the worse, but if I can pick up displaced old men on the highway, then I can be around Billy. Help me to have the courage to talk to him about you tomorrow. Amen.

42

⌒⊚⍟⊚⌐

It's a beautiful day and perfect to plant some marigolds. Henry grew vegetable plants from seeds under grow lights in the cellar. We enjoy French toast and bacon for brunch, and with help from the kids, our gardening wishes are fulfilled by 1:00.

"Daddy, can we go to the stable now?" calls Jane from the front steps.

He approaches her with his pail of garden tools. "They're expecting us at the St. James stable at 2:00. I know you're excited, Tot, but we have to wash up and change our clothes."

Peter rolls up the hose and joins his sister. "Do I have to go with you, Dad?"

"Yes, Son. This is something we can do together while your mother's working. I know you would rather be playing baseball with your friends, but family time is important."

"I could go with Mother and help her. Horses are too smelly for me."

I giggle, tapping my son on the head. "I'll be home before you. Go. Have a good time."

"See you later, Mom." They wave goodbye as they get into the car. I follow them out of our community until they turn right, and I go left.

Chapter Seven

The pine trees cast eerie shadows across the long driveway as I venture toward the house. Billy's van is the only car I see, but Jean's is probably in the three-car garage. Getting out of my beat-up old car, I wonder where the maid's car is because it's too far off the beaten track for a bus to drop her off.

Oh, that's right. It's Saturday. Probably her day off. Jean and her husband are most likely out back by the pool already. Gee, it's so quiet around here. Not even a breeze.

I ring the doorbell several times. No answer. I venture on the slate walkway to the side of the house, which joins a wooded path to the vast backyard.

"Violet, over here." Billy waves.

Reluctantly, but with my head held high, I walk over. "Hi, Billy. I don't have much time, so can we get right to work?"

He pulls the tape measure out of his toolbox. "Take one end and walk until I tell you to stop?"

Taking the tape as I walk, I call back, "Where's Jean?"

"Stop there. I don't think anyone's home."

For some reason, I want to drop the tape and run for my life. "Twenty feet," I yell back to him.

"Okay. Go around the curve of the pool until I tell ya to stop again."

With a clipboard in his hands, he walks back to the driveway. "Okay. The pool is thirty-eight by twenty. I'll

44

have to buy several curved tiles. They can be plain, but the same shade as the other tiles."

"That will work. My job will begin when you get the tiles to me. Here's my business card, Billy."

He takes the card. Good. You'll be hearing from me soon."

I turn on my heels as quickly as I can, open the back door of my car, and grab my pocketbook. *I must stop at the store and grab a vegetable for dinner.* All at once, I feel strong arms wrapped around my body and, within seconds, I'm lifted and thrown into the back of a smelly van.

I scream and I kick, but to no avail.

"Shut up, would you?" He holds me down with one hand and gags my mouth with a bandana.

Tears of fear begin to flow as I thrash my feet at him. He ties my feet together and binds my hands behind. My stomach flip-flops.

"No one can hear you. Jean left a note on the door. Everyone's at an away soccer game." He slams the door.

My helpless body is wedged between buckets, bags of tile grout and cement, a sledgehammer, and several pairs of dirty rubber boots.

Bump. Bump. Bump. *It feels like this van is pushing something. Oh, my God, protect and help me.* Breathe. Just Breathe.

Alan Freed, disc jockey for 1010 AM out of New York is playing the top forty rock and roll songs, but I'm scared for my life. "Maybelline, why can't you be free?" invades the space of the entire automobile.

"Talking about things you used to do," shouts my abductor.

The only windows other than in the front are the small ones on the back-panel doors. I wiggle myself from my side to my back as the anguish in my heart intensifies.

"Oh, Violet. Oh, dear Violet. You're all mine now," croaks the voice from up front.

All I can see are trees, trees, more trees and power lines. The sun has set. My hands are tied behind my back, so I can't get to my watch, but it's probably 5:00 by now. *Either we're almost to the city by now or he's driving on desolate country roads, because I feel like I've been back here for hours.*

He slows down and turns onto a bumpy, gravelly road. The trees are so thick over it, everything's pitch black now. My heart sinks into the pit of my stomach.

What's he going to do with me? I didn't do anything to deserve this. Jean will see my vacant car and call the police. Wait. He was pushing something with this van. Was it my car? There were sounds of cracking and breaking branches. The area around the Tish's is dense and wooded. They live in the wilderness.

The van stops. The front door slams shut.

I breathe a sigh of relief.

The door by my feet opens, and hands grab hold of my ankles. "I'll be back in a little while, my pretty one. I have to wait until the coast is 100% clear before I move you to your new home."

I squirm and mumble the best I can, "Let me go. Please let me go."

"Now, now, Miss Violet. Calm down. No one can hear you. Don't you know that by now?"

The door closes and locks as I continue to lay in this dark nightmare of fear.

Uncontrollable tears roll down my face, and the urge to go to the bathroom turns into a real act.

It can't be helped.

I vaguely remember being carried from automobile to bed. It was dark, cold, and unrecognizable. I must have

passed out from delirium because I now realize, I'm not at home.

The small room smells like a horse barn or maybe a machine shop in a barn? There are only two small windows at the top of the raised ceiling, and I know this because the room is illuminated by one lamp on a small dresser. Awake and confused, I throw the handmade quilt off me. As I look at my hands and feet, I realize I'm somewhat free. I run to the door and try to open it. Nothing happens.

"Help, help, help! Someone help me," I scream.

As I reach to my mouth and yell out again, I recognize the fact I'm free in this small space only. I fall to the floor with my back against the door and weep until the water from within is gone.

I pull myself up and walk around the room in muddled trepidation. A dilapidated kitchen table and chair adorns one corner, a makeshift open bathroom consisting of toilet and sink in another, a twin bed with a pile of clothes neatly folded on top. I talk softly to myself, "Why all the fluff if he plans on hurting me? Did he kidnap me for a ransom? What else could it be?"

"Mo-o-o. Moo," bellows the sound of a cow right outside the bed wall.

I run to each wall and pin my ear against it. Nothing, except a cow chomping on its cud.

"Is that my pocketbook on the chair? A pitcher of water and two deli sandwiches too."

Henry, Peter, Jane, my family. They must be frantic with worry. Billy's van is one of a kind. It won't take long for the police to track him down and find me. I might as well change my clothes and eat something. Dungaree coveralls and a flannel shirt? How feminine. A six pack of lady's underpants. My size. How did he know?

Curling up on the bed with my purse in my lap, I pull out the little leather New Testament I always carry with me. The Gideons came to our church last fall and left a box of them to distribute.

"Oh, my God," I cry out. "Why are you testing me? I'm prey to a deranged man, and terrified. Keep the evil one from this place, in Jesus' name. Please Lord, save this hurting man's soul. Don't let me fall into depression or any kind of mental anguish. Grant me words of comfort from your word. Amen."

I flip the pages to James 1:12. "Blessed is the man who perseveres under trial, because when he has stood the test, he will receive the crown of life that God has promised to those that love Him."

Peace overwhelms me as I dump the contents of my bag out on the bed. I grab my toothbrush, toothpaste, and hairbrush and head to the simulated restroom. Sudden fatigue hits me after cleaning up and rinsing out soiled clothing from the day before. The only strength I have left is to put everything back in my handbag and lie down.

I try hard to keep my eyes open, but sleep encompasses me instead.

I can hear birds tweeting in the distance as the leaves on the trees rustle from the wind blowing through. The cow must be someplace else in the pasture outside this barn. My eyes focus at the blue skies glistening through the tiny windows out of reach. I look at my watch: 7:30, *it must be Monday! I must find a way out of here today.*

I roll over on my side and gasp at the sight before me. Sitting in a chair, is Billy Weston.

Overwhelmed with sweat and anger, I crouch in the corner of the bed, folded up like a cocoon, except my head is at full attention.

In complete innocence, he smiles, "Well, good morning, beautiful. I see the sandwiches are gone. Good, huh?"

I clench my clammy fists. "Don't touch me. Keep away, you beast."

He laughs obnoxiously. "Now, is that any way to treat a gentleman?"

"You can't keep me here forever, Billy. The Tishs know your car and have probably called the police by now. Kidnapping will get you thrown in jail for a long time."

"That van is no longer in existence. I have a truck now. Oh, about your old jalopy, it's down deep in the woods somewhere in Ridge. So people will think you flew the coop."

Now, I want to rise like a gorilla and pounce on him. "You big brute! You might as well kill me and get it over with."

He shakes his head. "I will never hurt you, my dear girl."

"Then what are you going to do with me? Put me up for ransom?"

"Something like that."

Building up a little bit of courage, I bite my lip. "That's a laugh. A real hoot, if you ask me. I don't come from wealth of any kind. You might get a few dollars out of it. That's it."

"Oh, come on, Miss Violet. I happen to know that Mr. Kahn, the millionaire you did the fireplace mural for a few years ago, has a mad crush on you. He'll come through with my demand."

He rises from the chair, and I get ready to strike. "I'm not ready for that yet. All I want to do is look at you and gaze upon your beauty."

My mouth is dry, and cheeks are hot. "But why?"

His back is to me as he places his hand on the door.

"Billy Weston. Answer me. Why do you have to keep me locked up in here to do that?"

As he turns, his face is beet red, with anger in his eyes. "No more questions. No more. Do you hear me?" He starts coming towards me.

I grab my New Testament and hold it in front of me. "Stay away from me, in the name of Almighty God."

He drops his hands and head. "I brought a hot plate, instant coffee, and a few cans of soup for you. There's a pot too." He turns to open the door.

I take a deep breath, sliding off the bed. "Please, please let me go, Billy. I'll tell everyone I went to the city for a mini vacation." I scan the room quickly to see if there's anything that could be used as a weapon.

Billy Weston freezes in the doorway for a moment. "Bye, Violet. I have to go to work now." The door shuts and a deadbolt locks in place.

I fly to the hardwood door and bang with all the strength within me. "Let me go, please let me go," I cry out as loud as my voice will carry.

It's no use. I'm like Rapunzel waiting for my Prince Henry to free me. How can he? He has no idea where I am. My little girl will be lost without me. She lost her doggy, and that was hard enough, but losing me will devastate her for sure. Let's see, it's been two full days already. Oh, Father God, keep me strong through this pit of misery. Don't let me lose hope. Amen. Sighing deeply, I pull myself up once again and move around the small room, feeling the walls for holes or a hint of an escape. I look at the floor and realize it's brand new.

He carpeted this just recently. A pretty good job at that.

Getting on all fours, I pull a corner of the rug off the hard wood. I bang my fist on the small space.

It's hollow. That means there must be crawl space under this room. If only I had a saw.

50

Chapter Eight

When I awake on day three, I hear the door latch shut. Only God knows how long Billy sat and stared at me, but if that's all he's going to do, it's okay for a while anyway. He added a few things.

A red velvet robe hanging on a clothes rack, two magazines, and a transistor radio. He's thoughtful and caring in a strange sort of way.

"We interrupt this program to be on the lookout for a missing woman from Miller Place in Suffolk County. Violet Pearl Funk was last seen on Saturday by her family. She was meeting with Billy Weston, a mason contractor, at the Tesh home in Ridge. Mr. Weston claims he saw the postcard model drive away while he was packing up his van. Violet is thirty years old, has black hair, and brown eyes. Please contact the Port Jefferson police department if seen," conveys the news reporter as I flip on the radio.

I slump into the chair. "At least they're looking for me. If only someone would follow Billy."

I fiddle with the hard roll and butter he left on a nice china plate. "Nothing to use as a weapon, but maybe there is a loose floorboard somewhere."

Talking out loud clears my mind, and hopefully in doing so, I can figure a way to escape.

On my hands and knees once again, I crawl around the perimeter of the room, pulling up the carpet every so many inches. "He didn't do a very good job of securing this to the plywood."

About two o'clock in the afternoon after sweat and tears, I have a breakthrough. "Ah ha. A loose floorboard." I leap to my feet, run to the door, and press my ear to it. *I don't hear him yet, but Billy doesn't seem to come during the day. At least not yet.* I must be careful not to reveal what I'm doing in this spot. I pull the rug back several feet. Take a few deep breaths and pray. I pull and prod the sagging piece of wood. Fortunately, it's short, and the more I pull, the looser the nails get.

"I would think I would hear his car pull up, but maybe he leaves it somewhere and walks. I might as well talk out loud. After all, someone could hear me. I know I'm making noise; it can't be helped. It's a chance I have to take."

I take a break and leaf through a *Family Circle* magazine he left. I listen. The only sounds are birds tweeting and rustling leaves from a nearby tree.

I venture back to the possible escape route. With a little prying of the nails using a butter knife, I'm able to pull them out of the wood. Cautiously, I lift the plank out, and my heart leaps for joy at the sight below.

Dirt.

I don't know if I should jump with happiness, cover it up quickly, or step down. Choosing the latter, I plant one foot on the soft dirt and then the next. The space falls just above my knees.

Crunch, crunch. Crunch. The sound of footsteps seems to be getting closer.

My heart starts to race. I know there's a very small window of time to get myself out of this spot.

The footsteps are getting louder and closer.

I pull back up to the room as quietly as I can. Place the floorboard back. Then the carpet. I look down at my shoes, and they are covered with dark, moist dirt.

The lock on the door jiggles.

Panic consumes me as I pull off my shoes and flee to the bed.

Just as I shove the filthy footwear under the covers, the door opens.

He finds me digging around in my purse. *I'm so glad I keep this possession next to my pillow all the time.*

With squinted eyes, he looks around the room and to me. "There's no way out of here other than through that door, but then you already know that."

Does he see the bumpy carpet over there, or did he see me standing in the dirt from the outside?

Billy smiles and winks. "Here., I bought you something special. It will cheer you up, for sure."

I'm confused on how quickly he changed the subject, "I don't want your gifts, Billy. I just want to go home."

He's still holding the beautifully wrapped box. "You know that's not an option."

I throw a pillow at him. "I don't want your gifts."

Suddenly, he's sitting on the bed right next to me. Good thing the covered shoes are on the other side.

"Open this right now. You hear me?"

He smells of sweat and tile grout. A ferocious lion has better breath than this guy.

I start to pull away, but he grabs me.

"Yum. You smell so good, pretty girl."

Grabbing the box, I shift over the lump in the bed. "I'll open it if you get off this bed now."

"Ha. Ha. Ha. I have to respect your private space, for now anyway."

He watches me from the observation chair a couple of feet away. As I pull the ribbon apart, my nose takes in the aroma of an Italian pizza with all the trimmings. I glance to the table and see a cardboard box that confirms tonight's supper.

"Open it."

I lift the lid and peel back the tissue paper. "What did you buy, Billy?"

He beams from ear to ear with a sinister grin. "Aw, don't be such a sore sport, Violet."

Reluctantly and with trembling hands, I lift out a sheer black negligee.

He slides closer to me. "Do you like it?"

I fling the box and the gift at him. "Take your gift and get out of here."

His strong grip pins my legs to the bed. "Is that any way to show your gratitude? You'll wear that to bed tonight. "

Tears roll down my face. "I can't do that."

His face is so close to mine that I can see the evil in his eyes. "All pets obey their masters. So, kitten, see that glorified nightie? It will be on that curvy body of yours tonight. It's time to play."

Thank God that my thoughts are my own. I want to bury my face in my hands and cry.

Billy removes himself and gets the gift off the floor. He plops it on my lap.

"I brought a pizza. Enjoy it."

With my head down in total despair, I close my eyes and pray. *Lord God, help me get out of here before he comes back tonight. Please.*

He opens the door. "See you later, honey. Be ready for me, okay?"

All I can hear is the sound of footsteps on the wood leaving the building, then crunch, crunch, and crunch. Then silence.

Okay, Violet. It's time to make your move before that creep comes back. He plans on doing more than just watching me tonight. I have no idea how long of a crawl under this barn I have before a dead end.

Looking up at the ceiling windows, I see it's still dusk. *I can see for a while longer.*

I wolf down two pieces of pizza, pack up my pocketbook with my personal belongings, open the hole for the great exodus, and begin my journey into the unknown.

I slither along on my belly like a snake and stop every few feet to listen for any worrisome sounds. I can see the moonlight beaming through cracks in the wood ahead of me. I sigh.

Don't tell me. I must break the wood with my hands.

On my stomach, clutching the purse, I look to my left and then to my right.

There's a hole made by some animal. Hopefully, we won't run into each other. Could be anything.

I pull small chunks at a time, so the going is slow.

Getting bigger. *Not big enough for me yet.*

I want to sneeze but work hard at keeping it in. My hands are getting tired, and my body's aching.

Better rest for a few minutes.

My purse becomes a pillow.

Crunch. Crunch.

I pick my head up and squint in the direction of the sound. My heart races and fear takes over as the figure gets closer.

No turning back now. He'll find an empty room within minutes. I must squeeze through, or he'll have his way with me. God, reach out and lift me from this pit.

It's dark enough to get out and run.

All is quiet, and I can't see anyone. I stick my head out the hole and look. A mist is covering the cow pasture to my right, and dense woods are to my left as well as straight ahead.

I barely squeeze through the opening. As I slowly rise to my feet, I hear footsteps inside the barn behind me.

I grab my purse and bolt over a fence into the pasture, dodging the cows and their droppings. It's getting darker, but I don't dare look back. *I wish I had a flashlight, but then that would be a dead giveaway.*

Finally, I reach the end of the pasture but still no lights in sight.

Branches scratch my face as I plow through with my bare hands. It's pitch black now.

I sure hope Billy thinks I went through the other woods and not this way. Doggone it, there must be a road soon, but where?

Nearly tripping over a big rock, I catch my breath and sit.

"Who, hoot, hoot," bellows an owl in the tree over me. Goosebumps prick my arms. The wind's blowing through the trees as the night closes in on me. Sounds of crunching leaves from an animal or human being get closer.

I can't breathe. My heart is racing. I want to curl up in a ball and wait for my Henry to save me. No, I'm not going to sink into depression. I won't allow it. Lord, God, you helped me escape from that Billy, now help me find a safe place. In your name, Amen.

Standing and squinting around me in all directions, I realize that the moon is almost full, and it illuminates the direction to take. I startle a couple of deer, and they bolt right in front of me. I hold my head high and move through the woods. Leaves crunch behind me, but I'm too frightened to look back. Maybe a rabbit or a chipmunk or some other kind of animal. The partly covered moon provides faint illumination as I forge forward still clutching my purse.

I'm glad I decided to wear the flannel shirt and coveralls that creep gave me on the first day of captivity. At least, I'm keeping warm from the cool night, and the danger of getting poison ivy is slim. Good, it's quiet behind me now, and the woods are still.

A road. A road. Where am I? I wish I knew.

My heart races in hopes of flagging someone down to help me. I'm standing in the middle of the road, turning in circles.

Do I go left or right? I better stay to the side for safety reasons. I'll head this way.

I walk for what seems to be an eternity when my eyes focus on two headlights in the distance coming toward me. Do I take a chance and flag this car down?

The car is only a few hundred yards away now. *Can the driver see me?*

I start to perspire as I leap into the center of the road and wave my arms every which way. The car comes to a screeching halt, and I don't know whether to run towards it or freeze in place.

"Help! Help! I need help."

A figure gets out of the driver's side and starts to walk towards me with the headlights glowing behind.

"I need a ride to the nearest police station," I squeal.

I can see a muscular build of a man now. *Oh no. It's him.* Dread claws its way up my throat.

"You can count on me to help you, honey." He reaches out to grab me.

I escape from his clutches and take off in the opposite direction. I can hear the car door slam and the car motor roar behind me. Fear and trepidation overwhelm my total being. Not a house in sight, just a long road to nowhere.

"Where do you think you are going to go? Huh, Violet?" he shouts out the window of his car just feet away.

He's going to get me and have his way. I can't let him do that. I can't let it happen. Oh God, help me. This nightmare must end. I dart to the side of the road, down an embankment, and, once again, I'm in the woods, running for my life.

Another road already? Wait. The Miller Place Post office is over there. I know where I am.

Here comes a car. This time I won't wait to see who it is. I know this area like the back of my hand, because the kids and I walk this way all the time. Run, through those woods and wait at that old haunted Holiday Inn until daylight. He'll never look for me there. If he has been tracking me for a while, then he knows where I live. That's the route he'll take and if I'm right, a cop car is patrolling the area.

The driveway to this spooky place is covered over with weeds and broken-down tree limbs. My face is getting scratched as I pick my way through. The dark, eerie structure stands vividly under the glowing moon. Most of the windows in front are smashed, but the antique wooden shutters that survived the years of abuse are dangling in the wind. Creak. Creak. The five-story wood structure has been vacant since the '40s. "Evil lurks within the walls of that place," the locals say.

"And where the good way is, walk in it, and you will find rest for your souls." Psalm 25:4-11.

I can't keep my eyes open any longer, I must rest for a few minutes. Right here. My family must be so worried about me. Oh, dear Lord, I'm so scared. Please keep all evil away from me, in Jesus' name. Thank You that I got away from Billy's clutches. I'm fighting to keep my eyes open. I'm so sleepy, so sleepy.

The sound of crows flying above wakes me. I leap to my feet. *I did fall asleep.*

The air is still as I slowly look around, but all I see is the big, falling apart structure and the dense woods around it. *I better walk around carefully before venturing off. I don't want to let my guard down one bit.* Standing in the front of the inn, I can vaguely see North Country Road in the distance. The doors to the old place are boarded shut with signs: *NO Trespassing.*

I can hear a siren in the distance. I must build up the confidence to move on.

I venture down the old horse trail to Mount Sanai beach and run along the shore for two miles until I can climb the cliff behind our house. I glance behind me. No one. I scan the top of the cliff, but I only see trees.

"Be not afraid, the Lord is with you."

I look at my watch, "Its 7:00 in the morning. Is anyone home? Maybe the house is locked up and they all went to Aunt Flossie's. Billy could be waiting inside or at the top of the cliff out of sight for that matter," I mumble as I start the ugly, dirty climb upward.

Tears of pain from an aching body run down my cheeks as I paw into the sandy bluff. My feet keep sinking into the quicksand-like stuff, but an occasional small tree gives me leverage to hang onto. *Almost there. Maybe I should go to Leger's house first. Did I just think that? That won't work. No. What should I do?* Panic rises, and sweat overcomes my body. As I peek over the top of the fence to our backyard, I hesitate. Fencing separates each piece of property in Miller Place Park.

Oh, the Panose's are usually up. I can get there.

I decide to crawl across the yard through the screen door and into the porch. I wiggle the doorknob to the house. It's locked. *Oh, I wish I had a key, but it's on the key chain in the car.* I bang on the door with all the energy I have left.

I squint and look through the glass. Everything is quiet and dark. I don't dare walk to the front, because no doubt Billy is out there or nearby for sure.

With my back to the door, I slump down on the cement floor and look at the back yards to the left and to the right. I decide to go right.

After crossing over two empty lots, I drag myself to the back door of my Greek neighbor's house.

I can't bang on the door. No strength. I only tap, tap, tap.

They must be away or decided to go to work early today. Jim and Kelly, where are you? If they're not there,

I'll break in anyway. I can use their telephone to call the police.

Come on, answer the door, or I'll have to go to Freddy Leger's house.

Lost and dejected, I shuffle slowly away from this would-be place of protection.

"Violet. Violet Funk. Is that you dear?" yells the recognizable voice of my friend Kelly.

I turn and freeze in place as she rushes to me with a warm embrace. I melt in her arms as the tears of joy move us in unison into the safety of her house.

Chapter Nine

Even though Billy Watson was arrested after a good ole car chase down 25A, I still find myself in a state of depression, which leads to a lack of concentration. I can't focus on anything, much less an order that must be filled by the end of next week. The Tishs were nice enough to give me an extension on the tiles for the pool. They hired a new mason from the city with outstanding references and decided to pick up the completed order at the shop. News reporters and even a television crew wanted interviews right after the ordeal ended. Henry took a vacation week off so he could watch over me, so he says.

What should I do today? Catch up on my reading, paint tiles, or work at the shop for a while?

I cannot suppress this. No, I can't. My Father in Heaven will keep my mind on Him. Inspire me, Lord, that I may raise this voice, thy gift, in songs of praise. I never dreamed I could sing, but when Jesus came into my heart, I was able to croon for Him in the church choir. The piano Henry bought when we were first married is in our new living room. He helps me with the alto part of the hymns even though going to church is not his thing.

"Honey, the children are in school for a few more hours. Let's go for a walk on the beach?" he offers.

I pick a few notes on the upright. "I don't know. I should be painting a few tea tile orders."

"I have some silk screening to do downstairs. We can walk for an hour then work when we come back."

It's high tide, but the waves are rolling into the shore slowly and silently, giving a serene setting as we walk barefoot in the sand. I'm reminded of how much I love to swim when I see the graceful porpoises reel in and out of the water.

"In another month, you'll be out there with them," he says.

The dark part of the sound does not scare me. "I can't wait. I know it worries you when I do that, Henry, but God propels me forward, and the great fish seem to enjoy the company."

"I worry about leaving you for a second ever since the Billy Watson ordeal."

"The Bible says, 'Cast your cares on the Lord and he will sustain you.'"

"You really believe that God singles you out individually? If he's as powerful as you keep saying, then why did He let you go through that terrifying trial?"

I step into the cold salt water. "If we're inclined to worry, we can turn that over to the Lord. He's never too weary or too tired to pay attention to us. He has all wisdom and complete sovereign power."

Henry brings me into his arms. "You have been praying for me, haven't you?"

"Yes, for you and our children to come to know the Savior as I did. I could not have gotten away from Billy without God's help."

"Well, I've been thinking about coming to church with you and Jane. It won't hurt to try it."

My heart leaps for joy.

We have an early supper of hamburgers, homemade french-fries, and broccoli. *Jane will not eat broccoli, but if I put her in her room to eat it, somehow, she does. Funny thing.*

After the table is cleared and the dishes are washed, Henry helps his daughter prepare for an arithmetic test while Peter continues working on a model airplane. I set up a card table for him so he could leave his project there.

The doorbell startles us.

Peter runs to open it. "Mr. Leger?"

Henry picks up his head and darts to the entry. "What do you want, Freddy?"

"I have something for your little girl."

Jane and I are very curious. Glaring at a medium-sized box at the foot of the steps, I ask, "What do you want to say to her? I can't even imagine."

He's clean shaven and neatly dressed. "Um, I, uh, well. I'm the one that hit her dog. I'm so very sorry. I was drunk, and I admit that now. I know it has taken me too long to come over and apologize to you, little one, but I'm here now."

Jane's hiding behind me with her head peeking at our neighbor. She's trembling as she clings to me.

I scowl and step forward. "This little girl was beside herself, Mr. Leger. You took from her the one thing that made her happy."

He drops his head. "I'm sorry about that. Very unfortunate, and I am also sorry about what happened to you, Violet."

Peter stamps his foot. "I think you said enough, Mister."

Henry grabs the neighbor's arm. "Thank you, sir, for the apology, but it's best that you leave. Okay?"

Pulling away without incident, Freddie goes down the steps, picks up the box, and looks up at us.

"Hopefully, this will make up for my bad behavior." He climbs back up and puts the box at Jane's feet.

Before we could say any more, he's on his way over the fence to his house.

Peter picks up the box. "Ooh. Something is moving inside this thing."

"Bring it in the house, son," orders Henry.

As soon as we set it on the rug by the fireplace, we hear, "Yip, yip, yip."

Penny pulls open the flaps and lifts out the most adorable white and black short hair puppy.

Tears of joy and laughter roll down her soft cheeks as the small animal licks her nose. The pup becomes the center of attention as he wobbles across the floor, with the kids right on his tail.

Henry grabs an old newspaper and scatters it on the floor. "Put him on the paper in case he needs to go. I think this pup needs a name."

"Pups. He is Pups," squeals my daughter.

Peter giggles loudly. "Come on, so he's a puppy. You can think of a better name than that."

I pick up the little fur ball as he licks my nose. "Pups, it is. Perfect name for him."

Everything's relatively back to normal now as we plow past Memorial Day into June. The weather's warm and enjoyable with the excitement of planting seedlings in the gardens. Henry planted seeds under grow lights in February, and now the little plants are ready to put in the ground. He takes care of the vegetables, and my job is the flowers. Today, I'm planting marigolds once again along the walkway from driveway to the house. I count fifty plants.

"Vi, Peter and I are heading into the hardware store in town for some fertilizer." Henry waves.

I'm so thirsty, and I need to get off my knees too. Jane is at Mary Ellen's for the afternoon. Pups is fine on the back porch now that he's house broken.

The doorbell causes me to jump.

I look down at my dirty trousers and filthy shoes too. *I better not answer it. I look a mess.*

Whoever is out there is very persistent. Now, there's loud knocking.

Suddenly, I realize the door's open and the screen is transparent. I run my fingers through my hair and straighten my clothing the best I can. As I make my way to the door, I see a young man in his twenties dressed in a black suit, carrying a Bible. He's accompanied by an attractive older lady dressed very modestly with a sweet smile.

"May I help you folks?"

"My name is Dr. Russell Shed, and this is Lois Schmidt. We're from Port Jefferson. If you have a few minutes, we would love to share with you some exciting news about what God is doing locally."

I'm intrigued by the mention of God. "Please come in, but excuse my appearance. I have been gardening most of the day."

"We won't take too much of your time, Miss." Lois smiles.

"How rude of me. My name's Violet Funk. May I get you some iced tea?"

He looks out at the sound. "What a beautiful view you have here."

I motion to the couch. "Please have a seat."

"Iced tea would be lovely, Violet."

I'm glad Henry's not here now because he's still rather cynical about Christianity. I can't believe that young man is a Doctor of Theology. Handsome in his own way, but wow those ears are big.

"Doctor Shed has a vision for a new church in Port Jefferson. I met him at a friend's house last week and decided to join him in canvassing the area." Lois smiles.

He looks at me with intent interest "Do you know Jesus as your Savior and Lord, Violet?"

"Yes, I do. After a nervous breakdown and searching for the secret of happiness, I realized my life was a shamble without God in it."

Lois grabs my hand. "Praise God. You have a testimony to share with the brokenhearted."

"Do you have a good church you belong to?" he asks.

"Sound Beach Community Church."

"It's important that the message of salvation is preached wherever you attend, Violet."

I hesitate. "Well, I uh, don't ever hear that mentioned."

He hands me a business card. "Please pray for God's guidance. If you feel led to join us, call me at this phone number."

I look at the card and back at my guests. "I'm a ceramic tile artist, and I have been praying about turning this business into a witness for Christ. It will be called Tiles with a Testimony. I'll certainly pray for you."

Chapter Ten

The next day, after reading the Bible and praying for guidance in my life, I feel deeply moved to call Doctor Shed. Henry's back to work, and the children are at friends.

"Hello, Doctor Shed? This is Violet Funk in Miller Place.

"How are you doing, Violet?"

"I'm fine. How are you?"

"Several of us are gathering in Port Jefferson to canvas the area about our new church project. Would you like to come?"

"Yes. I am interested. Today?"

"Yes, around 12:00 at 25 Jayne Boulevard in Port Jefferson. Do you know where that is?

"I know where Jayne Boulevard is. Whose house is it at?"

"The Barlow's. Twenty-Five Jayne Boulevard.

I glance at the clock over the stove. "It's eleven o'clock now. If I leave in a few minutes, I can be there at 11:45."

"See you in a little while."

I hang up the phone and race into the bedroom to change from my paint-stained clothes to a pleated skirt and a buttoned-down cardigan sweater. Within minutes, I'm driving past the school towards 25A where I make a right and head to upper Port Jeff station. Little traffic this time of day. *Here's the street I'm looking for, Jayne Boulevard.*

THE BARLOWS. I knock on the white door a few times. A sweet looking, plain dressed lady opens the door. "You must be Violet. Come on in, dear."

The smell of oatmeal cookies gives me a warm, fuzzy feeling all over as I make my way to the small living room.

Doctor Shed reaches out his hand. "Welcome, Violet. You remember Lois? Then you met Betty Barlow a few moments ago. I find it best to go out in teams of two when knocking on doors. I have these tracts and flyers for you to hand out to the folks you meet today."

The flyer invitations say: *Come one, come all to an informal get together about a new church in the area. Place: Oddfellows Hall on Jayne Boulevard, June 10 at 6 pm.*

Lois gets up and grabs my hand. "You and I will go out together."

"Sure. Where do we go first?"

Doctor Shed chuckles, holding his hand on the Bible. "Let's pray first."

Mrs. Barlow hands out fifty biblically based tracts to each one of us. "Be sure to give one to each family."

Lois and I decide to stay on this street while the others head out to other areas. I'm focused on a split-level home right across the street because of the bright orange door. A short lady dressed in a turquoise top and red pants with black hair is pruning what appears to be rose bushes from my vantage point.

I tap Lois on the shoulder. "Let's start there."

The lady's' back is to us as we venture up the sidewalk. "Hello. It's a beautiful day, isn't it?" I call out.

She falls forward into the bushes. "Oh, my stars. You scared me."

I rush to pull her up. "I'm so sorry, Miss."

She brushes herself off as she turns to us. "*Buenas noches*, my name is Vicky."

"My name is Lois, and this is my friend, Violet. We are friends of your neighbor, Betty, across the street."

She looks at us with squinted eyes. "*Si*. Very nice lady."

I hand her an invite to the gathering. "Several of us in the community are getting together in expectation of starting a new church. We would love to have you join us, if you don't have a church home."

"What religion is this?"

"Baptist, but all denominations are welcome."

She shakes her head with a deep sigh. "We are Catholic."

I smile and hand her the pamphlet. "Isn't it wonderful that we all worship the same God, Vicky?"

She stares at the cover for a few minutes. "Would you like some iced tea?"

Lois nods. "That would be nice. Thank you."

We follow her through the garage and into the house. Shoes are lined up in perfect order, so we take ours off as well. The orange kitchen is immaculately clean and orderly with yellow café curtains adorning the two windows. A lovely aroma fills the entire room, but I cannot put my finger on what it is.

"What is that beautiful smell, Vicky?" I ask.

"Heno De Pravia, from Madrid."

"It's lovely." Lois smiles.

She serves us tall glasses of iced tea. "Do you have children?"

"A boy and girl. Jane is ten, and Peter is fifteen. How about you, Vicky?"

"Nelson is thirteen, and Maria is ten. We just moved here, so they would love to meet your kids."

Lois is grinning from ear to ear as Vicky and I converse about art and family. She's so polite not to interrupt, but lets the conversation continue.

I pull out a business card. "Here's my phone number at the shop. Call me next week and we can have lunch, okay?"

"I would love that."

The beverage is going right through me. "Can I please use your bathroom?"

"Of course. To the left, down the hall."

"Thanks. Lois, tell her about your family."

Lois and I canvass twelve houses on Maxwell. No one was home at three of them, two housewives screamed profanities at us for trespassing, but the rest of the folks were very interested and accommodating.

"The Smiths are strong Christians. Certainly know the Bible well," comments Lois as we walk back to our cars.

"They sure do. They are members of First Presbyterian but are praying about making a change."

"God is good. We handed out seven invitations, and the Kents accepted Jesus into their hearts."

"That was a great phrase you brought to their attention, 'Jesus is your Savior, *not* your religion.' Now, they're so hungry for the word of God."

I look at my watch, "I better get home before the children do. I must pick my kids up soon. Can you tell the rest of the team our good news, Lois?"

Only a handful of new people showed up for the first information night at Oddfellows Hall. Over two hundred invitations were handed out to prospective attendees, so it was a bit disheartening to see such a small turnout. We all decided to continue as a Bible study and prayer group at the Barlow's twice a month. Thanks to God, we grew from seven to twenty over the course of the summer. Folks sat on the floor in a packed Barlow living room, studying the Word of God.

Vicky Valladares and I became instant friends. I believe she knows the Lord as her Savior, even though her way of worshipping God is different than mine.

We sit on the beach as the girls build sandcastles. "Vicky, how does your husband, Val, feel about the Bible study at your neighbors?"

"I simply can't go if he's home. He thinks the Barlows are crazy people."

"Val is so hilarious and personable. I would think he would like everyone."

"Nada. He'll wave and smile, but trimming the hedges is more important than carrying on a conversation."

"Well, Henry's still not buying this idea about starting a church, let alone a Baptist one. The Bible's my guide for living the life God wants me to, and I pray I'll be inspired each day."

She speaks in a low tone. "I keep the Bible you gave me on the coffee table. Val never says a word."

I grab her hand. "Dear Lord God, thank you for my friends the Valladares. I pray that You will keep Vicky strong and close to You when she faces conflict with her husband. Amen."

We sit quietly gazing out at the peaceful, beautiful sound while the seagulls chirp above us.

"We better get going, Violet. I have to pick Nelson up at 3:00 when he gets off work."

I shake out the towels and fold the umbrella. "Jane, Maria. Time to go."

The girls flop into the water for one last dip and giggle with glee, splashing each other.

Vicky pulls on her sneakers and bolts to the edge of the water. "Maria. Get out of the water now. Your brother will be waiting for us at the market."

Jane scowls and continues to doggy paddle. Maria dodges the rocks with arms wrapped around herself for warmth. Vicky wraps her daughter in a light green beach towel as she pulls off the white bathing cap.

How will I ever get my child out of the water? She's like a fish.

"I'll call you soon, Violet. It will take us awhile to climb those steps," Vicky calls out as they leave.

"All right. Go ahead. I understand. Jane, come out of the water this instant."

The beach bag's packed as I make my way into the shallow water. "Your dog needs to go out, and I have tiles to paint. Let's go."

She ignores me completely.

I splash through the water and grab her wet arm. "Stop ignoring me. Look, Maria and her mother are halfway up the steps already."

Jane wiggles and squeals like an injured seal. "Ouch. You're hurting me."

I look up at my friend and daughter with humiliation as they stop and stare at us.

I turn back to the situation at hand with a vengeance. "Do I have to carry you out of the water?"

Jane whimpers as she stands up. "Why can't we stay longer than them?"

"You are making a scene, Jane. Honestly. Go. Get your towel."

As I put my sunglasses and hat on, I get a glimpse of our friends moving out of sight at the top.

It takes about ten minutes to climb from beach to hilltop if one doesn't dawdle along the way. My curly-headed daughter bounds ahead of me, skipping two steps at a time.

Bill Haley's "Rock around the Clock" is blaring away as we make our way into the cool house. Peter and his friends are dancing up a storm on the back porch. It's no wonder the neighbors haven't called the police for disorderly conduct.

"Turn that down," screams Jane.

Everyone freezes in place as the big brother lifts his sister off her feet. "You little brat."

The company freezes in place as the focus turns to the show at hand. Peter carries his screaming sister into her room, and I stand kind of helpless in place staring at the teenagers. Good thing Vicky and Maria are on their way home.

My mind is following my children but, somehow, I freeze in place. "Hi, kids, can I get you something to eat?"

Martha speaks for the rest, "Do you have any Coca-Cola?"

"I think we have a few bottles."

Everyone returns to laughter and a few whispers as I grab the bottles of soda from the refrigerator. *I better check on those kids of mine.*

As I open the door to my daughter's small room, my heart is tamed at the sight before me. Peter, Jane, and Pups are on the lower bunkbed in a loving huddle. *That little dog sure holds a key to instant peace.*

"Sis-o, I love you, but I have to spend time with my friends without my kid sister as the center of attention. They will only be here for a little while longer, okay?"

She keeps loving on her doggy. As he exits the room, I take his place.

"Let's get out of these bathing suits, get dressed, and you can help me in the studio for a while. How does that sound?"

Jane keeps her head nestled on top of the dog's head. "Okay."

I get up and pull a pair of shorts, underwear, and a shirt out of the drawer. "Pups come on. Time to go outside and do your thing. Jane, dear, please get out of that wet suit."

She reluctantly gets up and slides out of her suit as I walk out the door with the white and black pup.

A half-hour later, I'm sitting at my design table in my new studio meticulously working on the new design. "Prayer changes things." Taking a break, I glance at my skinny daughter all curled up on the couch with her cowboy coloring books. She did help put the hangers in the cork backs for ten minutes, but her short attention span moved her to what she likes to do the most.

Peter bursts through the door. "The gang and I are heading for the beach for a while."

I smile as I shake my head. "Okay, son. Please lather yourself with lotion. You know how prone you are to sunburn."

"Uh, I will."

I can't believe that boy will be a senior in high school next year.

Chapter Eleven

Before I surrendered my life and talents to God through Christ, I felt the only way to fame with my business was to attend tile conventions when I could. My dear Aunt Flossie has always believed in my artwork from the very beginning. If I didn't have enough money to go, she would give me the rest. I've traveled to California, Florida, and New Jersey in the past year, which generated a lot of new orders from all over the country. This next one will be the first interior decorator's convention I've ever attended.

Thank you, God, for a thriving tile business. I'm thrilled to work with local interior decorators on creating new or updated kitchens. Thank you for my beautiful studio with natural light flowing through the full-length windows. I have more work than I can handle, so I know attending conferences will be a thing of the past after this weekend.

I pray for safety as I fly and for the children to be obedient to Henry in my absence. Amen.

It's the crack of dawn on Friday morning as we pull into the railroad station. The children are fast asleep; hopefully, until Henry arrives back home to wake them for school.

"Oh, Henry, I'm so happy this convention in Dallas is my last. The business is thriving now, and I have good artists helping me too. I want to get that van and start my dream of *Heavenly Treasures.*"

He pulls me to him, stroking my hair. "I'm glad I had some vacation time left so I can stay home today to get the children off to school."

"Yes, I am too. Can you silkscreen a couple dozen each of the wedding and baby's birth tiles while I am gone? The orders for those keep coming."

The lights on the semaphore flash as the train pulls into a stop.

He kisses me. "I'll do what I can. Don't worry about anything, okay? You better get going."

He carries my suitcase to the porter, and I give him a hug. "I'll call you tonight."

Henry whistles to get my attention as I climb into the car. "You look sexy in that red dress."

I feel my heart skip a beat as I wave.

As the train rattles along to Grand Central, making numerous stops to pick other passengers up, I gather my thoughts about the posters I have to make, how I'll find a helper for the two days, and checking to see if tickets are where they should be.

Daybreak emerges as the train pulls into its destination.

I have two hours to get a cab to La Guardia airport, check my suitcase, and pull myself together before we take off. It'll be good to check in to the hotel a day earlier. I have so much to do.

The Adolphus Hotel opened its doors in 1912 as a luxury palace worthy of the Lone Star state. Elegance and splendor take place together in twenty-one stories. It's said to be the Grand Dame of Dallas hotels.

I'm swept away as I pull up in front the mighty structure enhanced with four sculptures of the early

American cowboy. As I walk into the striking entry way, I'm greeted with Flemish tapestries and an ornately carved Steinway in the center of the vast floor.

Observing the various folks at the hotel registration desk, mostly well-dressed cowboys, I take my place in line. Looking to my right, I spot a table with two ladies sitting behind it.

A sign on the table reads, "Conference temporary employment."

I better go there before I go to my room. The tiles were shipped here last week, so they should be either in the room or somewhere in this big place.

"Are you here for the convention?" an appealing voice from behind asks.

I turn and look up at a handsome, well-dressed man. "Yes, sir. I am." I blush.

He winks at me, and for some reason beyond my control, I stand speechless.

"You better go to the desk. They're waving to you."

Turning around, I see he's right. "Thank you."

"I'm Violet Funk. Did my shipment arrive?'

"Yes, Mrs. Funk. The shipment's in your room. Is there anything else we can help you with?" The check-in clerk smiles.

"Not that I can think of, but thank you."

"Here's the key to room 210."

Fumbling with the key, my pocketbook, and suitcase, I try to remove myself from the counter. *Of course, I'm looking down at my feet, as usual.*

With a clunk and a bump, I plow into that good-looking fella. "Oh, I'm so sorry, sir."

He flashes me a big Cheshire grin. "That's quite all right, Miss."

I don't respond but head over to the employment table.

"Good afternoon, ladies, how are you today?" I ask.

The blond with glasses reaches out her hand. "I'm Valerie, and this is Marion, from the Dallas temp agency. What is your name, and how can we help you?"

"Pleased to meet both of you. My name is Violet Pearl Funk, and I'm a ceramic tile artist. I would like to hire an assistant for the convention."

"We have a couple of very eager young women from the community college who are looking to make a few dollars."

"Wonderful. I'll be in room 210 for a while since it will take some time to unpack. I'm not at all fussy about who I hire except that she must have an outgoing personality and be quick on her feet."

Marion smiles and pulls an index card out of the Rolodex. "I will give this contact a call right now."

I grab my bags once again. "Thanks a million, ladies."

I move swiftly in the direction of the elevator and make it just before it closes. Feeling a bit bedraggled and overanxious at the same time, I let out a huge sigh.

A male voice to my right asks, "What floor are you on, Miss?"

Picking my head up and looking around me, I realize I'm on the elevator with one other passenger.

The fine-looking gentleman from moments ago. "Uh, uh. Two. The second floor."

"Oops. Sorry. I'm on the tenth, and it already passed your stop."

I smile lightly. "That's fine. I'll ride up and back down."

He laughs as the elevator comes to a stop. "My name is Bradley Cooper. Miss?"

"Hi, Bradley. My name is Violet Funk."

A young couple gets on as he walks off. "See you later, Violet."

Good grief. It looks like I must ride up to the twenty-first floor and back down again. I must go to the bathroom. I sure hope we don't have to stop at every floor. I'm going to order room service for supper tonight, because I have so much to do.

The couple gets off on the twentieth. *Good, I'm alone. Okay. Zipping down fast now.* Ten, nine, eight, and stop. Three older ladies get on. Three and two. *I want to scream out, "Hooray."*

The telephone is ringing off the hook as I open the door, drop my bags, and grab the receiver.

"Hello?"

"I can hear your heartbeat from here." The male voice chuckles.

"Who is this, please?" I pant.

"Bradley Cooper on the tenth floor. I do have Violet, right?"

I cross my legs as I sit on the bed. "Oh. Yes. Mr. Cooper, what can I do for you?"

How do I tell this stranger that I have to go to the bathroom?

"Several sellers are getting together for supper in the hotel restaurant at 6:30. We would love to have you join us. How about it?"

With a grumbling tummy and my eyes on the bathroom door, I quickly answer. "Sure, Mr. Cooper. I would love to meet as many company reps as I can. See you at 6:30."

"Great. See you in an hour. Oh, and please call me Bradley."

Click.

I flee to the commode and breathe a sigh of relief.

A knock on the door startles me.

"Coming," I yell, forgetting where I am.

I had better be cautious here. "Who is it?" I say through the door.

"It's Marion Ryan from the temp agency. They tried to call, but your phone was busy."

Unlocking the door and opening it, I gaze upon a tiny blonde with big blue eyes. "Come in, honey. I have a dinner engagement in forty-five minutes, but I can use your help right away. How late can you work tonight?"

"As late as you need me. I share an apartment with several girls three blocks away. Put me to work, Mrs. Funk."

Pulling a notepad and pen from the desk drawer, I begin to jot down instructions. "You're a darling, Marion. Please call me Violet."

She blushes as she plays around with her long curly hair. "Thank you. Do you need me to take anything to the ballroom?"

"I'm making a list for you to refer to while I'm gone. I should be back here no later than 8:00. You'll have enough to keep you busy until then. Can you be here at 6:30 tomorrow morning?"

"Yes, Ma'am. I can."

I hand her the list and point to the three boxes by the door. "Start with these. Open them and inspect all the tiles to be sure nothing is broken. Then sort by designs."

I fling my suitcase on the bed, open it, and pull out a purple dress and black patent leather heels. Marion is opening the boxes and scanning the tiles as I race into the bathroom.

I have twenty minutes to wash up, change, freshen my makeup, and head down to the restaurant. I must make a good first impression with potential customers. I really don't need any office furniture, so Mr. Cooper is just a liaison for me to meet other salespeople.

"Okay, Marion. You know where to find me if you need something. Do you need a sandwich?"

"I ate a big meal in the school cafeteria before I came, but thank you anyway."

The restaurant is dimly lit with candles in hurricane lamps on each table to light the way for patrons to find their tables. Dark, mahogany wood covers the walls with a few paintings scattered around. The maître d' is standing at attention at his lectern, peering at me over his wire-rimmed glasses.

"Can I help you, Miss?"

"Yes. I'm with the Bradley Cooper party. He has a 6:30 reservation."

"Certainly. Right this way." He motions, and I follow.

We wind around several tables and into the back room. Two large, round tables are filled with folks laughing and eating. Off in the far corner appears to be a booth, but my attention is diverted to an empty table set for eight. I slow down, ready to find my place.

The maître d' keeps moving to the corner. "Enjoy your dinner, Madam."

Bradley Cooper emerges out of the dark booth.

"Violet, I'm so glad you decided to come." He winks.

I am not amused but very curious.

"Where's everyone else, Bradley?"

"Come now. Would you have accepted my invitation if it was just the two of us?"

Turning to go, he grabs my hand. Goosebumps race up my arms.

"I have work to do, so I will order a sandwich to go. Good night."

"Look around you. There are lots of people in this room. I can see you are a married lady, so I would never consider this a date. Please dine with me. Think of it as two business associates sharing what they do."

I pull my hand out of his and let out a deep sigh. "All right. I guess it can't hurt anything, and I am famished."

He winks again and pats my back. "That's the spirit."

Sitting across from him, "I'll eat and run, though, because I have an assistant working in my room as I speak. There's a lot to do before tomorrow."

He raises his hand in the air calls, "Waiter."

The ornate ballroom is bustling with activity with forty vendors from all over the country and prospective customers milling about in the aisles. Some stopping to seriously chat with representatives while others move swiftly, as if on a mission. Dallas is in the middle of cowboy country, so there are many Stetsons within view. Marion and I were ready to set up at the crack of dawn.

"Violet, would you like some coffee and a doughnut?" she asks with a sigh of relief.

"I'm not usually a big one for doughnuts, but that sure sounds good right now. Here, let me get a few dollars for you."

She chuckles, and taps my arm. "It's all complimentary for the distributors. We just have to show our badge."

I love that kid. She's so eager to please, and being young and perky sure helps too. She certainly doesn't look like a college student dressed in that grey, pin-striped suit. The pale blue silk blouse under the jacket brings out the brilliance in her eyes. Look at that cowboy tip his hat at her as she walked by.

"Good morning, Violet."

My eyes are drawn to handsome Bradley. "Good morning. You must not be busy at your booth."

"I decided to make the rounds to see the displays. There are two salesmen in the booth. It gets a bit crowded with three of us."

I'm attracted to this man. I can't be. I love Henry with all my heart. God, help me stay strong. Good. Here comes Marion, and two ladies are looking at the tile rack.

"Thanks for dinner last night, Bradley. Hello, ladies. These are hand-painted, kiln-fired tiles and all original designs."

"They are absolutely stunning. We are decorators from New Jersey, and our clients would love to use your amazing artwork for fireplace facings. Do you do murals?" asks the tall one with glasses.

By the end of the day, we'd handed out over two hundred business cards to folks passing by and over fifty brochures to very interested clientele. The most promising was from a huge ceramic tile distributor in Houston.

The ballroom's almost empty now after the big cleanup and tear down. Marion is paid in full, and she is bringing the last of my parcels to the concierge to be shipped on her way out.

It's been a long three days, and I'm exhausted. My flight back home is in the morning. Good. I turn around and look at the vast room. *Goodbye, conventions. Goodbye, Dallas.*

I'm going to use room service tonight for sure. Do I have everything? Yes. Pocketbook. Portfolio with new designs. Good. Oh, I can't wait to get out of these pointy high heels. I ponder all this waiting for the elevator. The door opens. I step on. The door closes.

Suddenly great arms embrace me from behind. "Hey, girl. Fancy meeting you here."

I turn and come almost face-to-face with Bradley. I'm tongue tied and sweating.

Oh, no. I didn't push the number two for my floor. My heart's beating rapidly. Think, Violet.

He kisses my forehead.

I freeze in place. We're alone as the elevator moves upward to the tenth floor.

Why am I not fighting him? He's holding me with such gentleness.

"I knew you were attracted to me from the moment we met," he whispers in my ear.

"This is…not."

He lifts my chin up and plants a kiss on my cheek. The door opens, and without thinking, I find myself walking off the elevator with him, hand in hand.

There's not one person in the hallway and not a sound can be heard from the any of the rooms as we walk to his.

He opens the door.

I pull away.

He grabs my hand. "Just one night, Violet. Just tonight. It's okay. No one will know."

I step into the room as the door closes behind me.

"Come, darling. Let's order room service. The night is still young."

My back is stuck to the door as he walks away. I grab the knob, pull, and turn.

I want to run after him, but…

"Good night, Bradley. God knows, and that makes this whole thing ugly."

I flee to the elevator just as it begins to close.

Psalm 31:3 come to mind. *"Yes, God. You are my rock and fortress; therefore, for your name's sake lead me and guide me."*

Part Two

Chapter Twelve

1958

What will my son do with his life? He'll graduate from high school on Friday with no signs of college or a future, other than working in that gas station as a mechanic. It's a shame to see someone with such good grades in school mope around here in his spare time. Oh, dear God, please help Peter find a purpose for his life.

I watch him flop on the couch while I prepare supper. "Peter, did you talk to your guidance counselor today?"

"Huh? Why would I do that? I told you before that I love my job at Bill Roth's."

With a fork, I taste the stew and venture out of the kitchen to the sprawled-out figure. His eyes are shut, but I know he can't be asleep that fast. I can hear the *American Bandstand* theme song from here, so I know Jane is enthralled with her favorite show.

"Peter! Sit up, Son. We have to discuss your future." I wave my hand with the utensil.

One eye pops open. "What do you think you're doing? Coming at me with a fork?" He grabs my hand with great force.

"Ouch. You're hurting me."

He leaps off the couch and almost knocks me over in doing so. "I'm going over to Martha's."

With my hands over my face to hide my emotions, I fall into the couch. The tears flow silently down my cheeks as I ponder who might be able to talk to Peter and help him. *Oh, how he needs Jesus in his life. I wish he would come to church with us, but his heart has grown cold towards Christianity.*

The smell of something burning tickles my nose, and I bolt from the pit of despair into the smoky kitchen. In the nick of time, I'm able to salvage supper. I pull the pan off the stove, add a little water, and cover it. It's six o'clock. *Henry will be home in an hour. Good. Maybe, he can talk some sense into that boy.*

"Jane, I'll be in the studio working on a new design," I say as I buzz pass her.

"Uh, okay."

The black and white sketch shows a rock wall with a partially open gate. A rose bush, hydrangeas, and a blooming birch tree add foliage to the design. I smile in adoration at my artwork, but I know I have a challenge in creating perfect lettering.

In the garden of my heart, there's a little postern gate, which when I open it, leads into the presence of God.

"Yum. Something sure smells good. What's for supper?" Henry asks with a big bear hug.

"Beef stew and homemade biscuits. You have exactly five minutes to wash up, take off your tie, roll up your sleeves, and sit down." I chuckle. "Jane, come for supper, please."

I can't believe that she's almost thirteen. She'll be in the ninth grade in September. Where has the time gone? A few of her friends are boy crazy and they have late night parties, which can lead to trouble. It's hard to not let her go, but I always seem to give in.

"Where's my brother? At Martha's again?"

I let out a loud sigh. "I guess so. Don't worry about him and eat your supper. Henry, you're going to have to talk to Peter when he comes home. He got angry at me when I asked about his plans after high school."

"It depends on how late it is when he comes home. I do have to get up early to catch the train."

"Maybe Martha can talk some sense into him. She's college bound in the fall and very excited about it."

The front door closes with a bang, and Peter's bedroom door closes with a loud thud.

Henry throws his napkin on the table. "That's it. He must be dealt with now."

I run fast behind him. "Can't you eat while it's hot? Stay calm, Henry."

Henry's temper gets out of hand when he's hungry. Oh, Lord please keep them civil with each other. His face is beet red as he turns and shakes my shoulders and mouths, "Stay out of this."

I shimmer with a cold chill and take three steps back as Henry enters the room and closes the door. Since the door is rather thin, I decide to eavesdrop a bit. *Oh, God. Henry's so upset right now. He's tired from the long day at work and that long commute. He's dealing with a short fuse. Give him the right words to say. Amen.*

"Son, what is going on with you? Graduation is in a few days, and you don't have a clue what will happen after it's all over. Do you?"

"Leave me alone, Dad."

"No, I won't. Not until we have this long-overdue talk."

"Okay. Fine. I'm happy working at the gas station. You know how satisfying it is for me to fix things? I'm rebuilding an engine right now. Bill is so pleased with what I can do. He's putting me on full-time next week."

"You can get into almost any college with the grades you have. I find it a real waste for someone with your intelligence to work as a mechanic. Do it for the summer months, but then further your education."

"Mom's always bugging me about the same thing. I'm sick of it."

"Keep your voice down, Peter. She's only looking out for your best interest because she cares."

"I know, but she's always preaching at me about what the Bible says. I don't need to hear about hell, fire, and damnation in every conversation I have with her."

"I'll talk to her about that. I get a little tired of it, too, between you and me."

My heart sinks like a rock dropping to the bottom of the ocean. Tears well up in the corners of my eyes as I slink away into the kitchen.

It's a beautiful, clear Saturday morning on this 23rd day of June. A perfect day for an outdoor high school graduation and picnic celebration at home. I made the deviled eggs, potato salad, and molded the hamburger patties last night. At my son's request, I broke down and bought a case of Coca Cola. *Everyone in this household knows I believe in healthy choices, such as milk, fruit juice, or cool clear water. Several of his classmates will be coming over later, and they will be looking for the soda to quench their thirst.*

"Mom, Dad, I'll see you at school. We have to be in our caps and gowns and lining up no later than 9:30. See ya." He flies out the door.

We have no time to answer as we both look at the clock. "Jane. It's time to go."

She's dressed in black slacks and a white oxford shirt with her hair askew. *That kid never wants to dress up.*

A real tomboy. Always playing ball with the neighbor boys, climbing trees, or pretending she has a horse.

"Henry, I'll ride in the back seat with Jane so I can do something with her hair." I grab a scarf and brush from her room as I follow them out.

Moments later, my daughter squeals as I drag the brush through her knotted hair. "Ouch. You're hurting me."

"Sorry, honey, but your hair looks like you put your finger in an electric socket. Honestly, couldn't you wear a dress for your brother's graduation?"

She rolls her eyes in pure agitation. "I hate to dress up. Humph."

Fortunately, I have a small beauty salon in my pocketbook. I grab a can of hairspray and secure the scarf around her head.

"Now, there's my pretty girl."

She leans back in the seat, folds her arms, and pouts. "Is Grampa meeting us there?"

"Yes. Aunt Flossie and Daisy will be with him. They're spending the day with us. Isn't that grand?"

Henry turns slightly. "That ought to be interesting. Those three in the same car for a couple of hours each way."

"Now, Henry. Please be nice, all right? No matter what Papa says or does?"

"I'll try."

The cars are lined up on either side of the driveway as Henry maneuvers to find a place to park. The graduates are lining up in front of the school by the stairs going down into the field.

"Oh, there's Papa now. You can let us out here. We'll save you a seat."

Jane leaps out of the car and flies into her grandfather's arms. *Those two are two peas in a pod. He can make her laugh in an instant with all his corny jokes, and I love to see that kid of mine smile.*

I hug my sister. "Daisy, my you are such a beautiful young woman now. So tall and slender. I bet the boys are lining up at your doorstep to take you out on a date."

"Violet, I don't have time for any of that while I'm in med school."

Papa doesn't really acknowledge me as he heads down the stairs with his granddaughter. Aunt Flossie climbs out of the back seat of the car, and I take her hand for support.

"Hello, Toots. It's a beautiful day, isn't it?"

I hug her. "We better head down to the field and grab some seats. The ceremony will begin in fifteen minutes."

"It looks like Berto and Jane found a row of seats just for us. Peter is going on to college, isn't he?" whispers Daisy as we find our seats.

"I think not."

With a perturbed look, she folds her arms. "Just because you and Henry didn't advance your education, doesn't mean he doesn't have to."

The Earl Vandermeulen High School band hammers out "Pomp and Circumstance" as the graduates dressed in purple caps with gold tassels and gowns file two by two down the steps into their designated seats.

After a few speeches, two songs from the school choir, a gift to the school from the graduates, and two hundred diplomas handed out, it's over. Those clad in purple throw their caps in the air. "Hooray!"

Two hours later, our guests are relaxing now that their bellies are full. Some folks are sitting on blankets in the back yard, gazing at the waves roaring below. Auntie, Daisy, and I scurry about, putting food away, sweeping the floors, and tidying up a bit.

Auntie puts a few dishes away. "Toots, Peter doesn't want to talk about college at all. Why is that?"

"He's taking a year off and working at the gas station."

"You can't let him be just a mechanic. He is too smart for that."

"We aren't happy about his decision. He argues with us if we try to interfere. You know how he loves to work on cars."

"I can talk some sense into the kid if you want me to," Papa says.

Henry slams his hand on the table and rises. "You will do no such thing, Berto. You never give him the time of day when you visit, and you expect him to take your advice?"

"Look at you, Henry. You have all you can do to feed your family. You work many hours, but you have nothing to show for it."

Henry raises his fist, ready to strike, but I grab it in the nick of time. "You two stop it this instant."

A few guests gather in the doorway to the porch to watch the spectacle. Peter pushes his way through with a few of his friends at is heels. "Mom, this was a nice celebration, but it's ugly now. I'm going to Vinnie's party. Don't wait up for me." He hugs Auntie and leaves with all his friends.

He was never very fond of his grandfather.

"Oh, for crying out loud, Auntie. We didn't even cut the cake yet, and it's his graduation."

"I'll get the ice cream and start serving it anyway."

Papa looks around the room and out to the porch. "Where's Jane? She plumb disappeared after lunch. I thought we could play a round of Parcheesi before we leave."

"Probably in her room because she doesn't like hanging around with adults. Go get her, Papa. You always make her laugh."

I hear him say, "Hey, kiddo. Want to play a game with your cranky grandfather?"

Jane replies, "Chinese checkers. We can play right here. I'll sit on the bed, and you pull up that chair, Gramps."

Papa's jokes are so old, but it gets that kid every time.

"Hey, Jane? How high is up?"

She chuckles uncontrollably. *My daughter has a contagious laugh.*

Summer's in full swing on the North Shore of Long Island, and the biggest blessing we have is that the kids can literally go to the beach every day. Peter and Henry are almost finished building a hydroplane from scratch. They have been working into all hours of the night and weekends. If my son isn't working at the service station, he's in the garage sanding down his boat. A few of Jane's friends have horses, and she is feeling left out these days because we can't afford to buy her one, let alone find a place to board. Her whole life revolves around anything horse. *I can always tell when she has been around the big animals because a potent smell of manure encompasses her when she returns.*

Today, I'm filling an order for a dozen. "Prayer changes things" tiles in the brightly lit studio. I glance over at my daughter, who is curled up on the couch, reading *Black Beauty*.

"What are your friends doing today, dear?"

"Riding together. What else?"

"You mean to tell me Carol has two horses and didn't ask you to ride with her?"

"She has a cousin spending a couple of weeks at her house, so I'm out of luck, I guess."

"I have a meeting at the Barlow's this afternoon. I'm sure Maria will love to spend some time with you. The two of you are old enough to get together without parents around."

"She's boy crazy, Mom."

"What do you mean?"

"We used to play with dolls, but now she wants to plaster makeup all over my face and dress me up in skin-tight clothes. She invites the neighbor teen boys over whenever she can."

"When her parents are home, right?"

"Sure, for the most part, but they stay upstairs while the party roars on underneath. The rooms dimly lit and…"

Oh Lord, please don't let my daughter turn boy crazy. Not yet anyway. With a tray of painted tiles in my hands, "I have to get these in the kiln. Answer the telephone if it rings.

Lord, I pray that You will always protect my daughter from the sins of this world. May she accept You as her Lord and Savior soon. I know if I had You in my life at a young age, I wouldn't have encountered the demonic world or fallen prey to a mental breakdown. Please protect Jane from that. Amen.

The church group in Port Jefferson is growing with plans to start services in January. We meet for prayer every Wednesday and recently added a hymn singing with praise time. *I'm excited to see what God is going to do in this area.*

I still teach Sunday school at the Sound Beach church, and Henry sings in the choir. Jane loves to help in the nursery and has made a couple of friends in the youth group, so getting her up on Sundays is not difficult. I continue to pray for my son.

Pastor Barkley sits with us at the potluck luncheon after church. He announced his resignation today and will be moving to Florida in October. "Would it be all right with you both if I took Peter out to lunch this week?"

"Have you ever met him?" Henry asks.

"Yes. I have made it a point to buy my gasoline there on a regular basis and recently had a new muffler installed. Peter did a great job."

I smile. "I think it's a great idea, Pastor. If he would only say yes."

"Violet and I are concerned that he'll be working there indefinitely. If you can encourage him to do something else, we would appreciate it tremendously."

"I'll stop by tomorrow on my way into town. Lord willing, I'll have some success."

It's the night before school starts, and Jane is still not home. Her curfew is 8:00 on school nights and 9:30 on weekends. Henry's pacing back and forth. The dog can't seem to settle in one place because his pal is not in the house. *Where is she? Its 9:00 and no phone call. I know she's with Carol and her friends, but what are they doing? They know she won't walk home in the dark alone.*

94

Pups growls and barks at the front door.

Henry opens it. "Where have you been, young lady?"

Jane squeezes past him. "Over at Carol's, playing records. Her father dropped me off."

I grab her arm. "You're grounded for a week. You should have been home an hour ago. I have a feeling boys were there."

She bursts into tears. "There were. I'm so sorry. I won't do it again."

Chocolate chip cookies are waiting for Jane when she comes home from school the next day. I'm on my knees by my bed in prayer as I am currently most days. *I don't have to worry about her because she seems to have the same routine. A snack in front of the television will pacify her for at least an hour.*

I always pray out loud for some reason. Today's no exception. "Father God Almighty, I thank you for your constant love. Watch over me and my family. You're the Lord of my life, and all has changed since I asked Jesus into my heart a few years ago. I have learned through Your Holy Bible about You being the triune God, three in one. God, the father, Jesus, His son, and the Holy Spirit. Thank you so much for getting the ugly demon out of my life. Oh, how I pray for those I love to come to know You as I have. Henry knows You exist but doesn't have You in his heart. Peter's heart is hardened towards You, but Jane's so close to finding You, Lord." I continue to pray with tears of joy. I remove the shawl from my head, pull myself up, and blow my nose.

"Mom?" whispers Jane.

I jump up and spin to face her." Honey, you startled me."

"I heard you praying for me. How can I have Jesus in my heart like you do? You're so much happier than you used to be, and people sparkle when you walk into a room. I want this too."

I hug her with all my might. "Let's go into your room and find the Bible I gave you. I want you to read a verse out loud, okay?"

She finds the Bible in a desk drawer. We kneel at the side of her bed together. I open the black book to John 3:16. "Here, read this."

"For God so loved the world that he gave his only begotten Son that whoever believes in him will not perish but have eternal life."

"Repeat after me. Dear Jesus, please forgive me of all my wrongdoings and come into my heart. Help me to be the kind of person you want me to be. Thank you, Lord. Amen."

Chapter Thirteen

Through much prayer and researching the financial status of the Violetile's Shoppe, I decide to close in two months, on December 31st. My customers will be able to enter my well-equipped studio at home using the private entrance. I'll save a bundle of money on rent alone.

The leaves blow inside the door every time it opens on this autumn day. I closed the upstairs portion of the store in August, and most of the remaining merchandise is on sale. Looking around with a sigh, I realize it will be bittersweet to turn the keys over to the landlord. *Thank you, Lord, for all the friends and contacts I have made since the beginning of this endeavor. Continue to bring people into my life I can tell about your saving grace. Let my light always shine for you. Amen.*

As I strike a match to burn some lavender incense, the door opens. My eyes widen and my smile blossoms as I take in the sight before me. Three black ladies dressed to the nines fill the room with their radiant presence. "Good afternoon, ladies. How are you on this windy day?"

The heavy-set lady dressed in a black ottoman suit beams from ear to ear. "Are you Violet?"

"Yes, I am." I reach out and shake her hand. "And you are?"

"Gladys, and these are my sisters Althea and Bernadette. We were at the library and asked where we could find some Christian gifts. The librarian suggested you."

"I'm flattered. Please look around and take your time. Where are you from?"

"Copiague, near Babylon. We like to eat at the Schooner restaurant a couple of times a year. These roosters are beautiful, and the scripture verse from Genesis, 'and God created every living creature,' makes them a perfect gift."

"All the designs on the tiles are my creations, and I hand paint each one. We kiln fire for permanence."

"I'm going to get me at least a dozen of these before I leave this store. Do you have boxes?" Althea asks.

"Yes, I do. I can gift wrap your purchases, if necessary. Where do you go to church?"

"The African Methodist Episcopal Church in Copiague. Oh, how we love sweet Jesus. You must love Him, too, because most of your tiles have Bible verses."

"My life was a shamble before I asked Jesus into my heart. Without Him, I would be nothing."

"Oh, honey. Isn't God amazing to send His only Son into this world of sinners, but He can take the broken pieces and make it into something beautiful. Last week a young single mother was kicked out of her house by an alcoholic husband. She had no place to go except our church."

"My goodness. Is she all right? What about her children?"

"The parsonage is huge, with many empty rooms. Our minister took this family of three in off the streets. The mother, Eunice, is doing all the housekeeping in exchange for a safe place to live. The little ones are four and two. This woman was destitute and rarely smiled, but she has renewed her relationship with Jesus. She shines like a polished jewel. Like you."

"How sweet of you to say that. Yes, I can relate in the sense I was a shattered vase that God put back together into a unique masterpiece."

98

Bernadette puts her arm around me. "Althea, we should have Violet speak at our women's harvest luncheon. You know time is running out. It's in a few weeks."

I feel a bit flushed, "Uh, I don't know if I should…"

"Althea, what would the ladies think about that?" Gladys jumps in after giving me the once over.

I'm in a tough place right now. I hope this doesn't come to fruition, because I doubt if I would be well received as the only white woman in the bunch. Let alone the speaker.

"Sisters. sisters. Now, now. Let's go home, talk to the committee and pray about this before we make this final. What do you think about it, Violet?" Althea smiles.

"Well, I have not given my testimony in public yet. I don't know if I would be ready. When is this event?"

"Saturday, November 10th, at noon."

Looking at me with doubt in her eyes, Gladys turns and heads to the door. "I'll wait for you two in the car."

Bernadette lays her purchase on the counter. "Don't you mind her now, Violet. If it's God's will for you to come and speak, it will happen."

"I don't know about this."

Althea laughs. "We'll bill you as, *African Violet.* Perfect, don't you think?"

What happened here today, Lord? In a flash, I was invited to speak at an all-black church in a non-white neighborhood. Well, this is positively exciting, to say the least. In the sight of one hour, I made friends with ladies who shine with the love of Jesus. We hugged each other as though we have known each other forever. Oh Lord, I'm amazed by you. Amen.

"Jane, get ready for youth group. We'll be leaving in a few minutes."

"Do I have to go? Last week, there were only five of us, and it was so boring."

"Yes. You do have to go, and that's it. It's only one hour, Jane. Honestly."

I watch my daughter slink into her room to get her Bible. I hope.

Henry and Peter are watching boxing on the television as they do every Wednesday night. Peter looks my way as I put a few last-minute things in my purse. "Mom, don't make her go to that goofy group."

"She needs to be with Christian young people, Son. She'll cheer up once she gets there."

He taps his dad on the knee and chuckles. "Mom has become a holy roller."

I keep my composure but without a smile. "Okay, you two. See you later."

∽⊙≈⊙∽

Wednesday nights at our church are busy with youth group, two Bible studies, and Pioneer Girls, a program for girls ages two through twelve. I'm co-leader for the woman's study.

Sally grabs Jane's hand. "We're going to make ice cream floats tonight."

The pastor taps my shoulder. "Hi, Violet, can I pull you away from your group for a few minutes? I want to talk to you about Peter.

We sit in a pew in the sanctuary.

"I saw your son today. Did he tell you?"

"No, he didn't. How did it go?"

"He's going to meet me for lunch on Saturday."

100

"That's an answer to prayer, Pastor. The summer has come and gone. Now, we're fast approaching a new year, and he's still at the gas station. He'll be nineteen in a few months."

"I have a good rapport with him. I have been in prayer asking God for guidance on how I can direct him. You do know that I served in the armed forces, right?"

∽⊚⦿⊚∽

In bed that night, Henry and I talk about the events of the day. It's seems to be the only time we're alone to talk before he drifts off to sleep with a sermon of snoring. Most folks would think us unusual since we like to have a window open in the chilliest of weather.

We huddle under the covers in each other's arms "Honey, I forgot to tell you about the interesting request to speak at an upcoming ladies harvest luncheon I received today."

He yawns. "The Port Jefferson Ladies Guild, I presume?"

"No. The African Methodist Episcopal Church in Copiague."

He leans onto his elbow. "What? Are you crazy, Violet?"

"What's wrong with you? I think it's wonderful. Can't you be happy for me?"

"I'm in no way prejudice, but there has been a lot of violence in the news regarding that town lately."

"Oh, Henry. The event is during the day. We'll be all right."

"We?"

"Yes. I am taking Jane with me. There will be other girls there her age. It will be fun for her."

With a sigh, he rolls over. "I sure hope you know what you're doing. I don't like it though."

⌒⊙∽⊙∽

I ran an ad in the newspaper for a big sale at the shop. This is the busiest Saturday in a long time. I'm glad Astrid is helping as cashier today so I can replenish the stock as needed. Amazingly enough, people are asking for their merchandise to be gift wrapped in Christmas paper.

We aim to please the customers.

Astrid calls out, "Phone call for you, Violet."

"Hello, Violet speaking."

"How are you, my African Violet? This is Althea."

I chuckle into the phone. "It's so good to hear your voice."

"Can you take an hour off for lunch on Monday? The committee wants you to speak next week, and I want to give you directions and a preliminary copy of the program."

"The shop is closed on Mondays, so I won't be in town at all. Why don't you come to my house for lunch?"

"Really? I would love to. Where do you live?"

"At 48 Sea Cliff Avenue in Miller Place. Do you know where that is?"

"No."

"Jot down my home phone number, 216-7369, in case you get lost."

"I'm looking forward to it, honey."

Astrid leans in my direction. "I don't mean to eavesdrop. You told me about this new friend of yours, but is it wise to invite her to your house?"

"Why is that your concern?"

She pulls me into the corner. "What will the neighbors think?"

102

"Astrid, I'm surprised at you. Jesus teaches that we should love everyone, and that's what I intend to do. The color of someone's eyes, skin, or hair has no bearing on who they are as a person."

"I guess we found something to disagree about. What will your husband think of this?"

"Please join us on Monday, Astrid. I guarantee you'll love Althea the moment you meet her."

❦

"Mom, Dad, come here for a few minutes. I have something to tell you," Peter calls from his room.

I glance at Henry with a shrug. "Coming, dear."

Peter motions for us to sit down. "I had a great time with Pastor Barkley today. He's a very nice man and had some great advice for me."

"Really? What did he say? Please don't keep us in suspense."

"I'm enlisting in the Navy on Monday."

Chapter Fourteen

It's the end of January, and we are experiencing a big snowstorm. Henry took the day off from work to avoid long delays, which is common when weather paralyzes most of the island. It's been quiet around here without Peter. No more greasy clothes to wash after a day at Bill Roth's. He's in the fourth week of basic training with the Navy. It was good to hear from him last night. "Mom, we're in the tulles out here, and if I don't bundle up in my naval pea jacket, I'll freeze my backside. They shaved off my slick, thick hair and I have a buzz cut."

My speaking engagement at the African Methodist church went well. Their joy for the Lord was evident in the hand clapping, dancing, and shouts of Hallelujah. It was easy sharing my testimony after the time of worship.

As the three of us sit down for a nice breakfast of bacon and scrambled eggs, the lights flicker as the wind howls around the house. We glance at each other and continue eating. Pups is on his haunches waiting for a morsel to drop at his feet.

Henry takes a bite of toast. "It was so good to hear from Peter, wasn't it?"

Jane's eyes widen. "I didn't know you talked to him."

"It was after 11:00, and we didn't want to wake you. He'll be home in four weeks for furlough."

"That's a long time from now, Mom."

Henry grabs her hand. "Oh, don't fret, Tot. How about a game of Parcheesi after breakfast?"

The ring of the telephone startles us all.

"Hello?"

"Hi Violet, this is Althea."

"Althea, how are you doing in Copiague?

"We would love to have you lead a Bible study here. What do you think?"

"A Bible study? Me? I don't know, Althea. Can't you or one of your sisters lead it?"

"It was unanimous. Everyone wants you."

"I'll pray about it, my friend. Keep warm. I'll call you tomorrow."

Henry shakes his head as I clear the table. "What was that all about, Vi?"

"The ladies from her church want me to lead a four-week Bible study on Galatians."

"Can I come with you? Althea's daughter, Leora, is funny," Jane asks, munching on a piece of bacon.

"I don't know, Jane. It will be on Mondays, a school night."

Henry shakes his head. "Listen, Violet, I don't want you to do this. During the day okay, but not at night."

"Oh, Henry, I've been over there a few times and never had a problem. Let me pray about it."

"Humph. Go ahead and ask God what you should do. You'll do what you want anyway."

"If I can win someone to a saving knowledge of Jesus Christ or help them to grow in Him, I will take every opportunity to do so."

"Mommy, please let me go with you. I'll bring my homework with me."

"Honestly, Vi, I'm sure they have folks who can do this. Why you?"

"Henry, they love the tiles, and I have made some lucrative sales since I made the connection in Copiague."

The conversation ends abruptly once the Parcheesi game is placed on the table. I gather the dirty dishes and head into the kitchen to fulfill my role as housewife. The snow's falling, and the waves are producing huge white caps on the sound. For some reason, heaven seems a bit closer when gazing upon a huge body of water.

Lord, you know I have changed my thoughts and plans since You became the Lord of my life. Your Holy Spirit lives with me, and when I pray for Your leading, I'm granted peace one way or another. My daughter loves to be with children her age that love Jesus. How can I deny her that? I want her to grow up accepting people from all walks of life, no matter where they come from. I ask now for Your infinite wisdom to direct me to do the right thing. First, should I teach this study, and if yes, do I let Jane come? Amen.

I finish cleaning the kitchen and head into my bedroom to make the bed, put things away, and get dressed for the day. *I would rather stay in my pajamas, but it's already noon. This is a perfect day to organize the studio and catch up on some back orders. Maybe I'll call Lois first and ask her to pray for me.*

"Hi, Lois. How is at your place? We still have power."

"We were without power for a couple of hours, but everything's okay now."

"That's good. My African American friends want me to lead a Bible study in Copiague."

"Is it at night or during the day?"

"At night, but I think it's of the Lord, but Henry doesn't understand. Jane wants to come with me too. What do you think?"

"That's a rough area, Violet. If it's during the day, take it. Otherwise, I wouldn't."

"I do believe that God will protect us, and it's a good opportunity. Go ahead and pray. Please. I have to call her back tomorrow with an answer."

❦

Two Mondays have gone without any incident. I always call Althea before Jane and I leave home and vise-versa to Henry on our return. There are ten women who attend the study, not counting three teenage girls. We start with prayer and dessert, which never lasts more than twenty minutes. Rather good for a bunch of chatty-patty women. A good hour is spent digging into Galatians. Most of us must get up early to go to work or to get kids off to school, so we end at 8:00 on the dot.

"Lock your door, Jane, and the back door too," I say as I pull out of the driveway.

"Why did you turn here, Mom? Don't we usually go straight through town to the main highway?"

"Bernadette told me about this shortcut that will save us about ten minutes. Don't fret, Jane."

We pass a few boarded-up establishments and several abandoned cars. "She said to go through two traffic lights and turn right. Okay, good, a green light."

"This neighborhood looks creepy. Let's go back the other way. Mom, please?"

I approach the second light as it turns red. "Don't pester your mother. Keep quiet."

Five teenage boys appear to be waiting to cross the street, but instead they surround the car. There are no other cars in sight and no people either. As I look to my left, a lit house suddenly goes dark. They start pushing the car back, but I'm in a state of panic and don't remember how to step on the brake.

"Mommy. The brake. The brake." The car continues to roll. She flings over the console and presses her left foot on the brake. We jolt forward, and the two thugs on the hood fly off, shouting foul language.

The one with a baseball cap taps on my window. "Hey, lady. I think it is time you get out of that car, so we can have some fun."

I scowl at them through the glass. "You boys leave us alone."

"And what are you going to do about it if we don't? Scream? No one will hear you."

I look over at my daughter as she grabs my hand. "God, help us out of this safely."

They start rattling the door handles. My skin prickles, and I rub my arms.

"Mommy. I'm scared."

Pushing Jane's foot off the brake and replacing it with mine, I ease up slowly and gun the gas pedal to make the car bound forward, but right at that time something smashes the window on Jane's side of the car. Glass shatters all over her, and I am forced to stop the car. Panic rushes through me as someone's hand unlocks her door. Jane's blood-curdling scream sends chills down my back as she is yanked from her seat.

"Leave her alone. She's only a kid." Thinking quickly, I hide my purse under the seat, lay on the horn, and yank the key out of the ignition. Leaving it in my hand, I leap across the seat.

The five boys are laughing and drinking as they form a circle around us.

Jane's crying uncontrollably as I circle her in my arms.

"Oh, yeah, we are going to party with a mama and daughter. Hey, boys. This will be a night to remember."

Out of nowhere I am filled with courage. "God sees what's going on here. Yes. He knows everything." My cheeks are burning.

"What you know about God? He hasn't saved you yet," the tall one with a bat shouts in my face.

"No talking to our prey, Elroy. Time for the good stuff," yells the one with his body pressed against my back. I cringe at the alcohol smell as goosebumps climb my arms. Jane's so close to me that I can feel her relieve herself as it drops on my feet.

"God hates evil, and what you boys are doing is just that," I cry out. *Did I just say that?*

Hands from behind wrap around my chest, and I take one hand and try to pry them off. He removes one hand to play with my hair. Roars of laughter shatter my eardrums. "Come on, Lamar, give us a good show. Unbutton her coat. Uh, huh."

Good thing there's a streetlight a few feet away so I can get a glimpse of faces. Oh, God, please send someone to rescue us. These boys mean business. Oh, no. The younger boy is pulling on Jane.

"Don't let go of me, honey. Hold on."

She's pulling on my coat and crying as her enemy struggles to win.

"Jeffrey, that one is your size all right. You hold on a few minutes, little brother, and I will help you score. First, I'm going to enjoy her mama. Lamar moves directly in front of me and yanks the buttons off my coat. He pulls it off me. "Stop it. No. Leave my daughter alone. Please?" Lamar looks me over as he takes a swig of liquor. "Get ready, lady, 'cause I sure am."

"Lamar, a car's coming, man. It could be the night patrol," shouts Elroy.

He acts like he doesn't hear because he's kissing my head. I manage to fall to my knees, bringing my daughter with me.

"Get up now." He growls as he unbuckles his belt.

Jeffrey yanks Jane from me as she screams.

Lamar pulls me up by the hair. My knees turn wiggly.

I hear a siren in proximity.

"Scatter, everyone. Come on, Lamar. Get moving, Jeffrey." Elroy runs into a dark alley.

"Give me the key to your car, lady. Now." Lamar looks at the revolving red light a few blocks away.

"I don't have it. I dropped it somewhere. I don't know where," I cry.

Everyone's gone except the two brothers as the headlights shine on all of us. I pull away and grab my daughter. The police run after the guilty and grab them within minutes. My stomach is churning as tears fall from my eyes. "We're safe now, Jane. Everything will be all right." The bright, entertaining lights bring a few spectators out. I hear car doors slam and a couple of familiar voices, but my burning eyes are on my daughter.

"Oh, sweet Violet. Oh, dear Jane. Your husband called looking for you when you didn't come home at the usual time. Lavon saw you go in this direction over an hour ago. So, I called the police."

Breaking down in tears, we fall into her arms. "Althea, I don't think I can drive home. I'm so shaken, but I'm so grateful that God took care of us."

"Clarence will drive your car to your house. You and Jane can come with me, okay?"

"That's so nice of you. Thanks, Althea."

The flashing lights on the patrol car are off as the handcuffed brothers are moved into the back seat. One of the policemen approaches us. "I have to get a statement from you, Miss. It looks like assault and battery, but I must get all the details as it happened. Are you up to it?"

I pull myself together, holding Jane's hand in the process. "They didn't do anything physical but threatened to harm us. If you didn't come when you did, I would have been sexually assaulted. My thirteen-year-old daughter was traumatized as a result of this horrific event."

"Do you want to press charges?"

"They're teenagers who need guidance and something constructive to do with their time other than drink alcohol, which leads to trouble. I don't like the idea of jail, but at least they won't torment anyone else."

"Were they alone?"

I hesitate a moment. "There were five of them, but the brothers were the actual assailants."

He continues to write on a pad. "You look familiar. Aren't you the lady that was kidnapped last year?"

"Yes, I am."

"So sorry, Mrs. Funk, that you had to go through another ordeal. You have some good friends here. Lamar has been convicted of abusing women before, so I know what would have happened if we didn't get here when we did. I have all the information I need. Do I have your permission to call your husband to tell him you're on your way home?"

"Yes, of course."

"Here. I think this is the key to your car?"

"It is. Thank you."

I opt to sit in the back seat with Jane as Althea drives us back to Miller Place. My daughter is fast asleep in my arms within seconds after leaving the scene of gloom.

My friend belts out, "Praise Jesus for getting my African Violet out of Satan's clutches. Thank you, Lord, that Lavon saw her go in this direction so the police could find Violet in the nick of time. Oh, Blessed God, take care of Jane as she recovers from this nightmare. Amen. Hallelujah."

"Amen, amen," I whisper.

I sleep on the top bunk in her room so if she has a nightmare during the night, I will hear her.

Henry tosses the newspaper on the floor the next day and pulls me on his lap. "You can't save the whole world, so stay away from that part of the island."

Chapter Fifteen

1959

The heat's excruciating as we try to endure one of the hottest summers of the decade. We have several fans running throughout the house during the day to keep the air circulating, at least. Henry figured out a way to cut an opening on the studio wall for an air conditioner. He thought it was good strategy to keep customers and the ladies in my Bible study happy. Jane and I have been spending a lot of time in this room the past few days, not just because of the heat either. It seems that all her friends are busy doing other things, and my daughter isn't included. I look over at her eating her lunch surrounded by her horse books, crayons, and sketch pads. She certainly knows how to keep occupied and entertained.

"How are you doing over there?" I ask.

"Good. These tuna sandwiches are delicious. You make the best chocolate milkshakes too."

I bite into my sandwich. "They are pretty good. Aren't we lucky to have this nice cool room?"

"Can I sleep in here again tonight, Mom?"

"I don't see why not. You could call Paulette or Charlene and see if they want to sleep over?"

"Nah, all they do is talk about their horses and the new trails they ride on. I keep asking God for a horse, but nothing happens. I'd rather stay here and stay cool than to hear them brag."

"I'll be right back. I must put these tiles in the kiln in the basement*." It's much cooler down there for a hot kiln to do its work.* "If the phone rings, answer it."

My daughter has become such a homebody since school let out for vacation. She'll go to the beach if I go with her but not by herself. It seems to bother me more than her. I love how she prays out loud, but her cries for a horse wrench my heart, because I know in my heart it can't happen. There, tomorrow I'll cork back all these tiles and hopefully deliver to Patchogue Decorators on Thursday. What's that banging?

I run up the stairs, and as the banging gets louder, I realize it's coming from the front door. "Coming. Coming."

I open the door to three sweaty, frazzled young girls. "Mrs. Funk, is Jane home?"

"Yes, come in, girls. It's too hot there. Do you want a drink?"

Carol moves her hair from her face. "We can't because we have to watch the horse."

"Horse? What horse?"

Paulette nearly jumps out of her skin. "We have a horse for Jane."

I look over their heads and down the lawn. "There's a horse tied to our fence!"

Carol jumps up and down. "Mrs. Funk, that's a horse for Jane."

"Hang on. I'll go get her."

My heart is pounding and sweat drips from my brow as I run through the house. *The only thing I can think of is there's a horse right outside for my daughter. God does answer prayer.*

She's fast asleep on the day bed with *Black Beauty* in her hands. *I hope I don't startle her.*

"Jane, honey." I rub the curls away from her eyes.

Her eyes pop open. "What? Leave me alone. I just want to sleep."

"Your friends are waiting outside for you. They have a surprise too."

She sits up. "What kind of surprise?"

I all but pull her off the bed. "You better go right now, Jane."

She takes her time. I wish she would get past this inferiority complex she has. Always worried she'll be left out or excluded. This time her friends have her best interest at heart. I hope she sees that.

The girls are sitting on the front steps when she opens the door. "What's going on?"

They leap up and in unison say, "We got you a horse."

Jane turns to me with tears in her eyes and then turns back to them. "Leave me alone. What kind of joke is this?"

She starts to come back inside, but Carol grabs her hand. "Jane, look over there. What do you see?"

Reluctantly, she turns and looks. "Whose horse is that?"

"It's yours if you want him."

In an instant my daughter is transformed into a bubbly, happy girl. I watch as she sprints across the lawn to the animal.

I follow. *Where are we going to keep this horse? I just bought a van and a new kiln. There isn't any extra money for a horse. Yet, this is an answer to prayer.*

Jane's wraps her arms around the animal's neck. "What a nice boy you are."

It touches my heart to see the love my daughter has for this horse, but I'm disillusioned by his appearance. The fur is a dull grey, and since the horse is so thin, I can almost count every rib. *Oh, dear. Look at that huge sore right where a saddle would go. Time to get some answers.* "Carol, where did you get him?"

"From a man in Mt. Sanai who knows my father really well. He asked us to find a home for him. He doesn't have time to take care of the horse."

I finally get up enough courage to touch him. "Does he have a name?"

Keeping her arms around the horse, Jane answers. "It's Zorro, Mom. There is a Z on his rump."

"Uh oh, that's quite a sore he has up here. It looks really nasty." I sigh.

Carol rubs Zorro's snout. "Axle grease will take care of that in no time."

I look at her with a scowl. "You're joking, right?"

"Nope. I tried it on one of my horses, and it took away the sore within a week."

"Jane, let him eat some grass. He's probably hungry," Paulette says.

After some grazing time and several walks up and down the driveway, I realize it's late in the afternoon, and a discussion on where we'll keep this animal has to take place before it gets dark. *Henry will be annoyed, to say the least, if he comes home and sees a horse on our lawn.*

"Carol, we can't keep Zorro because we don't have a place for him. Surely, you knew that when you brought him here."

"My dad said Jane can keep him at our place for the summer and that will give you plenty of time to find a boarding facility before winter comes."

I look at my watch. "That's nice of him, Carol. I strongly suggest you kids get that horse to your place before folks get out of work and the traffic gets heavy."

I was completely amazed at Henry's reaction to Jane's new pet. He's going to call a few people in the

neighborhood for stable options. I called a few places, but monthly board is higher than most apartment dwellings. We can't afford that.

"I think I'll take the day off today. I could use a long weekend, and Jane really wants me to see that horse of hers," says Henry as we cuddle in bed.

"That is wonderful, honey. She's so excited."

"I have an idea. Why don't we all go? We can have a long overdue family day."

I give him a kiss and roll out of bed. "I need to go for a nice, long swim. You need to spend some quality time with your daughter. "

"You've been cooped up in the house for a few days now, and I know how much you love to swim. Let's get dressed and have some breakfast."

I throw my robe on, "I'll make some coffee."

"Daddy, I have to go and put that stuff on Zorro's cut."

"Right after we finish our breakfast, young lady. We need to spend some time with your mother before we all go in different directions."

My daughter wolfs down the remainder of her breakfast. "Can we go to the farm store after stopping by the Karney's house? I want to get my own brush and curry comb for the horse."

Henry smiles at me. "Sure, we can, Tot."

I stand on the front porch and watch them drive away. *I better get the dishes done before I get into my swimsuit. I know I have the whole day to swim, but I don't want to be out in the sun after noon. A sunburn is no friend of mine.*

A few people are in the water farther down, but there are no other people on the beach where I am. The water's relatively calm as the soft waves roll on to the sand in front of me. I lather myself with tanning lotion and lay back on the blanket to soak up some rays before it gets too hot. *I hope I don't fall asleep because I'll wake up as a cooked red lobster. Lord, I pray that we can find a reasonable place to board Zorro, so Jane will be happy.*

Keep them safe today as they spend time together. Thank You for this beautiful day and time to do what I love. Amen. I pull out my watch and see it is 10:30. *I'll read a bit before venturing out into the water.* I hear some kids run by, scattering sand all over me and my blanket. I sit up and soak in God's magnificent creation before me. Seagulls fly as they squawk about where the best fish are, the sky is a brilliant blue without one cloud, and the waves roll in a picture of absolute serenity. *Breathtaking. The porpoises are finally out there.* I take off my cover up, sneakers, and sun hat.

I'm glad it's high tide because there are no scraggly rocks under my feet. I dive under and swim out without looking back. *I'm close enough to the amazing fish. They always seem to ignore me. The water seems to get warmer the farther out I swim.* I stop after a few breast strokes to doggy paddle as I glance back at the shore. I turn and see the porpoises in a school of six or seven. I swim alongside, one vigorous breast stroke at a time. *It's amazing I don't have a fear of water. Most folks think I'm crazy to swim so far from shore, but I have never had a problem. This is so invigorating, but I better head back to shore in a few minutes. Ooh. What is that pain in my leg? Must be a charley horse.* I stop to kick it out. It's worse. My mouth opens unexpectedly, and I swallow a mouthful of water. I wave my arms over my head as I kick to stay afloat. *God, please take away the pain now. Don't let me drown.* I spin in circles, looking for a boat, another

118

swimmer, or a porpoise. My eyes are so bloodshot from the saltwater, nothing's clear. There's a motor sound in the distance. I'm alone in this vast body of water as it starts to go over my head. *No, I can't sink any farther.* Using my arms, I pull myself up enough to gasp for air. I don't dare grab my leg, but the pain is unbearable. *Don't inhale any water if you can help it.* I gasp for air as all the energy I have trickles out of my body. I do everything in my power to hold my breath as I sink, sink, sink. I shut my eyes to keep the salt from stinging them anymore. I try to paddle, but I can't use my legs, and my arms are motionless. *My life is over, and the Long Island sound will become my final resting place.*

Darkness consumes me.

"Violet? Can you hear me?" someone asks.

Everything is dark as I try to gasp for air. *Who is that? Where am I?*

"She's still unconscious, but our tests reveal she wasn't under the water more than five minutes. If it was any longer, Violet would not be with us. Your wife is in good shape and should pull out of this soon," says someone I don't recognize.

I try to blink my eyes, but I can't.

"Thank you, Doctor. My wife has many people praying for her, but I know you're doing everything you can to help her."

Henry. Oh, my husband. I hear you and want to hug you so much. My arms won't move. My legs won't either. I must be paralyzed or heavily medicated. A lonely tear rolls down my face.

"If you don't see improvement soon, I'll call in a neurologist from Smithtown."

"Violet's father, sister, and aunt will be here in a couple of days. They're worried sick."

"Please leave their names at the nurse's station. I have to check on a few other patients, but I'll be back later to see if you have any questions."

"Thanks, Dr. Kirby."

A warm sensation penetrates my forehead. "How does this warm washcloth feel, honey?

"The Lord is my light and my salvation; I will not fear. The Lord is the Refuge and stronghold of my life-I will not be afraid." Psalm27:1.

I can tell when night comes because it's quiet. I know my God has me in the palm of His hands, and I escaped death because of Him. I drift off to sleep.

"Her pulse is normal and heart rate is good. We took her off oxygen this morning, Mr. Funk. She's breathing on her own now and on the upswing."

"Thank you, Doctor."

"Jane, it's all right to go talk to your mother. I have your hand, but there isn't anything to be afraid of," Henry says softly.

"Mommy? Can you hear me?"

Oh, my sweet innocent girl. Why did your father bring you here? This is going to be hard for you to understand. I hope Auntie comes soon so she can take care of you. I pray God pulls me out. .

I don't know how long I've been lying here, but it seems like an eternity. I must have fallen asleep again, but for how long?

My eyes open to see Aunt Flossie looking at me. "Henry, she opened her eyes!"

I want to smile and shout amen. Nothing happens.

Henry comes around the other side of me and kisses my cheek. "My Violet, you're coming back to us. Thank God."

I'm becoming the center of attention as Papa, Daisy, Henry, Auntie, and Jane surround the bed. I can see all of them clearly. They stare in attention for the slightest change to happen. I flicker my eyes in approval, and a few tears fall. Papa wipes my eyes with a handkerchief.

"We need to get something to eat, Jane. The cafeteria has good food. Who else wants to join us?" Henry offers.

"I'll stay with her in case anything changes." My sister takes my hand in hers as the others disappear.

Oh, my dear sister, my God is right here, and I want so much for you to know Him like I do. A tear once again rolls down my cheek. I shift my eyes from left to right in total amazement. *Does Peter know I'm in the hospital?*

"Who rescued my daughter? I want to thank them," says Papa from a short distance away.

"It was me," says Henry. "I was taking the hydroplane for a spin to get it ready for Peter's leave next week. Luckily, I left Jane at her friend's house. I could see Violet swimming in the distance, and suddenly, she was gone. That little skimmer can cover a lot of space in a short span of time, so I revved up the engine. I saw her pop back up for air as I approached the scene, then she disappeared. Stopping the engine, I dove in. She was sinking fast. I grabbed her arm, pulled, and propelled my way to the surface. The boat drifted off a bit, but luckily, I had enough strength to pull us up on the deck. A fella with a Chris Craft

121

Capri with a V8 engine pulled up next to me and hooked up our boat to his. We took off to Port Jefferson as I tried to resuscitate her. The marina guard called for an ambulance."

My father hugs Henry. "Thanks, Son. She'll pull out of this. She's a fighter."

My heart smiles as my hands start to sweat. I can feel that. I squeeze my sister's hand.

She squeals, "Oh, my goodness, she just squeezed my hand. Violet's coming back to us."

Chapter Sixteen

The sun's beaming through the blinds, and the sheer curtains are dancing in the slight breeze blowing through the large, paned window. Muffled voices reach me from the other side of the sliding curtain that separates the two beds. My sense of smell has returned as I sniff in medications, bleach, and something edible, such as lunch. *Maybe.*

"It's a beautiful day today. If you could only eat something, we could take this ugly IV out of your arm. You're improving every day with increased mobility," Nurse Betty comments.

She's a beautiful lady inside and out. She reminds me of my black friends in Copiague. I bet she knows the Lord because she's always smiling and laughing. No matter what.

She cranks up the bed. "Okay, honey. Let's get you into the bathroom today. No more sponge baths for you. Yes, ugly old intravenous tube will go with us. Hmmm. Uh, ha."

She lifts me and puts me in the wheelchair. *I have enough strength to sit up, move my arms and legs. Praise God. I wish I could speak or even swallow something. Come on, please. I want to get out of here. I'm trying to swallow.*

"Okay, Missy, I won't look, so start taking off that gown so I can situate you on the chair in the shower. I know you can't tell me when you're ready, so I'll count to twenty-five, you'll be ready then."

I lift the arm without the IV and pull the gown off, and now the wires are in the way.

Good grief. Wait. Where is she going? I see her go around the corner. *Now what?* I try to maneuver the wheelchair but can't go very far. *I need help.*

Then, with all the strength I can find, I manage to say, "Hey?"

Nurse Betty darts around the corner with a teenager dressed in a striped uniform. "Did you say something, Miss Violet?"

I shake my head up and down, but words do not form. I manage to cover my private areas with my arms.

"Sally's your assigned Candy Striper for today. She will assist me."

Nurse Betty hands the soiled gown to Sally. "Please throw this in the laundry bin by the nurse's station. After that, I would like you to change the sheets on her bed."

"Yes, Nurse Betty."

The nurse takes out the IV line "There, we can keep this off until you're finished.

I successfully pull off my underwear and wrap my arms over my chest. *It's freezing in here.*

"Okay, honey, I'm turning on the water now. Oh, that feels warm enough. Here's a washcloth and soap. I will be standing right outside the curtain."

This feels divine. The water's just the right temperature. I muster up enough strength to stand up, holding on to the arms of the chair. *There, nice and clean.* I sit back down and wash my hair as the water flows evenly over my body.

I let out a loud sigh and surprise myself. Then, I shout, "Nurse!"

The curtain flies open, and she hands me two warm towels. "You spoke, by golly. Sally, Sally. Get Mrs. Funk a clean gown. She spoke."

"Nurse Betty, thank you," I mutter softly and slowly.

"Your husband took your family out for lunch and will be back soon. Now, let's get you in a clean gown and back into bed. I need to get a hold of the doctor and let him know your progress. Oh yes, he'll be thrilled."

Sally runs into the room. "Nurse Betty, the lunch trays are here."

"How about it, Violet, would you like to try and eat something?"

"Please. I'm starving."

"Let me get Doctor Kirby. Here put this gown on, and I will hold off on the IV until I hear from the doc."

In a few minutes, Sally returns. "Come, Violet. I'll help you back to your bed. I put clean sheets on, so everything's as good as new."

My stomach is growling. "I would like something to eat."

"Well now, that's good, but we must wait for the doctor's orders before we proceed with that. You have been fed intravenously for a week, so I'm sure small portions of food will be better to start with." She covers me and cranks the bed to a sitting position.

A stack of magazines catches my eye on the bed stand. *I really want to read my Bible.*

I grab the latest issue of *Look* magazine. *The new fall fashions are stunning.*

"All right my dear, here's a cup of chicken broth, a few crackers, and some Jell-O," Nurse Betty announces, carrying a tray.

"If you consume this, then no more IV for you."

"This is all I get?"

"Yes, Ma'am. Doctor's orders."

I drink the broth and nibble on a cracker. *My tummy feels a little queasy. I'll throw up if I eat anything else.* I push the table away, lie back, and close my eyes.

"It looks like she's asleep," Papa whispers.

I open my eyes and laugh. "Hi, Papa."

Tears shine in his eyes. "Welcome back, honey."

"I love you, Papa."

Henry comes around the other side of the bed, grabs my hand, and kisses my forehead, "You had a close call, but so many people were praying for you. God needs you here."

❦

I was released from the hospital a week later to recuperate at home. Henry bought a chaise lounge for the porch so I can enjoy the beautiful weather without going anywhere. Sometimes I take long naps, or I read my bible. The ladies from Calvary Baptist bring home-cooked meals every night so I don't have to cook. *I thank God my strength is slowly coming back. I could have died.*

Henry pulls up a chair. "Peter will be home the day after tomorrow, Violet. Is there anything I can do to help you prepare for his homecoming?"

"I'll make a grocery list so you and Jane can shop for what we need. The best thing is you took two weeks off and have been doing a lot of housework. What more could I ask for?"

"I keep going over and over in my mind about the events of that day when I rescued you. I hope you don't swim that far out anymore."

"If it wasn't for that charley horse, I would have been fine, Henry."

"You would have drowned, Violet, if I didn't get there when I did."

I sigh. "I guess I can look at the porpoises from the shore."

He pulls me over to him, and we hug. "I love you so much, and I don't know what I would do without you. My world would have been upside down."

"I love you too, Sweetheart. God isn't finished with me yet. I have many people to tell about Jesus and the gift of eternal life He gives to those that will accept Him as Lord and Savior."

"Althea and the ladies want to come and visit. Are you up for that yet?"

"I'll call her and tell her to wait until Peter goes back to the base."

Jane plops down between us. "Zorro is getting fat, and that ugly sore is almost gone. The axle grease really does work."

I caress her curly hair. "Did you find a place to board him yet?"

Henry shakes his head and takes Jane's hand. "Nothing yet."

❧

A few nights later, Henry and I cuddle in bed, as we often do while the summer breeze blows through our windows. Jane's room is in the original part of the house, which is a good distance from our bedroom. I usually wait until she's sound asleep with Pups at the foot of her bed. *Where would she be without that little dog?*

"Henry, what are we going to do if we don't find a place for the horse before winter?"

"It's going to upset our daughter more than we can imagine. She loves Zorro so much, but I don't see any solution currently. The horse will probably have to go back to the owners."

"The horse looks so good, and she just started riding him too. I heard there's a new riding stable in Rocky Point. You could try to ask there," I offer.

"I drove out there alone the other day and asked about boarding. Eileen, the owner, said they are open for trail rides only at this time. However, if Jane becomes horseless, she can work there for trail rides."

"Oh, Henry, I pray she can keep Zorro."

I can feel my husband's arms relax as a rhythm of snoring echoes in my ear. I smile and roll on my side. *I love this man so much, Lord, but his snoring can be quite annoying.*

Tossing and turning this way and that, I find myself wide awake. *I almost drowned in the depths of the Long Island Sound. I can still taste the salt and the burning sensation it gives to open eyes. God must know I have people in my life that don't know Him. People need the Lord, and my family needs me too.*

"In the day of my trouble, I will call to you, and you will answer me." Psalm 86:7.

I'm going to make some warm milk. Goodness, it's one a.m. already? Usually, this remedy of my mama's puts me right to sleep. I pray when I get to heaven, Mama's the first person I see.

"Yum, what smells so good, Mommy?" Jane shouts as she opens the refrigerator.

"Jane, don't be eating anything now. Supper will be served as soon as your father gets home from the train station with your brother."

She grabs the milk and the Nestle Nesquik. "What's for supper?"

"Peter's favorite. Pot roast."

"Yuck. Do we have any hard rolls?"

"I think you should drink your milk and change your clothes, my dear. You smell like a horse. You know how immaculate your brother is now that he's an Ensign."

She chugs her milk down. "Come on, Pups. Let's get ready for big brother's homecoming."

That girl is such a tom boy. She would have a menagerie of furry friends if we would let her. She'll be back to school soon, and I'm afraid homework will not matter at all.

The table's set with cut flowers from the garden and the antique dishes from my mother-in-law. *It's too bad all of Henry's immediate family members are deceased. He talks about cousins in Ithaca, but he's not the least bit interested in communicating with them.*

Pups growls, followed by a bark.

Curiously, I head to the front door, and my wondering eyes focus on my tall, handsome son in full uniform. "Peter, my son. I'm so glad you're finally home."

We hug for a long time.

"I love you, Mother. Let me look at you."

I step back, and he studies me. "You went through quite an ordeal a few weeks ago, but I must say you look wonderful."

He opens Jane's door. "Sis-o, come and give your brother a hug."

She leaps into his arms. "Welcome home."

With duffle bag in his hand, Henry sniffs. "Something's burning, Vi."

I'm able to salvage the meat by adding some water and turning it over. I decided to wait until the men in my life came home to boil the potatoes and carrots. *Good thing I waited.* I pour three glasses of red wine for the adults and ginger ale for Jane.

"Okay, supper's ready, everyone. I made your favorite, Peter."

"Beef stew? Yum."

"No. Pot Roast."

He laughs, taking a mouthful. "I hope you plan on making all of my favorites while I'm home."

"Wait, Son. Henry, will you please ask a blessing on the food?"

Peter almost chokes on his food." When did you start doing this?"

Henry smiles at me with a wink. "When your mother came through her near-death ordeal. I realized that only a Devine Creator could have saved her. Right after I accepted Jesus into my heart."

Peter rolls his eyes, puts down his fork, and stares at his dad.

"Lord God, thank you for bringing our son safely home. We are overjoyed he'll be here for ten days. Our prayer is Peter will come to know you the way all of us at this table have. Thanks for this delicious meal my beautiful wife prepared after recuperating from a terrible accident. Amen."

"Dad, that wasn't grace. It was a sermon."

I keep my head bowed and silently pray. *Oh God, I pray for Peter. He doesn't believe in You and how astounding You are as the Alpha and Omega. If it's Your will, may I have an opportunity to talk to him about You? Amen.*

Peter pokes me. "Mother wake up. Do you have any more potatoes?"

It's Labor Day weekend, and the weather's extremely warm with record breaking temperatures in the 80s. The beach is packed with families and their friends. The neighborhood boys are practicing gymnastic moves on the parallel bars and still rings installed by their fathers. Jane could care less, but her friends are mesmerized by the handsome gymnasts.

"Sis, do you want a ride on the hydroplane?"

"You go too fast, Peter."

"I promise to go slow. This might be your last chance, because I might sell it next year."

"Go ahead, Tot," Henry says.

She turns to look at the exposition quickly then joins Peter. "You better go slowly."

He gives her a life jacket and positions her safely in the cockpit directly in front of himself. Henry gives them a little shove; the motor turns over, and off they go. Jane's wish comes true as they glide slowly across the calm water.

Henry motions to me. "Vi, come on in. The water's just right."

Reluctantly, I wade in the water on the shoreline. He takes my hand and guides me until my waist is covered. "I'm right with you, honey. Don't be afraid."

Water never bothered me before, but I'm petrified beyond words now.

We swim together for a while. "I think I'll go and dry off, Henry. I really should answer that pile of mail on my desk. Look, here they come."

"Peter, you're getting a sunburn. Let me put some lotion on it before it gets out of control, okay?"

I lather his back and arms. "How does that feel?"

"Thanks, Mom. Hand me that tee shirt. It's best to be covered when I drive this boat to the landing. Dad's going to meet me there to help me carry it to the car. It's time to put it away until next year."

I fold up the towels as Henry takes down the umbrella. We pack up all our belongings and head to the long staircase going up the hill. I turn to get a glimpse of our son driving his boat away."

"His furlough sure went fast. It's hard to believe he is going back to the base on Monday."

The heat is bearing down on us as we make our way to the first rest area on the long staircase. The hydroplane is a small red dot in the distance.

Jane turns midway. "Carol's father needs to know what we are going to do with Zorro. He doesn't have enough hay for an extra horse this winter."

Henry pats her head. "I'm working on it, Tot. There's a place in Patchogue that boards horses. I'll check it out after I bring your brother to the train station on Monday, okay?"

"I guess so." She climbs up the steps, skipping every other one.

ꝏ

On Sunday morning, I knock on Peter's bedroom door. "We're leaving for church in a half hour. Everyone's so anxious to see you. because your mother has been bragging about her son, non-stop.

"You can come in, Mother."

"You're still in bed? You're coming with us, aren't you?"

"No, I'm not. Mother, you must stop badgering me about the Christian life. I'm not interested. I'm not sure there is a God, let alone go to church to worship one."

Chapter Seventeen

A couple of months later, I find myself on my knees by my bedside in the middle of the day. I lay out two pages of prayer requests to hold up to the Lord, with my Bible next to it. The house is quiet since Henry's at work and Jane's gone back to school. New designs will wait. There's nothing better than spending time in prayer and reading the word of God. I flip it to Romans 3:22, *"We are made right in God's sight when we trust in Jesus."*

"Oh God, I pray for my son Peter, that he will come to know You and trust You as his Lord and Savior. I know Your hands of protection are on him as he serves in the Navy for our country. May You bring Christians in his path to witness and encourage him?" I cry out loud. "Oh, and my dear Jane had to give Zorro back to his owners. We could not find a place to board the horse, and there was nothing else we could do. I pray that in time she will grow out of this horse craze." My knees start to ache, even though I shift from one to the other. *I have absorbed this prayer list and then some.* "Thank You, Lord. Amen."

The ringing of the telephone catches my attention, and I flee to the studio to grab it before whoever it is hangs up. "Hello?"

"Violet, my name is Beatrice Mackey from Stony Brook. "

"How may I help you today?"

"Lois Schmidt gave me your name as a possible speaker for our ecumenical Bible study."

"Oh, do you have a date in mind?"

133

"We'll be having a Christmas celebration instead of a study in two weeks. We're inviting you to give your testimony and share some of your artwork as well."

"Sure. I can do that. Let me write down the date, time, and address."

"Lois will pick you up. She has been here several times now. The date is December 10 at 7:00. You'll be given compensation for your time."

"How nice. I'm looking forward to meeting you, Beatrice. Lois has told me so much about you."

"Okay, we'll see you then."

"Good-bye."

Jane will be home in an hour; *I better get going on this new design based on the fruits of the spirit.in Galatians 5:22. This unusual tree will prove to be a quick sale for anyone who desires to be more like Jesus. The nine apples must be uniform in size with the words love, joy, patience, peace, self-control, faithfulness, goodness, gentleness, and kindness. Henry really mastered the art of silk screening, but this is the first tile with two colors, red and black.*

"Mom, are you in here?" Jane calls from the hallway.

"Yes. I'm working on a new design."

She leans over my shoulder, breathing heavily. "That's a weird tree."

"How was school today?"

"All right, I guess. The junior high basketball and volleyball teams have been selected."

"Did you try out for that?"

"Nah, but almost everyone I know did. I might try out for cheerleading next year."

"You should do your homework now so you can relax the rest of the night. I must keep working on this design so I can get a composite made for a new screen. Get yourself a snack. I'll be making supper in an hour."

134

"Oh, *American Bandstand* is on right now. See ya, Mom."

Homework is always at the bottom of her list, and the last report card was proof of her lack of interest in school. There's always a huge disagreement when I insist upon her doing schoolwork over anything else. For some reason, she works better with Henry.

I look down at my work and breathe a sigh of relief when I see the apples are perfect. Penmanship is one of my strong points, so I meticulously write each word, one apple at a time. *Good. I better quit and let the ink dry. If all goes well, I can get it to the copy company on Monday so they can make a new screen for me.*

⁓⊙⥁⊙⁓

The Mackey's house is a three-story colonial at the end of a long driveway embellished with perfectly formed pine trees. A Christmas tree loaded with colorful lights bids a welcome as it shines through a window on the main floor. Light snow covers the lawn as we walk up the sidewalk to the huge front porch.

"Look at these magnificent decorations, Violet," Lois remarks.

"Exquisite. I can't wait to see the inside."

She rings the doorbell.

A white-haired lady with a face of a saint opens the door. "Hello, Lois, and you must be Violet. Please come in and get out of the cold."

"You have a beautiful home, Beatrice. It's so festive and inviting," I say as I put down the box of tiles.

"Thank you. Let me take your coats. I set up a table for you in the family room so you can arrange your tiles. That's to your left. The refreshments are set up in the dining room so everyone can grab what they want and carry it into the living room. You'll be sharing your testimony in there. Everyone is expected to be here in a half hour."

"Violet, you go ahead and start setting up and I'll go and get the rest from the car."

"Thanks, Lois."

⤳⟍⟋⟍⟋⤶

A while later, I find myself intentionally pausing in amazement at the thirty people with their eyes fixed on me. *Either they're intrigued that I'm an accomplished artist or they never met someone who had a nervous breakdown.*

"I could not finish the face of the Jewish maiden on the fourteen-foot fireplace mural until I gave my heart to the Lord. I spent nearly a year completing this monumental task, but the face was not right. I wanted it to show serenity, contentment, and heartfelt joy. I couldn't achieve this because my own heart wasn't at peace. I picked up a book by Billy Graham, God bless him, called the *Secret of Happiness*. The title intrigued me because happiness was one thing that always eluded me.

"Oh, I'm probably boring most of you by now. Maybe, we should close in prayer, Beatrice?"

Someone shouts out, "Please continue. Your testimony is fascinating." Followed by a few more statements of interest.

"After I read the book, I fell on my knees and asked Jesus to be the Lord of my life. Peace filled my heart, mind, and soul. I had never known such joy in my entire life. I finished the mural a few days later, and the maiden's face reflected what was in my heart. She's more than that. She's a symbol of all the people who are waiting for the return of Jesus Christ."

I pause and drink a half a glass of water.

136

"My tiles are breakable things with no eternal value. Since then, I have turned Violetile's over to the Lord. God has given me a talent to reach others for His kingdom, *Tiles with a testimony.*"

Everyone in the room breaks out in a huge round of applause and a few shout, "Amen."

"Violet has her tiles for sale in the family room through that door. They make wonderful gifts for the people in your life who don't know the Lord. Feel free to grab another cup of coffee or a cookie and stay as long as you like," Lois offers.

Beatrice grabs my hand as I try to make my way to the tile display. "Violet, I want you to meet someone."

An adorable lady, with high cheek bones and hazel eyes, probably in her fifties, is sitting on the curved couch. "Violet, this is Clara Rubin. She's a Hebrew-Christian."

I feel an instant connection and sit right next to her. "It's a pleasure to meet you. I'm so intrigued by someone of the Jewish faith who calls themselves a Christian."

"Oh, Honey, everyone I meet says the same thing. Jesus is the Messiah, the Chosen One, but many of my Jewish brothers and sisters don't know it yet."

We both chuckle, and I take her hand. "Most people don't know this, but there's a German Jewess in our ancestry. So, you see, we're truly connected."

"Your testimony warmed my heart, Violet. Come, show me these tiles everyone is raving about.

My heart's bursting with joy on the drive back to my house. "Lois, they bought almost everything tonight. I think they would have purchased the rack and tablecloth if we put a price tag on those things."

She taps my arm. "You, my dear, have a gift in selling, which will lead to customers all over the state."

"I give back ten percent of everything I earn. The rest is deposited in a special account, earmarked for a new van. The old rat trap of one I have now is falling apart, needs new tires, and has almost 200,000 miles. By the grace of God, we keep rolling along."

As we stop in my driveway, she opens her door. "Let me help you in with everything?"

"No, no. I can manage. Really. After all, I only have six tiles left, remember?" I give her a hug, grab all my stuff, and make my way to the front steps. "Thanks, Lois."

Henry greets me at the door. "I was getting ready to call a search party for you."

I give him the boxes. "It was stimulating tonight, Honey. I met a Hebrew-Christian, and she was fascinated by my testimony. Her name's Clara Rubin. You'll love her instantly."

"How interesting. Where does she live?"

"Massapequa in Nassau County."

"Do you know that is one of the biggest Jewish populations this side of New York City?"

"No, I didn't know that. Is that a bad thing?"

"I doubt if it's life threatening for her, but I'm sure she is up against a lot of ridicule from local Rabbis and the Orthodox Jews"

"I'll soon find out, because she invited me to give my testimony to a women's group that meets in the Jewish Community Center near her."

"So soon? You just met her. I don't' know if I want you to do this, Vi. You could be going into a bee's nest, to say the least."

As I look in the mirror the next day, I'm caught off guard when I see the flab around my belly. *What in the world is this? I can't be getting fat. No, I won't allow it. What does the scale say?* I flee to the bathroom, strip down, and weigh myself. *Oh, no, I'm ten pounds overweight. No wonder my clothes are too tight.* Panic begins to overwhelm me as I'm taken captive by my situation.

"Okay, where did I see that article about that machine that removes unwanted fat?"

Henry's at work, and Jane's at school. I race through the house to the living room, stark naked. I grab all the magazines I can find, plop down on my bed and leaf through, scan, and toss. A half hour later, all wrapped up in the bedspread, my eyes feast upon the answer to my dilemma. *The machine of miracles.*

The ringing of the doorbell catches me off guard, and I look at the clock.

"It's 11:00, and Beatrice, Lois, and Clara must be here early," I mumble.

Ring, ring.

I get dressed in record time, comb my hair on the run, and slip into black flats as I make my way to the door. I take a deep breath.

"Hello. Do come in out of the cold. How are you ladies today?"

Lois gives me a scowl. "We almost left, Violet. What took you so long?"

Clara pats my shoulder as she passes by. "What a fabulous view you have, dear. If it wasn't for the fierce wind, I would go out there and enjoy God's creation."

"The coffee is hot. Who wants a cup?" I offer.

Beatrice takes their coats and lays them on the couch. "We were hoping you would say that, Violet."

We laugh and chat for an hour, and they feast on Entenmann's coffee cake, while I drink coffee with them. I can't help but look at Clara's excess weight. *She keeps on shoveling in that cake, and look at the butter she's piling on top. I sure hope I made enough tea sandwiches for lunch later. The rate they're going, I might have to scrounge up something else.*

Lois nudges me. "Earth to Violet? The girls are anxious to see the rest of the house."

"Violet, this place is a mess. You should have picked up. You had all morning," whispers Lois as we walk ahead of them.

I shrug my shoulders. *She sure is a crab today.* "This is our living room with a separate entrance to the back yard."

Beatrice hits a few keys on the piano. "You must like music. That's a nice Steinway, and your stereo system is marvelous."

"Henry built the hi-fi system himself and loves to hammer new songs for the choir on the piano. He's very handy and musically inclined."

"And this is our bedroom and master bath." I close the door quickly and scurry ahead of them. "Come and see my favorite room in the whole house."

Clara puts her arm around me. "So, this is where all of your creativity becomes a reality? This is astounding, and look at those picture windows. You must spend most of your time in here."

At least, this room is picked up and presentable. I hope they leave right after lunch so I can turn on the television to Jack LaLanne, my fitness hero.

"So, you only have this little kiln, Violet?" Beatrice asks.

"Of course not," I snap back.

Ida takes her hand. "Come girls. I'll take you downstairs and show you where Henry does all the silk screening and where large tile orders are fired. Violet, why don't you go get lunch ready?"

I freeze in place with embarrassment.

140

Instantly, Clara is behind me with her hands on my shoulders. "Are you all right?"

I look at my feet. "I'll be okay. Go with the girls. Lois is a good tour director."

"Yeshusa God, bring peace to my friend and lift her spirits. Amen."

We hug as silent tears escape my eyes.

"Clara, we're waiting for you. There's a lot to see in the basement," yells Lois.

My eyes follow her down the stairs, and she disappears around the corner. I flee to the bathroom and grab the three bottles of pills sitting out in the open. I open the linen closet and bury them under a folded hand towel. *I can't believe I left these out for everyone to see. Henry has no idea I have been going to a psychologist, who is also a medical doctor.*

The ladies are making a racket as they climb back up the stairs. "Something is wrong with Violet. I'm really worried about her," Clara says.

I want to shout out, "Mind your own business," but I don't.

Putting on my actress demeanor, I flit to the kitchen and busy myself like Betty Crocker.

"Are you ladies ready for some lunch?"

Beatrice smiles. "Can I help you do anything, Violet?"

I pull the tray of tea sandwiches out of the refrigerator and hand it to her. "Thank you."

I pretend that everything's fine and dandy as they nibble on sandwiches and sip on mint iced tea and homemade oatmeal cookies. *I really can't wait for everyone to leave so I can order that Relaxercizor.*

Ida picks up the dishes. "Clara, you have a drive ahead of you. We should probably get going."

Each one hugs me as they leave. I wave and shut the door.

I glance at the clock on my way back to the bathroom. "Jane will be home from school any minute. I don't think I took all of my morning pills," I shout out to an empty house.

The linen closet door is open. That's funny. The pill bottles are exposed too. "Here you are. My friends."

"All right, I took the big red one for sure. Another one tonight. This is the one I missed, the grey pill." I swallow it with a glass of water. "Now, the pink one is for tonight as well."

I look in the mirror. "In a week, you'll look better and feel on top of the world."

"Mommy, what are all those pills for, and who are you talking to?" Jane asks.

Chapter Eighteen

If I don't take these pills, I slip into the dark confines of depression and lose the will to clean the house, let alone my body. I'm ashamed that my daughter saw me with the bottles of the colorful tablets. I sure hope she believed me about them being vitamins the doctor prescribed for losing weight. I tried not taking them for two days and found I was gloomy and would cry at the drop of a hat. My brain felt as though it was absorbed in mud. I was lazy and would stay under the covers for hours after Jane went off to school.

It's the third Saturday in December, and the three of us are decorating for Christmas. Henry drops two big boxes of decorations in front of me. "There you go. Can you take care of the decorating, so Jane and I can hunt for a tree?"

I wipe the sweat on my brow. "I guess I can do that. Wow. It's blazing hot in here."

Henry puts his hand on my forehead. "You're perspiring. You should take your temperature, because you might have a fever."

I break out into uncontrollable laughter that causes me to wet my pants. I try to stop, but it's like a babbling brook with no end in sight.

"What has gotten into you, Violet?"

I wrap my arms around him. "Laughter's a good thing, Henry. You should try it sometime."

"Daddy, it's starting to snow again. Can we go and get the tree now?" Jane asks as she puts on her boots.

He gives me a peck on my cheek. "We won't be too long."

"Can Pups come?"

"I can't see why not, Tot."

Good, now I can hook up to the Relaxercizor and vibrate some of this excess fat off my body. For this to be the most effective, I must strip down to my birthday suit. I head to the bathroom to do so, attach the pads to the flabbiest parts of my body with the wires connected to the machine, and turn it on until vibration takes over. I can feel my heart start to race as the phone rings in the background.

"I'm not here," I yell out with a quiver.

The phone stops.

I must lose this weight so I can wear that slinky red dress I bought for Henry's Christmas party at the Met. I must be the most attractive lady there and the thinnest too.

The telephone rings again, again, and again.

There are red blotches where the pads are, and I'm perspiring from head to toe.

The ringing continues.

"Oh druthers. I might as well stop this charade and get the phone." I detach myself from the machine, throw on a robe, and race to the telephone in the studio.

"Hello."

I stand in shock as my ears pick up a dial tone.

I might as well get dressed before they return with the Christmas tree. Oh, I forgot about the decorations. Henry will no doubt ask me what I did while they were gone. Panic reaches into my core as I contemplate what to do first. Put away the pills. Yes. Of course. Now, the crazy fat dissolving machine.

The phone resonates.

144

I leap to get it. "Hello, Violet speaking."

"Hi, Vi, we're at the gas station getting a tree."

"Henry? Did you call before?"

"Just now. That's the only time."

"Only once. Hmmm. Someone else called. I wonder who it was."

"We'll be home in a little while. Do you need anything?"

"No, I'm fine. Did you forget to get a Christmas tree?"

"We have a small one, but it will have to do."

"Good. I'll see you in a couple of hours. Bye."

I race in high energy around the house with garland, Santas of various sizes, and assorted candles and plug in the illuminated snowman. *I feel like I'm in overdrive. Supper? What will I make for supper? Spaghetti with meat sauce always works.*

I'm startled by the chiming of the front doorbell. *Who can that be?*

"Coming."

I open the door and find Clara standing there. "What are you doing here?"

"Violet, I'm very worried about you. I tried to call, but you must have been out."

I squint at her suspiciously. "Are you alone?"

"Yes. Please let me pray with you, dear."

"I guess it will be all right. Come in out of the cold."

"I won't stay long. Your house looks so festive, Violet. I decorate for Hanukkah and Christmas to please all who enter."

"Can I get you some coffee, tea, or hot cocoa?"

"Come sit with me for a few minutes."

I follow her command and join her on the couch.

"Violet, do you know you missed the meeting at the community center on the 12th?"

145

I stare at the floor. "I forgot."

"Everyone was eager to hear your testimony. Luckily, there was a young Hebrew who recently became a believer in Jesus, so she jumped at the chance to share."

I fidget with my hands like a naughty child. "I forgot, Clara. I'm sorry."

She grabs my hand. "You look like you are worried about something. Are you?"

"I'm fine, Clara. You shouldn't trouble yourself about me."

"Look at me, Violet."

I reluctantly turn to face her.

She takes both of my hands. "Honey, I know you're taking some pills. I saw the bottles in your linen closest when I went to look for a hand towel last week."

The anger bubbles within me, and I want to pop her nose off her face. "Those are all vitamins. For goodness sake, Clara."

"Vitamins with a labeled prescription on each one? A Doctor Feinberg prescribed them, right?"

"They're special vitamins that you can't get over the counter, that's all."

She raises her hands to the ceiling. "Almighty God, may your Holy Spirit empower my friend, Violet, right now. In Jesus' name. Amen."

Trembling, I leap off the couch away from her clutches and fall face down on the floor. I kick, pound my hands on the scatter rug, and weep like a baby in need of a bottle.

Clara rubs my back. "God is working in you, let Him do what He needs to. Take all the time you need."

My body relaxes as she massages and hums, "Blessed Assurance."

Still on the floor, I mumble, "My husband and daughter will be home any minute."

"Do you want me to leave?"

"No. Please stay." I turn onto my side.

"I don't want to leave you like this. Can you feel the working of the Holy Spirit now?"

I pull a worn tissue out of my pocket. "Yes. Oh Clara, I let pride and physical beauty get in the way of my love for the Lord."

With one hand on the couch and the other on my head, she rises. "Oh, my knees hurt dear. I have to sit."

I get up and grab her hands. "Come. Let's go in the studio where we can have privacy. Please stay for supper, Clara. Besides, I want you to meet my family."

As we walk through the living room, I spot Henry and Jane coming up the walkway.

"Yes. I'll call Samuel and tell him not to expect me for supper. He'll worry otherwise. Can I use your phone?"

I feel somewhat overwhelmed now as I plop down on the office chair. "You can use the phone on my desk."

I watch Clara and listen to her talk to her husband, but then I'm drawn to my Bible sitting on the coffee table in front of me. I pick it up. *Lord God, I have fallen away from You in the last few weeks. Please forgive me for letting pride get in the way of Your redeeming grace. Thank You for my friend Clara. Speak to me through your word. Amen*

"I won't be too late, Sam, I promise. I love you," Clara says as she hangs up the phone.

"Thank you for coming when you did, Clara. I was falling apart on the inside but trying hard to stay a beautiful package for everyone to see on the outside."

"Listen, Honey, when the Lord tells me to do something, I usually jump. At least, I did this time. You're holding the Bible open. Did you find some scripture that you want to share?"

Not realizing the book was open, I look down at an underlined verse in Isaiah 42:16. I begin to read out loud, "I will lead the blind by ways they have not known, along unfamiliar paths. I will guide them; and make the rough places smooth. These are the things I will do; I will not forsake them."

"Powerful words written for you today, my dear Violet."

A tapping on the door jars my thoughts. "Come in. It's ok."

My handsome husband hesitates as he opens the door. "Is everything all right, Vi?"

I avoid his question. "Henry. This is my new friend Clara that I have been telling you about."

He reaches out to shake her hand. "I'm pleased to meet you."

"Jane is walking her dog but asked about supper. She worked up an appetite picking a Christmas tree."

"Give us a few more minutes, okay?"

With an inquisitive look, he says, "Well, all right, but it is 6:00 so don't be too long, please."

The door closes.

"Does Henry have any idea that you have been taking all those pills, Violet?"

"I don't think so. I'm a good actress, you know. I grew up on the Vaudeville stage with the strangest people doing very odd things. All I do is put a mask on to cover what is really going on inside my heart."

"I think it's time you dealt with your emotional issues using a healthier lifestyle. I know a wonderful Christian physician who is also a psychologist. I will go with you to get a thorough medical evaluation so you can get on a vitamin regimen and exercise program. Lord knows, I could use his help too."

"The pills Dr. Feinberg gave me make my heart race and move my energy level out of this galaxy. Maybe he's a quack after all."

"Could be, but I think you should dispose of all of the pills while I'm here. Otherwise, you will most likely resort to taking them again when some emotional issue attacks."

"I'll fall apart, Clara. If I throw them away, I won't be able to function."

"Now, now. Don't let your emotions get a hold of you again. Close your eyes and call out to God to rescue you, in Jesus' name."

"Lord Jesus, I ask You in Jesus' name to clear my body of the desire to take these pills. I pray that my life will be what You want it to be, free of this addiction to prescription medicine. Amen."

Clara pulls me up with a hug. "Amen. Now, let's go empty those bottles, okay?"

I open the door cautiously, and we creep into the bathroom. "Where do I start?"

"The first step is to flush the contents of each bottle down the toilet. Then, we will connect with each other on the phone every day. I will make the appointment with your new doctor for next week. You are going to be fine now, my friend."

After supper, Clara offers to clear the table, but I insist that she heads home and calls me as soon as she gets there. *I'm on a high still from the pills, but I know it will take a few days for them to disappear from my system. I must allow Jesus to take the wheel every moment of every day until I can see the new doctor.*

"She's a very fine lady, Violet. I can see why you are drawn to her for friendship." Henry smiles.

Jane flees to the box of Christmas ornaments. "I love the dreidel she brought with her. She said she will give me one of my own when we see her again."

"What in the world were you two talking about when I came into the studio earlier?" Henry asks as he leans over the table.

I pretend to not hear him and busy myself with stacking dishes and bringing them to the kitchen. He follows me with the empty platters.

"Violet, look at me. You were wiping your eyes when I walked in. The look on Clara's face was one of worry and concern."

I look over at Jane, who is engrossed in decorating the tree and back to the sink filling with sudsy water. "There's nothing to bother yourself with, Henry."

"Listen to me. We have been through a lot since we got married almost twenty years ago. You know that I have always been here for you even during the short separation when Peter was a baby."

I hold back the tears. "Everything was going fine until the lust of the flesh and my physical appearance got the best of me. I gained ten pounds, Henry. I sought out a doctor to give me some medicine to help me lose the weight and to keep me energetic. Up until today, I was taking six pills a day."

He wraps his arms around me. "I suspected something like this because your behavior has been unstable lately. Don't worry, Honey. We'll get through this together.

"Clara found the pills when she was here a few weeks ago. Her quest today was to get me back on track with the Lord.

"The pills are gone, but I'll be going through withdrawal the next few days. She's getting an appointment for me with a Christian psychologist. She knows him well, so it should be as early as next week."

Henry kisses my forehead. "Thank God, and thank you, Clara."

I watch him head out of the kitchen, thinking he wants to help with the tree but instead, he clears the table, brings the rest of the dishes to the sink, and proceeds to wipe down the table.

Miracles do happen when I least expect it.

I bow my head. *Heavenly Father, please hold my hand as I face the reality of the pain within me. Help me through the next few days as I go cold turkey off those awful pills. Forgive me for wearing a mask to protect my heart. Forgive me for letting my outward appearance become the ruler of my life. I know this kind of masquerade blocks my spiritual growth and intimacy with you, Lord. Amen.*

"Come to me, all you who are weary and burdened, and I will give you rest." Matthew 11:28.

Part Three

Chapter Nineteen

1963

Dear Auntie,

I'm writing this in a hurry, so please excuse any mistakes, as this typewriter is old. I desperately need a new one. Thank you for the generous monetary gifts for Jane and me. As you already know, I give all the money I make on tiles to missions other than car expenses, the phone bill, or necessary groceries. I'm convinced Henry's promotion to an office in Albany, is directly from God. He takes good care of us even though he's gone from Monday through Friday every week. Doctor Curtis is pleased with my progress, and I feel wonderful most of the time and I know it's because of the regimen of vitamins she put me on. We eat only brown bread, fresh or frozen vegetables, fruit, meat with the fat cut off, and plain yogurt, to name a few. Although, Jane cannot tolerate the white stuff even if it's covered with sugar. I'm so grateful to God and my friend Clara.

We enjoyed visiting with you so much. I wish we could see you more often. Please reconsider and hop on a train to Port Jefferson. You can stay overnight if you want. I faithfully pray for my loved ones to come to know the Lord.

All my love, Violet

"Mom, senior pictures are next week. I need to get a new outfit," Jane says as she flies out the door.

"Wait, Jane. You didn't finish your oatmeal." I catch a glimpse of her walking with Paula, our next-door neighbor. I shake my head, turn, and close the door behind me. *I'm glad she is out of that rough, reckless crowd she was hanging around with. It's almost too late to think about college.*

I dial the operator on the telephone. "Yes, can you connect me to area code 518?"

"May I have number, please?"

"Thank you. The number is 519-456-3732."

After several long rings. "Metropolitan Life."

"May I speak to Henry Funk?"

"He's having breakfast with his secretary. Can I take a message?"

"I'll call back later." *I hang up the phone, feeling bewildered or maybe jealous? Henry has only been upstate for a month, but he talks quite a bit about his red-headed secretary Barbara. I wonder if she's pretty or what? All I know is she's a single parent with a little girl named Andrea. I wonder why he must take her to breakfast.*

The ringing of the telephone catches me as I'm lost in my thoughts.

"Violet?"

"Hello, Henry."

"No, this is Pastor Strickland."

"Oh, I thought you were my husband, Pastor Strickland. I'm so sorry."

"I have a few people here that are interested in your idea of a bookstore."

"Really?"

"If you're not busy, can you come over?"

"Of course. I can be there in a half hour, okay?"

⚜

Several cars are in the church parking lot as I find a place to park my old van. A bit strange for a Monday morning.

As I walk in the meeting room, I see two unfamiliar couples, Clara, Lois, and Pastor.

Clara grabs my hand. "Good morning, Violet. Sit here, okay?"

"Violet's our creative friend who has a fascinating idea to present to all of us today. I know I'm putting her on the spot, but can you share with these fine folks your plan, Violet?" Pastor Strickland asks.

I fidget a bit and smile. "Sure, I'll be happy to."

"Wait a minute. Let me introduce you to these fine people. This is Joe and Edie Smith, the owners of the Christian radio station out of Smithtown. Mary and Timothy Cole own a coffee shop in Commack. Now, the floor is yours, Violet."

Luckily, there's a nice big chalkboard in the room. I grab a piece of chalk and write the words, "Heavenly Treasures."

"Now, I must say before explaining what these two words stand for, I'm extremely disappointed in my pastor for setting this meeting up without asking me first."

Lois puts her hand over her mouth. "Violet, please go no further."

"Since I came up with an idea, I must be the one to carry it out. I would have a much more thorough presentation today if I had time to prepare. I have diagrams, a financial plan, and other interested people who could have joined us today."

"You said you were free to chat about Heavenly Treasures today, Violet," Pastor Strickland says softly with a blushing face.

I glare at him and smile at the others. "Yes, that's true, but I thought it was going to be a conversation, not a presentation on my part."

Joe Smith looks at his wife and the other couple. "I think we'd better leave. This is obviously a mistake." They start to get on their jackets and get up.

I feel ashamed and angry with myself. "Please don't leave. I apologize for my rude behavior to you, Pastor, and to everyone else. I have a short fuse sometimes and should not let my emotions get the best of me." In tears, I fall into the chair.

Pastor and Clara lay hands on my shoulders. "Lord God, deliver our sister from the bondage of anger right now. Help her to know we're excited about her inspiring idea. If it's Your will, I pray she shares some of her testimony with the Smiths and Coles. So they'll understand our Violet. Amen."

Everyone in the room prays for me. I'm so overcome with joy, I can hardly breathe.

Pastor taps my shoulder. "Let's take a break while Violet gathers her thoughts."

"I can feel the presence of the Holy Spirit in this place now. The Lord's my rock and my strength who has delivered me from the clutches of the evil one, time and again. Several years ago, I picked up a book by Billy Graham, *The Secret of Happiness*. I read this little paperback several times before giving my life to Christ. I made telling others about Him my goal in life.

"Someday, I'll write a book that will help many people who suffer with emotional or mental issues of some kind. Right now, I want to open a glorified coffee shop and call it Heavenly Treasures."

Mrs. Smith wipes her eyes with a hankie. "You do have a story to tell, Violet. Please tell us more about this brainstorm of yours."

I get up and write these words on the chalkboard: Coffee, tea, Christian books, gifts, and music. Two or three offices set up for counseling. Comfortable chairs.

I turn and elaborate on each one. "Any questions?"

Mr. Cole raises his hand. "Yes, will there be access to Bible studies as well as live, local entertainment?"

I clap my hands with excitement, and everyone chuckles. "Absolutely. There will be an opportunity for both of those."

"Violet, you should tell everyone about the promotion Henry started a few weeks ago. It does have bearing on this project," comments Lois as she leaves the room.

I dismiss clouting her one. "Yes. My husband was recently promoted with Metropolitan Life to upstate New York. We're very excited that after all these years of being a loyal employee, he finally landed a supervisor's position. This does put a damper on my dream. I have to be honest and say, we'll be putting our house on the market in the spring and moving in June, after my daughter graduates."

I sit down not knowing what else to say. *I wonder if I will hear from Henry tonight.*

"May I interject here?" asks Mrs. Cole.

I nod with a slight smile. "Of course, Mrs. Cole."

"Please call me, Shirley, okay? The four of us have been praying for quite some time how we could pool our resources and open a place like you just described. I want to thank Pastor Strickland for doing his weekly Bible teaching at our studio, and because of that we have become good friends. God used him as a vehicle to share a very brief description of your vision, Violet. It was just enough to entice us to learn more." She looks at her husband. "Brian, do you have anything to add?"

The tall, distinguished looking man stands with a somber look. "Violet, although your idea is attractive to say the least, I must say you're not the right one to manage an endeavor of this magnitude. I would be afraid that you would go into one of your emotional episodes and berate a customer."

Silence fills the room as he sits down.

I close my eyes. *Lord, this man has no idea what it's like having to confront active emotions every day of your life. You have lifted me up out of the muck and mire, over and over. Thank you, Lord.*

The door opens, and Lois wheels in a cart with a pot of coffee and a platter of chocolate chip cookies. "I thought you could use a treat right about now. Help yourself, please."

I leap to my feet as if someone pushed me. "Thank you, Lois. I need to say something to Mr. Cole and everyone else. I don't want the responsibility that management has, even if the rest of you think I'm capable. My vision from the Lord is to have two locations for Heavenly Treasures."

"You mentioned it to be a non-profit organization, right Violet?" comments Pastor.

"Yes. With a board of directors."

"Then, it would make perfect sense to appoint you as chairman of that board. Until you move, that is."

Lois pours a cup of coffee. "I agree. Let's set a date for our next meeting. How do the rest of you feel about Violet as chairman?"

I grab a cookie. "I'll feel better if we vote by closed ballot."

Linda Smith tears five pieces of paper and hands one to each voter. "Yes, or no, does the trick. Fold up and place in this offering basket. Violet, can you call Edna, the church secretary in to tally the votes?"

A few minutes later, she announces, "Four say yes and one no."

Pastor smiles. "Violet is the chairman of the board for Heavenly Treasures."

Everyone but one cheers, "Hallelujah."

Chapter Twenty

Heavenly Treasures opened its doors on February 14, 1964, on the heels of the greatest tragedy to ever hit the United States of America. The nation's still recovering from the assassination of John F. Kennedy, the thirty-fifth president of our fine country. We devoted the front of the establishment to red, white, and blue to show our patriotism. The free lending library of Christian books proved to be the most popular section, and people came from miles around to sample our signature apple crumb cake. A young couple that graduated from Nyack Missionary College manages the entire operation. The board unanimously voted that I put the Heavenly Treasures logo on my dated Ford Econoline van since I still go out and evangelize with Christian books.

I'm tickled pink, my dream's a reality, and I hope to live to open a second one in the Albany area. God is so good. My heart melts every time someone less fortunate walks through the doors.

"Mom, is Peter going to make it home for my graduation?" Jane asks a few days before Easter.

"He's going to try really hard to get a couple of days furlough, but he won't know for sure until May. Meanwhile, you have an exciting event to look forward to this Sunday."

"I'm a little nervous about getting baptized. You know I don't like to be dunked under water, Mom."

I laugh and pat her curly head. "It's just for a split second, honey, but think of how special it's going to be to go through this spiritual experience with your father?"

"Why don't you get baptized, Mom?"

"I was baptized as an infant. I don't have to do it again."

"Pastor said, 'Baptism by immersion is an outward sign to show others that Jesus lives in our hearts.' When's Daddy coming home?"

"He will be home late tomorrow night for four days. I tried to get him on the phone earlier, but he was having lunch with his secretary."

"He's always talking about this Barbara person, Mom. Don't you get tired of hearing about her red hair?"

"Well, he's lonely, and she has been a big help to your father since he relocated to Albany."

"I would be calling him collect every night to be sure he's not fooling around."

"Jane. That's enough. I trust your father."

She wrinkles her brow and makes a weird face. "Okay, okay. Come on, Pups, let's go for a walk."

"I want you back here in a half hour to do your homework. I hope you hear from Cobleskill about your college application. It's been over a month since you applied."

She puts the leash on her dog and heads for the door. "Oh, I forgot to tell you that Carol will be here tomorrow afternoon to paint with you."

"I sure do need her help, Jane. I have several orders to fill with our newest tiles, 'Only One Life so soon is past' and 'Christ is the way.' I'm so thrilled to have assistance because she's so artistic and willing to help at a moment's notice." The words go out to an empty room.

Jane's been spending so much time with her boyfriend Danny, and her schoolwork's suffering for it. He's older than her and out of school. He works full time

160

for his mother's real estate company. Jane and I have a huge argument every time I try to set up ground rules and a curfew.

A tapping on the front door diverts my thoughts.

I open the door to Jack Karney holding a big mason jar. "Jack, Carol isn't here."

He laughs on the other side of the screen door. "I know she's riding her horse in the field as we speak. I brought you some homemade Manhattan clam chowder."

Reluctantly, I open the door. "Oh, how did you know this is my favorite kind of soup? Come in. Would you like a cup of coffee?"

He brushes past me, leaving a slight sent of alcohol behind. "When will your husband be back home, Violet?" I watch the tall, retired railroad man with glasses walk into my kitchen with the soup, remove his lightweight jacket, and settle himself at the dining room table. *How long does he think he's staying here, anyway?*

"Where's Jane today? I haven't seen her at our house in quite some time. She must not be interested in horses anymore, but then we only have Pride now."

"Jack, Jane was so upset when she had to give Zorro back to the original owners, and we thought the horse thing was over after that. In fact, she made some new friends, and high school soon became a priority."

"Until Carol bought Joy, a retired racehorse. Jane was at our house almost every day. There were a lot of sleepovers in those days. My wife, Roberta, was so healthy back then. No sign of ill health at all."

I realize I'm enjoying his company now. "I know how hard each day must be for you, Jack. How long has she been gone now?"

He breaks down in tears and then blows his nose. "It will be a year on Monday."

I reach out and grab his hand. "Can I pray for you, Jack?"

"I know you're a religious woman, Violet, but I don't understand why God would take such a vibrant wife and mother from this world so soon. She was only fifty-five."

"I know, dear. I know. You do have four lovely daughters to take care of you and the household chores."

He grips my hand and looks up at me. "Yes, and they're helpful in every way, but they can't fill the void of having someone my age to talk to."

I try prying my hand from his. "Oh, goodness. I forgot the coffee."

The grip gets tighter as his free hand goes on top. "Stay with me, Violet. I don't need any coffee. All I need is your companionship."

Pups trots down the hall, with Jane at his heels. "Oh, Mr. Karney. What are you doing here?"

Jack releases me, and I rush into the kitchen. "Mr. Karney brought us some soup, Jane."

"What kind?"

"Clam chowder. Your favorite."

Jack stands. "We don't see you around anymore, Jane. Is the person next to you the reason why?"

I'm intrigued by his question, so I step around the corner. "Danny? When did you get here?"

Jane rolls her eyes. "Danny, this is Carol Karney's father."

"Nice to meet you, Sir."

Jack puts his jacket on. "Violet, I'll take a rain check on the coffee. I hope you enjoy the soup. It's been nice spending some time with you today."

I blush as he walks out the door.

"You kids didn't answer my question yet. How long has Danny been here?"

Danny wraps his arm around my daughter's waist and gives me a smug look. "Oh, over an hour."

Jane giggles as she kisses his cheek. "You were having so much fun with Jack Karney, you never noticed the time."

I must break this up now before things get carried away. "Danny, please leave."

"I invited him for supper, Mother. He's staying."

I step in front of her, holding back the anger. "This is my house. I'm your mother and I make the rules. Do you hear me?"

"Jane, I better go before this gets any uglier. I'll call you later, okay?"

He kisses her on the lips, walks down the hall, and disappears out the door.

Jane stomps her foot and shouts, "I hate you!"

I decide it best to let her go in her room to have some alone time. I whisk past her room, shut the front door, and lock it. The evening breeze is cool, and keeping things locked up is a safety precaution as well. *Oh God, I worry about Jane being promiscuous with this boyfriend of hers. I have talked to him about spiritual things, but he passes the conversations off by saying, "I'm a Catholic." He's a bad influence on my daughter. It seems that her life is worthy of you when she's with her church youth group, but it changes when with friends who are worldly. Help her to walk in your ways. Amen.*

The biscuits are baking, and the soup is simmering on the stove. A fire's crackling away in the fireplace as I relax on the couch with the latest issue of *Woman's Day*. *This is a very cozy house.* The tap, tap of doggie paws with the scuffing of slippers on the linoleum are familiar enough not to cause alarm.

"I'm sorry, Mom. I didn't expect to see Danny tonight. I was walking Pups when he pulled up next to us on the road."

I pat the couch. "Come sit, dear. I don't like you to be alone with him. Things can get out of hand in the heat of the moment. That boy has had many girlfriends, I can assure you."

"I wonder about that sometimes."

"Jane, break up with him before it's too late."

"I'll think about it. Is something burning?"

Henry whistles at me as I walk into the living room on Easter morning. "You look beautiful, Vi. You're a real knockout in that flowered dress."

I kiss him on the cheek. "Thank you, and you're handsome in your navy-blue suit."

"Is Tot ready to go? This a double header, special occasion today. I'm getting baptized with my daughter on Easter Sunday. It's too bad your family declined our invitation to be a part of this."

"I keep praying for them to come to know Jesus the way we do. In the meantime, we better get to church on time. They expect a full sanctuary with overflow in the fellowship hall."

The church is packed when we arrive but, fortunately, the first two rows of pews are reserved for those being baptized and their families. I scurry to the second row and save two seats next to me. The organist belts out "Christ the Lord is Risen Today" as the five participants dressed in white robes march down the center aisle. My heart fills with joy at the sight of Henry and Jane walking side by side up to the front.

Pastor faces the congregation. "Please be seated. Welcome to this glorious Resurrection Sunday. If you're here for the first time, please raise your hand, and our ushers will bring you a special gift. Christ the Lord is risen today."

"He is risen, indeed! Hallelujah," echoes throughout the sanctuary.

"Our choir director will lead you in the next hymn, 'Savior, like a Shepherd Lead Us,' while I lead the participants to the baptismal font."

Pastor takes his position in the water. "Romans 6:23 tells us baptism is a personal identification with Jesus Christ. We believe it's an outward sign of salvation in our Blessed redeemer."

I'm deeply moved as I listen to the first few give brief testimonies followed by immersion. Henry and Jane step down into the font together, followed by elder Harold Kingsley. Tears roll down my face as they tell the congregation when they were saved.

"This is the first time I have the privilege of baptizing a father and daughter together. This moment is one I will cherish for many years," Pastor shares.

"I baptize Henry and Jane Funk in the name of the Father and Son and the Holy Spirit."

The men dip them in and out of the water in a most graceful motion. Jane wipes her eyes with one hand and pulls her wet hair away from her face with the other. A deaconess is waiting with towels as they step out of the font.

The choir dressed in red robes with white collars files down the aisle to the front, singing, "Crown Him with Many Crowns." My heart leaps for joy when my husband and daughter take their places next to me as the congregation stands to sing the last stanza.

This a perfect Easter Sunday, one that I will always cherish.

Chapter Twenty-One

For Sale: Beautiful custom-built, fully insulated, year-round ranch home on the North Shore of Long Island with an exterior of Redwood planking and asbestos shingles. Picturesque and peaceful view of the sound. Living, dining, and kitchen are combined, giving a feeling of spaciousness. Large fireplace and curved window seat with storage. Kitchen appliances are stainless steel, including a dishwasher and a three-foot chopping board complemented by a long, walnut, Formica breakfast bar. Three bedrooms, two ceramic tile baths. Large art studio/third bedroom with separate entrance. Full basement. Two car garage, $32,500.00

My husband and I are standing at the edge of the cliff looking at the quiet waves roll slowly into the shore. "Henry, I'm going to miss this place. We've made so many memories here."

"I've moved on, Violet, but you and Jane will have to take time to adjust to the move."

"I hope we can sell the house without a real estate agent. How hard can it be? It's only been listed in the newspapers for one month, but the height of the season is fast approaching."

"I don't want to put a sign on the lawn unless absolutely necessary because you're alone during the week. There are a lot of kooks out there so you never know who could pop up on your doorstep."

"I'll try to schedule potential buyer appointments on weekends when you're here."

He kisses my cheek. "I have to go. I have a four-hour trip ahead of me. Walk me to the car, okay?"

My heart sinks as I watch him drive away once again. *Oh God, I pray this house sells very soon. We can't afford two homes, and I don't like to be separated from Henry. Amen.*

I grab the mail out of the mailbox and head to the house.

The phone's ringing as if there is no end in sight.

"Hello?" I shout, out of breath.

"Violet Pearl?"

"Auntie?"

"I'm thinking about coming out for a visit for a few days."

"Now? Today? Of course, you can. Henry just left."

"No, tomorrow. Is that okay?"

"Of course. I'll be home all day. See you tomorrow."

I'd better change the sheets in Peter's room and tidy up this house. Auntie's staying for a few days, which is very unusual. She hasn't been out here for months and only comes for the day when she does. I must use this opportunity to talk to her about the Lord.

I knock on Jane's door. "You can take the car to school today. I don't need it."

When I hear no sound, I ask, "Jane, are you awake?"

"Huh?"

I open the door to a dark room and a daughter under the covers. I pull the covers back and roll her towards me. "Why aren't you up and getting ready for school?"

Her eyes are half open. "Leave me alone. I'm not feeling good. I need to sleep."

I feel her forehead. "You are as cold as a cucumber. Get up this instant. You're going to school. Playing sick worked when you were in elementary school, but not anymore. Your great aunt is on her way here to visit for a few days."

Jane shoots out of bed like a canon, flicks on the light, and opens the curtain. "Did you say I could take the car to school today?"

She scurries from bedroom to bathroom as I head to the kitchen. "I'll make you some cinnamon toast," I yell as I walk by.

Moments later, I'm sipping coffee as my daughter munches on her breakfast. "It's 7:30, Jane. You must be in your homeroom by 8:15. You're cutting it close, and you have to find a place to park too."

"Seniors have special parking privileges. Give me a break, Mother. I'll make it on time. Don't worry about it, okay?"

I look down at the mail. "Oh, there's something from Cobleskill. Do you want to open it quickly? I'm so anxious to see whether you got in or not."

With a scowl on her face, she grabs her school bag and pocketbook. "You can open it. Are the keys in the car?"

"They're in the ashtray. Be sure to come home right after school."

I hope she gets to school instead of hooking up with that Danny. I don't trust that fella. Jane has enough trouble with school, she doesn't need any more distractions. She can't flunk anything or there won't be a diploma in June.

I pick up the Cobleskill envelope and carefully open it, even though it's addressed to Jane Funk. I open the folded letter.

Dear Ms, Funk,

Thank you for your recent application to the two-year associate degree program at our college. We receive hundreds of applications every year, so we must be selective on whom we accept. We regret to inform you that we're unable to offer you placement for the school year, 1964-65. Thank you for your interest in our college.

The Cobleskill Board of Admissions.

I grab my coffee and plop down on the couch. "Oh, my Lord, Jane will be crushed when she reads this later. Then again, maybe I better hide it, so Aunt Flossie doesn't get ahold of it. She comes down hard on Jane about her schoolwork as it is." I shove the letter under the stack of magazines on the end table. Many times, when I'm alone, I pray out loud. "Father, I pray for an opportunity to witness to my aunt about salvation. Now, help me prepare myself and this house for her arrival. Amen."

An hour later, the sheets are changed, the last load of laundry is in the dryer, and a Dutch apple cake is baking in the oven. I breathe a sigh of relief when I look in the freezer and find several different possibilities for suppers.

The ringing of the doorbell gets my attention and I race to it because I'm excited to spend some quality time with my aunt.

"Jack? What are you doing here?"

"I brought you some fresh eggs. I know you like brown eggs better than store bought. I haven't had any breakfast yet. So how about you scramble up some eggs for both of us?"

I peer over his head to see if anyone is around. "I guess it's all right if you eat and run. I'm expecting my aunt soon, and I don't think she'll take it too kindly to seeing a strange man in my house."

I unlock the screen and open it.

He hands me the box of eggs, hugs me quickly, and walks past. "I promise not to stay long. I have to take whatever time I can get with you, Violet."

This man is incorrigible but perfectly sweet at the same time. I don't expect Auntie for at least another hour. He'll be gone by then, even if I literally kick him out.

"Thank you, Jack, for the eggs."

He gives me a wink as he comes in the kitchen. "All alone, huh?"

"Listen, Jack. I'm very uncomfortable with this arrangement. Please go and sit at the counter. I like my kitchen to myself when cooking."

"Tsk, tsk. All right, only because you said please."

I stand on my side of the counter while he gobbles down his breakfast on the other.

As I look at the clock, I realize a half hour has gone by already. "Jack, it's time for you to go now. No, leave the dishes right there. I'll take care of it."

"We didn't have any conversation, Violet. You seem so nervous today, all because your auntie is coming."

I follow him to the door. "It's not proper for you to be alone with me, that's all."

He swiftly turns and pulls me into his arms. "Can't you see, Violet? I'm crazy about you."

I try pushing the big man away, but his embrace is too strong. "Let me go."

"What's going on here?" Aunt Flossie yells through the screen door.

My face is burning with embarrassment as Jack releases me. "Auntie, you came in the nick of time. Mr. Karney, this is my aunt from Queens."

He opens the door for her. "Pleased to make your acquaintance, Ma'am. I was showing your niece some gratitude for her friendly hospitality. Yes, our Violet is one beautiful lady, on the inside and out."

Auntie glares at him and grabs my hand. "Good day, Mr. Karney. Come on, Violet, help me unpack and get settled before Jane comes home."

Jack lets out an obnoxious laugh and reaches out to stroke my face. "I'll be back in a few days to continue where we left off, Sweetheart."

I slam the door as he whistles down the steps.

170

"You have some explaining to do, Violet Pearl. Are you having an affair?"

I want to haul off and belt her one in the kisser. "Jack Karney is a big flirt, but I will not fall prey to it, Auntie. I'm surprised at you for even bringing such a thing up."

"Well, you're alone most of the time, so anything can happen."

"Listen, Auntie, I'm not the same person I was back in Richmond Hill. My life is focused on God and telling others about His saving grace. The Bible says, 'I'll enter not into the path of the wicked, and go not in the way of evil men, I will avoid it, turn from it and pass on.'"

"Tsk, tsk. You're certainly becoming a religious fanatic, dear niece."

Father God, minister to my wounded heart. Your love is more powerful than any other. May I rise above the ridicule from my aunt? Amen.

"Here's an empty drawer for you, and I put hangers in the closet too. I have a cake in the oven that I must tend to immediately before it turns to charcoal. It's a beautiful day to sit on the porch with a fresh glass of mint iced tea."

"All right, Tootsie. I'll join you in a little while. I'm a bit tired from the drive, so I may take a cat nap."

"Good thing I came to the kitchen when I did, or this cake would be overcooked," I mumble. I place it on a rack to cool. I grab the package of chop meat out of the fridge and begin the process of making meatloaf. *It's 4:30. I wonder where Jane is. She has been pretty good about coming home right after school when she has the car.* I fill the tea pot with water, turn the burner on and head outside to get some fresh mint from the garden. *Perfect. I better go around the front and be sure Auntie left enough room for Jane to pull in the driveway.* I squint and shield the sun from my eyes as I see my car parked on the front lawn. No one is in it. I hear giggling and soft voices coming from under the weeping willow tree. I creep closer, and my heart skips a beat when I set my eyes on my daughter and her boyfriend on a blanket in a very compromising situation.

"Jane!" I squeal.

The two continue to kiss and caress each other as if on a secluded island somewhere. Then the unspeakable happens, Danny rolls right on top of her, holding her hands down at her side. Jane cackles a nervous laugh as he kisses her neck. A car drives slowly past.

I stand over them. "Danny, get off my daughter."

He looks up at me with a sinister smirk. "Hi, Mrs. Funk. Nice day, huh?"

Jane wiggles out from under him. "Mom, how long have you been standing there?"

"Get in the house, Jane, but be quiet. Auntie's napping in your brother's room. I don't want to see you with my daughter again. Find someone your own age and leave her alone. The next time, I'll call the cops."

He raises his hands over his head. "Okay, okay. I'm going. Settle down, Lady."

I watch him get in his car and drive away. The neighbor across the street is staring with hands on her hips.

The tea kettle is whistling a tune of urgency when I enter the house, and Pups is standing on his hind feet trying hard to get at the ground beef. I can hear Jane's unpleasant tantrum, by way of slamming cupboard doors, from the kitchen and pray that Auntie naps through it all.

"Jane, please, please, settle down. Auntie's sleeping. She doesn't need to know about Danny, okay?"

She glares at me. "You humiliated me in front of my boyfriend. We weren't doing anything wrong."

"Listen, Dear, I can remember when I was in a compromising situation with my first boyfriend."

"Oh, so you are telling me you fooled around before you met Daddy?"

"I had boyfriends, but I worked hard at not letting my emotions lead into acts of sexual immorality. I knew it was wrong even before I came to know the Lord."

"But Danny says he loves me, Mom. That should count for something."

I turn her to me with tears in my eyes. "Honey, men will say that, so you give in to them. You're too young to understand what love between a man and women is."

"The prom is coming, and he was going to be my date. Now what am I going to do?"

I peer down the hall to see if the bedroom door is still closed. It is.

"Danny won't be back. I took care of that. Now, isn't there someone else you can ask to be your date?"

"What do you mean, he won't be back?"

"Shush. Not so loud. I told him to stay away from you or I will call the cops."

"No. Why? I'm not a baby. I would have broken up with him in due time."

"What is all the ruckus out here? I'm sure your neighbors are having a heyday today listening to your squabbles." Auntie perches at the counter.

Jane rolls her eyes. "How are you, Aunt Flossie?"

"I can handle anything since I took a nap, but I hope someday, you and your mother will learn to converse without arguing."

I bow my head. *Lord, please show me how to truly love my daughter unconditionally and to correct her with discernment. I don't want her to make the mistakes I did.*

"I'm sorry, Auntie. Neither one of us intended for you to hear our discussion. Supper will be on the table in an hour. Jane, do you have any homework?"

"How are your grades in history lately?" Auntie scowls.

"I do have a test tomorrow, but I have pulled my average up to a D, so I should be all right to graduate."

"Can Auntie help you study for your test?"

Silence fills the room.

"Jane?"

"I guess so, but I hope she doesn't get mad when I don't know the answers right away."

"You two can go in the studio for privacy, because I want to call your father to see how his day went. He should be at the boarding house by now."

They chat back and forth a mile a minute as they disappear into the confines of the other part of the house.

I smile and shake my head in approval. *Auntie will get her on the right track with her studying. Hopefully, Jane will get at least a C on the test. She'll find another date for the prom.*

I pick up the phone and call collect.

I listen to the operator, "Placing a collect call for Henry Funk."

"Please wait."

"Yes. I can wait."

I grab broccoli out of the fridge, open the package, and place it in a colander for rinsing.

"Metropolitan Life, Henry Funk speaking."

"Hi, Honey. How are you today?"

"Hi, Violet. I'm taking a short break. What's going on there?"

"Oh, it's been eventful here. Auntie's here for a few days, Jane and Danny were found in a compromising situation on our front lawn, and I almost burned the apple cake. How about you?"

"What? She's still dating that Danny boy? I told Jane I didn't trust that kid."

"Yes, but I sent him on his way and told him not to bother Jane again."

"I worry about our daughter and the fellas she attracts. Did Auntie tell you I talked to her yesterday?"

"No, Auntie didn't say anything about talking to you yesterday."

Henry sighs. "I asked her to loan me some money."

"For what?"

"The Property in Elnora?"

"Not that acreage on top of a hill? What does my aunt have to do with that?"

"I'm borrowing ten thousand dollars from her to put a down payment on the land."

"How could you do that? Why do we need so much property anyway? There are lovely housing developments all over the capital district within our price range. I can't believe this."

"I promised Jane a horse when we moved."

"For a horse. You bought this property so our daughter can have a horse? We have all we can do to get her graduated from high school."

I turn my back to pull out a pan for the broccoli.

"Is Daddy getting me a horse?" Jane squeals, with Auntie behind her.

"Henry, I'd better go. We'll be eating shortly. I'm very disappointed, to say the least, to hear you and my aunt did all of this without my consent."

"Oh, Vi, calm down. Everything will be fine."

"Goodbye."

I try not to slam the phone on the receiver, but the anger is very hard to compress at this point.

"Toots, please try to understand. Henry didn't want to lose the opportunity to buy the land. There were two other potential buyers, so wiring the money yesterday secured the sale. He led me to believe you knew all about it."

"Well, Dearest Aunt, you're wrong."

Chapter Twenty-Two

September 1964

I've been up to Albany several times to work out all the details with the builder. We had to sell our Long Island house to Metropolitan Life for thirty thousand dollars because we needed the money to proceed with the building process. The foundation was poured, and the concrete blocks were set, but the rest of the house was on hold until another payment was made. Not to mention the steep hill going up to our future home. Blacktopping it is out of the question, so we had to settle for a tightly packed gravel driveway. *I sure hope it won't be too much of a nightmare trying to get up and down the hill in the winter.*

"Mr. Gayer said that we should be able to move in no later than October first, Vi," Henry announces at breakfast on a cool Saturday.

"That's only a few weeks away. They must be working overtime to get to that goal."

"Landscaping will have to wait until spring, but we are saving some bucks by doing it ourselves. I know how much you love gardening and have an incredible knack for arranging shrubbery artistically."

"I'm still a little sore at you for insisting on that property. We could have been all moved in by now if we purchased a home in a development. A half-acre would have been more than suitable for our needs, Henry."

He takes a bite of a pancake. "All right, all right. That's water over the dam now. Once you are settled in your new place, everything will be great. You'll see."

176

"Good grief. It's ten o'clock, and Jane is still in bed. I better get her up."

"Why? It's Saturday. She's done with school. Let her sleep."

"Carol's coming over at noon to help me fill an order, and Jane is supposed to put cork backs on the tiles."

"I hope you're paying these kids to help you, Violet."

"Of course, I am. No kid works for free anymore."

The rock and roll music's blaring throughout the entire cellar as all of us move about filling the orders that might very well be the last for Miller Place. Henry is silk-screening "God Bless Our Home," "God is Love," and wedding tiles. He's determined to fill the sixteen shelves with full trays of tiles. *I'm so blessed to have a husband that loves to do this on his weekends home.* Jane's chomping on gum as she glues the cork backs to the tiles. They must lie face down for at least twenty-four hours before packing to ship. Carol's sitting directly across from me. She fills in all the colors other than the reds and places the freshly painted tiles in the ceramic rack, ready to fire.

"Mrs. Funk, has my father been over here visiting you during the week?"

I see Henry turn and look at me, but he turns back to do his work.

"A couple of times, Carol. Only to give me some homemade clam chowder."

"My sisters and I are concerned about that. He's becoming a lonely man seeking female attention, but we tell him Violet Funk is a married lady."

"It's all very innocent, dear. I've been talking to him about God, and he's interested in learning more about the Bible."

Henry stops what he's doing. "Think about what this looks like to the neighbors, Violet. They know you're alone during the week."

"He must come here when I'm working at the bakery because I rarely see him," Jane adds.

I burst into a loud laugh. "He knows I'm a happily married lady. I think Jack needs a lady friend, maybe a widow."

My cheeks heat up as I run to Henry and hug him.

Carol shakes her head. "He talks to you on the phone, though. You have been telling him about some camp in the Adirondacks for older teens like Jane and I."

"I promise you that it's all very innocent, Carol. I talk to him about God and how much I love my husband. I wink at Henry. I did tell your Dad about wonderful Word of Life camp near Schroon Lake in the Adirondacks. You and Jane would love it there."

Jack is a big flirt, but I'm so glad Henry is my knight without the shining armor. No need for anyone else.

It's a beautiful fall day, with the leaves on the trees burning in various colors of oranges and reds. The early morning sun is beaming down to give the right amount of light to make a monumental job go smoothly. The Mayflower Moving truck is backed into our driveway with four muscular guys transporting furniture and boxes from each room to the truck. Henry left yesterday to prepare the new house for our arrival tonight. His car was loaded to the roof and then some, with boxes of important files and a few pieces of heirloom porcelain bisque packed expressly by yours truly. Fortunately, he's taking a few days off from work.

"Mom, where in the world will we fit Carol in our van anyway?" yells Jane.

"Calm down, dear. The men will get the big kilns on the truck. We must take the cases of tiles with us because I don't want them to get smashed in transit. Everything going in our van is in boxes by the cellar door for the guys to load for me when finished with the truck."

"Pups needs a bed in the van plus three suitcases too. It will never work. You'll have to tell Carol to take the Trail Ways bus."

A dark-skinned man whisks past us and winks at Jane.

"Mom, did you see that?"

I put a finger to my lips. "Shush. Please go and look in every nook and cranny in your room and Peter's to be sure everything is empty. Okay?"

"I'm keeping Pups in my room until the movers are gone. All right, I'll check it out."

The ringing of the telephone catches my attention.

"Hello."

"Jack?"

"Can I come over to help you move things to the truck?"

"No, I don't need any help, but thanks for asking. We did tell Metropolitan Life that you would be checking the property, doors, and windows for any damage."

"Yes, Henry gave me Metropolitan's phone number."

"Henry and I will be back to turn in the keys and leave for good."

"You're a very special lady to me, Violet."

"Stop it, Jack. Any one of your daughters might hear you."

"I really, really like you."

179

"You're a friend. That's it. I love my husband very much."

◦◎◠◎◦

Jane and I stand in the empty house gazing at the bareness of the place. *So many memories of family and friends over the years took place in these rooms. We had no money when we moved in, but look how God blessed us. Once again, we are tight for money, but I know things will turn around once we settle in.*

"I'm going to miss swimming in the sound, Mom."

I pull my daughter to my side. "Me too. Saratoga Lake is only twenty minutes away from our new home though, Jane. There are two lovely beaches there."

"Ma'am?" A voice from the front door summons my attention.

I open the door and look out. "Hi, Leonard, are you all done loading my van?"

"We packed it as tight as we could, leaving room for the dog's bed and one person in the back."

I follow him down to the cellar. "Oh, there are a few boxes left?"

"Your tires need air, and you'll have to drive mighty slow with the load you have."

"Well, these boxes will have to stay until we return next week. The rest of the house is empty. Let's walk through the garage before you take off, okay?"

"Sure thing, Mrs. Funk."

I look over and see there are only two fellas by the truck. *Where's the young one who was eyeing Jane?*

"Looks good, Leonard. You must be eager to get some lunch for your crew and get on the road."

He smiles, handing me a clipboard with the contract to sign. "If you'll sign here to verify, we can move on."

I sign the document, and he gives me a carbon copy. "My husband will give you a check when you arrive in Elnora. God bless you."

"Hey, Mac, where's Joe?" he shouts as he approaches the truck.

Something tells me I'd better see if Joe is bothering Jane. I fly up the walkway and up the steps.

Jane's giggling. "Oh, you better go before my mother catches you."

He gives her a hug. "But you're so cute. After today, I'll know where you'll be living."

"Get your hands off of her," I shout.

"See you later, Jane," he yells, flying past me.

"Why do you always spoil my fun?"

"Am I going to have to keep you under lock and key when we get to our new home? Come on, get your dog and suitcase and get in the van. I'll double check that all windows and doors are locked. Then we'll be on our way."

Fifteen minutes later, I find myself locking the front door and walking down the marigold-laden walkway. I don't dare look back. *It's time to trust God with this new adventurous journey to beautiful upstate New York.*

Jane hangs her head out the window. "I wish we had air-conditioning in this car. It's so stuffy."

"Once we're on the road, you'll be fine."

We pile Carol and her belongings in the over-packed van after she hugs her family good-bye. Jack slips me an envelope with the words, "Open tonight," written on it.

Jane and Carol are jibber jabbering, so they don't even notice it.

"Good-bye, Jack. May God keep you all healthy." As we back out, I see him pull out a hankie to wipe his eyes.

Chapter Twenty-three

The nine-year-old, grand Tappan Zee bridge crosses over the majestic Hudson River. Each time I cross it, I'm amazed how it spans for three miles and the swift connection it makes to the New York State Thruway. Pups has settled down, Carol's sleeping in the back, and Jane's flipping through pages of old issues of *Seventeen* magazine. I packed a cooler full of sandwiches and fruit, as well as thermoses filled with water and chocolate milk.

"When are we going to pull over for lunch? I'm starving," Jane whines.

"Shush. Carol's sleeping and so is your dog. There's a rest area ahead. They have picnic tables and bathrooms too. Good place to stop, eat, and take the dog for a walk."

"How far is that?"

"Oh, about an hour."

"Are we going to be in our new house before dark?"

I reach over and tousle her straightened hair. "Long before it gets dark, Jane."

This old van with the bald tires has been good to me. Great. The rest area's only ten miles from here. Once everyone empties their bladders and fills up their tummies, we'll be good to go.

Pups plows between the seats and climbs on Jane's lap. "Only a few more minutes and we can all get out and stretch our legs, even you, Doggy."

Looking in my rear-view window, I can see Carol yawning and stretching. "Hey there, Sleepyhead. Are you ready for some lunch?"

"I have to go to the bathroom really, really bad. How much longer, Violet?" Carol asks as she fans herself from the heat.

"We'll be home in less than two hours, but there's a rest stop up ahead, so you can use the restroom." *Is that smoke coming from under the hood?*

I glance at the gas gauge and wonder why the needle hasn't moved since we left the bridge. *There was a half a tank. I know there was.*

Pups is wedged between the seats, panting as if lost in the middle of a desert. Jane is sighing and mumbling as she stares out the window, twitching to the left and right.

"I smell something burning. Look, there's smoke coming from the hood," shouts Carol.

"Mom!" screams Jane.

"Oh, the van's slowing down even with my foot on the gas pedal. We must get off at the next exit, which looks like...Ravenna. Hang on, kids, we should be able to pull into a gas station and get the thing fixed."

The cars whiz past us as I creep over to the shoulder of the busy highway. "Oh God, please get us to a place of safety before this car dies. Amen."

We roll off the exit and coast our way down into the small town. The smoke's starting to seep into the cab and the smell is almost too hard to bear. We're going ten miles an hour with only a police station, a boarded-up gas station, a small A&P market, and no hotel in sight.

I pull up next to a teenager riding a bike. "Is there another gas station open for business in this town?"

He chomps on gum and pops bubbles. "Yeah, take a right at that stop sign and go straight. You can't miss it."

"Thank you."

The van putts and shimmers as we pull up to the old, dilapidated, white with red trim building with two pumps in front of it. The place looks deserted and so does the whole town, for that matter. *I start to think that maybe this is a bad idea. I need to look for a phone booth so I can call Henry. He'll call a tow truck for this rat trap of a car and then come and get us.* I turn off the ignition and get out to see if I can locate a mechanic.

"Stay in the van, kids. I don't think we'll be staying very long."

I hear the panel door of the van slide open as I walk to the partially open entrance, but I keep focused. "Hello, is anybody here?"

The small office/store reeks of motor oil and gasoline. There's a small dusty desk, two chairs, glass display case with a few candy bars, and a Coca Cola machine. I turn to look back at the van. Good, the kids are still in their seats. I hear a radio blaring from the garage. "Hello. Can someone help me?" An old '57, banged up Chevy is on a lift, and a Ford Station wagon is jacked with legs sticking out from under it.

"Excuse me, sir? Hello. Can you hear me?" I shout.

Suddenly, I feel a very warm, sweaty hand on my shoulder. "Hey Missy, maybe I can be of service to you."

I leap forward, turn, and face a scary fella with red hair and a beard to match. His face and farmer jeans are covered in grease. He winks at me, which makes me want to flee.

The wheels of the undercar creeper squeak from behind me as the redhead roars with laughter.

"Earl, what are you doing to this poor woman anyhow? Sorry, Ma'am. I thought my brother was in the office where he's supposed to be."

He wipes his hands on a clean rag and reaches out for mine. "Hi, I'm Grady, and this is my brother Earl. What can we do for you?"

184

I form a fake smile as I head to the door. "Our van overheated on the Thruway and I had to coast most of the way here. We need to get to our home in Elnora just north of Latham."

"Let me look. We close in an hour, but if it's something simple, you'll be on your way soon."

The hood's steaming as he reaches out to touch it with his gloved hands. "Give me a hand, Earl, would you?"

"Girls, get out and take Pups for a walk, but stay where I can see you, okay?"

As they lift the hood, the hot smoke pours on them, causing them to jump back. "We have to let this thing cool down a while before checking it out. Is the key in the ignition?"

"Yes, it is."

Grady gets into the driver's seat and turns the key. Nothing. He tries again. Dead.

"Maybe your battery or transmission. You might not be going anywhere, Mrs...?"

"My name's Violet. Oh dear, where's the nearest phone booth? I must call my husband."

"Right there next to the ice machine, but it's out of order."

"Do you have a telephone I can use and call collect?"

"We forgot to pay our bill, so it was turned off."

Panic and fear begin to penetrate my thoughts as I watch the girls chat away as they walk. I can't form the words as the two men stare at me with squinted eyes.

"Earl, check the oil. There's a working phone booth outside the police station, or you can use the one at our house, two blocks over.

My stomach flip flops.

"Oil's okay, Grady." The two ding around with the nuts and bolts of the transmission as I walk to meet up with the kids. "We have to find a telephone booth to call your father, Jane. The car won't start at all now."

Carol places her sunglasses on top of her head. "This town is dead. Only a few cars in sight, and the last time I looked at my watch it was 5:00. People should be coming home from work, I would think."

Jane looks back at the men working on the car. "They look like two bozos if you ask me, Mom. There must be a phone in that place somewhere."

"Out of order. Now, listen. You two wait here while I grab my purse. Do you need anything of importance from the van, girls?"

"I better get my travel case and pocketbook," Carol says as she wipes her forehead.

We walk back to the van to get our personal belongings as the sun disappears behind the clouds. The two men are arguing with each other, and their hands are waving in every direction.

"I have bad news, Violet," Grady says.

The girls squeeze next to me with the dog panting between us. "Oh, no. What's wrong with my car?"

"You'll need a new transmission. Your alternatives are that you wait until tomorrow for us to tow the vehicle to your house in Elnora or you can hang out here until we can get the replacement. There's a junkyard at the end of town where we can get a used one, but it goes on lockdown in ten minutes."

"I have to call my husband and tell him all of this before I make a decision. Is there a hotel nearby if he suggests staying here?"

Earl lets out a hurly-burly laugh. "There ain't no hotel in all of Ravenna. No, Ma'am."

"Let's get you to a telephone first, okay?" Grady smiles.

Jane fidgets with her hair. "You must have a diner here? They'll have a telephone for sure."

186

"The Shady Tree Eatery is open until 6:00, and they do have an inside phone booth. Come on, I'll drive you all over there because the restaurant will be closing in fifteen minutes," Grady says, running to a dilapidated green Ford truck.

"What about our dog?"

"Take him with you. Hurry," he shouts.

He turns on Main Street where there's a bit more activity with a few people leaving the restaurant. Grady pulls up to the curb. We all pour out and run into the tiny café.

"Sorry, Grady, we're closing in five, and no dogs allowed," yells a pink-clad waitress with blond hair.

"Mable, these people need some food and have to make a phone call too. It's an urgent situation. Her car broke down, and we can't fix it until tomorrow."

"Come on, Grady, I have a date tonight. I'll have to ask Charlie."

"Violet, grab the phone and try to call your husband, okay? I'll see if Charlie can make you some burgers," Grady says.

I race to the phone booth and plop several coins in the slots. *Good, a dial tone.* I dial my new telephone number. "It's ringing," I mumble as I watch the girls spin around on the seats at the lunch counter.

The ringing never ends. *Where's Henry? It's 6:15. He should be worried sick about us by now. Come on, answer the phone.* More ringing. *Maybe he went to the office, but why? Oh, I better try. He isn't home for sure.*

No answer there either.

A middle-aged man, who must be Charlie, is giving the girls hamburgers and chocolate malts. "What can I get you, Ma'am? Grady told me your dilemma, so order anything. It's on me."

I breathe a sigh. "I guess I'll have what the girls are having. You're so kind. May God bless both of you kind gentlemen for helping us tonight."

"My pleasure. The Bible does say do unto others what you want them to do to you. I'll be right back with your order."

I smile. "Amen."

"Did you get ahold of Dad?"

"No, he's not home or at the office. He must be outside or something."

"He's probably with that secretary again."

"Jane, that's enough."

Carol giggles with her hand over her mouth.

Grady sits down next to me. "It looks like you're going to be spending the night in Ravenna. The question is, where?"

I wipe away the tears that are forming in my eyes and hold my head up high. "Is there a rooming house or something of that sort?"

"Uh, no. I share a very small bungalow with my brother; otherwise, I would let you all stay there."

I stare at him with a scowl as agony rises in my heart. "You have got to be kidding. How far is it to a hotel?"

Charlie leans over the counter. "Nearest motel is an hour away. Ma'am, I suggest you and your girls go over to the police station and ask for assistance there. Our sheriff is a very nice, accommodating American citizen who goes all out to help his fellow man. Uh, woman."

Grady puts down his glass of water. "Come on. I'll take you over there and introduce you. He may even decide to take you all home tonight."

I wave to Charlie. "Thanks for the meals."

The grey, box-shaped cement building sends a chill up my spine as we pull up in front. Two empty, white and black police cars are parked at attention, waiting for an urgent call to report to the line of fire.

Pups growls as we follow Grady into the cold building.

Chapter Twenty-four

"Hey, Sheriff, this lady's van broke down and I can't fix it until tomorrow. She can't get a hold of her husband but would like to get home tonight. Can you or Deputy Carl take them to Elnora, just north of Latham?" pleads Grady.

The tall, muscular man dressed in black and wearing a shiny badge smiles. "I see, ho hum. I could send Carl on this little errand, which would take him away from his post for at least two hours. I don't know, Grady. You know we have had a lot of trouble on the other side of the railroad tracks lately. It's been quiet over there for two nights now though."

The girls move, emotionless, to an old wooden bench along a cement wall. *I sure wish things would be different for them. This is an awful experience, for sure.*

A tall, lanky looking fella comes out of a telephone booth-sized bathroom. "Are these women prisoners, Sheriff?"

Just the thought makes me cringe.

After twenty minutes of deliberation and pacing back and forth, the sheriff scratches his chin. "Okay, take them back to the van to get any belongings that can fit in the squad car. Take them home but come right back. The night is still young. If there's going to be trouble it will happen after midnight."

The fresh air is soothing to my soul as we step into the car.

190

Grady pats me on the shoulder. "Don't worry about your van, Miss. Violet. My brother and I will push it in the garage tonight. I'll call you when it's ready to pick up."

I want to hug him, but I don't. "Thank you. I'll always thank God for your help."

The deputy starts the car. Suddenly, the sheriff is waving and shouting something from the open door. "Stop, Carl. We have a problem on Watkins Street again. Someone has a gun. You must come with me. Grady, take them inside and lock the door."

"My father would be horrified if he knew I was in a jail," whimpers Carol.

I stare at the cold grey cement floor. "I'm so sorry about all of this, Carol. Thank God we're safe and that everyone has been truly gracious in this little town. God is with us right now, right here. Let's get some sleep. This is by far the safest place in town."

I look at Jane all curled up on the paper-thin mattress, covered by two wool blankets. *She hasn't said one word since we walked into this place a few hours ago. I guess it is better to let her sleep.*

The big clock on the wall is at 10:00, and Grady is snoozing behind the sheriff's desk. *At least the jail cell door is open so we can use the bathroom. Pups finally settled down on the small braided rug in the compact kitchen area.*

I creep over to the telephone and dial the operator. I pull the long cord over to the cold bench. "I would like to make a collect call. Yes, the number is 518-383-2522. I'm Violet Funk."

I can hear the ringing on the other end. *He'd better answer.*

"Violet, is that you?"

"Will you accept the charges, sir?"

Finally, I can hear Henry's voice. "Yes, I will accept the call."

"Violet? Where are you? I've been worried sick about you and the girls. You should have been here hours ago."

The adrenaline boils inside of me, and my body is on fire with sweat. "Where were you today, Henry? I tried the house a few times and even the office. No answer."

Grady opens his eyes but drifts off again.

"Uh, ah. I was cleaning up outside after supper."

"Well, I sure hope you enjoyed your supper. The van broke down, and we're stranded in Ravenna."

"What are you talking about?"

"It's the transmission. It's shot. The local mechanic is going to get a used one from the junk yard first thing in the morning. He assured me we would be on our way home by noon."

"How are you going to pay him? Do you want me to come down there?"

"Too late, don't you think? I have the business checkbook, but I hope I have enough in there to cover it."

"Where are you calling from, Vi?"

"The jail."

A loud pounding on the front door causes me to jump and drop the phone.

The doorknob jiggles.

I fly over to Grady. "Grady, wake up. Someone's at the door."

"Hello. Hello." A muffled Henry can be heard from the receiver on the floor.

"Whoa. What?" Grady shouts.

The door bursts open and the sheriff and his deputy push two coarse-looking looking characters into the room. I'm close enough to smell the alcohol oozing from their bodies.

"Ooh, you're a pretty one," the taller one says with a wink and a loud belch.

"You two are spending the night and will be arraigned in the morning when the judge gets in his office. Lock them up, Carl, and throw away the key."

Sheriff Murphy looks at me. "So much for a peaceful night, huh? Go ahead, Grady, and get some sleep so you can get to her car first thing in the morning. What's the phone doing on the floor anyway?" He moves to pick it up. "Only a dial tone."

By this time, Carol and Jane are huddling together on the bottom bunk of our glorified hotel room, with Pups in their laps. *I try hard to keep my composure, but it's very hard to do. God's been with me through a kidnapping, almost drowning, and a near brutal attack of Jane and me. He'll get us safely through this messy situation too.*

Luckily, there's a wall between the two cells, so the creeps are out of view. My eyes are burning from lack of sleep, and I feel grubby from head to toe. I motion for the girls to come over to my bunk, and they do.

"Lord, help the three of us to get some sleep now. Daylight will come in a few hours. Take away any fear the girls might have and help them to trust in You. Amen."

"They're fast asleep after their drinking frenzy, and their cell is locked. I'll be here for the rest of the night. So please don't worry, Mrs. Funk. Try to get some shut eye, okay?" Sheriff Murphy says as he walks to his cushy chair behind the desk.

"You sure you don't want me to stay with you, Sheriff?" asks the deputy.

"Go home, Carl. Come back in the morning. We have the culprits under lock and key now."

The deputy leaves as the sheriff turns off a few lights and locks the door. The big man settles into his chair, leans back, and shuts his eyes.

"Girls, we're safe now. Go and get some sleep."

Carol hugs me and climbs to the top bunk across from mine. Jane quietly makes her way to the bottom bunk and turns toward the wall with the blanket pulled over her head.

I want to grab her and let her sleep next to me, but the bed is the smallest twin bed I have ever seen. Best to leave her alone until tomorrow. A good night's sleep and a big breakfast will do the trick. I lay down, facing my precious cargo. Pups curls up on the floor next me. The place is relatively quiet, except for the harmonious snoring coming from Sheriff Murphy and the two outlaws.

I drift off to sleep.

Chapter Twenty-Five

Elnora, New York

The nightmare comes to end as we make our ascent up the steep driveway to the new house. Grady filled the car with gas, put air in all the tires, and replaced the transmission to the fine tune of three hundred and fifty dollars. He thinks the van has a new life and will last for at least another year. *We'll see.*

Henry's standing by the open garage with his arms folded. "So, here are the long-lost travelers. Welcome home."

With the window rolled down, I say, "Hi, Honey, it's good to see you."

"Bring the van in the garage. We can unload it later. The furniture should be where it's supposed to be, but there are a lot of boxes to unpack."

The girls disappear into the house while Pups begins a sniffing frenzy on the gravel driveway and beyond.

Henry kisses my forehead. "Father God, forgive me for not hearing the phone last night. I should have rescued my ladies, so they didn't have to go through such an ordeal. I thank you for keeping them safe and getting them here today. Amen."

"I really think there were angels in disguise in that town, Henry. The deputy and Grady, the mechanic, took the perishables out of our coolers and put everything in their refrigerators overnight. There's plenty for all of us to have a decent lunch."

The compact kitchen flows into the living room and dining room, divided by an L-shaped, Formica, bar-like countertop. Four tall, wooden stools with backs stand at attention waiting for their first customers.

I start putting the food away in the new refrigerator. "Lunch will be ready in a little while, folks. Meanwhile, unpack your suitcases. There should be a dresser in each room."

The view from the kitchen windows brings me back to another time when I gaze upon the vast field of cornstalks waiting for the harvest. Although we have good old clay in place of sand around the house, we are sitting in the middle of green pastureland. I smile as I lean on the sink and remember where we came from and the astounding possibilities in upstate New York.

Henry grabs a glass of water from the tap. "You must be exhausted from that ugly ordeal. I'll clean up the kitchen after lunch so you can rest."

I place a platter of ham and cheese sandwiches on the counter, cut up a few apples, and pour chocolate milk into thermos cups. "Girls, come and get something to eat."

Carol grabs a sandwich and sits at the counter. "Yikes, there are a lot of boxes to unpack, huh?"

Henry sits down next to her. "That's why we brought you here. Jane tells me that you and your sisters are extremely organized in your house."

She laughs and looks out the sliding glass doors to the back of the house. "This is a perfect place for a horse. Look at that beautiful pastureland."

Henry chuckles. "Yes, Jane will have her horse. We bought this property so she could bring her dream to reality."

Jane bolts to the counter. "Are you getting me a horse, Daddy?"

196

I'm not in favor of getting any horse, because we can barely afford to pay the mortgage and landscape around the house.

"Maybe in the spring, Tot. There's a lot to do around here before that happens."

I bite into my sandwich. "Carol, you should call your father and tell him you're safe. Use the telephone in the new art studio, through this door."

Jane scowls at me. "As soon as you hear the word horse, you change the subject."

The rest of the afternoon is spent unpacking boxes, making beds, and putting every effort into making some sense of organization in the living room area. The cross ventilation from the opened screened, front door, and the sliding door in the back oozes fresh fall air. I'm amazed at Henry and his talent for high-fidelity equipment. He loves his classical music so much that he hooked it all up yesterday. Beethoven and Bach create a fabulous background to keep us moving on with our work.

"The dishes, glasses, pots, and pans are put away. Where would you like me to go next?" Carol asks with her hands on her hips.

I pat her on the shoulder. "Thank you. You're so quick. Stack all the empty boxes by the sliding door. Henry's going to burn them tomorrow."

Carol's a small girl but very muscular. *Must be from lifting those bales of hay.*

"Hey, Vi, come down in the basement and check out where the movers put the kiln. I have most of the silk-screening equipment set up," shouts Henry.

The spacious basement is cold due to the cement blocks surrounding it and the newly poured floor of the same bond. Henry's workbench is to the right, and his screening apparatus is right next to it. The big kiln is on the opposite wall.

Henry whistles. "Come over here and see this."

At the far end of the basement there's an opening in the cement wall about four feet from the floor. He climbs up into it. "This is a crawl space designed for extra storage."

"It's dark and dingy in there, Henry. What in the world would we need this for?"

"Oh, once I get some lights in here, you'll fill it up with something."

"In about ten years maybe. Not now. Come on out of there, okay?"

"I plan on putting a door on this opening in the near future to keep the main area of the basement warm."

Carol takes in a deep breath as we climb up the stairs. "The van's empty now."

"It's time to call it a day, Dear. You have worked so hard. Where's Jane anyway? I haven't seen her since lunch."

"She was making her bed the last I knew, but I'll go check."

Henry and I collapse on the new, curved sectional couch that faces the fireplace.

"I don't want you to cook tonight. How about if I order a pizza? A new Italian restaurant opened on Route 146."

"That sounds great."

"Jane's sound asleep and so is her dog," whispers Carol.

Henry hands me a glass of water. "I'm going to take a ride to the pizza place and order the pie. I might as well wait there for it. Do you need anything else while I'm out?"

"You go ahead. We do need milk, eggs, and bread, but I can get that at Rosen's Store on the corner. It looks like a short enough walk, plus I could use some fresh air."

Henry kisses me on the cheek. "I'll be back in about an hour."

"Carol, you look like you need to rest. Please feel free to curl up on the couch while we are gone."

"I would like to walk with you, if it's all right."

"Sure, you can. Let me peek in on my daughter first. Hang on."

I tiptoe on the slate floor hallway to her room and peer through the crack in the door. *Good. She's snoring up a storm. Poor kid needs to sleep from the horrid ordeal we went through yesterday.*

The new clock in the kitchen reads 6:30.

Rosen's Store is on the corner of Vischer Ferry and Grooms roads. It's a small, crammed space from ceiling to glass door, refrigerators stocked with dairy products, soda, and beer. The aroma of fresh baked bread and fresh brewed coffee fills one's nostrils as they walk in the door. Shelves stocked with a variety of canned goods line three walls, and an old register on a beat-up counter occupies the other wall. A short, stocky, grey-haired lady smiles at us as we search for the groceries.

"These are pretty nice postcards. Come look at them," calls Carol, as I grab a gallon of milk and a dozen eggs.

"We'll have to get out and explore the area while you're here. These historical pictures of Vischer Ferry Township look so interesting."

"I forgot my wallet. Can you cover me for a few postcards?"

"Of course. I'm sure your family will be thrilled to get cards from you."

We pile our goods on the counter as the cashier proceeds to ring up each item. She peers over the top of her granny-like glasses. "Are you new to the area?"

"Yes, we moved here from Long Island yesterday. My name's Violet Funk. What's yours?" I reach out my hand, but she doesn't return the favor.

A few moments of silence follow. "Is this young lady your daughter?"

"No, my daughter's home resting, but this is Carol, her friend."

"That will be five dollars and fifty-five cents."

I count out the cash and hand it to her. "I'm glad this little store and gas station is so close to us. I'm sure you'll be seeing a lot of us. Have a blessed evening."

She scowls at me. "Next, please."

The house is dark when we get back, so I flick on the switch in the kitchen.

Jane leaps off the couch in a frenzy. "Where have you two been?"

Chapter Twenty-Six

November 10, 1964
Dearest Auntie,
I know it's been a while since I have written to you,
but I ask you to forgive me. It seems I can say so much
more in a letter than what I verbalize over the telephone.
Carol Carney stayed here for two weeks and helped us a
lot. We've been attending a little church five miles away
called Clifton Park Baptist Church, founded in the 1700s. It
has narrow pews that you can hardly fit your bottom on. I
hope you're doing well. I love and miss you, Tootsie.

"Mom, there isn't any water coming out of the faucet in the bathroom," Jane wails as she bursts into my small art studio. I fold the letter to Aunt Flossie and put in the envelope.

"Go try the bathroom sink here."

"Only a trickle's coming out."

"Okay. Daddy won't be home for a few more hours, so we'll have to go fill some containers with water at Rosen's Store."

"It's a pain, Mom. Luckily, I was able to get the crème rinse out of my hair before the shower went dry."

I pat her shoulder. "Our house is built on solid clay, which makes it almost impossible to find water."

⌒⊙℞℧⌒

Avis Rosen told Henry about an old hermit who lives in a deserted chicken coop in the woods who's a dowser. I slump into a chair and pray for a miracle.

"Hey, Vi, come out here for a few minutes. I have someone I would like you to meet," Henry calls through the opened back door.

I pull on my winter coat and head outside. A heavy-set man dressed in faded, blue jean coveralls peeking out of a ragged wool coat smiles at me with a near toothless grin. I'm greeted with a nauseating chicken coop-like odor as I get closer.

"Pete, this is my wife, Violet."

"Pleased to meet you, Ma'am."

I cringe a bit and shake his hand. "So, Pete, can you find water for us? I see you have a dowser. Do you mind if I watch you?"

He nods his head in approval as he begins to walk around the back yard. Henry and I follow in silent attention. The sun has set, and darkness is close at hand.

I lean towards my husband. "Does this fella come with any references?"

"Yes, I talked to a couple of people who swear Pete is reliable and trustworthy. Look, he's putting a stake in the same place the other two did. I took the stakes out and left a rock there, so this isn't a coincidence."

A Bible verse comes to mind. "If two or more agree about anything, it will come to pass."

Old Pete grins. "Ah, yep. This is the spot. There's water here."

"I'll call the well driller in the morning. Thanks, kind sir. Come on, I'll give you a lift home." Henry smiles and shakes the old man's hand.

202

"No, Sir. I prefer to walk. I might be getting old, but my feet have a lot of miles left."

After a few days of drilling and three hundred feet into the ground later, we're able to put in a new well. Henry purchased two empty containers to use as cisterns to collect rainwater. It won't do any good when the temperature drops to the freezing point but worth its weight in gold the rest of the year.

"I'm calling it a night, Violet. Are you coming to bed now?"

"Not yet, I have some work to do in the studio as well as filing. The new six-drawer filing cabinet will certainly come in handy."

He gives me a big wet kiss right on the lips. "Don't stay up all night. Okay?"

Good. I'm finally down to the last file. Oh, letters from my son. I'm so glad he's coming home for Thanksgiving in two weeks. What's this?

Dear Mr. & Mrs. Funk,

It gives me sincere pleasure to inform you that your son graduated as the "outstanding student" of his U.S. Naval School, Pre-flight class. Peter attained this honor by his excellent academic performance and his outstanding morale and military conduct. He has earned the privilege of wearing the naval aviator wings. Please accept my congratulations.

Sincerely yours,

J.H. Caldwell, Captain, U.S. Navy

Oh Lord, My God. I'm so proud of my Peter. You have blessed him with intelligence and determination. I pray he comes to know you as his Lord and Savior. May you continue to protect him? Amen.

I stretch my arms and rub my eyes. *Tomorrow's another day. I must do something with all those apples I picked from Kawecki's orchard, which happens to be across the street.*

Once I turn off the lights and lock the doors, I notice a light shining from underneath Jane's door. *It's 12:00. What is she doing up this late?* I open the door only to find her sound asleep. I tiptoe over to the lamp on her desk and turn it off.

As I make my way to the master bedroom, I turn off the hall light switch. Suddenly, a mumbling voice and footsteps are prevalent behind me. A hand on my shoulder causes me to gasp.

"Why did you turn the lights out, Mom?" my scowling daughter asks.

"Shush. You'll wake your father. I thought you left them on by mistake. You did, right?"

"I want them on. I need light."

"Let's talk in your room," I whisper.

I follow her back down the hall and watch her flick on the light in the bathroom.

"Sometimes I get up in the night that's why I need a light on."

"Are you afraid of the dark, dear?"

She turns away from me and climbs back in bed. "Of course not. What makes you ask me a question like that?"

"One light would suffice to show you a path to the bathroom, but you're using three.

"Okay. Fine. Leave the lamp on in here and leave the others off."

Deciding it best not to upset the apple cart, I cover her and whisk the hair from her eyes. "Dear Lord, I pray that Jane has a good night's sleep and that you would take away any fear she might have. Thank You for your love watching over her. Amen."

"Good night, Mom. I love you."

"I love you too. If you're frightened in the future, read the Twenty-third Psalm. The verses will always comfort you."

⌒⊙⌒⊙⌒

The aroma of fresh brewed coffee and the rays of sun peeking through the drapes prompt my eyes to open. I glance at the clock with half-open eyes and read ten minutes after eight. *I have an order to fill and close to rotten apples to tend to. Saturday's the only day I can count on Henry to catch up on silk screening.*

I grab my lavender bathrobe, yank on my matching slippers, brush my tangled hair, and sail into the warm, inviting kitchen. My husband is relaxing on the couch with his newspaper.

I love how I designed this part of the house. The kitchen, dining room, and living room all meet as one. Perfect for entertaining. I can visit with my guests as I cook.

"Good morning, Sleepyhead. The coffee's hot and waiting for you."

"Thank you, Honey."

"What time did you go to bed last night?"

"About 12:30."

"Really? Why so late."

"Jane was having some issues about sleeping without lights on."

"I saw the light on under her door when I went to bed but thought she was reading, so I didn't bother her."

"I'll see if I can get a nightlight for her room. We can't afford a high electric bill."

With a hot cup of coffee in hand, I join him.

"Isn't this nice? I don't have to rush off to the office, Jane's sleeping in, and you and I can have some much-needed quality time."

"You do need to catch up on the silk screening though." I stretch my legs on the couch as he puts his arm around me.

"Relax and enjoy this valuable time." He kisses my cheek.

"I'm so proud of Peter. He's at the top of his class and a pilot in the Navy. It was just a few years ago when we were at our wits end with him."

"I sure miss that boy."

"I do too, Henry. How about some scrambled eggs and rye toast?"

"I love holding you in my arms. Things have been so hectic around here with getting settled into our new home and drilling for water, over and again."

"God has been so faithful in providing for us. We cannot forget that."

"I thank God every day for His great provision. Now, you can go make those eggs."

The butter's melting in the frying pan, as I scramble the eggs, salt, pepper, and heavy cream together. I pop four pieces of bread in the toaster. "Come sit at the counter, Love. Breakfast is almost ready."

The front doorbell chimes and catches us both off guard.

We both look at each other and shrug our shoulders, in hopes that whoever it is will go away.

Ding dong.

I pull my robe tighter around my waist and comb my hair with my fingers.

The doorbell is relentless.

"I'll get it. I'm half-dressed anyway," he whispers.

I want to run and hide in the studio, but instead I watch him open the door.

"Berto. Daisy. Come in out of the cold."

Chapter Twenty-Seven

Papa and my sister stand in the foyer like misplaced sheep, probably because Henry and I are lost for words. My father looks at me and shakes his head, but no words accompany his action. *Honestly, why couldn't they call first? If they weren't my blood relatives, I would ask them to come back later. Someone please speak.*

I glance over at the breakfast on the counter demanding some attention, but I know full well the garbage can is its destination. A jolt of exhilaration races up my spine.

Daisy whisks past me. "Seriously, Violet. Where are your manners? We drove two hours to see you and your new home. The least you can do is offer us some coffee."

"Of course. Let Henry take your coats. Come, relax at the table. I'll get you some hot coffee and apple cake."

Papa gives me an emotionless hug. "Good to see you, Daughter. Where's my granddaughter?"

I stand motionless as I watch my husband disappear into the bedroom wing.

I pour the last two cups of coffee. "She's still sleeping. I'll have to wake her because she'll want to spend time with you."

My sister's eyes are boring a burrow right through me. "Are you going to stay in your bathrobe all day, Violet?"

Papa sips his coffee. "I hope you're going to show us the whole house. We didn't travel all this way to sit around at the dining table all day."

Same ole, same ole. They sure know how to cut me down. Lord, help me to rise above their constant ridicule. Amen.

I stand over my father with my arms wrapped around him. "The Bible says in Romans 8:31, 'If God be for us, who can be against us?' Excuse me for a few minutes while I go and get dressed for the day. I love you, Papa."

Jane springs past me, nearly knocking me over. "Grampa, did you see the rest of the house yet?"

Her grandfather puts his arm around her shoulder. "Not yet, Honey."

I flee into the bedrooms, make the beds, pick up a little, and manage to get dressed. Why didn't they let me know about this visit?

When I return to the table, I find a chatty daughter smiling from ear to ear. "Let's go on tour by starting in the studio and garage. Follow me."

Keys on the piano ring out a familiar sound. "How about 'Chopsticks' with your grandfather?"

A loud burst of rare laughter fills the room off the kitchen. "Sure. We can do that."

"Where did everybody go?" asks my husband as he pours another cup of coffee.

"Jane's giving them a tour of the studio and basement, then the rest of the house. I haven't seen her this happy in a long time."

"Your father and sister aren't nice to you though. I don't like that."

"I pray that we'll be a witness for the Lord today, Henry."

Giggling and mumbled voices can be heard as they ascend the stairs.

Daisy pats Henry's shoulder. "I don't know how you can work in that frigid environment."

208

"I wear flannel shirts and turn on the space heater, Daisy. It's extremely comfortable down there."

Daddy leans on the kitchen counter. "This is a tight space. Only room for one or two people in here. The contractor must have made a mistake."

"I designed this whole house, Papa. I have received many compliments since we moved in. I would love to serve you and Daisy a special lunch. Can you stay?"

"Please, Grampa. Have lunch with us? You and Aunt Daisy can stay overnight. I'll sleep on the couch, and the bedrooms are yours." Jane snuggles up to him.

Daisy stretches out on the couch. "That's out of the question, Jane. I must be back to work tomorrow morning. I worked hard to get in the residency program at The White Plains Hospital. Today is the first day off in months."

"We can stay until four o'clock, Violet Pearl. Lunch would be nice," Papa says.

I give him a peck on his cheek. "I'll have to go to the store and get some cold cuts and rolls. Do you want to come with me, Daisy?"

"Sure. We need to catch up. It's been awhile since we chatted, Sis."

"Jane, get out the Scrabble and play a game with your grandfather, okay?"

She ignores me as the two of them start their overdue duet of "Chopsticks." I catch Henry darting down the stairs as we walk into the garage.

There's scarcely any traffic as we drive to the new Price Chopper supermarket. Only ten minutes from home. Very convenient. They have an in-house bakery and a magnificent deli too.

"This is a nice store, Sis. I might buy some bread and take it back to my apartment."

"Go ahead and look but get a loaf of rye bread for the sandwiches."

I scan all the different meats and cheeses behind the glass case. My mouth waters as I breathe in the aroma of delectable pastrami and provolone cheese.

A handsome young man from behind the counter asks, "Can I help you, Miss?"

"Yes. Please give me a pound of boiled ham and a half-pound each of pastrami and genoa salami."

I smile as I glance at my sister piling things in her cart. *The prices must be right here. She's a very picky person.*

"Here you go, Ma'am. Anything else?"

"Oh, um. How about a pound each of Swiss and provolone? I'll take two pounds of potato salad too."

Moments later, after checking out, we're in the car on our way back to the house.

Daisy's looking to the left and right. "Do you like it here, Violet?"

"I love it, Daisy. Oh, I must show you where we go to church. It's right down this road on the right."

"Papa tells me you have become a religious fanatic. Always in church, he says."

"I love Jesus. He's my stronghold, Daisy. Here we are. It's usually unlocked so you can see the inside. It's a historical landmark."

"Clifton Park Center Baptist Church. You are a Holy Roller, Violet. I don't need to get out. I saw enough. I'm hungry, and I know Papa is too."

We drive in silence for a few minutes until I spot Old Pete walking on the opposite side of the road. I pull the car on the shoulder.

"What are you doing, Vi? This is one scary looking man. Probably an ax murderer or something. Step on the gas."

I roll down my window. "Pete, hop in the car and have lunch with us."

He smiles with his big toothless grin. "Uh, I don't think so. Good day."

I smile and wink at him. "Aw, come on, Pete. I'll bring you home later."

He sways back and forth. "I guess it'll be all right."

"Hop in the back."

Daisy slumps down in her seat and covers her nose as he slowly maneuvers his way in the back seat.

"This is my sister Daisy, Pete."

"Pleased to meet you, Ma'am."

"Humph."

I hit her arm. "Daisy."

Upon pulling the car in the garage, Daisy leaps out and bolts into the house without uttering a word. I turn to look at my other passenger, only to find him rocking back and forth with his arms crossed. *Poor old guy.*

"Come on, Pete. Let's have some lunch, okay?"

"Pete wants to go home."

I go to his side of the car and open the door. "This is my house, and you are my guest. Don't pay any attention to my sister."

Reluctantly, he gets out and follows me into the house.

Voices are escalating as we come through the house. Henry grabs a bag of groceries from me and smirks when he spots Pete.

"Nice to see you again, Pete."

Jane puts her hands on her hips. "Mom, how could you do this? We have company.'

I arrange the cold cuts on a platter, place the bread in a decorative basket, and spoon the salad into an attractive glass bowl.

"Come and eat, everyone."

Henry and Pete are sitting at the table, chatting away as I serve the food and sit down. At this point, I wonder why the rest of the people in the room are not trying to join us.

"Uh, hum, Daughter. We have a long ride. I think we better leave."

"What? I have this wonderful lunch all ready for you. Have something to eat with us and then you can be on your way."

My father squints at my other guest and shakes his head with a disgusted look on his face. "We'll stop somewhere on the way back to Mount Kisco."

Daisy grabs her bags of groceries. "We should be your priorities today, Violet. It's plain to see, you prefer other folks over your own flesh and blood."

"I can't let you leave like this."

Jane positions herself between her grampa and me. "Mom loves oddball characters. Please don't go, Grampa."

He pulls her to himself. "Goodbye, Jane. Your grampa loves you."

She bursts into tears as she pulls away from him. "I love you too."

Abandonment and rejection consume me as I watch my loved ones walk out the door. *I don't hate them; I feel sorry for them. Yet, I'll continue to pray for them.*

Chapter Twenty-Eight

The stuffed turkey is baking in the oven and pies are covered waiting for someone to steal a slice. The table's eloquently set for seven. I sent an invitation for Thanksgiving to Papa and Daisy right after they left two weeks ago. I haven't heard from either of them, but it would be like them to show up anyway. Everything hurts. My heart really hurts.

I purposely got up at 7:00 today to spend time with the Lord before prepping for the big day. I met Auntie at the Greyhound bus terminal in Albany on Tuesday. I must be quiet since she's sleeping in the studio, right through these doors. Although, I knew Peter would be arriving late last night, I had no idea it would be after midnight. Good thing I told him to come through the front door.

I pour myself another cup of coffee and head to the couch for a break. I lean back into the soft, comfy array of throw pillows and stretch out my legs on the coffee table. The house is so quiet and still.

The sound of the folding door opening behind me causes my antennae to rise.

"Good morning, Toots."

"Auntie, what are you doing up so early?"

Her long grey hair is pulled to the side in a braid, and her blue eyes are enhanced by the light blue robe she's bundled in.

She sits beside me. "I want to help you with Thanksgiving, Dear."

"That's sweet of you, but everything's done for now. You can take care of the cranberry sauce if you want to later."

"Do you have fresh berries?"

"Yes. In the refrigerator."

"Everything looks nice in here, Toots."

"Thank you. Would you like me to make a fire?"

"I'm a little chilly. Are Daisy and your father coming for dinner today?"

"I haven't heard from them since they left in a huff a few weeks ago. Did they talk to you, Auntie?"

"Daisy called a few days ago to tell me about her new beau, but I forgot to ask about today."

"She has a boyfriend?"

"Yes, a surgeon from Phelps Hospital."

"Is it serious?"

"Oh, you know your sister. She doesn't intend to get married, only an occasional fling."

"She needs the Lord."

"Now, now. Let's not get judgmental, Dear."

I poke the wood to stir some sparks. I let out a deep breath. "Can I get you a cup of tea?"

"I can get it, Toots. You relax."

I let her do it as I close my eyes to pray. *Lord, I pray my father, sister, and aunt will experience the gift of eternal life through salvation soon. In Jesus' name. Amen.*

My handsome son sits proudly at the head of the table. "You outdid yourself again, Mother, with this wonderful dinner. Please pass the creamed onions."

I smile at him and pat his shoulder, "Thank you, Peter, but hang on before you eat, so your father can ask a blessing on the food."

He puts his fork down after consuming a mouthful of giblet stuffing. "Sure thing."

Henry bows his head. "Let's hold hands around the table. Lord God, we thank You for the bountiful array of scrumptious looking food on the table before us. Thank You for bringing our son home safely last night and for the privilege of having Aunt Flossie with us too. You have blessed us with so much. Thank you, Lord. Amen"

Peter lets out a hearty laugh. "Whoa, Dad, that was almost a sermon. The food is probably cold now."

Jane grabs a bun. "Where are Grampa and Aunt Daisy? Shouldn't we wait for them?"

"Let's eat while the food is warm. If they aren't here in a half hour, I'll call."

Auntie plops a scoop of sweet potatoes on her plate. "My brother-in-law is always late for everything. However, Daisy Miss Prompt is another story. I wouldn't want to be in that car right now." Her frown deepens.

After a long silence, Peter speaks up. "Sis, how are the extension classes going at the high school?"

Jane fidgets with her fork. "I quit those last month. I'm working full-time at the luncheonette on the corner."

Auntie sighs. "Jane, why? How will you ever get into college now?"

I can see that my daughter is ready to bolt from the room but grabs a slice of turkey instead. "I need to save money so I can buy a car."

"That's okay, Sis. Remember, I worked in a gas station for a year before enlisting. Take your time. You're young enough to decide what you really want to do."

Auntie shakes her head in disapproval and remains quiet for the rest of the meal.

I look at the clock and realize it's an hour past the time I asked everyone to be here. *Time to call Daisy and see what's going on.*

"Excuse me for a few minutes. I'm going to call and see what happened to our other guests."

In the other room, I dial and wait for an answer on the other end. *Maybe they're on their way after all. I might as well hang up and put some food in the double boiler to keep warm.*

The ringing stops, and my sister's voice resonates in my ear. "Hello."

"Daisy, this is Violet. I was planning on you and Papa for Thanksgiving."

"We changed our minds at the last minute. A colleague from the hospital invited us to their home in Pleasantville. You should have seen this place, Vi. Absolutely gorgeous."

How hurtful. "You could have called, Daisy."

"Look at it this way. You have plenty of leftovers now."

I'm lost for words as I experience sudden nausea.

"Violet, are you there?"

I clear my throat and wipe my eyes with my sleeve. "Can I talk to Papa?"

"He's not here at the moment."

"Did he go back to Brooklyn?"

"He went for a walk with the widow down the hall."
I hate being a part of this crazy family.

"Wish him a Happy Thanksgiving for me. Goodbye, Daisy." Anger rises inside of me.

Everyone's intently listening to Peter share about his experiences in the Navy when I return to the table. *My heart's heavy with disappointment, but I'll manage to paint a smile of approval on my face.*

"Eventually, I was encouraged by the other pilots in the squadron to apply for flight training, and I did. I followed up on this right away."

Henry leans towards his son. "I'm sure Auntie wants to hear what happened next, but I have to say your mother and I have been praying for God's will to be done in your life."

"Hmmm. Well, Aunt Flossie, several months later I was accepted into the flight training program and began the greatest adventure of my life."

Jane surprises me by taking some serving dishes to the kitchen. *She must be bored.*

Auntie wipes her mouth with a linen napkin. "The Daily News predicts the United States will send troops to Viet Nam. I hope you won't be sent there."

"I graduate from flight training in January. I have no idea what my assignment will be after that."

I put my hands on my son's shoulders. "Fascinating. I want to hear more, but can you all move into the living room while I clear the table and put away some of this food?'

Auntie picks up a few dirty dishes. "Let me help you, dear niece."

"Okay. Thanks, Auntie."

"I'm taking Pups for a walk," shouts Jane as she flees from the scene.

I'm thrilled to see father and son engaged in conversation in front of the fireplace.

"Did you ever get ahold of your father?"

"I talked to Daisy, Auntie."

"What happened to them anyway? This was a rare chance for them to catch up with Peter."

"They were invited to a doctor's estate for an early dinner in Pleasantville at the last minute. I guess we're not classy enough for them."

I was fading, going somewhere dark.

Chapter Twenty-Nine

Winter 1965 was relatively mild compared to most. At least that's what the locals said. Henry made good use of cold weekends by creating a grow light system in the basement for seedlings he grew from seed. Today, on the first day of spring, he's roto-tilling a good-sized plot so he can plant tomato, cucumber, snap beans, green peas, and green pepper seedlings. It will be twice the size of our Long Island patch.

I hate to bother him because he's so involved with his new machine. I'll wait until he turns this way. As I gaze upon the Lord's creation, I realize our house sits in the middle of a green oasis, surrounded by a forest of evergreen, birch, and maple trees. The only house we can barely see is Alexandrine's.

"Hey, Violet."

"It looks great, honey. There should be a bountiful harvest in the fall."

"I'm thinking about putting a fence around the whole thing. I want to protect it from deer and other destructive animals."

I shake my head and chuckle. "I'm going to drive up to Keeseville with some tiles. Reverend Meek told me about a couple who opened a Christian book and gift shop there."

"Where is that?"

"About two hours from here, near Schroon Lake."

"I heard on the radio this morning there's a storm brewing in Vermont and heading towards the Adirondacks. Do they know you are coming?"

"Yes. I made an appointment for 1:00. I'd better get moving, so I can get back by tonight. I left a sandwich in the refrigerator for you."

He waves me off as he starts up the tiller once again.

I smile, throw him a kiss, and take off with a couple of boxes of tiles in his car.

It's raining profusely as I pass the Glens Falls exit on the Adirondack Northway. I can barely see twenty feet in front of me. *I may have to get off in Lake George if it doesn't let up by then.* The windshield wipers swish back and forth as the deluge continues. I turn on the radio in hopes of finding a weather report for this region. *Static only.*

A flash of lightning brightens the road ahead for an instant, as a bang of thunder bolts me upright, sending two hands onto the steering wheel.

"It's two o'clock now. I won't be at Keeseville until dark if I continue at this rate. The shop will be closed anyway." *Okay. Lake George, two miles. I'm going to get off and see if I can get a hotel room. I've heard a lot about this town, and this is a good time to check it out.*

Not a car in sight. Several motels have *closed for the season* covering the signs I can see. A police car passes with red lights flashing but going in the opposite direction. The gas gauge reads a quarter of a tank. *Great. Maybe, I should turn around and follow that cop.*

Another crack of lightning. The wind howls around me as I creep north on Route 9. *There's a Howard Johnson's, and it looks like it's open.*

I pull my spring jacket over my head, grab my purse, and bolt into the brightly lit restaurant. I'm greeted with the enchanting aroma of fried clams, French fried potatoes, and bacon. Two older gentlemen are seated at the curved soda fountain counter while a blonde waitress chats with them. The lights flicker as the storm rears its ugly head around the building.

"Can I help you, Honey?"

I peer at her name tag "Yes, Gladys. This storm doesn't look like it's going to break up soon. May I see a menu?"

"You got that right. Here, take a look, but not everything on the menu is available."

A tall, skinny man with a mustache bigger than his face plops down on the stool next to me. As I examine him out of the corner of my eye, I see he is drenched from head to toe.

He pulls a cigarette from his pocket and pops it into his mouth. "Hey lady, do you have some matches?"

Gladys ignores him as she serves bowls of soup to her other customers.

He pounds his fist on the counter. "Waitress, I need a cup of coffee and a match. How about it?"

I pretend to mind my own business, but I really want to slug him one.

The lights flash on and off.

Gladys glares at the grouch. "Okay, settle down. Here's your coffee and matches."

"Now, Missy, did you decide on what you want?"

"What kind of soup do you have today?"

"Tomato."

"I'll take a bowl and a small order of fried clams. Oh, by the way, are any motels open in town?"

"Yeah, the Lido going north on 9, on the right. A few other folks headed there about a half hour ago. I sure hope there are some rooms left. I'll put your order in."

The sleaze-ball next to me blows smoke in my face. "Hey, can I hitch a ride with you? I need to get out of these wet clothes and bed down for the night. How about it?"

I take a deep breath and a sip of water. My palms are spouting geysers.

"Come on, little lady. Don't pretend I'm not here."

I want to leave, but the soup sounds too good right about now. "Well, I—"

Suddenly, the whole place is pitch black.

"Oh, good gracious!" I shout.

A hand rubs the back of my shoulder vigorously, and I try to pull away. Feet scuff on the linoleum, the rain beats against the windowpanes, and a few matches light up the surroundings to some extent. I try blinking my eyes to see who is clutching me but can see only shadows. The cold, damp clothing of the one next to me pierces my body with chills. A warm, foul breath puffs on my neck. My insides feel like they're on fire.

"It's been a long time since I've been this close to a lady."

It's the creep sitting next to me. Lord, help me now, before it's too late. In Jesus' name, hear my prayer.

"Gladys, don't you have a kerosene lamp or a flashlight around here?" yells a male voice from a short distance away.

I use all the energy I can muster, spin the stool around, and flee from the strong clutches of this restaurant gorilla.

"Now, little lady, is that anyway to treat a gentleman? I can protect you through the ugly storm." He strikes a match, and I see him stand. It goes out.

Suddenly, a hand grabs mine. "Honey, it's me Gladys," she whispers.

I can feel the counter with my right hand as she guides me with my left. I feel a door close behind me as I trust my leader to get me to a safe place. I bump my hip on the corner of something. She flicks on a flashlight.

"Okay. We're safe now. Harvey, the cook and manager, is out front with a kerosene lamp. Since we are

221

the only ladies in the joint, he said to hunker down in here until the electricity's restored."

She flicks on a flashlight and closes the door to what appears to be a well-stocked storage room filled with canned goods.

"My purse? It's out there. My keys and wallet are in there." I start to leave, but she holds me back.

"Listen, Dear, what's your name anyway?"

"Violet. I have to get my pocketbook, Gladys."

"If it's on the floor where you were sitting, it will be there later. The grizzly guy sitting next to you is more interested in you than the purse. He's wanted by the law."

Goosebumps break out all over. "How do you know that?"

"The sheriff was in here moments before you arrived with a wanted poster. We didn't get a chance to put it up. Look."

My eyes pop wide open. "That's him all right. Gladys, if I didn't get away from him when I did, no telling what would have happened."

"He escaped from the Adirondack Correctional facility."

"Did you lock this door?"

"Look, it has a dead bolt on the inside. We're safe."

"Sal Gigli. Charged with three counts of assault and battery. Dear God, thank You for protecting Gladys and me. May you keep this man from harming anyone else. Amen."

Gladys nudges me as we sit on the cold cement floor. "Are you one of those Bible thumpers?"

I chuckle under my breath. "I believe in Jesus and the Holy Bible, if that's what you mean."

She taps me. "Listen."

Ear splitting pounding on the door and relentless jiggling of the doorknob permeates the air around us.

Chapter Thirty

"Open the door, girls, or I'll huff and puff and blow your house down," shouts the creepy but recognizable voice.

We grip each other, trembling in utter silence.

"Don't worry, he can't get in here," she whispers.

The sound of his body slamming against the door, once then twice, I can't speak. The words won't come. This is a nightmare. "Is there any other way out of this room, Gladys?"

"Harvey claims there's an entry way to a crawl space over there in the corner, but I never paid attention to it. I think it best to stay put for now. I wonder where Harvey is?"

"Shh, shh. I think he's gone."

Again, total silence embraces our existence as we sit in a state of bewilderment.

She flips the flashlight on and stands. "I'm looking for that other way out. It's too quiet out there."

The walls are built like Fort Knox, with cement blocks all around. Three large cardboard boxes filled with toilet paper are stacked in the corner.

"Gladys, did you hear that noise at the door?" I whisper.

"What noise?"

A picking sound near the dead bolt on the door catches her attention. She grabs my hand. The picking is getting louder. She covers the flashlight with her hand to dim the beam.

I point to the screw turning.

She nudges me and points to our escape route.

"How do you know this is the spot?" I whisper.

She shines the light up to the ceiling, where there's a plastic covered opening about three feet square. Gladys climbs on the box. "Hold the flashlight. I'm going up."

My knees are weak, and I'm shaking like I put my finger into an electric socket.

She scales the boxes with her hands and feet, with her wobbly ladder beneath her. The noise at the door causes the flashlight to detour from its focal point. The doorknob's jiggling, but the person on the other side can't get the best of it.

"Violet, give me some light, will ya?" she softly shouts.

As I shine the light on the spot, all I see are her feet pulling through the hole out of sight. *It's either now or never. Oh, Lord, give me a boost. Get us both to safety.*

The door's heaving in and out as I follow Gladys up the make-shift steps. I catch my foot on my skirt and everything wobbles. I freeze in place.

'Violet, hand me the flashlight."

I look up at the face of Angel Gladys, and I realize I'm close to freedom.

"Hurry."

She lends me a hand, and I drag myself into the attic. We flick the light off, cover the hole, and sit in silence above the clatter of a broken-down door below us.

Gladys nudges me with a finger over her mouth. I know to be quiet.

Police sirens are sounding off outside. The flashing red lights illuminate the attic, but we sit and wait.

"Sheriff, in here."

"This is a storage room, Deputy. Loaded with goods, no people, let alone a convict."

"Scan every corner. Harvey told the ladies to stay in here but no sign of them."

"The door was broken down when I got here, Sheriff. Maybe Gigli has the women."

"The power company's working on restoring the electricity, but until then we have to rely on the headlights from our cars."

I start to move, but Gladys pulls me back. "Wait a little bit. Harvey knows about the attic. He'll tell the cops. That hoodlum could be hiding in the kitchen somewhere."

"Look, could we crawl out that window onto the roof? We can call for help when we see the police leave."

"It's pouring rain out there," she whispers.

Silence controls us as we wait and wait. *For what? I must call Henry. He must be frantic.*

A gun shot startles both of us.

"Come on. Your idea of the roof sounds good right now."

We crawl on old carpet remnants to the window, lift the bottom pane, and, one behind the other, crawl onto the roof. The rain immediately saturates us as we watch the two cop cars fly out of the empty parking lot to pursue their target.

"I live just over there. We should be able to scramble down the side of the building on the brick side. I go out there to take a puff now and then. The bricks jut out in places."

I wipe wet hair from my eyes. "What about this Gigli fella?"

She points in the direction the police went. "He's long gone. Follow me."

Shivering from head to toe, we hike our skirts up above our knees and take two bricks at a time. When we finally reach the ground, we hug like two drowned rats.

She peeks in the windows. "Everyone's gone. Harvey must think we got away."

"The rain's letting up, and the wind has subsided. I think the storm's over."

"Gladys, I'm still frightened out of my wits. That felon could be hiding anywhere."

"Oh, he probably ran along the railroad tracks to catch a freight train to Canada. Relax, Violet. The lights will come back on soon, and everything will turn back to normal."

A car passes as we walk up the path to her house, with the flashlight beaming a path to follow. She unlocks the porch door and locks it immediately after us.

"One more door. I'll get you a change of clothes. You and I are about the same size. She shines the flashlight on her watch as we squeak along with sopping wet feet.

"Do you think your telephone's working, Gladys?"

"Let's try, okay?" She takes the receiver off the wall and listens.

"No dial tones. I should know better. When the lights go out, so does the telephone."

I sneeze several times as I shake to my core. "My husband must be sick with worry. I should have been home hours ago."

"Here, a dry pair of trousers, brand new underwear, and a warm sweater should do the trick." She lights several candles to illuminate the small living room, dining combo. "You can change in the bathroom to your right. Take the flashlight."

"Thanks. You'd better change too."

The small, blue-toned bathroom is immaculately clean with a seashell shower curtain completely covering the bathtub behind it. *He could be hiding there.* Goosebumps cover my arms as I yank the plastic aside.

I gasp. *I'm worrying about nothing. God forgive me for not trusting You. I thank You for my angel in disguise, Gladys. I pray I can lead her to You, Jesus. Amen.*

I'm amazed at how well the dry clothes fit. I wrap a towel around my wet hair, hang my wet ones over the shower bar, and proceed out the door.

Gladys is not alone.

"Violet, I can explain why he's here. Harvey and I have been dating for a long time. He was worried about us when we weren't in the storage room."

I pull the towel off my head and breathe a long sigh of relief. "Did they apprehend the criminal? I was wondering why you didn't come to our rescue, Harvey."

"That jerk hit me over the head with a frying pan when I tried to apprehend him. There's an all-points bulletin out for his arrest. Is this your pocketbook?"

"Yes. Thank you. My car keys are hopefully in here."

"Is your car a grey 1959 Chevy?"

"Yes, why do you ask?"

"It was the only car in the Ho Jo parking lot when I left."

Gladys and I chuckle. "We didn't even notice. Our only interest was to get away from Gigli as fast as we could and get out of our drenched clothes."

I look at the contents of my purse. "Keys, intact wallet, sunglasses, several paperback New Testaments, and map. Yep, everything's here."

Gladys lights a kerosene lamp. "Harvey is going to sleep on the couch tonight. Do you want something to eat before you turn in, Violet?"

Even though her hair is bleached blonde, she has a wrinkled face.

"You're so nice, Gladys. God placed you in my life at the right time. He knew I needed someone to help me get to safety. I wasn't about to let myself get kidnapped a second time."

"You were kidnapped?" They both sit at attention.

"Yes, a few years ago when we lived on Long Island. Through prayer and trusting in God, I was able to escape after ten days of captivity."

Harvey grabs his girlfriend's hand. "Tell us more about this God of yours. You talk like He is a real person or something."

"The Bible says God is triune, meaning He is three people in one. God the Father, Jesus the Son, and the Holy Spirit."

"Which one do you believe in?"

"When I accepted Jesus into my life, I got the whole package."

A tea kettle whistles from the kitchen, and Gladys runs for it. "Got to love Sterno. Works every time."

A few minutes later, we are sipping hot tea, enjoying each other's company, and forgetting completely about a storm or an escaped convict.

"We've been holding off getting married because he's Catholic and I'm not. He goes to his church, and I go when I feel like it."

"It's not about a church or religion. It's about a relationship with Jesus and growing spiritually by reading the Bible."

Gladys blows her nose as tears stream down her cheeks. "How can I know Jesus, Violet?"

"I John 5:12 says, 'He that hath the Son hath life; and he that hath not the Son of God hath not life.'"

Harvey kisses her on the cheek. "Tell us how we can be sure Jesus is in our lives."

My heart is overjoyed as I lead them into a prayer of acceptance of the Savior.

The Lord God lights up my darkness. The electricity's restored.

Chapter Thirty-One

"It was an awful night, Henry. If it weren't for my new friend, Gladys, I don't know where I would be right now."

"Henry clears his throat. "I warned you about the storm, Violet."

"I know. I had no way of getting a hold of you. The power was restored up here a little while ago."

Gladys motions for me to eat some bacon and eggs.

"Please come home, now, Vi."

"I'll be home by noon, Honey. I better eat something before it gets cold."

"Okay. I love you."

"I love you too."

The three of us enjoy hot coffee, rye toast, crispy bacon, and scrambled eggs with chives. We laugh about the escapades the night before but thank God periodically that Sal Gigli didn't abduct either of us.

Harvey takes a sip of coffee. "I wonder if they captured the bum yet. I'd better turn on the radio, or better yet, I'll call the police station."

"Are you still going up to Keeseville, Violet?"

"I would like to, since I am so close, but my husband thinks I'm on my way home."

"Well, I have the day off if you want some company."

"Hmmm. What time is it?"

"Eight-thirty."

"Okay. Let's do it. Can we get out of here within an hour?"

"You bet we can. After all, we are quite the team after last night."

As we clear the table, Harvey's disturbed look catches our attention. "What did you find out?"

"They couldn't find a trace of Gigli anywhere until an hour ago. He was found sound asleep in your car, Violet."

∞⦿♋☜∞

All that was left of the creep by the time we arrived at my car was his repulsive body odor. We leave Lake George with the windows down.

As we head north, we find many trees down and crews working hard to clean it up. The sun beams down on the wet macadam, and the smell of pine seeps into the car through opened windows. The dense forest creeping up the Adirondack Mountains lines either side of the road.

Gladys pats my shoulder. "There doesn't seem to be any power lines down up here."

I sigh. "Isn't this an absolutely beautiful drive? I've heard so much about the beautiful colors in the fall and how magnificent White Face Mountain looks in winter, but it's amazing how fresh spring appears."

"Look, finally a sign. Keeseville. Population: 875."

"The place looks deserted, Gladys. How in the world will my tiles sell way up here?"

"Yeah, I'm thinking the same thing. Where is everybody?"

"The bookstore is supposed to be to the right after crossing Main Street Bridge."

"This bridge sure is old. Hope it doesn't collapse while we cross."

"There it is. Keeseville Christian Books and Gifts."

Bells jingle and wood floors creak as we walk through the door. Soft classical music fills our ears as we are greeted by a variety of unusual gifts, and the aroma of fresh coffee grabs our attention.

An attractive, pleasantly plump lady with a big smile appears from behind a rack of cards. "Can I help you ladies today?"

"Yes, I have an appointment with Ida Davis."

"Are you Violet Funk?"

"I am. This is my friend Gladys."

"Pleased to me you. I'm Ida. We were worried when you didn't show up yesterday. Then, we heard on the radio about the awful storm that swept through the Lake George, Lake Luzerne area, leaving the whole area without power. I hope you didn't get anywhere near that escaped criminal."

Gladys chimes in and tells the story as Ida hangs on every word. They don't pay any attention to me going back and forth to the car for boxes of tiles.

"Do you need any help?" a dark-curly-haired gentleman with horn-rimmed glasses asks.

"Oh, thank you. Can you take the rack out of the trunk?"

"Sure. I'm Lenny Davis. You must be Violet."

They purchase a rack and enough tiles to fill it. They're so impressed with Gladys and her new-found faith in Jesus. She's been talking nonstop since we got here.

"Here is a new King James Bible for you, Dear." Lois smiles.

"I've never owned my own Bible. Can I pay you for it?"

"It's a gift. I always tell new believers to start with the book of John because it explains in depth why we must be born again."

"Are you ladies hungry? I bet you haven't had any lunch."

I grab the empty boxes and head for the door. "We really should be going. I told my husband I would be home by noon, and it is well passed that now."

"I think we could spare another half hour for a quick bite, Violet. I'm starved. What do you say?"

"I guess its okay. Where's a good place to eat in this town?"

"We close the store for an hour every day for lunch. Lenny, put the sign on the door so we can treat these ladies to a Davis kind of meal."

They lead us to the back of the store and up a flight of stairs to the most adorable apartment I have ever seen. Everything is white with shades of blue for drapery and accents. A well-appointed kitchen blends nicely into a dining space and living area. A wonderful aroma of onions and garlic makes my tummy flutter.

"Lois, can I use your telephone to call my husband?"

"Of course. It's right around the corner in the hallway. You go ahead and dial direct. No need for calling collect."

"I'll call collect. It will be an expensive call from here."

"I won't hear of it, my dear. You gave us a huge discount on the tiles."

Not knowing what to say, I stammer and fiddle with my hair.

"You better make that call, Honey, before your hubby sends out the cavalry," says Gladys.

Shaking my head, I make my way to the telephone. It sits on an antique desk with a small tiffany lamp, and I pull out a charming upholstered chair to rest my bottom on.

I spin the numbers, one by one, on the dial. After a long pause, ringing greets my ears.

"Hi, honey, How's the weather there?"

"Where in the world are you, Violet?"

"Whoa. Settle down. Give me a moment to explain."

"Please tell me you're almost home."

"No, I'm in Keeseville, delivering the order."

"You should be home. Not gallivanting. Do you know where Jane is?"

"Isn't she in her room?"

"She's been gone all day, and I know she's not at work."

"Maybe she's with her new friend Anita."

"First time I heard about her. Where does this girl live?"

"She lives on Kinns Road. Anita is horse crazy and has one of her own. Look around for a note. It's not like her to not come home without letting us know where she is."

"This is ridiculous. I want you home, Vi."

"We are getting a bite to eat, but I promise to be on the road in a half hour. Her last name is Pillar. Should be in the phone book."

"I'm sorry if I sound cross, but I worry about my girls when they're not home. I love you, Honey."

"I love you too. See you soon."

The table is dressed in an ivory lace tablecloth. Chicken salad sandwiches and steaming bowls of onion soup are ready for the taking. All eyes are on me as I take my seat.

"Lenny, will you ask the blessing for us?" Ida asks.

"Dear Lord, thank you for getting Violet and Gladys through the horrendous storm last night and for getting them safely here today. God bless Violet as she serves you with her ceramic tiles. We ask that You bless the food before us, and we thank You for it. Amen."

Gladys rubs my arm. "Is everything all right at home?"

"My husband worries when I'm out for long periods of time. He'll be fine when I'm home safe. It's my daughter, Jane. She didn't come home last night."

Ida lets out a long sigh. "Oh, God, we pray for Jane's safety and that you will return her home safely. Amen."

I glance at my watch and take a sip of the delicious soup.

"If I'm lucky, I should be home before dark, if we leave in a half hour."

Lois passes the sandwiches. "Violet, have you gone to the bookstore at Word of Life camps?"

"Yes, I have because I investigated the island for my daughter. Do you think they would be interested in the tiles?"

"Absolutely. They have three camps on Schroon Lake. It's right on your way to Lake George. The main store is at the Inn. Isn't it open until 5:00 during the week, Lenny?"

"Yes, it is. You should stop on your way."

I sip my coffee. "It does sound like a good place for my tiles, but I better get home."

The grandfather clock in the corner chimes three times. I jump to my feet and a half-cup of coffee slides off the table to the floor. "I'm so sorry."

Immediately, Gladys picks up the broken cup and mops up the liquid with her napkin.

"You have a lot on your mind, Violet. You two had better get going. Lenny will take care of everything so I can open the shop." Ida smiles.

∽☙❧∽

I find when I'm driving alone praying out loud makes the time go by. I don't worry about what other people think when they see my mouth moving with no one in the car. Little do they know, God's right next to me.

"Lord, this has been a crazy two days. I was almost abducted again, my car could have been hijacked, the power was out during a horrific storm, and I was stranded in Lake George overnight at someone's house I just met. You took care of me. Thank you, Jesus. The Davis's bought tiles, which more than paid for the trip. I pray Gladys and Harvey find a good church so they can grow spiritually. Lord, I ask that my daughter be home when I get there. Amen."

Chapter Thirty-Two

The house is dark when I pull up and open the garage door. I flick the light on, grab my bag, and shut the overhead door. Pups lets out a huge howl, which sends my heart in a grand leap. *Why is the place like a tomb?*

"Henry, Jane? I'm home."

The television blares static, and the smell of burnt toast permeates air. "Hello. Is anyone home?"

I turn down the television so I can hear anything that tells me I'm not alone.

Bang. A door slams from the bedroom wing.

Henry plows through the double door and heads directly to the refrigerator for a cold Coca-Cola.

"Is Jane in her room, Henry?"

He all but drops his drink as he turns on a pivot. "Vi, when did you get here? You scared the wits out of me."

I rush to his side and fling my arms around him, although I feel like I'm hugging a tree. "It's so good to be home. Where's Jane? Did you eat supper?"

"Slow down, woman. Your daughter's impossible to deal with, and she won't tell me where she was last night. When I look in her eyes, I see an incredibly sad girl." He pulls away, turns up the volume on the television, and parks himself in his worn-out recliner.

The six o'clock news. Everyone must be quiet, including me.

I open and close the refrigerator two times, clean off the counter, and stare into the darkness out the window. "Jane? Supper? Which?" I mumble.

I venture down the dark hallway and knock on the mahogany door in front of me. "Jane, it's Mom."

"Leave me alone."

I fidget with the door but, unfortunately, it's locked. "Please open. I want to talk to you."

No answer.

"Don't you want to hear about my escapades over the past couple of days?"

"Not really."

"I passed a dude ranch coming back from Lake George today. There were at least a couple dozen horses grazing in one of their pastures."

Thump, thump, thump. The door flings open to a dark, dreary room with an odor enough to choke a cat. Pups leaps off the bed and darts past me. Clothes are strewn everywhere, open bags of chips sit on the floor next to the bed, half-filled Coca-Cola bottles wait on the debris-filled desk, and she is wrapped up in her blanket like it's a cocoon.

I sit down next to her and rub my hands through her thick, curly hair, wondering how I can help this child. *Lord, I pray mental anguish doesn't rear its ugly head in my daughter.*

"Maybe you can go with me to Word of Life next week. They may be interested in the tiles. If we leave early enough, there should be time to stop at the dude ranch on the way. How about it?"

Her body trembles, accompanied by muffled whimpering. "You know, I have to work almost every day. So how can I go with you, huh?"

Lord, help me here. Please. Jane needs to know how to lean on You. Help her snap out of this depression.

"I'm going to make supper now, Jane. Unless you have something you want to say."

She doesn't move or speak, but I decide to turn on a light and open the door.

"I wasn't with Anita last night. I was with Bruce."

My heart skips a beat, and I want to let out a scream. Instead, I stand in silence.

"Aren't you going to say anything, Mom?"

"Did you sleep with him?"

She sits up on the edge of her bed. "No. We were playing cards with his mother and aunt. Time ran away from us. It was too late to call home. Don't worry, I slept on the couch. By myself."

I rush to her side and hug her. "You have been spending a lot of time with Bruce. I have told you so many times, things you don't want to happen very often do in the heat of the moment."

"It's so hard when you love the person."

"Oh Jane, he's your first serious boyfriend. Be careful. Has he told you that he loves you?"

"Not really."

"Bruce is a very polite fella, but he's a mechanic. Maybe you ought to spread your wings a little and date some other people."

"No. No. No. He treats me like a princess. Someday, we'll get married. You'll see. Who cares what he does for a living?"

A wave of anger and sadness washes over me. I want to say more but the words don't form. "Your father is hungry, and it has been a long day for me. I must go make supper. Please clean your room and join us in a half hour, okay?"

"I'm not hungry." She falls back in bed.

I decide it is best to leave her be to avoid confrontation. I escape to the kitchen to finish the task at hand. *If I know my daughter, she'll be out here as soon as she smells the onions and garlic frying.*

Frozen hamburgers come in handy at a time like this. They slowly brown as they thaw in the electric frying pan. *These green beans are still fresh. Good.* I pour cooking oil into a large pot and set the burner on low while I cut potatoes into strips for French fries.

Henry plops himself at the counter with confusion written all over his face.

"What's the matter, Dear?" I ask.

"It's almost 8:00, and I'm famished but also concerned about our daughter. She spends far too much time with that Bruce fella. I listened at the door."

I look past him to be sure the double door to the hallway is shut. "It's been hard for her since we moved here, you know. She only has one girlfriend, Anita. If she didn't get that job as a type setter at Cromwell in Albany, she wouldn't have a boyfriend."

"Have car, will travel. Sometimes I wonder if I did the right thing by loaning her money so she could buy her first car. Always gallivanting here, there, and everywhere."

I turn to flip the garlic burgers and slice up some onions to fry with them. "Stay right there, because dinner's almost ready."

"She loves that Dodge Dart convertible, Henry. We have to pray for Jane to get involved with some Christian young adults."

I carefully lift the fryer out of the oil, drain the fries, blot the grease off with a paper towel, and scoop a batch on a plate with the other food. "Here you go, Honey."

He bows his head. "Thank You, Lord, for the food before us. Thank You for getting my beautiful wife through another ordeal and back home safely. We pray for Jane to find some Christian friends. In Jesus' name. Amen."

Boom! The double doors burst open.

"I hope there's enough for me. I'm starving," Jane blurts out as she plops down next to her dad.

The ringing of the telephone catches us all off guard, as we are so engrossed in eating our long overdue supper. We all have mouths full of food as the ringing relentlessly continues. I swallow the last bite and grab the phone off the hook. "Hello."

"Hello, Mrs. Funk. Is Jane there?"

"Just a moment."

Reluctantly, I wave the phone at my daughter. "Jane. It's for you."

"Who is it?" She mouths without sound.

"It sounds like Bruce."

She waves her arms emphatically and shakes her head to imply a firm no.

"Bruce? I'm sorry, but Jane is not able to come to the phone at this time."

"Please tell her I called, okay?"

"I can do that. Goodnight."

"What did he want?"

"You, of course. He wants you to call him back."

"Got any more hamburgers? I'm still hungry."

The kid is like a bottomless pit. Eats and eats but stays slim.

After dinner, I fill the sink with sudsy water. "There's a few chocolate chip cookies left and ice cream in the freezer. Otherwise, the kitchen is closed."

Jane leaves her dirty plate on the counter, grabs cookies, whistles for Pups, and scampers out of sight.

The last dish is put away, and the counters are wiped down. I'm exhausted. *I'll always praise You, Lord, for getting me out of two hair raising situations unscathed. If You weren't the Lord of my life, I would be back in a sanitarium.*

After taking a quick shower and getting into my leopard silk pajamas, I join Henry in the living room with a hot cup of milk.

"Oh, it feels so good to relax in the safety of our home. I can't get last night out of my mind and that I could have been kidnapped once again. God is so good to me, Henry."

Is he sleeping? If he is, he isn't snoring like he normally does.

"Henry?"

He turns to me slowly with a very disturbed look. "I'm trying to watch the rest of Perry Mason. Please be quiet."

I swallow my heart.

Chapter Thirty-Three

1966

The wind howls around the house as a blizzard of astronomic proportions dumps snow everywhere. Thank God, we still have power, and the refrigerator and pantry are fully stocked. Henry was able to shovel a substantial area on the deck for Pups to do his thing.

"Is that dog scratching on that glass door again?" Henry roars.

I shake my head. "He's one spoiled dog, but you can't blame him for wanting to come back in. I know I wouldn't want to be out in this stuff either."

"That hill is dreadful to get up when there's the slightest bit of snow on it," Henry adds.

"The weatherman says the storm will continue for at least two more days. Jane's car is stuck at the bottom of the hill until the neighbor can plow it. I trudged down there early this morning to make sure the emergency break was on and the doors locked."

I hand my husband a fresh, hot cup of coffee. "I'm glad it's New Year's Day with blizzard warnings because she'll have to stay home all day."

We both chuckle while the dog sprawls out on the rug in front of the warm fireplace. The wood pops sparks as it burns colorful shades of yellow, orange, and red.

I rest in his arms as the snow continues to fall outside, and overwhelming peace fills the household. "Did you see the invitation to Daisy's wedding?"

He kisses my head. "Valentine's Day, huh? I didn't think your sister was a romantic of any sort. In fact, I was beginning to wonder if she would ever have a social life outside of the hospital."

"It's going to be a small wedding with immediate family only. Doctor Albert Roth is an only child, but his parents live in New Jersey, so they'll be there."

"I hope we don't have another snowstorm to prevent us from going."

"Now, now. Don't be so negative, Honey. I must get there. After all, I'm the matron of honor. How about some pancakes and bacon?"

"Let me hold you for a little bit longer."

The telephone catches our attention, and I leap off the couch to get it.

"Hello?"

"Hi, Mother."

"Peter?"

"I see on the news that you're getting blasted with snow. Are you alright?"

"We're fine, Son. Dad loaded up the wood box with plenty of logs to burn, and I went shopping and loaded up on every supply you can imagine. How are you?"

"I hope you're sitting down. I have some news for you."

"Why do I have to sit down? I'm making breakfast. I'm giving the phone to Daddy. He's anxious to talk to you."

"I love you, Mom."

I love you too."

Henry's beaming from ear to ear as I hand him the phone. "Hi, Son. They're not shipping you out again?"

"I decided to leave the Navy."

"What? You're being discharged from the Navy?"

"No, Dad. I served my time and then some. I'm leaving active duty, but I'll stay in the Navy reserve. It's time to move on with my life."

"You make it sound like this is a good decision all the way around."

"I hope you understand. I'm going to fly for commercial airlines."

"Will you be able to come home soon? For your mother's birthday?"

"Is Mother right there?"

Yes, she is."

"I'm coming home in a few days."

I lean into the phone and perch on the stool. "I love you, Peter. God has a plan for your life."

"I want you both to know that I gave this a lot of thought."

"I'll be all right after it settles in my mind for a few days. Your room will be ready for you when you get here. Here's your father." My mouth's dry. I didn't know what else to say.

"I'll pick you up at the airport, Son."

"Bye, Dad"

We sit in silence for a few minutes, holding onto our thoughts.

Jane bursts into the room. "Got any bacon left? I'm starving. Why didn't you wake me up?"

"We wanted you to catch up on your sleep, Dear. Come sit at the counter. I'll make you some breakfast. You can see we are snowed in, so there's no need to get stressed out. I haven't seen a snowplow go by once."

"Our hill is ridiculous. I can never get the car up, even when there's a dusting of snow."

Henry takes the last bite of pancake and swallows with a swig of coffee. "Tot, be grateful you have a roof over your head and parents who love you, even when things are not going so good for you. I'm going to take a shower and get dressed."

I hand her a plate of food. "As soon as the snow lets up, we'll all venture down the hill and clear off the driveway. Let's put it this way, if you came home at a decent hour last night, your car would be at the top of the hill."

She starts shoveling the food into her mouth as if someone might take it away from her.

"Jane, please take the time and say grace."

"Grace."

I shrug my shoulders. "Lord, thank You for this warm house and for the food in front of Jane. I pray You would bless it to her body. I pray for Peter, who'll be home in a couple of days. I pray he comes to know You as his Lord and Savior. Amen."

When I open my eyes, I find my daughter staring at me. "Why is Peter coming home, Mom?"

"Peter's leaving active duty from the Navy. He served our country by flying a hundred missions and had a lot of close calls. He's going to fly for commercial airlines."

"I know he wrote you and Daddy a long letter about what happened on the Oriskany, but I never read it. Do you still have it?"

"I do. It's in my Bible on the end table next to the couch. Go get it and read it to me while I clean up the kitchen."

She returns to the counter with my favorite book. "Wow, Mom, you have this thing all marked up. Is it okay to write in a Bible like this?"

I chuckle as I load the dishes into the sudsy water. "When God speaks to me through His word, I must write it down. Did you find the letter?"

She pulls out a folded piece of paper and opens it. "This is his handwriting."

"I'm listening."

"Dear Mother, I've been lucky with the near-death experience I have encountered. I'm still recovering from the October 26, 1966, nightmare on the USS Oriskany. The ship caught fire early in the morning, not far from my compartment. I woke up early because I was assigned to fly to Subic Bay, Philippines, to pick up an overhauled aircraft. The fire killed forty-eight sailors, most pilots, like me, lived. The fire almost destroyed the entire ship. I'm lucky to be alive and glad to be back in the states. I love you, Peter."

"Peter's making the right decision. I needed to hear those words again to put me in that frame of mind," Henry comments as he puts his hat and coat on.

"Where are you going in this storm, Dad?"

"I'm going to try to get your car up the hill."

The sun's shining, the sky's brilliant blue, and the long, hilly driveway is clear of the white stuff. Mr. Alexandrine was Johnny on the spot when the snow ceased from falling. He saw Henry shoveling a small patch at the bottom of the hill and offered to plow the entire mountain for fifteen dollars.

"Thanks, Mother, for the clean towels and loads of hangers in the closet. You remembered how I like to take all my clothes out of the suitcase and hang them up." Peter hugs me tight.

"I'm so happy you're home with us for a few days. God answered our prayers and kept you safe through all of your challenges."

"Something saved me from death, but I'm not sure what. I have some great news to share with you and Dad. I'm so excited about it."

"Your father won't be home for another hour. Please tell the news."

"You have to wait, Mom. What are you making for supper? Something smells mighty good."

"Pot roast. Your favorite."

"Where's my little sister? Out with that boyfriend of hers again?"

"Isn't she in her room?"

"No, but it sure is a mess in there. If I didn't know better, it smells like a cat's litter box when you open the door. She should be grounded until she cleans her room."

"Check and see if her car is in the garage."

"Already did. Car's gone."

"She has disappeared every Friday night for the past month, other than the night of the big blizzard."

"What? You mean to tell me you let her get away with that?"

"I'm going to check out her room and see if there are any phone numbers or something marked on the wall calendar."

I dart around her room, picking up clothes, and begin to organize the closet. That's when I see it. A litter box. For cats. I turn on my heels with my hands on my hips. *Does Jane have a cat in here?*

I close the bedroom door and make the bed.

Meow.

I lift the bed ruffle and crouch down on all fours. A very scrawny, orange kitten darts past me into the closet. *Henry will be horrified to know there's a cat in this house.*

I slink over to the closet and sweep the small animal off its feet and into my arms. "Hello, little one. I don't know how long you can get away with hiding out in here. I guess you're Jane's and my little secret."

A gentle knock on the door startles me, so I hide the cute animal in a dresser drawer. "Is that you, Peter?"

He opens the door a crack. "Wow, sure looks a lot better in here. Did you find any clues that could help us figure out where she is?"

Lord, please keep that kitten quiet, because Son isn't crazy about cats. "I'll be with you in a minute, Peter."

I uncover a January calendar and see every Friday filled in with the words, *GO, GO Dance at Finnegan's bar and grill in Troy, 8-midnight.*

Closing the bedroom door behind me, I knock on my son's door. "Peter?"

"Come in, Mom."

"You're not going to believe this, but your sister is a go-go dancer at a bar and grill every Friday night."

"Jane's a sneaky one. Where did you and Dad think she was anyway?"

"She's been dating Bruce for quite a while now. We thought she was with him on these nights."

"I don't like this at all, Mom. She's in a vulnerable situation being the young, attractive girl she is, with men of all ages looking her up and down, as she shakes her booty."

I sit down on the bed. "Jane's always trying to find a way to get people to like her. She's the limelight in this situation, for sure. Some drunk could grab her when she walks to her car."

"We better go tell Dad."

Henry and Peter decide to go and get her immediately. I call the place to get directions and send them on their way. "I'll be praying you there and back, boys. Be careful."

Chapter Thirty-Four

It's 11:30 pm and still no word. I heat up some milk in a saucepan and glare out into the darkness, with the moon glimmering on top of the swaying treetops, dancing in the wind. *Oh Lord, my God. Help my daughter to find stability in her life and to realize how valuable she is to You.*

Warm milk always relaxes my entire being. I lean back on the sofa and close my eyes for a minute or two or more.

I hear voices, but it's hard to discern if I'm dreaming, or are they real? I try talking, but my mouth only moves. *Wake up, Violet.*

"I can't believe how you embarrassed me tonight, Big Brother. Really. Couldn't you at least wait until my shift was over?" Jane screeches over me somewhere.

"You have no business being in a bar, nevertheless, working in one. That dress was mighty short, even if there were shorts underneath," growls Peter.

I wake up with a start as the blanket falls to the floor. "What's going on here?"

Jane's curled up on the couch with tears glistening down her face. "Ask your son."

I look around the room and find the men are gone. I put my arm around my daughter and pull her to my side. *Lord, help me to choose my words carefully.*

After a brief silence. "I was going to quit tonight anyway, Mom. Peter made a big scene."

"Oh, Honey, I'm sure you thought it was all in fun, but you were putting yourself in a very vulnerable situation. Your brother was very worried about you because he knows full well what happens to men when they have too much to drink.'

"You know how much I love to dance, Mom? Discotheques and go-go boots are all the rage right now. Sally from work has been dancing there for a year and never had one problem."

The grandfather clock strikes twelve with consecutive gongs. "Are you hungry, Jane?"

"I could eat a sandwich. How about you?"

"Ham and cheese on rye sounds swell right about now."

Pups jumps up on her lap as I bolt off the couch with an extra burst of energy. *It's late, Lord, but the quality time with my daughter is irreplaceable.*

We munch on our sandwiches and sip glasses of milk. Moments of silence still find a path to the bond we're finally building. The dog's head rests on her lap as she feeds him bits of ham. I grin from ear to ear. *She loves her dog. Oh, my goodness, the kitten.*

"Jane, I know about the kitten in your room."

She nods. "I tried to hide her, but the truth is out, huh? Does Daddy know?"

"No, he doesn't, but you better tell him. She's an adorable little thing, but you know how your father feels about cats."

"I couldn't resist taking her home with me. She appeared, all scraggly and skinny, when I was at the laundry mat. I popped her in the laundry basket, and you know the rest of the story."

"Listen, Dear, I'll show the kitten to your dad after Peter leaves. He knows how much you love animals and that might soften his heart to let you keep her. Do you have a name?"

"Not really. I call her Little One."

I squeeze her and rub her head. "How about, Poosie?"

We both laugh as we watch the embers on the logs in the fireplace burn out.

"I think we better call it a night. It's 1:30 in the morning."

As I turn off the lights, she turns to me and whispers, "Mom, the owner of Finnegan's wanted me to wear a very skimpy costume the next time I danced. He was pushing for me to make the change tonight, but I refused. This was long before I was dragged out of there by my brother. I wasn't planning on going back."

Peter left after a long weekend, and we never told him about the cat. It turns out that Henry couldn't say no to his little girl, after all. Oddly enough, the dog and the growing kitten get along like two peas in a pod. All of us are getting a kick out of watching the kitten play with Pup's tail.

"I'd like to make a long-distance phone call please. Yes, I can wait."

"The number, please?"

"It's 212-555-1616. Daisy Moretti."

I wonder if she's home, as the ringing continues to burn in my ear.

"Hello?"

"Daisy? It's Violet."

"It's good to hear your voice."

"I know it's been awhile since we've talked. How's Papa?"

"Papa is ill, Violet."

251

"Oh, no. I wish he would answer the phone. What's wrong with him?"

"Sick to his stomach and diarrhea."

"Stomachaches? I know he eats a lot of rich foods. Italian one night, Chinese the next, pastrami sandwiches in between, not to mention homemade knishes his Jewish friends give him."

"He's starting to come out of it now. He wants to take us all to dinner."

"You want us to have dinner with you, Albert, and Papa?"

"Yes, this Saturday at Jack's Oyster house in Albany."

"We can meet you in Albany, sure. When?"

"Seven. I'll bring your dress for the wedding."

"I can't wait to see it."

"Okay, we'll see you at Jack's at 7:00."

"I love you, Sis."

"I love you, Daisy."

Well, that's a switch. Usually, I'm the one that says I love you first, without a response back.

"Who were you talking to?" asks Henry, coming from the garage.

He catches me off guard while I'm checking the meatloaf in the oven. "Ohoo, you scared me. I wasn't expecting you until 7:00."

He gives me a peck on the cheek. "So, who were you talking to?"

"Daisy."

"The wedding's in two weeks. Is she ready for it?"

"They want to take us out to dinner at Jack's Oyster House on Friday night. She's going to bring my dress so I can try it on."

"Will it be Albert and her?"

"Papa's coming with them. He stays at Daisy's a lot these days."

"Maybe I should let you spend time with them alone. I can come home and make a sandwich or something."

"I want you with me, Henry. You're my husband after all."

"What about Jane? I hope she's invited. She loves her grandpa and would be upset if she's left out of this occasion."

"We're a package deal. It's all of us or none. She can invite Bruce if she wants to."

"Where is she anyway? I didn't see her car."

"With him."

"You don't sound too excited about it. I have to say she has been much better to deal with ever since that go-go dancing ordeal."

"She has been dating Bruce, on and off, for at least a year, and he never asks us for her hand in marriage. He clearly loves her, and she seems to feel the same way. I'm impressed that she's always home at a reasonable hour too."

A lightly snow-covered sidewalk greets us as we get out of the car and make our way to the glass door entrance to Jack's. The restaurant is known for fresh oysters, either raw in the half shell or in potato stew. The aroma of fresh brewed coffee and homemade bread embraces us as we move our way to the maître d'. *A cup of that coffee sounds good right about now.*

The reserved-looking gentleman dressed in a starched black tuxedo jacket, white shirt, and black bowtie grimaces. "Do you have a reservation?"

"We are with the Moretti party," Henry offers softly.

He looks at us with admiration as though we're wearing crowns. "Please, follow me."

A large, round table set for seven occupies the farthest corner of the dimly lit room. Jane and Bruce gravitate to Papa instantly. She hugs her grampa and introduces her date to everyone.

"Hi, Papa," I say as I kiss him on the cheek.

"Daughter, it's been a long time. Nice to see you."

We start with Manhattan clam chowder and a tray of assorted relishes. Most of us have the oyster stew, but Jane, Bruce, and Henry have filet mignon. I notice Papa's appetite is not what it used to be, and his suit jacket appears to be two sizes too big for him. The glass of white wine seems to appeal to him more than anything else.

"Grampa, you're not eating," Jane remarks rather loudly.

He winks at her. "I'm savoring this glass of wine before I indulge, my dear one."

Bruce puts his arm around her chair as he takes a bite of steak. "I can't believe how fast you eat, Jane."

"My granddaughter loves to eat, Son. How she stays so slim is beyond me. She takes after me for sure. Never been crazy about vegetables but everything else goes down the hatch without a hitch."

Laughter encompasses the table, but Jane drops her fork with a clunk on the plate. She pushes herself away from the table and flees toward the restroom.

Papa starts to get up. "What? Where is she going, Violet?"

"You know how sensitive your granddaughter is, Papa. You embarrassed her in front of her boyfriend."

Papa pats my sister's shoulder. "Daisy, go see if she's all right?"

I take a bite of salad. "No, Papa. Leave her be for a little bit. If she doesn't come back in ten minutes, I'll go and get her. Everyone, please enjoy your meals." *Should I stay or should I go?*

The seconds roll into minutes, and no Jane. The waiter starts clearing the table, but I stop him from taking her plate. "Can you please wrap this up for us to take home? My daughter's not feeling well."

The quiet, half-hour ride home is almost unbearable, but the steady snow fall keeps everyone on the alert. A few cars pass us on the Northway and the oncoming headlights shining into our car expose the two love birds in the back seat. As we approach the twin bridges, I know home is only a few minutes away.

"So, did everyone enjoy their dinner tonight?"

"Yes, Mrs. Funk. It was delicious and my first time at Jack's. It was nice of your sister to pay for my meal and I'm not even family."

Simple but lovely describes my sister's wedding, held in the Sleepy Hollow courthouse with Judge Bricker presiding. Two big arrangements of red roses and baby's breath adorn the courtroom. I stood next to my sister in a pink, lace, ankle length dress. She looked stunning in her designer, white brocade gown and a simple veil that enhanced her brown curly hair. The men all looked handsome in their black suits, starched white shirts, and red bow ties.

A scrumptious, catered lunch was brought into their new two-story Tudor home. The house sits on ten wooded acres that has a creek running through it. Six furnished bedrooms allow us to stay overnight.

The newlyweds are gone when I make my way to the kitchen the next day.

"Good morning, Auntie. Did you see the happy couple before they left?"

"No, but the coffee was still hot in the percolator on the stove. We must have just missed them, Toots."

"How have you been feeling these days, Aunt Flossie?"

"This emphysema gets me down sometimes. I must stick my head out the door and breathe in fresh air, several times a day. Clean air's hard to come by in Queens, with all of the vehicles burning oil, buses leaving exhaust behind, and thick smoke from the trains."

"You really should think about moving in with us after the addition is complete. My office will become a guest room, or you can sleep in Peter's room. He rarely comes home since he started flying commercial planes for Pan Am."

She pours a second cup of coffee. "I'll think about it. Maybe in the summer. Your father has been in the hospital two times in the last six weeks. They had to feed him with an IV tube."

"What? Why didn't anyone tell me? I'm surprised at you, Auntie. I write to you all the time and tell you all kinds of things. I'm so frustrated right now. Always-left-out-of-the-loop Violet." I tack on a smile, hoping it's enough to mask my disappointment.

"You have your hands full with all of Jane's antics and the tile business."

My heart starts to pound ferociously as cold sweats break down my back. "I would put everything aside where Papa's health is concerned."

"Honestly, Violet, you don't have to get so worked up."

256

Tears burn my eyes as I look at her. "Just keep me informed about my family. That's all I ask."

"Mom, come quick! Grampa's vomiting in the bathroom. The door's locked, and I can't get in," screams Jane.

I rush to the bathroom door with Auntie and Jane at my heels. "Papa, open the door. Please." *Where's Henry? Is he keeping himself unavailable because of Papa?*

The toilet flushes. "I'm all right, Violet. Just a little upset stomach."

Auntie pushes her way to the door. "Berto, let's get you to a doctor."

He opens the door. "See for yourself, Flossie. Don't you ever eat something that doesn't agree with you? Honestly, a man can't even have some privacy to do his business."

A strong odor follows my pale, piqued father as he slowly passes me. I rush into the bathroom to clean up the mess on the floor around the toilet. Panic shoots through my insides.

Chapter Thirty-Five

It's June 27, 1967, and Jane will be celebrating her twenty-first birthday. Her friend, Carole, from New Jersey will be spending one night with us. Papa's attempting the drive from Brooklyn by himself because my sister must work. *I pray he'll decide to stay overnight after all.*

"So, my dear wife, how do you like your new art studio? Everything's right here at your fingertips. I love having my silk-screening right here too. No more lugging stuff up and down the stairs."

I turn to look at him as I sit at my art table. "It's more organized than the Long Island one because of all the wonderful shelves to store everything."

"He pulls up a chair. "What time is the big party?"

"Three to seven."

"I suppose we'll have a house full of young adults listening to Elvis and The Beatles in high volume, blaring from the record player."

"I plan on making it as special for her as I can. I don't think you have to worry about loud music."

"Who's all coming?"

"Papa's on his way as we speak. Carole from Hackensack, Bruce and us. Anita had to work."

He shakes his head. "Do you think that boy will ever ask her to marry him?"

"Mom, I don't want to wear a paper dress. Come on. I can't believe you found such a thing. I'm twenty-one, not twelve."

"You'll be a big hit. The colors are bright and cheerful. Perfect for a birthday party."

She plops on the bed with a look of defeat. "One time only. I guess it can't hurt anything. How come Auntie isn't coming?"

"She couldn't bear the long trip in the car with your grandfather. She sent you a card, though."

"Oh, that's ridiculous. Grampa's a gentleman and would treat her like a lady. He's her brother-in-law, for crying out loud."

I glance at my watch. "It's time to get dressed for the party, Dear. Carole will be here shortly, and I still have to frost your cake."

She flits over to the record player and places a 45 rpm on the spindle, and as I walk out the door, I hear the rhythmic sounds of the Temptations singing, "Get ready, here I come." *That girl loves Motown music. It's engrained in her.*

I hear talking as I return to the living room. "Why, hello, Papa and Carole. When did you two get here?"

Carole's big smile is infectious, as usual. "Can I help you with anything, Mrs. Funk?"

I give her a big hug. "Honey, let me show you to your room so you can settle in. Maybe you can help Jane get ready. She's probably dancing in there forgetting that it's her birthday."

"You keep on getting things ready. I'll get her going."

Lord, it's amazing how a college graduate with her first teaching job in September can still have time for my Jane. Miles separate them, but they have kindred spirits.

She grabs her overnight bag, "I'll follow the music."

"Uh, hum. Can you spare a few moments for your old papa, Violet?"

I race to hug him. "I'm so sorry, Papa. Come sit down and let me get you a nice cold glass of mint iced tea. You must be exhausted from the long drive."

"I stopped a couple of times to stretch my legs, but I haven't had anything to eat since last night."

"I made deviled eggs. Do you want a couple to hold you over? We'll be eating when everyone gets here."

He crinkles up his face and sits at the counter. "Do you have any ginger ale?"

"Why? You love my iced tea."

"My stomach has been playing games with me. Nausea all the time."

"Oh, let me look." I move things around in the fridge and find an unopened bottle in the back. I pop it open and pour it over ice.

"Thanks, Daughter. Where's the birthday girl anyway?"

"She's in her room getting ready."

I jump when the phone rings. My hands are covered with ground chuck from forming hamburgers on a cookie sheet. It keeps ringing angrily, like it's going to leap off the wall.

"Hello?"

"Hi, Mrs. Funk, this is Bruce."

"Yes, Bruce. Are you coming for the party?"

"I'm at the drag strip in Lebanon Valley."

Okay. Are you coming or not?"

"I'll be there late, so don't hold dinner for me."

"I see."

"Please tell her happy birthday, and I'll give her a present when I see her."

"I'll give her the message. Be careful." A flash of anger burns in my belly.

Henry sits with Papa. "It smells good in here. I'm getting hungry."

I scoop the Lipton's French onion soup dip in a bowl and pile chips around it. "Try some of this."

"Was that Bruce?"

Henry pops the delectable snack into his mouth. "I bet he's not coming. This sure is good, Honey."

If I tell Jane her boyfriend isn't coming to her party, she'll go ballistic.

"Wow. Look at our beautiful girl, Vi."

Jane's beaming from ear to ear with her brown hair pulled back, enhanced by a headband that matches the flowered paper dress. She's arms in arm with her friend.

"Happy birthday, Sweetheart." Papa rises and pulls a small box from his jacket pocket.

She wraps her arms around him. "Should I open it now, Grampa?"

"Sure."

I place hamburgers on the buns. "Hamburgers are done. Let's open presents later."

Jane sits at the table, pulls away the wrapping, and opens the small box. She carefully lifts a fourteen-karat yellow gold, pearl pendant. "It's beautiful."

"Allow me," he says. She turns so the necklace can be placed around her neck. With her hand on the pearl, she turns to him. "I love you, Grampa."

Henry smirks. "Before we enjoy this beautiful meal, let me ask a blessing over it."

Papa grabs a deviled egg and bites into it.

Henry's a little jealous of Papa and Jane's closeness. I don't know why it bothers him so much.

"Heavenly Father, thank You for this beautiful June day, which is also our daughter's twenty-first birthday. I pray You'll bless her and help her to grow spiritually each new day of this year. Thank You for bringing Berto and Carole here safely to help us celebrate this special day. We thank You for the food on the table, and may You bless the hands of the cook, my dear wife. Amen."

Papa's snoring like a roaring chainsaw when we start passing the food.

⤖

The gifts are open, the food's put away, and the table cleared for the birthday cake. I look out at the back deck and see everyone chatting and laughing. *Papa seems to be feeling better now. His entertainment background allows him to be the life of any party.*

Standing inside the screen door, I ask, "How about some songs around the piano, Papa?"

Jane lends Papa a hand. "Come on, Grampa. Show Carole your stuff."

We gather around the piano as Papa hits the black and ivory keys. He plays a medley of show tunes as we rock back and forth to the rhythm. Jane looks around the room with sadness written all over her face.

"Where's Bruce? He should have been here a long time ago."

I put my arm around her. "He won't—." A knock on the door stops the words.

Henry opens the door, and a disheveled looking boyfriend holding a brown cardboard box with a red ribbon around it enters. "Sorry I'm so late."

Jane runs to him. "Bruce, where have you been? You're a mess."

"At Lebanon Valley, racing."

"Those cars are more important than my birthday?"

He grimaces, "Here. Happy birthday, Jane."

She reluctantly takes the present, but instead of opening it, sets it on the couch.

Bruce wobbles back and forth like a lone ship sailing through stormy seas. His hair is askew, and a few greasy smudge marks tarnish his handsome face. The blue

262

tee shirt under the loose-fitting plaid shirt enhances his blue eyes. Jane sandwiches herself between Carole and her father. I try to smooth the goosebumps along my skin.

I take the young man's hand. "Come with me, Dear, you need to freshen up. I saved you some food. I'm sure you're famished."

Papa pounds out, "You are my Sunshine," on the piano and those around him follow in melodious voices.

Carole and Bruce strike up a conversation as he wolfs down the array of food on the plate in front of him. She seems intrigued by his racing stories.

Jane and Papa go outside and sit on the deck to enjoy the beautiful weather.

I smile with attentiveness as I stand inside the screen door, not to eavesdrop, but to learn what the bond is between them.

"I'm so happy you came for my party today, Grampa. I didn't think you would come by yourself."

He grabs her hand. "You are my special girl. Always have been, always will be."

"I love you, Gramps. Thank you for this beautiful necklace. I will always cherish it."

"I wonder if your mother still has the pink pearl necklace I gave her when she turned thirteen? It was a long time ago, but I saw her wearing it, even when we weren't getting along."

"She really wanted to be a ballerina, huh?"

"Yes, she did, my dear, but I was headstrong and stepped in her way. I know now, I was wrong."

"My mother's so talented and popular, Grampa. I wish I was like her." She bursts into tears.

I want to go out there and pull her in my arms, but instead, I cry silent tears.

"Don't cry, Janie, I never made it through the tenth grade. You have a kind, warm heart for animals. I have watched your love for horses grow over the years, and I wish I could have bought you one of your own." Papa reaches down and pets Pups.

"Daddy promised me a horse when we moved here, but he ran out of money putting in three wells."

"It's a shame, too, because you have the land for a barn and a nice pasture."

"I guess I have to settle for a cat and a dog for now." She sniffles.

"If I had the money, I would build a beautiful stable out there with a white fence surrounding it. It would be filled with horses."

Chapter Thirty-Six

I love to wake up an hour earlier than usual, so I can spend time with the Lord and pour through pages of Scripture. So many times, new ideas for tiles have been uncovered as I read and meditate. *Oh, Lord, open my eyes to where and what I can do to spread the gospel to the children of this neighborhood. We have this beautiful house that needs to be shared for Your glory. Amen.*

Mark 1:17 catches my attention. "And Jesus said unto them, come ye after me and I will make you fishers of men." I doodle a few fish on a piece of scrap paper and ponder a moment. Like a lightbulb the "I will make you fishers of men, if you follow Me" song comes to mind.

"That's it!" I whisper with a smile. "The Fishermen Club will be my neighborhood ministry. Henry can copy leaflets at work tomorrow, and I can start ringing doorbells on Saturday." *Oh, Lord, thank You for the artistic ability You have blessed me with. May You fill this house with boys and girls who are hungry for Your word? Amen.*

"Mom, is Auntie coming here for a few days?"

"Yes, she is on the Trailways bus as we speak. I'll be picking her up at the terminal in Albany at 11:00. Do you want to come?"

"No, I'm going up to the dude ranch in lake George to go horseback riding with some friends. I'll be home for supper."

"Be careful. I hope you cleaned your room, as well as the stinky litter box."

The tooting of a car horn causes her to fly out the door. "See you later, Mom."

I whiz around the house as fast as a rabbit running from a fox, moving clothes and toiletries to the guest bathroom. Henry will sleep in the spare bedroom, and the sofa bed in the office will be where I rest my head for two weeks.

"How was the bus ride, Auntie?"

"It was rather bumpy at times, but once we got on the thruway, it was a pleasant ride. Albany's a quaint little city compared to the noisy, crowded streets of Queens. I'm looking forward to spending some time in the country, Toots."

She has aged around her eyes since the last time I saw her. Her solid head of grey hair is always wrapped in two braids on her head, but her complexion is still flawless.

I touch her arm. "I'm so happy you're staying with us for a couple of weeks. It's so peaceful out on our back deck. You'll love the flowers in the window boxes too."

"Now, I won't have you catering to me every five minutes, Dear. I'm perfectly capable of making my bed and doing my own laundry."

A few days later, on Saturday, the first session of the Fishermen's Club is about to begin. I have no idea how many will show up, but I managed to hand out over fifty flyers. Aunt Flossie decides it best to stay in her room for the two hours because she thinks the noise would be beyond her comfort level.

"Henry? Jane? Are you in here?" I call down the hallway.

I call again as I move from room to room, only to find total emptiness. *Hmm. I wonder where they disappeared to.*

I tap on Auntie's door. "Auntie, do you need anything before I let the kids in?"

She opens the door with a slight grin. "I'll be fine, Violet. I have my tea, a good book to read, and the chair with an ottoman will give me total comfort."

"Do you know where Jane and Henry are?"

"I don't know. I thought Jane was going to help you."

The doorbell catches my attention. "I better go. Feel free to join us at any time, okay?" The door closes before any more words can be said.

"Come in, kids. Let's get a name tag on each of you, so I can remember your names. Five overly excited children, ranging all sizes, file into the foyer.

"Wow, Mrs. Funk, this is a beautiful house," a skinny redhead chimes out.

"Thank you, Honey. What's your name? I'll make a name tag for you."

She giggles. "It's Samantha."

"Put this tag on. Is this your brother?"

"Yes. His name is Tim. He's kind of shy though. My cousins are visiting for the weekend, so I brought them along."

Fifteen minutes later and after a snack of oatmeal cookies and lemonade, we gather in the living room for the

Bible story from Mark 1. The flannel board is set up with a blue background and each piece depicts the story about Jesus calling the disciples to be fishers of men. The five children face me with their mouths wide open as they hang on every word.

"I'm going to teach you a song that will be our theme song each time we meet, okay?"

Little Pam, who appears to be the youngest, raises her hand. "I don't know how to read."

I pat her on the head. "That's okay, Sweetie. You'll learn it as we go along. I'll sing it first, so you get the idea."

The words are painted neatly on poster board.

"I will make you fishers of men, fishers of men, fishers of men. I will make you fishers of men if you follow me. If you follow me, if you follow me. I will make you fishers of men, if you follow me."

"Okay, let's stand and try to learn it. Throw your arm out like this to pretend it's a fishing pole. Good. Now reel in your big catch."

I'm bubbling over with joy after the children leave because when I shared how much Jesus loves each one of them, they hung onto every word. When I asked if anyone would like to ask Jesus into their hearts, Samantha bolted to her feet. "I want to."

She repeated the sinner's prayer with me. "Heaven's rejoicing over you, Samantha. The simple prayer of asking Jesus to be the Lord of your life is cause to celebrate."

⊂╸◎℞◎╺

Henry's voice startles me. "How did it go?"

"I was looking all over for you and Jane earlier. She was supposed to help me."

"I was in the garden and puttering around in the garage. How did the kids like the Fisherman's Club?"

"One girl accepted Jesus into her heart. They're going to invite friends to the next club meeting."

He hugs me with his sweaty body. "I saw Jane take off in her car a few hours ago."

"Whew. You need a shower. On your way through, knock on Aunt Flossie's door to tell her the coast is clear."

I have a couple of hours before supper. This is a good time to call Papa to see if he's all right.

The office chair invites me to take the load off my feet. I dial the number and lean back in the comfy seat.

It rings, rings, and rings. *Come on, Papa. Where are you?*

After a dozen rings, I give up. *That's odd. He's always in his apartment every night at this time. I hope he's all right. Lord, please be with Papa right now.*

"Toots, where's Jane? With that boy again?"

"I don't know where she is, Auntie. I don't think she's with Bruce because he's usually at the drag races every Saturday. Hopefully, she'll be home for supper."

"I hope that girl is helping you with the housework. She seems to gallivant a lot with no rhyme or reason why. Her conversations are all over the place."

"Well, she's holding down a full-time job at Cromwell Business Forms. Oh, I forgot to tell you, she got into the Junior College of Albany for the fall semester."

"Really? How did that happen?"

"She pulled her grades up with the post graduate course at Shenendehowa High School. She'll be taking a two-year associate degree course on preschool education."

She sighs. "I'm impressed and happy that Jane's finally going to make something of herself."

"She'll be able to get a good job in a nursery school or maybe go on to a four-year school."

The studio door slams and stirs Auntie into a frenzy. "What was that?"

Jane leaps into the room with a huge smile on her face. "Mom, I bought a horse."

"You what?"

"I went back up to the dude ranch and rode a big black horse that I absolutely fell in love with. The owner said I could buy him for a hundred and fifty dollars. Since I just got paid, I gave him one hundred and will pay the rest when I pick up the horse."

Auntie fans herself to ward off the distress. "Ye gods, Jane. How could you do such a thing without asking your parents first?"

Jane scowls at her. "It was a deal I couldn't pass up."

I shake my head. "Where do you think you're going to keep this horse, anyway?"

"I don't know that yet, Mom. I'll have to ask around. Maybe Anita's."

Auntie shakes her head. "I'm getting your father."

"I'm starving. Can I have a snack?"

"Jane, a horse is a big expense. You should have consulted us first."

She flings open the refrigerator door. "I have been waiting for years for my own horse. Daddy promised that when we moved up here, I would get one. I'm so excited about this, Mom. I have a week to figure out how to get him here and where to keep him."

I hug her, even though I'm filled with chagrin over her actions.

"What's this all about, Jane?" asks Henry.

"I bought the most beautiful black horse, Dad. His name is Ebony. Wait until you see him. You'll want to ride him right away."

"Okay. We'll figure something out. I know this is a dream come true for you, so let's see what we can do to get a barn built in record time."

Auntie sits at the counter. "It costs money to do all that, Henry. You're just about making it now."

Jane bursts into tears. "Please don't burst my bubble of happiness, Aunt Flossie."

"Humph. You can be so inconsiderate, Jane. Doing things on the spur of the moment can lead to trouble. I'll be in my room. Let me know when supper's ready, Violet."

I watch with dismay as she disappears into her room and mumbles. "Honestly, this whole horse idea is total nonsense if you ask me. Only the wealthy can afford to board horses."

"Listen, Vi, I promised the kid a horse when we settled into this place. We have been here four years, and it's still not a reality. What could it possibly cost to put a small shed up and bush hog an acre of land back there?"

Jane's sobbing becomes an opera of rhythmic sniffles and sighs. My heart softens as I think back how long she has waited for this moment.

I slice an onion and green pepper from the garden. "Okay, you won my heart, you two. However, I'll pray you find a place to keep this Ebony until a shed can be built here. I'm too busy to trot around the countryside looking for a boarding facility. It sounds like you have your work cut out for you. I sure hope it all works out." *This sounds like an instant replay of that Zorro horse on Long Island. I pray this has a happy ending.*

Part four

Chapter Thirty-Seven

1969

The barn raising event proved to be an expensive one, but I was able to hire two college boys to paint it red. The footing was almost impossible to lay due to the hard clay soil. Henry insisted on digging a trench all the way to the barn from the house, so the plumbers could lay the pipe and hook up the water. I wince internally.

Jane's so happy these days. She takes good care of Ebony, and it's a joy to be able to look out and see her riding in the backyard.

Henry wraps his arms around me. "See, wasn't it all worth it?"

"What?"

"The horse, the barn, and your jubilant daughter?"

I giggle as he tickles me. "Yes, things are going good for her now. An answer to prayer if you ask me. I had no idea a horse could provide one girl such happiness."

"She starts the junior college of Albany next week and is holding down a part-time job at Macy's. How will she find time for this horse?"

"But Bruce is still around and no engagement in sight."

"Here she comes, Honey. We better change the subject."

She jumps up on the deck with a bounce. "Good morning, you two. Were you watching me ride? Come on, Mom, admit it. Ebony's growing on you."

I take a deep breath before I speak. "Jane, I love seeing you happy."

The stack of mail on my desk calls to me as I sit after cleaning the kitchen. *Junk. Junk. Macy's advertisement. What's this? A letter from Daisy.*

Dear Violet,

I trust everything is all right with you and your family. Auntie told me about Jane's horse and the expensive barn you had to build. Honestly, Sis, don't you think you got in over your head with all of this? I know you'll tell me that God is in control. Is He going to throw some money down from the heavens? I'm happy Jane's going to college, long time overdue. I'm too busy to call you these days, but I wanted to update you on our father. He's been in the hospital twice, and the tests revealed a debilitating liver disease. Can you break away from your obligations and take a trip to Brooklyn? He hasn't been taking very good care of himself.

Love, Daisy.

"Why so glum, Mom?" Jane interrupts my concentration.

"Oh, your grampa's not feeling well. I have to go to Brooklyn."

"Oh, no. I wish I could go with you. When are you going?"

"I'll call him in a few minutes, but he doesn't always answer the phone. I should go as soon as possible, maybe tomorrow."

"It's Christmas in July at Macy's, and now that I'm shift manager, I can't take time off. He's my only grandfather. I hope he'll be all right, Mom."

"I know, honey. Let's say a prayer for him before I call."

"I have to go to work, but I'll pray on the way."

I pick up the receiver and dial. After a few rings, I hear heavy breathing.

"Papa?"

"Is this you, Violet?"

"Yes. It's your flower, Violet. Daisy said you're not eating. You must eat, or you'll get sick. Daisy's busy and can't break away from her practice. Papa, are you there?"

I hear several raspy coughs. "Hang on a minute."

"I'll hang on."

Oh, Lord, help my father right now. He's not doing well at all and is all alone. Give me wisdom to know what to do. He needs a Savior more than ever.

"I'm coughing up blood, and I threw up earlier."

"I'm coming down tomorrow."

"Can you bring Jane? You know how much I love to see her?"

"Jane has to work. I'll leave first thing in the morning. Try some dry toast and tea."

"I love you, Flower."

"I love you too, Papa."

I'm glad I ended the Fisherman Club. There were twenty-five kids at the last meeting. Most of them are attending local church Sunday schools. Thank you, Lord.

Driving over the Kosciusko Bridge into Queens, I smile at the fact I missed the rush hour work traffic, but it quickly fades when I think of Papa. The rugged, old apartment buildings creep their way to the blue sky while folks stand on street corners and wait for a bus. Yellow taxi cabs rush about, beeping their obnoxious horns at anything blocking them. *I sure hope I can find a parking place near*

Papa's place. I have plenty of loose change for the meter, but I don't want to drive all over the place to find one.

"Wonderful. Someone's pulling out."

I grab my train case, lock the door, and check the meter to find it has two hours left. The three-story brownstone building comprises of D'Auria's Deli on the ground floor with apartments above. *Maybe I should buy some groceries first.* The salami and cheeses hanging in the window make my mouth drool, but I resist the urge to go in.

I jiggle the doorknob to find it locked. I knock.

No answer.

That's right. He leaves an extra key on top of the door frame.

"Papa?"

The windows in the small living room are wide open, with all the sounds from the street charging in. Dirty socks are strewn everywhere. I trip over a heaping basket of dirty laundry. Boxes of records and books are stacked on the cushions of the tattered couch. "Papa?" I whisper.

I turn to see his bedroom door is closed. I gently open the door to find him cutting Zs, lying on top of his crumbled bedding. *Why is he sleeping in a coat in August?*

The ringing of the telephone catches my attention. I gently close the door and leap over the laundry basket to get it. "Hello?"

"Oh, good, Violet. You're there."

"I just got here, Daisy."

"How is Papa?"

"He's sleeping. I'm not going to wake him."

"Call me later, okay?"

"I promise to call you later."

Where do I start?

I turn the light on in the cubicle kitchen and pause as my eyes adjust to the mess in front of me. The sink is loaded with crusty-laden dishes and coffee cups with grounds clinging to them. Ants are enjoying the picnic of crumbs on the counters and floors. Spaghetti sauce is splattered all over the stove top. I lift the lid of a pan. *Ugh. There's mold on this macaroni.*

Two hours later, with my feet raised on the ottoman in front of me, I marvel at how clean the place looks. *I can hear Papa snoring from here. I'll have to wake him up soon if he doesn't get up on his own.*

I open my Bible to First Corinthians 13:5, "Love does not insist in its own way, for it's not self-seeking; it is not touchy or fretful; it takes no account of the evil done to it."

"Heavenly Father, I'm here to help my father. He's a lonely man who's not in the best of health. I pray I can be useful while here, but more importantly, may he come to know You as his Lord and Savior. Amen."

I lean back in the timeworn wingback chair and close my eyes. *I'll rest for a few minutes, then wake Papa.* A cool breeze tickles my nose as I drift away for...

"Violet, wake up. Let's get some Chinese food for supper."

I try to open my eyes, but they appear to be glued shut. *I better see where Jane is.*

I feel a firm hand on my arm. "Flower? Are you all right?"

The dark brown eyes of my father bring me back to reality. "Papa, you're finally awake. You had a good, long nap. How are you feeling?"

He slowly sits on the cleared couch. "I'm always cold, Violet Pearl. I had awful cramps earlier and I decided to lie down until they passed. I put my overcoat on to ward off the chills. I'm fine now. I know a great little Chinese restaurant around the corner. Are you hungry?"

"Are you sure spicy food is good for you right now? I can cook something healthy here, Papa."

"Oh, I'm all right now. Daisy calls two times a day and treats me like one of her patients. I take an Alka-Seltzer as a quick cure for what ails me. Come on, let's go for a walk and find that restaurant."

"I guess I can't stop you if you're feeling up to it. First, you must call Daisy. I promised to check in with her when you woke up. It will put her mind at ease if you talk to her."

He bolts to his feet and walks swiftly to the bathroom. "I'll be right back. Nature's calling."

I catch a strong whiff of an active bowel as he passes me. *Lord, please help my Papa. I'm going to try to convince him to come back home with me for a while. My husband many not approve, but I can keep close watch on Papa if this happens. Amen.*

"I'm fine, Daisy. Really. Stop your worrying. Violet will be staying here for a few days so that alone should put your mind at ease." Papa rolls his eyes, shaking his head. "I promise to call the doctor's office if things flare up again. Daisy. Stop hounding me. Let me take care of myself. I'm not an invalid."

I get up and motion for the phone. He hands it to me. "Sis, it's Violet."

"Did you clean up the apartment, Violet?"

"Yes, I cleaned the apartment. I have a load of laundry to do tomorrow, and I have to check his food supply tonight."

"Please keep a close eye on him."

I watch Papa pace back and forth. "Listen, we're going to go and get some supper. I'll call you if there are any changes, okay?"

"Where are you going?"

"Papa's taking me to a nearby Chinese restaurant."

She yells in my ear, "He has no business eating that rich food."

"He's hungry. Some white rice and hot tea should be just what the doctor ordered. You can't rob him of everything he loves to eat."

"Violet, tell her you'll call tomorrow. We might not get a table if we wait any longer."

"Daisy, I have to go. I love you."

She ends the call without uttering a word.

Chapter Thirty-Eight

"Here, Papa, I found a pair of clean pajamas. I will change the sheets tomorrow and head to the laundromat. The refrigerator needs a serious overhaul before I get some groceries for you."

He sits next to me on the couch. "Why are you doing all of this for me, Flower? I haven't been the nicest father to you."

"I love you, Papa. A day hasn't gone by where I haven't prayed for you. If God can forgive me of my past and the mistakes I made, He can forgive you too."

"I'm an old man now, and I have a lot of time to think. I want you to know I'm immensely proud of your accomplishments as an artist, mother, and wife. Will you ever forgive me for all the years I have treated you unkindly?"

I lean my head on his shoulder. "The Bible says in Colossians 3:13, 'I am gentle and forbearing with others and, if someone has a difference against me, I readily pardon him; even as the Lord has forgiven me, so must I also forgive.'"

Kissing my forehead, he slowly gets up. "I admire your strong faith in God. You're following in your mother's footsteps. Keep praying for me, but I'm not ready for the church life yet. I'll see you in the morning."

I wipe the moisture from my eyes as I watch him go into his room.

"Good night, Papa."

Thank you, Lord, for guiding me here. Papa's so close to accepting You.

Dear Auntie,

Papa's mellowing in his old age, and he seems to be feeling a lot better. I have been in Brooklyn for four days, but I must go home soon because several orders must be attended to and I need to help Jane get ready for college. The apartment is in tip-top shape, there's food in the refrigerator and non-perishables in the cupboards. We are getting along so well. I'm going to try to get Papa to come home with me for a couple of weeks. Don't be concerned how Henry will take this big change, I trust God that it will work for the best. I pray you'll meet some nice people at the Episcopal Church you're going to. I love you. Remember to take your vitamins.

Tootsie.

It's 9:00, and Papa's door is still shut. He is always up and dressed by 8:00 at the latest. *I hope everything is all right. I'll give him a few more minutes.*

I pour another cup of coffee, fold up the blankets on the couch, and open my Bible to the Psalms. My eyes are drawn to chapter twenty-three, and memories of my dear mother dance in my mind. *Will I see her in heaven one day?*

"The Lord *is* my shepherd; I want for nothing. He refreshed, restored my life, and I no longer fear evil. God is always with me.

"He helps me prevail over those who mock me. I am truly blessed. Goodness, mercy, and unfailing love have followed me to this point of my life. The house of the Lord will always be my dwelling place."

I tap on Papa's door. "Papa?'

I turn the doorknob and open the door quietly to find him sitting on his bed all hunched over. "Papa, what's wrong?"

"I'm in severe pain, Violet. I tried calling for you, but I couldn't muster up enough strength to yell. I soiled myself too."

I rush to him. "Oh, I have to call the doctor as soon as I help you out of these wet clothes and strip your bed. Take my hands and try to stand."

I manage to change him and get him into the armchair in the living room. "Here, take your medicine with this glass of water. Hopefully, it will take the edge off your discomfort."

"Doctor DeMarco's office."

"Hello, may I speak to Doctor DeMarco?"

"Is this an emergency, Miss?"

"Yes. It's an emergency."

"Ouch, oh," groans Papa.

"Can you please hold for a few moments?"

"Yes, I can hold for a few minutes, but my father is in severe pain. Papa, can you get yourself to the couch?"

He shifts himself and tries to stand but falls back into the chair.

"This Is Doctor DeMarco. To whom am I speaking?"

"Hello, Doctor. This is Violet Funk, Berto Moretti's daughter."

"Oh yes, how can I help you, Dear?"

"My Papa is doubled over in pain and cannot stand without help. He was up all night with excruciating discomfort."

"I'll see him right away. When can you get here?"

"I don't think I can get him down the steps."

"I'm right around the corner. I'll come there."

"Papa, Doctor DeMarco's on his way. He said to get the hot water bottle and apply it to your stomach to ease the pain." I manage to help him to the couch and help stretch his legs out.

281

By the time I heat up some water and pour it in the rubber container, he's fast asleep. *Oh, good. He needs to take a nap before the doctor gets here.*

"Come on, Daisy, pick up the phone," I whisper. All I get is constant ringing on the other end. I lean back in my seat and sigh.

I never thought to take his temperature. Good thing there's an oral option these days. I flip through *The Brooklyn Times* and a new *Women's Day.*

I jump when the intrusive doorbell rings.

"Who's there?" Papa groans.

The short, stocky Italian doctor bursts over the threshold, carrying his black leather medical bag. "Where's my patient?"

He rattles something in Italian to Papa.

"Si, grazie," he groans back.

"What's going on, Doctor?" I ask.

"Your father's having problems going to the bathroom. I'm going to take his temperature and listen to his heart before I give him any new medication."

Papa clings to the hot water bottle with his life as the doctor performs his job.

He pulls the thermometer out of Papa's mouth. "He does have a slight fever of 101, but his heart rate is normal."

"How are you feeling now, Berto?"

"Still in pain."

"I want you take two Bayer aspirin right now to bring the fever down. I'll wait here awhile before I take your temp again. Hopefully, the new medicine I leave will help you go."

"Violet, get the good doctor a glass of Chianti, and bring me some water, please?" murmurs my father.

Doctor smiles. "Oh, I shouldn't drink while on duty, but one little glass won't hurt."

I am amazed at how quickly the aspirin worked because, within a half hour, Papa's sitting up and gulping down another tall glass of water. The two converse in Italian.

"I better get back to the office, Berto, but if you experience any more pain after the new medicine is in your system for an hour, get yourself to the emergency room at Brooklyn Hospital."

"Gracie, Salvatore. I mean Doctor."

"Oh, you can call me by my first name since you knew me all my life. You're lucky to have your daughter staying with you indefinitely."

"She's the best nurse in all of Brooklyn. Why don't you come back for some Manicotti and sausage? Violet's a great cook."

Wow, what a switch. Papa gave me a compliment.

He turns and shakes his finger at Papa. "No more rich foods for you, Berto. You must go on a bland diet to keep those bowels from being obstructed."

"I can't do that. I love to eat."

"You must change your eating habits if you want to live a longer life. Violet, he can have another dose of medicine in four hours."

"Hogwash," yells Papa as I walk the doctor to the door.

"I have to leave in a couple of days. Do you think it's okay to take him with me to my home upstate for a while?"

"As long as the medicine works, and he has a good bowel movement before you leave. It might do him good to get out of this apartment."

"Good. I'll have to convince him to go, and that might be difficult."

"I'll call tomorrow to see how he's doing. Good luck."

⤳⦷⧉⦷⤶

With the Lord's help, I was able to convince Papa to come home with me. The new medication seemed to help him, so the doctor gave us a green light to travel. Henry was a bit annoyed at first, but when I broke down on the phone, he relented.

"Well, we're almost home, Papa."

"My home's in Brooklyn, but I promise to put my best foot forward to make this my second residence. I'm probably going to be bored out of my mind living in the country."

"Daisy and I both agree that you are better off with me while your health is so questionable. We're within minutes of Albany Medical Center, one of the top hospitals in the country."

"Are you sure it is all right with your husband? It's no secret that we just tolerate each other."

"Oh, Papa. Henry has changed since he became a Christian. He's choir director, a deacon in our church, and we pray about everything together."

"Now, now. Church isn't in my schedule while I'm here."

As we drive up the driveway, he lets out a huge, "Wow."

"What, Papa?"

"You added on since I was here last. Is that your new studio with the big picture window?"

Jane's beaming from ear to ear as we pull into the two-car garage. "Grampa, I'm so glad you're all right. I was worried about you." She takes his hand and helps him to his feet.

"I'm going to be okay, my dear granddaughter. No need to worry your pretty little head."

284

I'm left to carry the suitcases and three bags of perishable items from the apartment. *I can make a nice chicken soup with the leftover chicken for supper.*

"Grampa decided to take a nap, Mom. Can we unpack his suitcase when he wakes up?"

"He can't sleep too long, or he won't be able to tonight."

"Can you go to the store and get a loaf of Italian bread for supper?"

"I guess so. What are we having?"

"Chicken soup."

"Yummy. I'll pick up a chocolate cream pie for dessert. I'm going on a blind date tomorrow night."

"What about Bruce? Forget the pie. Your grampa is on a strict diet. Sweets are not on the list."

"Anita planned this whole thing. Bruce doesn't have to know. Does he?"

Chapter Thirty-Nine

"Well, my beautiful wife's finally home. Things were quiet around here while you were gone. How was the traffic coming out of the city today?" Henry cradles me in an enormous bear hug.

"Hi, my love. I missed you terribly, and it's good to be home. My bed will feel good tonight after sleeping on Papa's couch for a few days. There were a few snarls coming out of Brooklyn, but once we got over the bridge, everything was smooth sailing. I never thought I would be able to convince Papa to come home with me, but God interceded and allowed it to happen."

"Where is he? I thought for sure he would be sitting in front of the television watching *The Mike Douglas Show.*"

"He's taking a nap, but I need to wake him for supper. I thought he would sleep in the car, but his eyes were wide open all the time."

"I'm going to change, but I promise to be really quiet." He kisses me on the nose.

I follow him on my tiptoes and head to the guest room to find the door wide open. *He must be in the bathroom.*

"Papa, are you all right in there?"

"All is well. Is it time for another pill? The cramps are starting up again."

I look at my watch. "You can take it in a half hour. I made chicken soup for supper. Our old family recipe seems to always do the trick."

The toilet flushes and the shuffle of feet on the tile floor can be heard.

"You look tired, my daughter. I hope you can get to bed early tonight. Is Henry home yet?"

"Come on, Papa, let's find one of your favorite shows so you can relax a bit before supper."

I settle him on the couch, click on the evening news, and run quickly to clean up the mess around the toilet. *Poor Papa. He probably thought he did a thorough job of cleaning. Good thing I have some good Air Wick spray and bowl cleaner.*

"Nice to have you here, Berto. How are you feeling?" asks Henry as I walk back into the living room.

"So-so, Henry. My daughter's an excellent nurse though. Thank you for inviting me to stay for a week. I could have taken care of myself simply fine back home, but my daughters are so concerned about my well-being."

Jane bursts in and scares me to death. "It smells good in here. When's supper?"

"Let me make some garlic bread. You go visit with your grandpa for a few minutes. Did you feed your horse yet?"

"Yes, I did. He's all set for the night."

She plops down on the couch next to him. "Did you have a nice nap, Grampa?"

"I slept a little, but I spent more time tossing and turning. When am I going to see your horse? Ebony, right?"

"Tomorrow. I will bring him up to the deck so you can pet him. How does that sound?"

"Tsk, tsk." Henry shakes his head in annoyance because he can't hear the news.

"Okay, come and get it while it's hot," I say.

Papa appears to be perky and happy this morning, which causes my heart to leap for joy. *Maybe he's getting better.* I'm stronger than my fear.

"Are you hungry, Papa?"

He perches on the stool at the counter. "Not yet, but I would love a cup of coffee. It smells so good."

"Here you go. Just the way you like it, one sugar with a bit of cream."

"There's a beautiful view from here, isn't there, Flower?"

I look at the corn fields getting ready for harvest. "It's God's country, Papa. We're so blessed to live here where we don't have to deal with heavy traffic or long commutes for Henry."

The sliding door slides open. "Grampa, come and meet Ebony."

I do a quick spin when I see the black horse's head and two front feet inside the house. "Jane, what do you think you're doing? Get that horse out of here, this instant."

Papa rolls himself off the stool into a lively laugh. "This is just like the vaudeville days when animals occupied the same space as the human entertainers."

Ebony snorts as Jane holds his halter with both hands. "Come over slow, Grampa. This is all new for him."

I shake my head with disgust. "I'll say it is. This is a one-time event, Jane. That beast better not go any farther."

Papa lets Ebony sniff his hands. "You're a nice, gentle horse. Aren't you, fella?"

Jane pulls a sugar cube out of her pocket and plants it in Papa's hand. "Give him this."

"I'm so happy for you, Jane. Your dream finally came true."

I turn for a moment to top off my coffee and, in that instant, find the horse completely in the house, with his tail raised.

"Okay, that's enough, you two. Get him out of here this instant, Jane, before he leaves a deposit on my clean carpet."

She backs the big, black animal out on the deck, laughing all the way. "Good boy," she utters as she leads him back to the barn.

Papa's standing on the deck in his pajamas and robe and hands on his hips, beaming from ear to ear.

This was a priceless moment for a man not in the best of health. My joy's contained.

"What's all the commotion about out here?" asks Henry.

I kiss him on the cheek. "I'm not sure you want to know."

"Try me, but first tell me, why is your father standing out on the deck in his pajamas? Isn't it cold out there?"

"He just met Ebony. It's a big deal to watch his granddaughter with her own horse."

Papa shuffles back into the house. "Good morning, Henry. You just missed all of the excitement."

"You seem to be doing much better today, Berto. I'm delighted to see that."

"Thank you. I'm feeling a lot better, and the new medication has something to do with it. Jane's ecstatic with that horse of hers. That's the first time I witnessed an animal of that magnitude inside a house."

Papa only asked to go back to his apartment one time during the ten days he has been here. He misses *The Brooklyn Times.* I was able to pacify him with our *Times Union* and back issues of *The New York Times.* He complained a few times about a constant diet of poached eggs on toast, vegetable dinners, and oatmeal.

"I would love a salami and provolone sandwich on Italian bread for a change, Violet. Your homemade whole wheat bread is delicious, but I miss the fresh white bread from Angela's bakery."

"You lost a little weight since you have been here, and I rarely hear you complain about stomach pain."

"True. It's too quiet around here now that Jane's in school during the day and working at Macy's on the weekends. I want to go back to Brooklyn, Violet."

"We'll talk it over with Daisy when she comes this weekend. She wants to take you on a drive up to Lake George to see the foliage. The colors are at their peak."

"Is she actually staying overnight?"

"Not here, Papa. She's staying at the Century House in Latham."

"I honestly don't know what happened, Daisy. He was fine a few days ago. The medicine was working until yesterday. He was literally doubled over in pain, and I couldn't keep up with the incontinence issues. I had no choice but to call an ambulance."

My sister and I sit silently in the stark white waiting room at Ellis Hospital in Schenectady for a few minutes. *This is almost an instant replay of when Mama died.*

"You have done everything humanly possible to help Papa, Sis. I'm worried that he has something more serious than we anticipated. Doctor DeMarco prescribed the right medication to alleviate the pain. It was only a matter of time before things would go downhill."

A tall, skinny young man in a lab coat and a stethoscope around his neck approaches us. "Are you Berto Moretti's daughters?"

We stand at attention and simultaneously say, "Yes, Doctor."

He ushers us into a small conference room and closes the door. "We put your father through a series of tests over the past twenty-four hours. The results are back."

I lean forward with tears in my eyes. "Please give the news to us. My sister's a doctor from White Plains."

He shakes her hand. "Feel free to give your opinion. Your father is suffering from ulcerative colitis and cirrhosis of the liver. He's a sick man."

Daisy and I hug each other and weep.

"I'm sorry, ladies."

"How long does he have, Doctor?" Daisy asks with complete composure.

Chapter Forty

We stay with Papa until he is stabilized and sleeping soundly. The registered nurse on duty reassured us she would call immediately if there was any change. The hospital corridors are quiet and empty as we make our way to the elevator.

"It's late, Daisy. Why don't you stay with us tonight? I'll change the sheets when we get back. It will be midnight before you get back to your hotel."

"I was thinking the same thing. I'm exhausted, Sis. It's best we are together if something happens during the night." She sighs.

The parking lot is brightly lit, but my car's the only one there.

"Do you think Papa will be released from the hospital any time soon?"

"Why? Are you willing to get nursing care for him at your house?"

"You know he never liked hospitals since our mother passed away."

"I know. I think I can convince Doctor Bricker to release him in your care if you can provide for his needs."

I burst into tears as I grip the steering wheel. "Our father is dying, Daisy."

She hands me a Kleenex and sniffles. "We need to make him as happy as we can for the remainder of his days. I hope Henry will be okay with bringing Papa to your house in his declining condition."

"I think you and I should pray about that right now."

"No, no. You can do that when you get home. Right now, you need to concentrate on your driving. It's pitch black and no cars in sight. Keep your eyes open for darting deer."

Forever, Lord. Grant me wisdom as I prepare to talk to my husband about setting up a hospital room at our house for Papa.

Silence plagues the car for the rest of the ride home.

Much to my amazement, Henry's watching the *Johnny Carson Show* when we arrive back home. The dog is wagging his tail, hoping one of us will let him out or plant a biscuit in his open mouth.

"Is Jane sleeping, or is she out?"

"She went to bed about a half hour ago. Don't worry about the dog. He did his thing an hour ago. How's your father?"

"Um, Daisy is with me. I need to talk to you about Papa."

A commercial fills the screen, and he turns his body. "Hi, Daisy, I didn't know you were here. Please, come sit for bit."

She reluctantly joins him, but if I know my sister, she would rather turn in for the night than to watch television.

"Daisy will stay the night with us, Henry. I don't want her driving to Latham this late. You two chat while I make up her bed."

A half hour later, alone in our room, with the moonlit night shining through the windows, Henry and I settle down under the covers.

I grab his hand, "Honey, Papa's dying. I want to bring him here, so he isn't alone. Please pray about it."

"Ouch. Do you know how difficult this will be for you? Jane and I will be gone all day. You'll have your hands full with your business, household duties, and nursing your father."

"The hospital recommended a visiting nurse organization in our area. I would have a registered nurse come in five days a week in the mornings. Our office would have to be turned into a bedroom with a hospital bed."

"Where would everything in that room go?"

"I'll show you in the morning. Right now, we both need our sleep. This arrangement must be good for all of us or it won't be for Papa. I love you, Henry. I know my father has been difficult over the years, but he needs us now. If we don't take him in, then he must go to a nursing home. He can't afford that."

"I guess it's all right, Violet."

Dear Lord, I pray that your will be done as far as Papa's concerned. He's so alone in that hospital bed and in desperate need of a Savior. Grant me peace, one way or another, about him coming here to die. Amen.

Two weeks have passed since Papa moved into the transformed office area of our house. We were able to rent a beautiful hospital bed and wheelchair from Taylor rental. Henry seems okay with the arrangement, but I think he agreed to it to make me happy. *Thank you, Lord, that he can get himself in and out of bed at this point. I love to watch him gaze at Jane riding her horse.*

"Papa, are you warm enough out there?"

His head is drooping downward, and from the back, it looks like he's sleeping. I open the screen door and step in front of him. "Papa?"

"Ha, I fooled you. I'm not sleeping. The sun's in my eyes."

"It's a little nippy out here. Do you want a sweater or blanket?"

"Oh, I'm fine. It's mid-October, so we can expect cooler weather."

I grab his hands. "Your hands are cold. I'm getting you a blanket."

"Tsk, tsk. You are like a mother hen, Daughter."

"Here, this will keep you warm and cozy for a while." I wrap a red, plaid wool blanket around his shoulders and over the front of him.

"My granddaughter sure loves horses. Look at her go."

"She has a new boyfriend, so this love for horses may just disappear."

I watch my daughter vanish into the treed area around the barn. "I'm starting supper now. Do you want to stay out here or come in?"

"Come get me in a few minutes."

The beef stew is simmering in the electric frying pan as I tidy up Papa's little room. He's looking at an *I love Lucy* rerun and nodding off occasionally. Jane whizzed in and changed her clothes in record time to dart off to her shift at Macy's.

"Hey there, Sweetheart," chimes Henry.

"Whew. You caught me off guard, Honey. How was your day? You must have passed your daughter. She just left."

He wraps his arms around me and plants kisses on my cheek. "Yes, she gave me a quick wave. You must be making my favorite. It smells so good."

I flee from his grasp. "Go say hello to Papa. We can continue this love fest after the 11:00 news."

He smirks at Papa. "Time for the news."

I'm appalled to watch him step in front of my father and change the station. *That's a real switch. So loving to me and the next minute rude and inconsiderate to Papa.*

"Humph. You don't like Lucille Ball, do you?"

"No. I don't. You know when I come home from a long day at work, I must relax and watch the evening news. You can watch television all day."

"Henry, why did you allow me to live here? You despise me. I can see I'm a big bother to you."

"Boys, supper's ready. Henry, I think you better go change and come to the table."

"Yeah, yeah. Don't touch that dial, Berto. I can listen to it while we're eating."

"I'm sorry about all of this, Papa. Henry owes you an apology. Come on, I'll help you to the table."

"I regret all of those years of not being kind to your husband, Violet. I'm sure he's getting back at me."

The loud newscast stifles any conversation around the table. Papa and I know enough to wait until the commercials to talk.

"Papa, why aren't you eating your supper? I made one of your favorites."

"I'm not very hungry tonight. Maybe a little ice cream if you have it?"

"No desert until you eat some potatoes and carrots. I'm worried about you."

"Shush. The news is on," scolds Henry.

Later that night, when the house is quiet, with everyone, even the dog, sound asleep, I wander into the spare bedroom. I set up a dressing table with all my organized jewelry displayed in each corner.

I've created my own little haven in here since Peter seldom comes home anymore. Flowered curtains, bedspread, and the antique lamp from my girlhood bedroom are so elegantly displayed. Makeup is right at my fingertips. I'm so mad at my husband right now. I'll sleep in here tonight. Oh, I haven't looked in this drawer in a long time.

"Hmmm. What's in this velvet box?"

I flip open the top gently. "It's the pink pearl necklace Papa gave me for my thirteenth birthday." I grasp hold of it and cry with all the memories of years gone by racing through my mind. I slump back in the chair as tears well up in the corners of my eyes.

Chapter Forty-One

Papa's getting weaker all the time, and I'm finding it harder and harder to get him in and out of bed. His incontinence issues are getting worse, but I do the best I can to keep him clean. Lord, I must call the visiting nurse organization today.

Its eight o'clock in the morning, and he's sound asleep after a horrendous time in the bathroom. A fresh pot of coffee is brewing when Henry scurries into the kitchen.

"Did you come to bed at all last night? Your side seemed untouched."

"Papa had another rough night. He had to go to the bathroom three times. I decided to nap on the couch so I could hear him. I'm exhausted, Henry."

"He's becoming a handful for you, Dear. I think we better find a nursing home for him."

"Shush. He might hear you. Let's go into the bedroom to talk. You do owe him an apology, Henry. You've been quite rude."

"I'll apologize to him, but do you think you can continue catering to his every need, day after day? Please call the home health organization."

"I'm planning on calling the home health care group this morning. Hopefully, I'll be able to hire a nurse quickly."

Back in the kitchen, he pours a cup of coffee and sits at the counter. He sips a few slugs. "Please make that call. I better get to work."

"You didn't have any breakfast."

"I'll get something at the cafeteria. Don't worry about me. Make that phone call."

⚬⚬⚬

Three days later, a wide-eyed, grey-haired lady marches through the front door. She came highly recommended from the agency, and all her references were positive.

"May I take your coat? My name's Violet. You must be Nurse Betty Price."

She hands me her wool tweed coat. "It's nice to meet you, Mrs. Funk. You can call me Betty if you like."

Her uniform is a two-piece white pantsuit, and although she's a bit plump, I find her rather attractive for her age. "Betty, can I get you a cup of coffee?"

"No, thank you. Where is my patient? I'm anxious to meet him."

"Certainly, follow me."

"Papa, this is the nurse I told you about. She will be taking care of you a few days a week now."

"Hello, Mr. Moretti. I'm Nurse Betty. How are you feeling today, Sir?"

"Terrible, Betty. Terrible."

She turns and scowls at me. "Can you leave us alone for a while, Dear?"

I stammer a bit. "Sure. I'll be in the next room if you need me."

I close the door but listen on the other side.

"Mr. Moretti, I need to listen to your heart and take your temperature too."

"You don't have to do that, Nurse. I'm all right."

A normal routine is established, and Nurse Betty seems to have a good influence on my father because he seems happier and more content with his surroundings. She has been on duty for two weeks now with no problems, except Papa's losing weight.

"Can I speak to you for a few minutes, Mrs. Funk?"

"Oh, please call me Violet, Nurse Betty. After all, you have been with us for a while now."

"You're right. First name basis. I'm very worried about your father. He's getting weaker all the time, and I can't get him to eat a few crackers, let alone a meal. I give him water, orange juice, and ginger ale as beverage options, but he takes a sip and that's it."

"I know. I have noticed the same thing when you're not here. What can we do about this?"

"I will confer with the doctor first, of course, but I think he needs to be fed via an intravenous tube. He's not getting any nutrients at all, and I am fearful of the outcome if things continue like this."

"I see. My sister's a physician, so I will talk to her tonight about his decline. Please make the call to Doctor Paul Bricker to get his opinion about my father."

The dark, dreary morning sky hovers over the area as we wait for an early snowfall that could be significant. It's Saturday, so Nurse Betty has the day off. Jane's working and Henry's at the hardware store buying rock salt and another snow shovel. I pour another cup of coffee after looking in on Papa. He's taking his usual morning nap.

Poor man hooked up to that IV contraption. He needs a bed pan most of the time now and, even with that, has accidents.

I flip open my Bible to Psalm 147. Verse three catches my attention, "He heals my broken heart and binds up my wounds, curing my pains and sorrows." *Oh Jesus, sweet Jesus. If it's Your will, heal my father so he can enjoy more time on this earth. I pray for an opportunity to lead him to a saving knowledge of You. Amen.*

"Vi-let. Vi?"

The room's even darker with the blinds closed as I find my way to his bedside. "Yes, Papa. What is it?" I feel along the top of the dresser to find the lamp. "I'm right here."

His face is an ashen-beige, and his eyes are mere slits. "The pain is unbearable. Is it time for my medicine?"

"Not for another hour, Papa. How about the hot water bottle to lay on your groin?"

"I don't know if that will do any good. Ow. Oh, my. I don't know. How can I keep going like this?"

I grab his hand. "Papa, do you know where you will go after you leave this earth? Do you have peace in your heart that you will see Jesus?"

He turns his head away. "Must you preach at me now? I'm a sick man, and I can tolerate just so much. I have called out to God to heal me, but I keep getting worse."

I fall into the chair beside the bed and lay my head on his lap. "Papa, God is loving. Maybe he's yearning to heal your soul."

He rubs his hand across my hair. "I do want to know Jesus the way you do, Violet Pearl, but it's probably too late."

I lift my head to lock eyes with his. "Pray this prayer with me, Papa. Jesus is calling for you."

"Okay," he whispers as he squeezes my hand.

"Dear Jesus, I know that I am a sinner. Please forgive me for the things that I have done. I believe You died on the cross and rose again to pay for my sins. Thank You for healing my soul and giving me the gift of eternal life. Amen."

He slowly repeats after me, along with several deep breaths and a trickle of tears flowing from his eyes. "Amen."

"I love you, Papa, but now I have peace knowing you'll be with Jesus for eternity."

"Medicine, please."

⊱⊰⊱⊰

"Is Grampa dying, Mom?" Jane asks a few days later.

"Yes, Honey. He's getting ready to see his Lord."

"I can't go in there. Death is so scary."

I pull her next to me. "I know it's hard for you, Jane, but he has been asking for you every day. I don't think he understands your fear. Have you asked God to give you peace?"

"Nurse Betty always glares at me when I even try to step foot in there. Has Daddy seen Grampa lately?"

"Yes, they have made their amends with each other."

"Oh, Mom, will you go in there with me?" Her voice is chipped, with hands knotted together.

"Sure, I will, but first ask God to give you strength, okay?" Prickles of sweat bead up on my face.

"Jesus," she sniffs. "My Grampa is dying, and I'm so scared. He must be too. I pray that you would give me strength as I go in to see him. Help me bring peace into the room, so he will feel Your presence. Amen."

302

The tape recorder's playing soft, classical music as we open the folding door. The nurse stands at attention, stepping towards us. "I just got him settled for the night." She mumbles with a scowl.

"Grampa?"

A slight curve etches around his mouth, but his widened eyes say it all.

"Jesus loves you, Grampa."

He raises his left hand and drops it. "Jane, you came."

I watch his chest heave up and down as he tries to say something else. "What, Papa?"

He whispers, "I love you, Jane and my dear Violet flower." I look away, vision blurring.

Jane bursts into tears and her body trembles as I pull her in my arms once again. "Come on, Dear. Your grandfather must rest now." Reality rushes over me like an avalanche.

Chapter Forty-Two

My papa, Berto Moretti, slipped into eternity a few hours later. *Somehow, I knew it was time when I left the room with Jane, but I made sure she was sound asleep before I went back in. It was a bittersweet moment because I knew it would be the last time I could speak to him, but he was saved before he left this world.*

"Are you sure you don't need any help cleaning out Berto's apartment, Toots?" Auntie asks a few days after the funeral.

"Thanks, but Daisy will be there to help. I'm grateful I can stay with you for couple of days though. The Salvation Army will be coming in the morning to cart away the furniture we don't want."

"Are you going to save the secretary desk? That's an antique. Oh, what about all the Depression glass and that old china? That old man didn't have much, but there's value in those things for sure."

"Oh, Auntie. I'm not interested in treasures of this earth, only what I can store up in heaven."

"My dear niece, you always find a way to weasel into the conversation something about the Bible or the Great Almighty. I think you put way too much time into that."

I wrap my arms around her. "Well, you can't stop me from praying for you."

Later that afternoon, my sister and I make record time packing up everything but the kitchen sink for the Salvation Army truck, the junk yard, or the few things worth saving as our own personal memories. My recollections of this place snatch my soul, and I shiver.

"How are you doing in there, Violet? I've made two trips to the car with the things that are important to me. You can have the rest."

I sit in bewilderment on the bare mattress in Papa's room, holding three bankbooks. *How could you do this to me, Papa?*

"Didn't you hear me calling you, Violet? I'm getting ready to leave."

"Did you know about these, Daisy?"

"Where did you find them? I looked everywhere. Give them to me."

I clutch them with all my might. "No. I deserve an explanation."

She lunges forward to grab the thin, black books, but I instantaneously place them underneath my buttocks. The tears well up from my soul as she stands over me.

"Let's not be childish about this, Violet. Papa told me about these bankbooks a few years ago when things were so unsteady between you two. You have the secretary desk, the china, and Depression glass. If you need any money, you just have to ask me."

"I don't need any money from you, Daisy. Here, take your precious inheritance and put it with all your other riches. I pray God will become the Lord of your life one day, so you realize His love is more priceless than money or any shiny ruby."

❧

My great aunt's house is exactly how I remember it when I was a teenager. The small, old fashioned kitchen still consists of a chipped, white enamel sink, a dated white refrigerator- freezer combination, and a small table and chair set for two on a linoleum floor. I did manage to convince her to get a new stove a few months ago.

"It's like old times, staying with you, Auntie. It seems like yesterday when that thief broke into the house when we were asleep in the middle of the night."

"That was scary for sure. Then, the time you fell off the horse and got kicked in the chin and needed a few stiches two days before your engagement party."

"Oh, yes. The party you planned so beautifully for us that my own father and sister never came to. I really thought things changed between Papa and me over the past few months before his death, but I'm not sure about that after today."

"What do you mean, Toots?"

"Did you know about any bank accounts my father had?"

"Berto? Bank accounts? He was a poor man. He lived like a pauper to prove it."

"That's what I thought all these years too. However, that's not the case."

"You must know something, I don't. Please tell."

"When I flipped the mattress in his place today, three bankbooks fell on the floor."

She pours two cups of tea and sits across from me. "That sneak. How much did my brother-in-law leave you?"

"A total of $5,000 in cash in an envelope addressed to me."

"Ha, ha. Now you can buy that new van you have been eyeing for over a year now. I'm so happy for you, Violet. He wasn't so bad after all."

"I wish it were as good as that, Auntie, but it's not. The bankbooks were in Daisy's name."

She slams her hand on the table and the teacup splats the hot liquid all over. "This is a nightmare. Your sister will split it with you, for sure."

"She said to ask her when I need some cash."

She gets up and begins to dial a phone number. "I'll ask her to give you half."

"Auntie put the phone down, please. I got along without this money up until now, I can continue without it." I grab a sponge and clean up the mess.

"Tomorrow I'm going to make sure my will states my estate will be divided equally between you and your sister. Berto should have done the same thing. He was a wolf in sheep's clothing if you ask me."

⚬⊙⚭⊙⚬

He owns the cattle on a thousand hills, I know He will care for me.

As I pull into the garage of our beautiful home, I breathe a sigh of relief.

I look at the clock on the dashboard and discover it's five o'clock. Supper time. *Henry will be home in an hour. Jane's car is still here, but that doesn't mean anything. She might be out with Guy.*

"You who, Jane? Are you home?"

I quickly pass through the room that once belonged to my father, flick on the kitchen lights, close the drapes, and call down the empty hall, "Jane?" No answer.

Pups lets out a few barks, and Poosie rubs against my legs. "Okay, you two. I'll feed you, but outside with you first."

As soon as I open the front door, Pups flees, but the cat disappears somewhere down the hall. *This place is too quiet. Almost spooky, but I know better.*

I turn on the outside lights to illuminate the area around the house. "Oh, what's there to be afraid of anyway?" *I did lock the door from the garage to the house. It's been a whirlwind two weeks and hardly a moment to shop for groceries. I must scrounge up something for supper. Hmm, what's in the freezer? Ah, frankfurters. I'll make them in a barbecue sauce with mashed potatoes, and here's some frozen peas.*

Pups howls outside, causing me to leap and drop everything on the floor. Then, a door slams from the garage, thumping footsteps, and the rattle of the doorknob sounds from the next room. *Too early for Henry. Pups never barks at Jane.* I grab the biggest knife I can find in the drawer, and I wait in agony of who's entering uninvited.

"Hello, Mother. What are you doing with that knife in your hand?"

"Peter! What are you doing here? You scared the wits out of me. How did you get in?"

"I'd love to give my mother a hug, but I'm afraid to get stabbed in the stomach. I tried calling, but the telephone kept ringing and ringing. Dad gave me a key a while ago."

I throw the knife in the sink and run into his warm embrace. "I'm so happy you're home. How long will you be staying this time?"

"Only a few days. I was able to get a flight into Albany before I head to Miami. I'm sorry about Grampa. Maybe I can help dismantle the hospital bed and help you get back to normal while I'm here."

"That would be wonderful. I want to remember him at his best, not lying in that bed waiting to die. Are you hungry?"

"Famished. Do you still have some of my casual clothes hanging in the closet of the spare room?"

"Yes, your dungarees and denim shirts are right where you left them last time you were home. Go change, your father will be home any minute."

He smiles. "I love you, Mother." He disappears through the hall door.

I feel my mouth pull into a smile to match his.

"The roads are getting slick out there. I barely made it up the hill. I saw tracks coming up the driveway, but Jane's car is gone."

Henry hugs me from behind. "How are you?"

"Hi, Honey. Peter's home. He had a key and let himself in, but he scared me for sure."

"Really? That's swell."

"Dad, there you are. So good to see you. I tried calling you at work, but there was no answer. Luckily, I was able to hitch a ride."

"Come sit down, fellas. Dinner's ready."

"Where's my sister?"

"At Macy's. She usually comes right home after it closes, but with the slippery roads, it will be around ten o'clock before she pulls in the yard. Are the garage lights on?"

"Don't you worry about her all alone out there on the highway?"

"Oh, she'll be all right, son. Jane's a good driver. She'll be home before you go to bed. So, don't worry, okay. Tell us what you have been up to since we last talked."

"Wow, Mom, these hot dogs are scrumptious. I haven't had this since I was a schoolboy. I miss your good ole home cooking."

"Thanks. I'm glad I made extra. Otherwise, you would be eating tuna fish sandwiches for supper."

"I guess I better let you in on the latest endeavor in my life. In my spare time, I manage an apartment complex in Miami."

Henry drops his fork on the plate in front of him. "How in the world do you find time to do that when your flight schedule is so grueling and demanding? I would think that you would be exhausted after flying those big planes every day."

"I get my own apartment free in exchange for being the manager. I have an answering machine, so if there's a problem, the tenants leave messages. Everyone has the number for the owners, in case something major happens."

"Hey, Vi, look out the door and see what the weather's like. I'm getting worried about Jane. I guess what you're doing is a good thing after all, Peter. You get a nice place to live out of it."

"There's a spare room and guest bathroom for you and Mom to come visit. Florida's beautiful when it's freezing cold up here."

"It's snowing pretty heavy, Henry. Pups was covered with the white stuff when I let him in."

"When does the store close?"

"Nine o'clock, then it takes them a half hour to close out the registers and clock out."

"Dad, its only 9:00 now. I'll bet my sister will be home safe by 10:00."

I start clearing the table. "I pray you're right."

Chapter Forty-Three

The two policemen stand on our front porch with creased eyes. Henry and I freeze in place as Peter steps in front of us. "Please come in out of the cold, Officers. What can we help you with?"

In robotic form, they remove their hats and stand solemnly at attention. "There's been an accident on the twin bridges, and it involves a Jane Funk. Are you her parents?"

Despair rises inside me like bubbling tar. "Is she all right? Where is our daughter?"

"The ambulance took her to Albany Medical Center. Her car is in pretty bad shape, but she's lucky to be alive."

I rush to the closet and pull on my boots and coat. "I have to get to my daughter. Now."

"The roads are pretty treacherous, Mrs. Funk. It might be a good idea to wait until tomorrow."

"I can't do that, Officer. Peter, please take us there right now. Jane needs us."

"Okay, Mom. Dad. Let's go."

The policemen escort us down the highway. It's nice having them so close just in case we find ourselves in a bad situation. "It seems like an eternity getting to the hospital in this weather, Peter."

"I know, Mom, but if I go any faster, we may find ourselves in a ditch. It's best I take it real slow. There's a lot of snow for the beginning of November."

"Poor Jane. I hope she's sedated. Otherwise, she'll be in a panic state. Dear God, we pray for our girl, right now. We ask that You embrace her with Your love and protection. She has endured a very traumatic experience. We pray for our safety on these treacherous roads but thankful Peter's driving. Amen."

Henry taps Peter's shoulder. "Okay, good. We're finally on New Scotland Avenue. We should be at the hospital in fifteen minutes or so."

"I'll drop you and Mom off at the emergency entrance and park the car. Gee, I hope my sister's all right. The squad car's gone."

I look behind us. "You're right. I wonder when they left us."

Henry yawns. "Albany Medical Center. We're finally here. It took over an hour."

The emergency room is teaming with patients of all ages. A young mother, no more than eighteen, is cuddling a newborn on her heaving chest, while a stout, grey-haired man coughs profusely into an enormous handkerchief and a very pregnant woman is moaning as she waits in a wheelchair.

Henry and I make our way to the glass-enclosed nurses' station. "My daughter was brought by ambulance two hours ago. We must see her," he says.

"Name?"

"Jane Funk."

"They just brought her to ICU on the third floor. You can take the elevator up there. It's down this hall to the right, but it is past visiting hours. Don't be surprised if you can't get into her room," she says in a huff.

"Oh, my goodness. She must be in critical condition." My legs wobble beneath me as I hold back the tears.

Henry waves his hand, "Here comes Peter. Let's get up there."

As we approach the nurse's station on the third floor, my heart skips a beat as I notice all the blinds are drawn in the rooms surrounding the small area. I look at my wrist and realize I don't have my watch, then I glance at the big clock on the wall. It's 12:30. *Where's my daughter?*

A perky, young nurse leans across the counter. "Can I help you folks with something? It is past visiting hours."

Peter smiles, winks, and pulls his shoulders back. "My sister, Jane Funk, is in one of these rooms. She was in a car accident a few hours ago and brought to the emergency room by ambulance. I know it's past visiting hours, but I'm sure you can make an exception, Nurse." He gives her a wink.

She fidgets a bit and straightens her white uniform. "I guess I can allow one of you in at a time, but please be quiet. She was sleeping when I checked last."

The men elect me to go in first. The dimly lit, disinfected room gives me an all too familiar feeling of deja vu when I walk in the door. The streetlights outside twinkle dancing shadows across the bed as I approach my daughter's side. *Good, she's sleeping. Her arm is in a cast, her face is badly bruised, and her head is wrapped in white gauze. Oh, her beautiful, curly hair is seared with dried blood. Probably from a shattered windshield.* Tears trickle out of the corner of my eyes as I take her hand in mine. I swallow the lump in my throat.

"Lord, thank You my daughter is going to be fine. She could have been killed tonight. The roads are treacherous. Jane must have been sick with worry when brought to the hospital in an ambulance. Thank You that Peter is with us. Amen."

We each had a fifteen-minute vigil with the patient as the early morning hours grabbed ahold of us. Peter and Henry look positively exhausted, yawning every few minutes. A trip to the all-night cafeteria and several cups of coffee later, we have a decent conversation.

I yawn. "How about it if you fellas go home and get some sleep? I'll stay here. There's a nice chair in Jane's room where I can take a good nap. No sense all of us hanging around feeling useless. Goodness, it's 3:00."

Peter looks out the window. "It's not snowing anymore, and the roads seem to be plowed down to the pavement. I think it's a good idea, Mom. What do you say, Dad?"

"To tell you the truth, I don't like leaving your mother and sister at a time like this. You just went through a hospital undertaking with your father, Vi. Are you sure you want to stay here alone with Jane?"

The emotional roller coaster ride inside of me causes a huge avalanche of waterworks. "I don't know. I sat by my father's side in a hospital, but this is my little girl. I can't leave her. The nurse told us she has a concussion, but until I can speak to Jane and her doctor, I don't know what to expect."

Henry brings me to his chest. "You're exhausted, Honey. You need to curl up and close your eyes for a while. I'm sure you will feel a lot better after a few hours of sleep."

I can barely keep my eyes open as I yawn once again. "I'm tired. I can make it to her room fine now. You go home. I'll call after the doctor does his rounds in a few hours. I may need you to bring a change of clothes for Jane and me."

I walk them to the elevators We hug and say goodbye as the door closes.

The rattling of gurneys and food carts and people chatting in the hallway causes me to wake with a start. I squint my eyes as the bright sun radiates on my face. It takes a few seconds to realize where I am. *Jane. How is my daughter?* A nurse must have drawn the curtain between my chair and the hospital bed.

"You're a very lucky young lady, Ms. Funk," a strong, masculine voice remarks.

I pull the curtain aside with eyes open wide in surprise at the young man lifting my daughter's hospital gown.

"Mom, how long have you been here?"

The handsome, black doctor smiles and reaches his hand out to me. "I'm Doctor Otis Griffin. You must be Mrs. Funk."

"Pleased to meet you, Doctor. I'm glad to be here for your diagnosis. We came as soon as we heard about my daughter's accident."

I grab Jane's hand and rub it on my face. "Oh, Honey. I'm so happy you're okay."

Her eyes are filled with fear, but she gives a half smile. "My car skidded on the ice and rolled over twice, Mom. I was petrified. Do you know how many times you and Daddy asked me to buckle my seatbelt? For some reason, the bad weather triggered a desire to do so."

The bottled-up tears from hours ago sting my eyes once again.

"Your vitals are all normal now. You suffered a mild concussion."

"How long do I have to stay in this place, anyway?"

"Well, Jane. You can't take a concussion lightly. We need to keep you here for forty-eight hours to be sure there are no other complications. Bed rest is the best thing. Do you have any pain?"

He presses the switch to bring the bed flat, turns back the sheet, and presses his hands all around her mid-torso. "Do you feel any discomfort?"

"No, no. Not yet. Ouch. That hurts."

"You may have a broken rib or two. Let me get the nurse to order an x-ray."

Panic rises all over her. "I'm so scared, Mom. Are they going to have to cut me open to repair my ribs?"

"Try not to worry, Jane. We must trust God and the medical team here."

"Ebony. My horse needs to be fed."

"Daddy or Peter will take care of him. Pups too."

"Peter?"

"He surprised us yesterday. He's home for a few days."

"Okay. Your x-rays are ordered, and the nurse will be taking you there shortly. Broken ribs usually heal on their own, but your activities will have to be minimal through that process." Doctor Griffin smiles.

Chapter Forty-Four

Jane's Dodge Dart had some major damage to the front, but her life was spared, thank God. She was in the hospital for two days and was released in our care. Complete bed rest for one week, which meant she had to miss some classes and work.

"Dad, can you please bring Ebony on the deck so I can pet him?"

"How 'bout it, Vi? What do you think?"

"Tsk, tsk. Only on the deck, mind you."

"I'll go get him before I go screen some tiles. He's been whinnying a lot, so I know he misses you, Jane."

Henry bundles up and heads out into the cold November weather. *At least the sun is shining as the snow glistens on the landscape around him.*

Jane pulls the quilt around her. "I'm glad Peter was able to spend time with us before he left. Did he tell you what he thought about Guy? He's always so serious when it comes to my boyfriends."

"Here, drink this glass of water, please. You're not drinking enough fluids, Jane. He thinks your boyfriend is the nicest one you ever dated. Of course, he's only met a couple of them." I chuckle.

"I'm crazy about him, Mom. Did you see the beautiful pink, mohair sweater he gave me last night?"

"Yes, a nice gift. I invited his parents over for dinner next week. I know you'll be back to work, so I made it for a Sunday night. Did he tell you?"

Clunk, clunk, clunk. The loud clip-clop of horse's hooves grabs our attention. We both burst into gales of laughter as we head to the open door. Jane's face beams with excitement.

She rubs her nose against the big black horse's snout. "Hi, Boy. I sure missed you. Mom, get me a carrot, please."

❧

The ham's been baking in the oven since this morning, the potatoes are ready to mash, and the green beans are in the pan, ready to steam. A two-layered chocolate cake is on the buffet ready for the desert portion of the meal. I bring a bowl of fresh fruit to the table and marvel at how attractive the table looks.

The sound of high heels on the flagstone floor causes me to turn and look. Jane's dressed in a frilly, white, long-sleeved blouse and a purple, pleated mini skirt. Black stockings cover her slender legs.

"Smells so good in here, Mom. They should be here in a few minutes, huh?"

I look down at my soiled apron. "Should I change my clothes? You look so beautiful and very dressed up."

She studies me from head to toe. "Ditch the apron and you'll be fine."

Georgette Lieteau is a petite lady with a very pleasant smile. Her short, light brown hair accentuates her beautiful hazel eyes. "It's so nice of you to invite Albert and me for dinner. I put a long day in at the hospital, and sometimes I find cooking supper an agonizing chore."

"We love having you both. Jane and Guy are spending a lot of time together these days, so it's about time we all get to know each other. What do you do for a living, Albert?"

318

The slender, grey haired man across from me blushes. "Work at the mill in Cohoes. I've been there for thirty years."

"Oh, that sounds interesting. Maybe, you can tell us later what they manufacture. Henry, will you please ask the blessing?"

"Lord God, thank You for the food before us and for the privilege of dining tonight with some new friends. May You bless the conversation around this table? Amen."

As I lift my head, I see our guests cross themselves.

Jane and Guy are spending more time giggling and flirting with each other than eating. Things are getting serious between these two.

"Everything is delicious, and I admire your knack for decorating too." Georgette smiles.

"Thank you. I'll have to show you my studio so you can pick out a tile to take home with you. Albert, you might like to see Henry's silk-screening operation."

"Guy and I will clear the table, Mom, so everyone's free to explore the studio."

"Whoa, that's a switch. I must say I like that idea. While you're at it, unload the dishwasher too."

Everyone spouts off with laughter like kernels of corn popping over an open fire.

I turn to my guests. "Right this way."

They follow my husband, but I pause and turn to find the two young people embraced in each other's arms.

"These are beautiful, Violet. I see you have many with quotations from the Bible. I never saw anything quite like these. Are all of these designs yours?"

"Yes, God changed my life after a nervous breakdown. I'm saved by the precious blood of Jesus, the Lamb of God. Our new slogan is, Tiles with a testimony. It's not about a religion but a relationship with the triune God. Where do you go to church?"

319

Georgette fidgets from one foot to the other as she puts the "God is Love" tile back on the shelf. "Uh, um, we're Catholic."

"I believe the word Catholic means universal church. Don't we all worship the same God?"

Her eyebrows furrow together as her mouth forms a jagged scowl. "I think it's time to go. Thank you for a nice dinner. Albert? We must leave."

Albert peeks from around the screening area. "Why? Henry's showing me how to silk screen. Just a minute," he says in his broken English.

She spouts something off in French, but it's too fast to catch any of the words I learned as a teen.

"Wa, wa. In a minute, Dear."

Georgette turns on her haunches and whisks into the other part of the house.

Do I go after her or let her be? Sometimes, Lord, I know I can be too pushy.

"Guy, we're leaving this instant."

The two love birds are cuddling on the couch and leap to their feet as if caught in an embarrassing moment. Jane straightens her skirt. "What's wrong? You didn't have desert yet."

"Georgette, please forgive me. I didn't mean to upset you. Stay for some cake."

"I would like to have my coat."

Guy stands. "What's the hurry, Mom? It's only seven o'clock. Why are you so agitated?"

"I'm not going into detail right now. I'll tell you on the way home. Please get your father, Guy."

Jane pulls on my arm. "What happened in there? Why is Mrs. Lieteau so upset?"

Georgette glares at me and shakes her head. "Religious differences caused a disagreement, I would say."

320

I reach my hand out to her. "I apologize, Georgette. Henry and I have many Catholic friends. We simply respect each other's beliefs, allowing God to bridge over the gap. Please, stay longer."

Reluctantly, she takes my hand and sighs. "I over-reacted. I'm sorry for getting so huffy. I would love a piece of that chocolate cake."

A smile tugs at my lips.

Later that night, before going to bed, I see Jane's light on in her room. "It was a lovely night with the Lieteau's. Do you think they had a good time, Jane?"

She's clad in flannel pajamas and sprawled out on her bed. "They're strong Catholics, Mom. There's a crucifix hanging in every room, statues of saints around, and the same priest visits once a week."

I perch on the side of the bed. "How serious are you and Guy?"

"I love him, Mom, and he loves me."

Chapter Forty-Five

Be ye not unequally yoked together with unbelievers; for what fellowship hath righteousness with unrighteousness? And what communion hath light with darkness? 2 Corinthians 6:14

"Oh, my Lord and God, my daughter is in love with a wonderful boy, who comes from a loving family, but they're Catholics. Henry and I must be prepared for the day Guy will ask for her hand in marriage. They will have a huge strike against them if they marry. Grant us all wisdom and guidance. Amen."

Henry joins me on the couch. "Why so glum, my dear?"

"I have a strong feeling Guy is going to ask us for permission to marry Jane."

"Isn't that a good thing?"

"Yes, of course, but the difference of religion can cause a huge problem for them. His mother was very offended when asked what church they go to."

"Is that what happened when they were over for dinner? I don't think Albert had any idea what happened. He's a delightful man and so interested in the silk-screening process. He screened a dozen tiles in that short period of time. Georgette hardly speaks with an accent, though born and raised in Canada. She's an intelligent woman. Yet, Albert speaks very broken English. His family comes from a little town, called Joliet, north of Montreal. Interesting people."

"Henry, I agree with you, but the Bible speaks against being unequally yoked, and it will be disastrous if our daughter marries into this family."

"Oh, come now, Vi, let's take one day at a time, okay? We don't even know if they are that serious. How long have they been dating?"

"Close to six months now. I think we better have a talk with Jane soon about all of this. She needs to be prepared."

"I think you're taking this way out of proportion, Vi. Catholics are not bad people, and you know that. We all worship the same God in different ways. Listen, my dear, you have witnessed to many different types of people from all backgrounds. My advice is to commit this matter to the Lord, and I will too."

I throw my arms around his neck. "Thank you for your inspiring advice. I have decided to call myself a missionary to the oddballs, fully aware that I'm the oddest of all. One thing for sure, our daughter is incredibly happy these days."

Dearest Violet,

I have been thinking about you a lot lately. I am still distraught about the bank books you found at your father's apartment. I have since changed my will to read fifty-fifty. You and Daisy will get equal shares of my estate. The emphysema is really bothering me, and I can't seem to get enough fresh air. I feel good other than that. Jane wrote and told me about her new beau. Sounds serious. Are there wedding bells soon? I would like to come up and stay with you for a couple of weeks, weather permitting. It's very lonely around here since most of my friends have died or moved away. It seems undesirable folks are moving into this neighborhood more and more. I keep the lights on all through the night and I have the telephone next to my bed. Thank Henry for putting that jack in for me when he was here last. Well, let me know when I can come to visit.

    I love you,
    Aunt Flossie.

"What are you doing, Mom? I've been standing here for a few minutes and you didn't even notice. That's unusual."

"Oh, sorry, Jane. I'm reading a letter from your great aunt. She wants to come and stay with us for a couple of weeks because she wants to enjoy the beautiful fresh air of upstate New York. What do you think?"

"Geez. She's so picky about my life. I don't think she approves of my lack of intelligence. I feel so stupid when I am around her."

My eyes widen as I fold the letter and focus on my daughter. "Honey, she loves you very much. Aunt Flossie only wants the best for you. She's thrilled that you are going to college for preschool education, and she's eager to meet Guy. Here, read her letter while I make supper. Are you working tonight?"

"No, but I'm going over to Guy's house for supper to meet his aunt for the first time. Yikes, I'm nervous." She fiddles with her hair.

She unfolds the letter and squints her eyes with curiosity. "Emphysema, huh?"

This might be the perfect time to talk to her about her relationship with Guy. "What time are you supposed to be there, Jane?"

"Six."

"We need to talk, dear, after you finish reading."

"About what? How long would she stay with us?"

"Keep reading. I'm going to start browning some ground chuck for spaghetti sauce. Come and sit at the counter when you're done, okay?"

Lord, grant me the wisdom to talk to my daughter about what the consequences will be if she marries into another religion. She's in love and I don't want to upset her.

"Wow. Now I feel sorry for Aunt Flossie, Mom. I think it's a great idea that she spends some time here."

"I'll call her in the morning. She'll be here in a few days, I'm sure."

"Jane, are you and Guy getting serious about each other?"

She giggles and rolls her eyes. "Of course, we are. I love him, Mom."

"You do know his family are devout Catholics?"

"So what?"

"Plain and simple. You're not."

"It's not like they have the bubonic plague or something."

"The Bible's very clear about being unequally yoked."

She slams her fist on the counter. "Guy told me you were very pushy about religion when his mother was here. She acted like everything was fine when she left, but she was very disturbed about your conversation. I won't let you come between us."

"Listen, Honey, your father and I want you to be happy, but we know two people from two different religions can bring havoc on a new marriage. It's important that you think this through before doing anything hasty."

"If two people love each other, isn't that enough?"

"Your father and I have always loved each other, more than life itself, but when I was going through a very dark time in my life, it was my faith in the Lord that pulled me out of it. I know that the Lieteau's believe in God, but it's the way they worship that is different from ours."

"Okay, okay. That's enough, Mom. I don't want to hear any more of this. Guy hasn't mentioned anything about marriage. After all, we have been dating for only a few months. I better go feed Ebony before I leave."

Jane's a little naïve, to say the least. Poor kid. Henry and I do need to be prepared if her boyfriend decides to pop the question.

❧☙

A few days later, on a frigid November mid-morning, I find myself heading to the bus depot in Albany. We've been blessed not to have any snowstorms lately or any in the future weather reports. *Oh, Lord, I pray you would grant me wisdom as I drive to pick up Aunt Flossie. You know, Lord, I have prayed for her for years and talked about the power of the triune God. Yet, she comes so close to accepting You as her Lord and Savior. She'll be staying with us for a couple of weeks, a perfect opportunity to talk to her.*

"Goodness, the bus must have arrived early. There she is."

I put the car in park and leap out the door. "Oh, Auntie. How long have you been standing here? You came earlier than expected." I give her a hug and lift the cumbersome suitcase into the trunk.

"I just got here, Toots. The fresh, cool air feels wonderful."

"It's so good to see you and especially great that you are staying with us for a while. I worry about you alone in that big house with all of those oddballs moving into the neighborhood."

"Mrs. Abernathy, my neighbor next door, is watching the place for me."

"You went through that checklist I sent you, right? Doors and windows locked, hall lights left on, all mail on hold and..."

"Yes. Yes, and yes, Violet Pearl. I even called the police station and asked for a patrol car to pass by the house on occasion. I'm not worried at all, and you shouldn't be either."

"I shouldn't doubt you, Auntie. You might be getting older, but you still have your wits about you. It sounds like you have all your bases covered. Did you bring some warm clothes?"

"I could use some new flannel nightgowns. Other than that, I have everything I need in case of a snowstorm that keeps us housebound for a number of days."

We both giggle over that and other things as I pull into the Kirker's steakhouse parking lot for lunch. "Let me treat you to some nice Manhattan clam chowder. It's delicious here."

"I hope you'll be comfortable in our room, Aunt Flossie. The sheets were changed this morning and I put an extra blanket on the bed too. Come look in the closet, as I moved most of our clothes into the spare room so you would have plenty of room to hang your clothes."

She perches on the edge of the bed and shakes her head. "I feel terrible that you and Henry are giving up your beautiful bedroom for me. If I knew you were going to do that, I would have stayed in Richmond Hill. You have bunkbeds in that room for goodness' sake, twin beds mind you. That's not right for a happily married couple like you two."

I place my hand on her shoulder. "We're so happy you're staying with us for a while, Henry will sleep in there and I might sleep on the sofa bed in the office. I put a six-drawer dresser in there for my clothes yesterday. So, my dear aunt, you don't have to worry about a thing."

327

"You are so good to me, Violet. I appreciate you so much. I hope you know that."

"Look, I even cleared off my dressing table for you. I know how much you love the one you have in your house. I'll bet you have your favorite perfumes, brushes, and hair ribbons in your train case."

She rises to her feet and sits on the small, cushy chair and looks in the mirror with a huge smile on her face. "I'm ready to unpack and settle in now. Go and take care of those orders you need to fill."

I strain myself as I lift the big, heavy Pullman suitcase on the bed. "Take all the time you need, Auntie. You even have time to take a nap before supper."

She waves me away with a smile, but as I shut the door, I watch her lift a large, black metal box out of her suitcase and clutch it in her arms.

Chapter Forty-Six

"How long is Auntie going to stay here, Mom? Honestly, I'm having a real hard time being in the same room with her."

"Jane, please lower your voice. She might be able to hear you." I motion for her to follow me to the studio. "Now, what's this all about?"

"She's always telling me to put my shoulders back, sit straight, smile more, and to stop rolling my big, brown eyes at everything she says."

"Oh, Aunt Flossie means well, Dear. She and my mother were raised to be proper ladies. She wants the same for you."

"Well, I certainly hope she doesn't scold me in front of Guy when she meets him for the first time tonight. Does she know he's coming for dinner?"

"Yes, she knows. Now, go and set the table."

She turns on her haunches, into the house, and slams the door behind her. Disappointment washes over me.

As I sit down to put the final colors on the "Have you prayed about it?" tile, I check the time and note that I have one hour before dinner. The spaghetti sauce is simmering, the meatballs are baking, and the salad is in the fridge. *I only have the garlic bread to do.*

The fire's crackling as we all sit on the sectional, eating apple crumb cake with vanilla ice cream. Guy and Jane are huddled close together. It's a wonder they don't spill the dessert all over the place.

"This is delicious, Toots. You have the Moretti gift for cooking. I'm going to gain some weight while I'm here." Auntie winks. "So, Guy, Jane tells me your parents were born in Canada?"

He pulls himself straight. "Yes, that's right. My dad's people come from a small town called Joliet, north of Montreal, and my mothers are from the city."

"How far from here is it?"

"About four hours, depending on the weather."

"Really? Let's take a trip there, Violet. What do you think?"

I collect the dishes. "Maybe in the spring, Auntie. The roads can be treacherous at this time of year. It's pretty barren from Lake George to the border too."

"Do you have a lot of relatives that still live there, Guy?"

"Tons of cousins. Jane will get to meet many of them at a cousin's wedding in April."

"Sounds like you plan ahead, my boy. This is November and April's months away."

⚬⚬❀⚬⚬

A few days later, after stepping out of the shower, the annoying ringing of the telephone catches my attention. I wrap a towel around myself and flee to the kitchen where the closest phone is. "Hello?"

"Mrs. Funk. How are you?"

"Guy?"

"Yes, I would like to talk to you and Mr. Funk alone."

330

My voice wobbles with emotion. "Tonight? Jane will be working at Macy's."

"That's great."

"You want to talk to her father and me? About what?"

"I want to tell you in person, if that's okay."

"Oh, I understand."

"How about 7:00?"

"See you then."

Auntie opens the front door and takes a deep breath of cold fresh air. "I heard the telephone ringing, but you got it before I could. Toots, you're dripping wet. You better get into something warm, before you get sick."

"I think Guy's going to ask us if he can marry Jane."

She grabs my hand and pulls me to the spare room. "Here, put this robe on before you catch your death. Pneumonia took your mother's life, let's not let it take yours, my dear."

I wrap the robe around me, and turban wrap my hair with the towel. "It will be a disaster if they marry, Auntie."

"Put on your slippers. I see two young people madly in love with each other. He has a good job, comes from a good family, and is a very polite young man. A perfect mate for Jane."

"I wish it was that simple. There's a huge religious difference that will cause strife from the get-go. Henry and I have been praying for God to give us wisdom for this upcoming conversation, but now that it's here, I'm fearful of the outcome."

"Do they believe in God?"

"Of course, they do."

"Tsk, tsk. Then what are you worried about? Get dressed, Toots. I'm ready for some breakfast. It's hot in in this house. I think I'll turn down the thermostat."

Okay, Lord, in a few short hours Guy will be here to talk to Henry and me. I pray for Your infinite wisdom once again to have the right words to say. My husband is so much better with words, so maybe I'll force myself to keep quiet. You know how hard that is? If this union is right in Your eyes Lord, I pray for peace. Amen.

✺

The day whizzes past as I fill a few orders, vacuum the entire house, and tidy up the office. Auntie enjoys putting the hanging jiggers in the cork backs while I paint across from her. Beethoven's 5th Symphony chimes a classical music aura throughout the room.

"Gee, it's five o'clock. I hope Henry's on his way home."

"I smell something burning, Toots. Do you have enough water in the Dutch oven for the pot roast?"

I race to the stove and find an almost burnt roast. "I got it in time, Auntie. Thanks for catching it for me. Where's my husband?"

I fumble with the telephone and dial the number to the office.

"Hello, Metropolitan Life."

"Henry? Why are you answering? Where's the receptionist?"

"I'm working late tonight. I'll grab supper later."

"What? You won't be home for supper. When will you be here?"

"I'm not sure. Why?"

"I'm glad I called you or I would have been wondering what happened. Can you be here by 7:00? Guy is coming over here to talk to both of us tonight."

"Calm down, Vi. Take a breath."

"Really?"

"Yes. Where is Jane? Call Guy back and make it another time."

"Jane's at work, and I don't know his telephone number. You must get here. You simply have to stop what you're doing so you're in this house when he arrives."

"Okay, I'll get there when I can."

"All right. I'll let you get back to your pressing project. Goodbye."

An hour later, Guy and I are sitting in the office alone. Small talk about the cold weather and a possible snowstorm tomorrow is chewing up some time. Auntie excused herself a few minutes ago.

"Um, when will Mr. Funk be home from work?"

"He had an important project at work, Guy. He just couldn't break away from it. If you want to come another time to talk to us, that's okay."

"Well, I've been rehearsing in my mind over and over how I was going to talk to you about something that concerns your daughter and me."

"Let me make it easier for you, okay? Do you want to marry Jane?"

He takes a big gulp and wipes his forehead. "Yes, I love your daughter and wish to marry her. With your permission, of course."

Father God, give me the right words.

I join him on the love seat and pivot his way. "Guy, Jane's in love with you too. However, her father and I are concerned about your religious differences. The Bible speaks against people who are unequally yoked joining together in matrimony. You would be starting off your marriage with a huge strike against you."

"My mother said the same thing, Mrs. Funk. What am I supposed to do? I know we're right for each other, and we both believe in God."

"Well, let's not talk about religion. Do you believe in Jesus as your Savior?"

"I know who Jesus is. I was baptized as an infant and I was confirmed."

"Those are sacraments in the church, but I'm talking about a personal relationship with Jesus. Have you ever heard of 'The four spiritual laws'?"

Guy reads each Bible verse and application on every page. He doesn't ask any questions, and when we come to the last page where the salvation prayer is offered, he prayerfully repeats each word after me.

Tears of joy trickle down my face as I hug him.

He lets out a sigh.

"The angels are rejoicing because you gave your heart to Jesus. Welcome into the kingdom of God. He loves you, Guy, and has a marvelous plan for your life."

"I'm tongue tied at the moment, Mrs. Funk."

"Do you have a Bible?"

"Uh, a big family Bible."

"Here's a copy of *The Good News for Modern Man*. It's a paraphrased New Testament portion of the Bible. Easy to read and understand. You can keep it."

He goes through it and smiles at a few of the illustrations. "Thank you. Now, do I have permission to marry your daughter?"

The door bursts open. "Well, well. Did I make it in time?" smiles Henry.

"Guy accepted Jesus as his Savior tonight. Isn't that wonderful, Henry?"

He reaches out and shakes his hand. "Great news, Son, and I'm sorry I'm late."

"I really came over tonight to ask permission, from the both of you, to marry Jane. We have looked at rings, but she has no idea when I will pop the question."

"Well, Vi. What do you think?"

The tears of joy send my heart into flurries of peppy heartbeats. "Yes. Yes. Yes."

"You may marry our daughter. This is cause for a toast. Do we have any wine, Dear, and where's Aunt Flossie?"

"I'll get her. She's probably in her room."

"Congratulations, Guy. I hope I'm still here when you actually give Jane the ring."

"It's not a secret. I'm planning on asking her this weekend. I'm taking her to a special place for dinner, Miss. Thomas."

She takes his hand with a giggle. "Please call me Auntie. Everyone else does."

Chapter Forty-Seven

In these early morning hours, the house is quiet as I sit at my desk contemplating a few new designs. The picture window overlooks the driveway and the grove of evergreen pine trees. I can look to my left and down to the bottom of the steep hill and to my right where glistening snow covers the summer grass. Aunt Flossie has been with us for a month, and her health seems stable for the moment. *Thank you, Lord. I'm filled with unspeakable joy as Jane and I plan a June wedding. We have the Clifton Knolls Country Club reserved for the reception but, Lord, where will they get married?*

The door behind me opens with a squeak. "Food for thought, my dear?"

"Honey, you startled me. You're up early for a Saturday."

He wraps his arms around me. "I miss my bride."

"Thanks, Sweetheart."

"Has Jane talked to you about getting married at the Community Church yet?"

"She keeps avoiding the subject and fills the void with wedding magazines, brochures about honeymoon getaways, and who will be her bridesmaids."

"The months will fly by and this wedding will be upon us. They must set up an appointment to talk to Pastor Whitman soon. Does he even know about the wedding date?"

"Yes, he does but is concerned about repercussions from Guy's family."

"Jane was bubbling over with excitement after the big Catholic wedding she went to with Guy. He was an usher at his cousin's wedding, and it was in St. Joseph's Catholic Church in Troy. Her eyes got as big as saucers when she described the bride walking down the aisle with her Dad."

"Are you talking about me again?"

"Jane, Honey, good morning. We do need to talk about the church."

She fiddles with her curly hair. "I know, it could be a problem."

"Why do you say that?"

"Come here, give your old Dad a hug, and let's talk about this."

She leans into her father's arms. "Guy insists we marry in Saint Mary's Catholic Church. I would have to go talk to the priest about converting."

I diffuse my anger with a deep sigh. "Do you want to become a Catholic, Jane?"

"Not really, but I love Guy, Mom."

"I know you do. Your father and I have been praying that you two would find a peaceful solution to this. We want you to be happy."

"I'm so torn by all of this. Everything's falling into place for a June wedding, but we can't agree on where the ceremony should be. Maybe we should elope." She bursts into tears.

"Do you think Guy will at least meet with Pastor Whitman about this?"

The sound of a door slamming shut arouses our interest. "What was that?"

I jump to my feet to find Auntie leaning against the front door. "Are you all right?" I ask.

"Uh, uh, um. I think so," she mumbles as she fans herself.

"Were you outside?"

She grabs ahold of my arm. "I needed some fresh air, Toots. Maybe if I eat something, I'll be all right."

Her skin is as white as the snow-covered ground, and continuous deep breaths are a cause for concern. Slowly, we make our way to the table, where she takes a seat. "How about a nice cup of hot tea and an English muffin?"

"That would be nice. Is anyone else awake?"

"Henry? Jane? Please come in and join Aunt Flossie for some breakfast. I'm pretty hungry too."

Henry rubs Auntie's shoulder. "How are you today, Flossie?"

"I'm having a hard time breathing this morning for some reason. Fresh air is a relief. I'll do better as the day wears on."

"Jane and Guy are having a hard time making a decision on what church to marry in. Who wants some scrambled eggs?" I say.

"A church wedding is nice. It doesn't matter where. Does it?"

"Must you always do that, Aunt Flossie?"

"I'm sorry, Jane, do what?"

"Smooth everything over as though there wasn't a problem at all. Honestly. The church issue is huge, and I can't sleep at night because of it. All you see is a nice French-Canadian family who settled in America."

Flossie smiles. "Love conquers all."

"How would you know? You never married."

"Jane, that's enough. You better apologize to Auntie, right now."

I look at composed Aunt Flossie as she calmly eats her muffin. *My daughter lashed out at her, and she still manages to keep it together. It's amazing how rare any emotion gets the best of her.*

Jane kisses her on the cheek. "I'm sorry, Aunt Flossie. I shouldn't have said that. I better go take care of my horse."

A few silent tears roll trickle down my Aunts face.

The kids went to talk to Pastor Whitman last night. According to Jane, they talked about football and hunting for a while before going into religious things. It was a nice move on the pastor's part, but an ice breaker can last just so long. Jane came home right after the meeting and ran to her room in tears. Of course, I tried to console her, but nothing I said worked.

It turns out that Guy refused to marry in the Community church because his family would never be able to accept it. Jane was so upset and fearful that she would lose the love her of life, that she decided to go talk to a priest with her fiancé. The only way we found out about this meeting was by sheer accident. A friend of mine just happened to drive by the Catholic Church rectory when she saw Jane and Guy going in.

"Jane, can I talk to you?"

"I know. About the church? Right?"

"Yes. In a roundabout way. Yes. Mrs. Nosal saw you going into the St. Mary's rectory with Guy. Do you want to talk about it?"

"It's complicated and frustrating at the same time. Guy said he was willing to go to my church, so I should return the favor and go to his. It comes down to one thing, Mom."

"What do you mean?"

"I would have to agree to become a Catholic. I can't do that. Why is this happening? There has to be a solution soon or the wedding will be called off."

I take a deep breath and pull her next to me. "Let's pray about it. Okay?"

"I did that already."

"Matthew eighteen, verse nineteen says, where two or three agree about whatever they ask for, it will come to pass by our Father in Heaven."

Much to my amazement, Jane leans forward with her hands folded and head bowed. "Dear Lord, thank You for a Christian mother who loves You. Please help me to be bolder in my faith and grasp opportunities to tell others what You have done for me."

Tears ignite as I sniffle. "Yes, Heavenly Father, may we never forsake You even when trials of all kinds come our way. We come before You today with heavy hearts about the church for the wedding. Thank You that Guy accepted You as his savior. He's the perfect man for my daughter, but religious differences are coming between them. We ask in Jesus' name that they find a solution to this problem very soon. Amen."

"Amen. Thanks, Mom, but I better get ready for work."

"I love you, Jane."

Chapter Forty-Eight

God answers prayer in His perfect timing and infinite ways, not always in the way we would like them answered. The Bible says, "Be thankful in all things." This is one of those times. The kids sought out a compromise pleasing to everyone involved, at least for the moment. Jane stopped at the Saint George Episcopal Church to talk to the priest, and he's very receptive to marrying them. All they must do is attend five marriage classes at the church. I never thought in my wildest dreams that Guy would go along with this, but he did. So, the June twenty-seventh wedding will be held at the Episcopal Church. *Will this just put a Band-Aid on the problem, Lord?*

"The snow is really coming down out there, Toots."

"I know. We're supposed to get six to ten inches by midnight."

She opens the front door, sticks her head out, and inhales, gasping for air. I turn from browning meatballs on the stove and sprint to her. "Auntie, come in out of the frigid air before you get sick. You don't even have a coat on."

Her chest burrows in and out as she inhales profusely. "Ah, uh, ah. I can hardly breathe, Violet Pearl. When I get like this, the only thing to do is go outside."

I pull her in and close the door. "Here, wrap this blanket around yourself and sit on the couch. I'll bring you a pot of hot tea. I think we better get you to the doctor as soon as possible, Auntie."

"Oh, I'm fine now, Dear. You don't need to fuss over me, but I will take you up on your tea offer."

"Is the fire still burning or do I need to throw on a few more logs?"

"It's glowing and radiating enjoyable warmth," she squeals as she takes in some air.

"Did your great-niece share the exciting news with you?"

"She avoids me at all cost, Tootsie. What is the great news that you are bubbling over about?"

I join her with two piping hot cups of lemon tea. "The wedding is set for June twenty-seventh at the Saint George Episcopal Church. So far, no one in Guy's family is disputing it."

"Tsk, tsk. Why would they contest a wedding? The Lieteaus are such pleasant people and seem like they love Jane. Is it a high Episcopalian service?"

"Yes, it is, and that's the whole reason why the Lieteaus are happy with it."

"It's close to a Catholic mass, from what I understand. All right, now both of you can concentrate on the important things, like the dress, flowers, and the meal."

"Jane wants to make her own dress. I'm making the veil."

"I hope I will be here for this grand occasion."

"Of, course you will be, Auntie. We'll shop for dresses together, okay?'

The new European Health Club is fifteen minutes from our house, kind of over the river and through the woods a piece. Auntie seems perfectly content in the office with the typewriter and her many books of choice. I left the phone number for the gym right next to the telephone, in case she needs me for anything.

I'm so happy I joined last week. This is the best time to come here. Mid-morning. Businesspeople are at work and young moms are doing housework or running errands, which leaves most of the machines open. One wall is covered with a floor to ceiling mirror accompanied by a ballet barre. Individual mats are available for stretching and various exercise maneuvers. Weights ranging from one to ten pounds are available for ladies to use for toning muscles. I opt to do some floor exercises to warm up.

I lie down on my back and spin my legs up into vigorous bicycle rotations, *one, two, three, four, the numbers turn into teens, and soon I'm at one hundred.*

"Hi there, have you been coming here long?"

I always close my eyes for some reason when I exercise, so I'm not sure if I'm the one being spoken to. I keep in motion.

"Yeah, I've been coming here since the grand opening two weeks ago. Do you live around here?"

She must be talking to me. I pull myself to a cross-legged position and turn towards the unusual but attractive lady right next to me. "I live in Elnora, the other side of Rexford. My name's Violet. What's yours?"

She's a petite woman with dark hair piled on top of her head in a beehive style. Her makeup is applied as though she's ready to take center stage on Broadway. Perfect eyeliner, black mascara, and plenty of rouge. "Twyla DuBois, from Alplaus."

I lean closer to her. "Do you take the exercise class or do your own thing when you come?"

"I try to do both. How about you, Violet?"

She must be a smoker because she reeks of it.

"I spend an hour using the machines, weights, and sauna and my own repertoire of stretches on the mat. I've never been one for group exercise classes."

343

"Well, I think it's about time you try one. The next class begins in ten minutes. What do you say?"

"I guess I better finish my routine and get out of here, so I'm not in the way. My aunt is staying with us, and she's not in the best of health. I don't like to leave her too long."

A few more ladies pull out mats to do warm-up stretches as the young instructor clad in black tights and a purple leotard organizes her music tapes.

I head to the rowing machine but with a corner of my eye on the synchronized group following their fearless leader. I thrust my legs back and forth in tune with the peppy rock and roll music. One, two, three…ten…fifteen. *Come on, Violet, push harder. Fifty is the magic number.* Twenty, twenty-five…

"Violet Funk? Is there a Violet Funk here?" shouts the receptionist from behind the counter.

With sweat dripping from my brow, I answer, "Right here. I'm Violet."

"You have a telephone call. Sounds pretty urgent."

Suddenly, Twyla's by my side, reaching her hand out to help me up. "I hope everything's all right."

I race to the phone and pick it up. "Hello?"

Panting sounds fill the phone, "Tootsie, I'm not doing so good."

"Auntie, what's wrong?"

"I can't get enough air. I managed to call for an ambulance."

I hear a lot of shuffling and muffled voices. "Hello? Aunt Flossie?"

"Hello, are you Ms. Thomas's niece?

"Yes. I'm Flossie's niece. Who's this?"

"I'm Mark, the ambulance driver. Can you meet us at Ellis Hospital?"

"Yes, I can. Is she going to be okay?"

A buzzing sound floods my eardrum, "Hello?"

I grab a towel, head to the locker room, and strip off my leotard. *Oh, Lord. Help me get to Ellis Hospital before the ambulance. If it's Your will, please allow the doctors to help my auntie.*

"Violet, do you want company? I can drive you to the hospital if you're too upset," Twyla offers while I am doing a miraculous change.

"Ellis is only a couple of miles, so I'll be fine."

I fly out the door, flinging my arms into my plaid winter coat while juggling purse and workout bag. The cool air blasts me in the face as I shuffle my way through the packed snow to the car.

"Dearest Aunt Flossie, please don't leave me yet. No. You must come to know Jesus first." The tears fall free from my eyes as I grip the cold steering wheel. "Oh, Sweet Jesus, prepare her heart now for you. She comes so close to you but then puts her hand out to keep you away. I know Papa's with you for eternity. Is Mama with him? I won't know until the day I breathe my last." I pull a hankie out of my pocket and wipe my eyes and nose. "If it's Your will, Heavenly Father, open the doors for Auntie to make that commitment. In Jesus' name. Amen."

An ambulance is pulling away as I pull open the glass door to the emergency room. The room's full of people ranging from infants to a very frail, white-haired lady in a wheelchair. DO NOT ENTER signs growl at me to keep from entering the double closed doors. I pivot in every direction to seek out a nurse or anyone who can give some ray of direction. Nervousness tickles the back of my throat.

A tall, thin nurse in a starched white uniform with clipboard in hand shouts, "Darlene Treater."

A very heavy-set lady, coughing profusely into a blue towel, waddles to the nurse.

"Follow me, Dear."

I grab the nurse's arm. "Please help me. My aunt was brought here by ambulance. I must see her now. She has nobody else."

Her eyes are narrowed, rigid, cold, and hard. I'm her enemy. She brushes my hand from her arm. "You must wait just like everyone else."

She disappears through the door. Everyone in the waiting area scowls at me. I slink into the nearest chair, with my hands over my face. *Now what do I do?* I don't have strength to argue.

I wait in my own little world for a while. I'm afraid to move. The only thing I seem to do is check the time on my watch. *I have been sitting here for twenty minutes now. Come on, Violet, do something.* "Lord, get me out of this slump before I sink deeper," I whisper.

"Violet Funk?"

Did someone say my name? I must be imagining it.

"Mrs. Violet Funk? Is there a Violet here?"

I pick my head up and watch a nurse in a white uniform turn on her heels.

"Wait. I'm Violet Funk."

"Follow me. You're aunt has been asking for you, but we had to get her as stable as possible before getting you."

The smell of Clorox tickles my nose as I follow her. There are several curtain-enclosed areas, a nurse's station, and an actual room with drawn white blinds. She knocks on the door, opens it, and motions for me to go in.

My legs wobble as I inch my way to Auntie's side. *She looks so pale and thin.*

"Auntie, I'm here." I grab her bony hand.

She turns her head and smiles with her eyes. "So glad you're here."

An IV is dripping slowly into the tube that connects to her other hand. Oxygen is pumping air into her lungs via a tube in her nose as she drifts off to sleep, wheezing with every breath. *I feel like I'm experiencing an instant replay of what happened to Papa just a few months ago. Oh, Lord, please give me a chance to share the gospel with Aunt Flossie one more time.*

"Excuse me, Mrs. Funk, but can I speak to you in the hall for moment?" whispers a man dressed in a long, white coat with a stethoscope around his neck.

I nod as I gently remove my hand.

"Your aunt's blood pressure is quite low, and she is running a fever of 103. We are medicating her through the intravenous tube, which should help, but we won't know the outcome for a few days. The nurse has the admission papers for you to fill out."

I glance at the name tag. "Thank you, Doctor Abbot."

Chapter Forty-Nine

Fortunately, I have an extra change of clothes, toiletries, and some makeup in my gym bag. I escape to the cafeteria to find a phone booth to call Henry. *I'll change later, as soon as I see Auntie's resting comfortably.*

"May I speak to Henry Funk, please?"

"Who may I ask is calling?"

"This is his wife, Violet. I need to speak to him. It's urgent."

"He's in a meeting and asked not to be disturbed."

"You must disturb him. My aunt is ill, and it's imperative I talk to him, now."

"Okay, please hold."

"Of course, I'll hold. Please don't drag your feet."

My hands turn clammy as my heart rate escalates. *Oh, come on. How long can it take to get a message to him?*

"Hello, are you still on the line?"

"Yes. I'm still here. Of course. Now, get my husband."

I feel like I'm alone on a deserted island as I tap my fingers and wait.

"Violet? What is the urgency?"

"Henry? Finally. I'm at Ellis Hospital. Auntie's terribly ill."

"My secretary said you were very rude."

"I wasn't rude to your secretary. Honestly, if anything, she was very inconsiderate of me."

"I'll pray for Aunt Flossie. She'll be fine with the fine care at the hospital. I must get back to the meeting, Vi."

"You have to go already? Well, I won't be home tonight. I'm staying right here with Aunt Flossie. Goodbye, Henry."

I slam the phone on the receiver, grab my things, and dart back to the elevator.

The dark clouds disappear into nightfall as I sink into the reclining chair next to the hospital bed. I glance over at the frail, untroubled body under the starched white sheet. The constant beep of the oxygen tank reminds me she's not able to breathe on her own. Every gasp of air catches my attention, but she continues to sleep. *I should have purchased some magazines. I don't dare turn on the television.* I lean my head back and close my eyes, in hopes of catching a few winks myself. *Dear Lord, if it's Your will, let Aunt Flossie get better so she can dance at Jane's wedding. Amen.*

"To-o-t?"

I pull my chair close and smile. "Auntie, how do you feel?"

She takes several deep breaths and gasps with a wince. "So weak. Can hardly move."

I hold a cup of water with a straw to her mouth. "Here, try a sip."

She turns her head away, as my emotions play havoc on me. *I must share the peace that only God can bring to her, right now, right here.*

Without much ado, I skirt around the foot of the bed to the other side. Her eyes are closed. "Auntie? Can you hear me?"

She flickers her eyes open.

"Jesus loves you, my dear Aunt Flossie. All you must do is accept Him as your Savior and Lord. You will spend all of eternity with Him if you do. Do you believe?"

My aunt Flossie slipped into a coma on that cold November day and passed away a week later. *I will never know until I go to my eternal home with my Savior if she accepted Him on her death bed or not. My heart burns with anxiety if I allow myself to dwell on it. "I am not anxious about anything, but in everything, by prayer and petition, with thanksgiving, I present my requests to God. And the peace of God, which transcends all understanding, will guard my heart and mind in Christ Jesus." Philippians 4:6, 7.*

My mission is to share the gospel to anyone who wants to listen. Twyla, from the health club, and I have become good friends. I'm not thrilled with her occasional foul language, constant cigarette habit and the gobs of makeup she wears, but she's fun-loving and interesting to be with. Everyone does matter to God, and it's always a privilege leading anyone to the throne of grace through Jesus. Twyla shared with me today all about her past affairs, with tears rolling down her face. "I want to know God the way you do, Violet. You talk about Him like He's your closest friend. You reflect a glow of happiness, and I want what you have."

"Twyla, do you believe that Jesus Christ is God's son?"

"Yes."

"Do you believe He paid the penalty for your sin and that He gave His life on the cross so you could be forgiven?"

"I never thought about it that way, but now that you said it, yes."

"First John 5:12 says, 'He that hath the Son hath life; and he that hath not the Son of God hath not life.' All you must do is invite Jesus into your heart and accept Him as Lord of your life. Are you ready to do that, dear friend?"

She breaks down and bawls like a baby as I embrace her with compassion and joy. "Take a few minutes to pull yourself together."

"Okay, I'm ready."

"Dear Lord Jesus, I turn from my own way and, by faith, invite you to come into my life."

She slowly but audibly repeats the words.

"I now receive you as Savior and Lord."

"Welcome into the family of God. The angels are rejoicing over you right now."

I have always been fascinated with bears, from the time I was a little girl, it was fuzzy teddy bears with red satin ribbons and then, I found myself drawing scads of pictures of black bears of all sizes. *Turf Trailer Park is loaded with children who need to know Jesus. Help me, Lord, to be the witness You want me to be.*

"Bear Witness" is born. I grab my friend, Merle Fritz, the seamstress. I bombard her with my zany idea of dressing up like a brown bear and calling myself, "Bear Witness." Merle is very conservative in manner and the way she dresses, but we hit it off like two peas in a pod. I certainly wouldn't call her odd by any stroke of the word.

"So, you want me to make you a bear costume?"

The soft, brown, furry material lies in bolts on the huge tables at the fabric store. "Yes. You know when God gives me an idea, Merle. I must follow through on it."

"You'll burn up in this material. It's heavy. I strongly suggest that you keep your face free, and apply some whiskers and eyeliner for special effects. Otherwise, you'll be extremely uncomfortable, Vi."

"I can live with that. How long will it take you to make?"

"Give me a couple of weeks. A lot of it might have to be hand sewn due to the heaviness of the fabric."

"I'm so excited about this new venture. You can dress up like a zookeeper, and we can entertain the kids together. What do you say?"

She smiles from ear to ear. "You can count on my prayers when you go out there, but that's it, dear girl."

Some of the trailers are dented, old, and in need of paint. As I drive into the entrance all decked out in my bear suit, I see a few older children stop and laugh at me. *I know there's a playground in the back part of the park. There should be some children playing there. It's a beautiful day, even though a bit nippy.*

A toothy kid shouts, "Hey look, there's someone dressed like a bear."

"Hi, kids, my name is Bear Witness. I want to tell you some stories from the Bible."

Much to my surprise, they come close enough to touch my costume. Three girls and two boys. Maybe in the four to seven age bracket. The smallest girl giggles.

"Come sit at this picnic table. I have some crayons and paper. You can draw while I tell you about Noah and the big boat."

I whip out my flannel board and the manila envelope that holds all the pieces to the story. They throw themselves into their drawings, like they never saw crayons. "Can you tell me your names?"

"I'm Sally Ann. This is Mary Lou."

"My name is Randall. I'm one of the oldest around here. That's my cousin Jacob. He's four."

"Maybe you can tell your friends about today and tell them the bear lady will be back again next Saturday. There was a man called Noah. One day God called from heaven, 'Noah? Can you hear me?'" I shout the line with excitement and authority. All at once, crayons drop, mouths pop open, and all eyes are on me.

"This is good."

I continue with the story, asking for volunteers to act out the animals I mention. The two lanky, older boys who were mocking me when I entered the park sit within hearing distance on the dilapidated swing set.

"On the fortieth day, God sent a rainbow as a sign that He would never flood the earth again. Well, kids, that's the story of Noah and the ark." I pull out my satchel and open it wide. "Come and get some candy."

"Is it free?" yells the tall, skinny boy with horn-rimmed glasses.

"Of course, it is. Please take a flyer that tells who I am and my telephone number, just in case your mother and father want to check up on me."

"I don't have any parents. I live with my grandmother," Sally Ann says softly as she reaches in the bag.

"My mother works all the time, and I never met my father. I have to go soon, so I can lock myself inside my trailer," mumbles Randall as he stuffs his jacket pockets with candy.

"I'm going to pray for all of you this week. You have my phone number. Call me if you need anything. In the meantime, I'll be praying for each of you." Without a word they scatter.

Chapter Fifty

The Lord answers prayers beyond measure. Every Sunday for the past two months, I manage to pack seven kids in my little Ford Escort and take them to Sunday school. They wait for me at the bus stop. I made sure a parental guardian signed a permission slip to take the children off the premises.

"Mom, are you really driving across town in that bear suit?"

Laughter rises from the pit of my stomach. "Of course, I am, Jane. I'm using the community room at the trailer park now, since we have so many kids attending Bible class. You should come with me sometime."

She rolls her eyes and sighs. "The wedding's in two months. I don't have time for anything goofy. Have fun, Mom. By the way, did you get a dress for the wedding yet?"

The phone bellows a steady ring.

"I'll get it," Jane mutters as she runs to grab it.

"Hello."

"Hi, Daddy."

"She's in that bear costume again."

"I'll tell her. I should see you before you go to bed tonight."

"What did your father say, Jane?"

"He won't be home for supper. He's working late."

"That's the third time this week."

I was totally exhausted last night, so I did something I never do. I went to bed at nine-thirty. I heard

354

Henry and Jane talking, but I rolled over and let sleep take over my entire existence. The last thing that was on my mind was, *Will my husband sleep in here tonight or in the guest room again?*

Loud purring and a furry tail in my face cause me to wake the next day. "Poosie. Honestly. How did you get in here?" She continues to rub up against my face, then settles on my tummy. I turn over and glance at the clock. "Eight o'clock. I almost slept twelve hours. Too long." I grab my robe, close the window, and head to the kitchen.

Henry's settled into his recliner with newspaper in hand on this Saturday morning. "I made you some coffee. I thought you would never get up today."

I get a cup. "You're working late a lot. Why is that?"

"I'll answer your question with one. What did I tell you I would never do when I got transferred to Albany?"

"Bring your work home?"

"Bingo. See, now I can relax all weekend."

"Did Jane go to work or is she out at the barn?"

"You just missed her. At Macy's, all day."

I sit across from him with a cup of steaming hot coffee in one hand and *Streams in the Desert Devotional* in the other. "So quiet and peaceful. Thanks for the coffee."

"What did you do yesterday, Violet? The dirty dishes have been in the sink since yesterday morning. It smells atrocious in here, like something died. Is it that litter box again?"

He's been very picky and grumpy lately. "I was with the children in the trailer park after school. Oh, they're so hungry for the word of God, Henry. I think we need two cars to pick them up for Sunday school."

"We? This whole thing is your idea. Don't pull me into this. I have all I can do to get to choir practice before Sunday school. You can't tell me that some of those parents don't have their own cars?"

I shake my head. "Forget it, Henry. I'll figure something out. Maybe Jane will help. She should do something to serve the Lord. All she talks about is that wedding."

"It's in two months. Is everything in place? She claims you have not started on her veil yet. Is that right?"

"Stop badgering me, Henry. I'll have it finished in plenty of time."

"I'm getting the mail. I'm sure you didn't check that mailbox in a few days." He pulls his coat and hat on and slams the front door.

My throat is so tight, I can't speak. I put the book on the end table and decide it is time to tackle the kitchen. "It is a mess in here," I mumble under my breath. Hot water and bubbly dish detergent flows over the sink full of dishes.

"Here's the mail." Henry slams it down on the counter. "Looks like you got a letter from your sister. How long has it been since you talked to her?"

I shrug. "It's been at least two months, but I sent her a letter last week. I wanted to make sure she had the wedding on her calendar. I'm surprised she didn't call."

"It will be amazing if she shows up with her busy schedule. Where is that odor coming from?"

"It's the compost. Your responsibility, right?"

He pushes me aside and pulls the bag out of the plastic container. "I'll take care of it."

He keeps his distance, which is fine with me. An hour and a half later, I marvel at how tidy the kitchen is. I even cleaned out the refrigerator and the oven. *Wow, I'm on a roll, and it's only twelve o'clock.*

I grab the mail and plop down at my desk with a loud sigh. "Junk, junk, phone bill. Oh, Daisy's letter."

Dear Vi,

Thank you for your letter. We have Jane's wedding on the calendar. Hopefully, both of us will be able to come, but if not, at least one will be there. I was going to call you, but it's better I write my thoughts to you because phone conversations don't always go well for us.

You must stop preaching to me. I'm getting very tired of getting religious periodicals from you almost every time I go to the mailbox. I have no time for anything religious, church or otherwise. Honestly, your constant badgering about where I will go if I die drives me away from you. Please don't send me any more of this propaganda. I'm happy that your faith in a higher power has kept you from another nervous breakdown. If you send me any of this kind of material, I will dispose of it immediately.

Love,
Daisy

Chapter Fifty-One

I have all the windows down as I drive back from delivering an order to Word of Life on this squelching hot July day. *What will I come home to? Jane and Guy are enjoying marital bliss in their adorable apartment in Halfmoon. Peter managed to come home for the wedding. Henry and I are like ships passing in the night, rarely conversing with each other, and dinner alone is the name of the game. The cat was my constant companion until last week when she got hit by a car. I had to ditch the bear suit because the heat was too unbearable. I thank God every day for the steady tile orders to keep me from getting depressed. The house sure is quiet these days.*

As I approach the Clifton Park exit, I'm reminded of a new place I heard about that was once an active farm. They sold most of their acreage for residential housing, but the farmer's wife decided to turn the barn closest to the road into a country store. *Maybe they'll give me an order.*

I pull into the dirt driveway and up to the rustic, brown wood structure. A few old milk cans, rusty farm tools from days of old, and other assorted antiques dot the green lawn leading to the door. The door jingles as it opens. A wonderful aroma of baked bread and apple pie greet me as I enter the establishment. Corn husk dolls adorned in flowery dresses dance from the ceiling above, and jars of honey dot the counter directly in front of me. I twirl the rack of postcards as I look at local historical attractions.

"Can I help you with something?" barks a gravelly voice from somewhere.

"Uh, yes. Well, I think so." I peer all around me.

"I'll be right down."

In the far-right corner, I see a wooden ladder heading into a loft of some kind. Soon someone with unkempt blond hair in a ponytail, in overalls and brown laced boots, descends.

"Sorry, I was getting fall decorations organized. How can I help you?"

She's rather attractive with big brown eyes and a beautiful smile. A few wrinkles indicate a lot of time in the sun, probably cultivating crops.

"My name's Violet Funk, and I'm a ceramic tile artist. You have a remarkably interesting place, but some local artwork might add some flavor to your inventory. I'm definitely going to buy a loaf of bread and maybe some honey too."

"I just opened last week, Violet, but I'll be glad to take a few tiles on consignment, to see how they sell. You probably don't have any with you."

"Actually, I do have some in my car. I just came back from delivering an order to a Christian camp in Schroon Lake. I don't usually do consignment, but since I live around the corner on Vischer Ferry Road, I can make an exception. I have a few left in the car. I'll be right back."

"These are lovely. Do all your tiles have a Bible verse on them? I'm not much of a religious person, but someone might like these." She picks up a "God Bless our home," a rooster tile, and a few four-inch tiles. "You can leave these. Do you have a business card?"

I hand her a few. "I'll check back with you next week."

There's something strange about that lady. She seemed so nervous and troubled. Lord, I pray for an opening to tell her about You.

The phone's ringing off the hook when I open the door to a quiet, dark house an hour later.

"Hello?"

"Peter. How are you, Son?"

"I'm calling from the airport in between flights. Can you and Dad come to Hawaii for a vacation?"

"Really? I don't know if I can get your father to take that much time off from work. He works many late nights, and I seldom have dinner with him."

"Well, I'm going to fly for another airline and still have a lease on the Oahu apartment."

"How much longer is the lease?"

"One month."

"That's wonderful. You still have one month left on your lease, but you'll be flying with a new airline. I'm so excited. I'm going to let you go, so I can jump in the car and go talk to your father about all this in person."

"Do you still have all of the information about flying standby?"

"Yes, I do, your address in Hawaii, and your telephone numbers as well. Hopefully, we can get over there soon. Thank you so much."

"I love you, Mom."

"I love you too."

My heart's pounding as the excitement wells within me. "Hawaii. A perfect place for Henry and me to pull our strained marriage back together." I glance around the quiet house and, without batting an eyelash, I pull a suitcase out of my walk-in closet and start packing. *Wait a minute. I better go see Henry before I jump the gun. Maybe I should call him. No. I'll get that secretary of his. Let's see. It's four o'clock and it takes me a half hour to get to his office. Perfect. We can go out for an early dinner together and plan this trip. Underwear, two nighties, three pairs of shorts, and matching tops. That's a good start.*

I change into a maxi flowered skirt and a white peasant top. Brush my hair and apply some fresh makeup. "Okay. Let the games begin."

The elevator takes me to the third floor, and I take a right through the glass door. The receptionist smiles at me as I walk by. Henry's office door is closed, but a young, attractive girl is sitting at the secretary's desk.

"Can I help you, Miss?"

"I'm here to see my husband, Henry Funk. Are you new here?"

"Nice to meet you, Mrs. Funk. My name is Lila Grant. You just missed him."

I laugh. "He must be on his way home, right?"

She hesitates. "No, he and Barbara went out for a business dinner at The Stone's End restaurant. I guess he didn't call you after all."

As I walk to my car, the dark sky above sends a deluge of rain down on me. By the time I close the door, I'm sopping wet. *Oh Lord, what do I do now? How much more of this can I take? Is Henry having an affair with his secretary? It sure points in that direction. Should I go to that restaurant or go home and wait for him? I wish I could just fly away, fly away.*

The granite stone restaurant sits at the end of a dead-end street. The establishment has a wonderful reputation for gourmet food at a reasonable price. I pull the shawl I just so happened to have on the passenger's seat around me. My heart's racing a mile a minute as I approach the front door.

"Can I help you?" The maître d' glares.

"I'm here to dine with Mr. Funk."

He looks me over from head to toe and then some. "Just a moment, please."

I follow him anyway.

Soon, we're in a dark corner of the place. A dimly lit booth with a single candle burning in the center of the table illuminates the two faces sitting across from each other. The maître d' leans in to whisper to my husband, but I push him away.

"Henry! How could you? You're having an affair, aren't you?"

Barbara slinks down in her seat as Henry pulls me down next to him. "Stop making a scene. Do you hear me? I can explain. If you give me a minute to do so."

I slap him across the face. "This candlelight dinner says it all. I'm leaving, Henry. Enjoy yourselves." I wiggle my way out and flee the scene, without looking back. I could feel a few eyes of other customers bore through me.

I manage to stay on the road as I cry my way all the way home.

The phone's ringing off the hook. I reluctantly answer it. I pour my heart out to Twyla, and within a half hour she's consoling me in person. My bags are all packed, reservation to JFK all set, and a quick phone call to my son complete. I keep my composure during the conversation.

"Are you sure you want to do this, Violet?" pleads my friend.

"I have to, Twyla. I need this time to think. You won't tell my husband, will you?"

"I won't, but we better get a move on because he'll be here any minute."

"Because I have set my love upon the Lord, He will deliver me; He'll set me on high, because I know and understand His name. I shall call upon Him, and he'll answer me; He will be with me in trouble." Psalm 91: 14

I'm sitting on the airplane as it ascends into the night sky over Albany. I grabbed the last standby seat with the only airline leaving tonight. "I'm flying away, Lord, flying away."

Chapter Fifty-Two

My eyes simply won't close, so sleep doesn't come. I wonder if I did the right thing. I left Henry many years ago because I was not in my right mind, but that changed when God came into my life. Oh sure, there have been countless times when I felt the enemy of despair circling around me. Each time, I asked Him to lift me up out of the muck and mire, and He did. Oh God, what have I done?

"Can I get you anything, Miss?" asks a stewardess with bright red lipstick.

"A glass of water, please."

The man next to me is still cutting Zs and the rest of the passengers are silent as the plane glides through the air. I glance through the small window into the vast darkness and wonder, *Where's heaven anyway?*

She hands me the water. "Can I get you anything else?"

"No, thank you."

A tall, handsome man wearing a cowboy hat squeezes past the stewardess and heads to the lavatory.

"Ladies and gentlemen, this is your captain speaking. We'll be landing in twenty minutes. Stewardesses, prepare the cabin for arrival."

JFK airport is filled with people from every walk of life, going here there and everywhere. It's ten o'clock at night, and the gates are packed. I look for my next flight set to leave at midnight, via Denver and Los Angeles then Honolulu. I'm riding standby, but seats were plentiful the last I checked. I freshen up in the lady's room and grab a tuna sandwich and a cup of coffee. I settle in at the gate.

The handsome man on the Albany flight sits across from me and winks. I blush and continue to munch on my supper. *I wonder if Henry even cares that I'm not home.*

"Violet Funk, please come to the podium."

I pretend not to hear the call, so I can finish my meal.

"Montgomery Jackson, please come to the podium."

I watch the cowboy saunter over to the counter. I'm too far away to hear what is being said, but he's issued another boarding pass. He disappears down the corridor toward baggage claim.

"Violet Funk. Violet Funk. Please come to the podium."

I throw away the trash, pick up my belongings, and head to the counter. "I'm Violet Funk. Is my flight on time?"

"Can I see your boarding pass, please?"

I give it to her but am curious as to why she needs it.

"I'm sorry, Ma'am, but we have to bump you to the next flight. This one is full."

"What? You have got to be kidding me. There were plenty of seats when I booked this a few hours ago. I must get on this flight. That's all there is to it." My cheeks are flaming.

"There are no more seats. I can give you a boarding pass for the flight at five o'clock to Minneapolis. That's the only option with a connection to Los Angeles."

"Let me speak to your supervisor."

She squints her eyes and forces a smug grin. "I am the supervisor."

"Listen, I'm exhausted and stressed out. I can't wait until five o'clock. I must get on this flight." A smile tugs at my face when I think about it.

"Here's your new boarding pass, Mrs. Funk. I'm sorry for the inconvenience, but there's a lounge for employees and their families. Now, please step aside so I can serve the people behind you."

⚬❦⚬

I'm greeted with cigarette smoke and the aroma of coffee when I walk into the brightly lit lounge. A few people are sprawled out on the sofa-like chairs, while others are reading newspapers or magazines. I spot a grey recliner by the window and beeline over to it. *Ah, rest at long last. Sleep will come quick now.*

"So, you're in my boat, huh?"

I keep my eyes closed, but my ears alert to the conversation so close by.

"Yep, we sure have a long wait until that five o'clock flight, don't we, Violet?"

Is he talking to me? A man with a southern drawl knows my name. How odd is that? I open my eyes out of curiosity and see the man from earlier, right next to me.

"Um, yes. I'm glad I can rest in here for a few hours. Where are you headed?"

"Denver, by way of Minneapolis. I have a ranch there. Where are you going, pretty lady? It looks like you're traveling alone."

"I'm going on a much-needed vacation in Hawaii. My son has an apartment there."

"Is your son a pilot?"

"How did you guess, Mister...?"

"Montgomery."

"Yes, he is. That's how I got the standby tickets." I yawn.

"You look exhausted, my dear. I think you should take a nap. I'll wake you at four, so we can get on that flight together. How does that sound?"

Somehow, I really trust this guy. "Thank you, Sir. You should rest too."

"No, Ma'am. I might catch a wink or two, but someone has to watch the time."

I pull my pocketbook close to me and curl up in the chair. The sounds around me slowly fade away.

The cowboy and I get on the Minneapolis flight without a hitch. Even though there are a lot of empty seats, we decide to sit next to each other. I rattle on and on about my whole life story. He attentively listens to my every word and rarely interrupts. He grabs ahold of my hand when I talk about my mental breakdown. I break down in tears. My whole body reacts to his touch.

"I'm so sorry you endured such heartache, Violet. You have an amazing story that should be put into print someday."

"I have thought about it, but I hope to publish a children's book with my daughter before I write my story."

He leans closer and squeezes my hand. "Your husband sounds like a real anchor for you. Why isn't he with you on this trip?"

"Our marriage was pretty solid until he got a promotion in his company. He spends more time with his secretary than he does with me. Things are strained between us, and I need a break."

"Hawaii's a beautiful place to go with someone special. Not alone."

I smile at him and lean my head on his shoulder. "You could come with me." *Did I just say that?*

"Funny girl. I'm a bit sleepy. Wake me up when we land, okay?"

He pulls his hand free.

I shift myself away, and clamp my mouth shut.

"Another delay? Really?" Montgomery asks the airline representative.

I pat his shoulder. "Maybe we can have some breakfast. My flight doesn't leave until eleven."

"You have yourself a date, my dear Violet."

We order scrambled eggs, toast, and coffee in the nearest café. We laugh and chat about our businesses and children. *I wonder if he's married. No wedding band.*

"Have you ever been to Hawaii, Montgomery?"

"No. I would love to go someday."

"Well, there are two bedrooms in the apartment, so you have a place to stay. I bet you could get on my flight. It's wide open."

"You're exceptionally beautiful, Violet. Your invitation is very tempting, but I'm a happily married man with three great children. I have a strong faith in God, and I try to live a life pleasing to Him in every way. I ride standby because my wife works for American Airlines."

I want to bolt from the scene, but the bond between us keeps me in place.

"Forgive me, Montgomery. I'm ashamed of my behavior. Jesus is my Savior and the Lord of my life too. I have drifted away from His teaching, and my spiritual life is somewhat stagnant."

"Can I pray for you before we part?"

I nod, with tears rolling down my face.

"Father God, please help my sister in Christ, as she goes through this short separation from her husband. She has an amazing story that You orchestrated from beginning to end. I pray for a reconciliation between Violet and Henry. I ask this in Jesus' name. Amen."

I squeeze his hand. "Thank you."

He turns on the heels of his boots. My cheeks burn.

Chapter Fifty-Three

As we start the descent to Honolulu, I gaze out the window at the pristine, turquoise blue water, lush green landscape, and the outlines of sandy beaches. Sailboats and catamarans dot the water below. *I can't believe I'm arriving in Hawaii by myself.* The sounds of ukuleles and bongo drums fill the airport as I head to baggage claim. I take a deep breath. It seems so real. Too real to be a dream.

A heavy set, dark skinned Hawaiian lady dressed in a moo-moo places a lei around my neck. "Aloha."

"Thank you." My eyes light up in response.

The eighteen-story apartment building overlooks the Pacific Ocean, and Waikiki Beach is right across the street. The dwelling is immaculately clean, with bamboo furniture throughout, and pale blue walls enhance the light green carpeting. Sliding glass doors open to a small patio. The floral hammock will be a great place to catch up on reading.

"I'll need to shop before I rest," I say to no one. I open the refrigerator and much to my surprise, I find it stocked with skim milk, orange juice, cottage cheese, and eggs. A loaf of whole wheat bread sits on the counter. *How did this get here?*

I sleep the day away. *Must be the jet lag.*

∾◌℞ᏰᏰ

The next day I browse through all the shops on the strip, swim in the warm, Olympic size pool, and run along the beach. I find a used bookstore and purchase a few novels.

A few days roll on, but thoughts of Henry fill my mind. *Is he living with Barbara now? Am I a figment of his imagination?*

There's no place on this earth that has sunsets like Hawaii. *I think I'm going to sit on the beach to watch it set tonight.*

I find a knoll to spread my beach towel. The turquoise ocean waves splash along the shoreline. People are laughing and talking as they walk on the sidewalk behind me. The palm trees are blowing in the gentle breeze over my head.

I whisper, "Oh, dear God, save my marriage. Please Lord. Henry has always been my knight without the armor. My stronghold, after you, of course. Maybe, the dinners with his secretary are totally innocent. If I'm wrong, I pray for forgiveness. In Your name, amen."

The tears flow from my eyes as I watch the great big sun sink slowly into the horizon. I curl up like a cocoon on the soft beach towel. I cry myself into a catnap. I'm so broken.

∾◌℞ᏰᏰ

"I've been looking everywhere for you, Violet Pearl."

Am I hearing things? Sure sounds like my husband. Can't be.

371

A hand touches my back, and I get goosebumps.

"If the front desk clerk didn't see you come here, I would not have found you."

"Henry?"

"Yes, I came to rescue my damsel in distress. Peter called when I got home after you left and told me where you are."

He lies down next to me and pulls me into his arms. "Why did you doubt my love for you? I love you and only you."

"Oh, my dear Henry, I love you with all of my heart. Prayer does change things. I prayed that you and I could enjoy this paradise together and here you are." I blink back the tears.

"I want you to know, Honey, Barbara made all the arrangements to get me here as fast I could. As for the dinner at Stone's End, Barbara needed to talk to me privately about her abusive boyfriend. They gave me a bonus at work which covered the airfare. I have three weeks off. I love you more than the world wrapped in a big red bow."

I plant a kiss on his lips and snuggle into his arms. "There's nothing wrong with me, wrong with me, wrong with me."

THE END

"People make plans in their minds, but only the Lord can make them come true. Depend on the Lord in whatever you do, and your plans will succeed."

Proverbs16:1&3

Acknowledgements

Special thanks to my husband, Tom for being my sounding board and shepherding me to the finish line. His loving support kept me focused.

The story you are holding in your hands, is due in large part to my editor, Sara Foust, also a published author. Her critique and advice made a solid story.

My brother, Peter for his inspiration and encouragement.

My amazing street team, Mission Possible, for encouragement. Too many to mention, but know you're appreciated. Thank you for good reviews of *Laugh Clown Laugh*. I hope you enjoy the pages of the sequel, *Missionary to the Oddballs*.

Thanks to Hannah Linder Designs for a beautiful cover. Your patience meant a lot.

I give thanks to God because He is good! (ALL the time)

About the Author

Penny N. Haavig is the author of *Laugh Clown Laugh*. She resides in Minnesota with her husband, Tom.

Penny was born in New York City and grew up on Long Island. Besides writing books, she loves to horseback ride, and dabbles in art as a hobby.

You can visit Penny at her website, www.pennynhaavig.com.

I enjoy reading reviews on Amazon and Goodreads. Thank you.

Violet Moretti's colorful life is a flight from emotional madness to sanity. Available at Amazon.com and barnesandnoble.com

www.ingramcontent.com/pod-product-compliance
Lightning Source LLC
Chambersburg PA
CBHW020819180626
46814CB00001B/24